praise f

"Sumptuous detailed descriptions of clothing and of sewing and fashion design are what make this story a cut above other gay romances. Wakefield develops the relationship between Kit and Barker in tandem with the filming of the episodes of a reality TV show and that device adds interest and tension to the story."

— *The 2021 BookLife Prize Fiction Contest Critic's Report*

"A heart-warming gay romance in a fresh and vivid setting."

— Amazon Reviewer

"Everything was good: the characters, the pacing, the conflicts, the humour, the banter, all of it."

— Amazon Reviewer

behind the seams

stuart wakefield

Copyright © 2020 by Stuart Wakefield

All rights reserved.

No part of this book may be reproduced in any form or by any electronic or mechanical means, including information storage and retrieval systems, without written permission from the author, except for the use of brief quotations in a book review.

For Hannah, who helped me start.

For Debbie, who helped me finish.

For Krete, who supported me through it all.

one
. . .

KIT BELTED DOWN THE STREET, juggling his suit carriers and bag to keep from tripping. Under his waistcoat, his shirt clung to his back. What was he thinking, staying in his work suit on a scorching day?

He clocked the time on a bus stop display. An hour late. A rusted metal sign lashed to a peeling fence caught his eye. Was that it?

He hurried through the gate, then slowed to a stop. Anonymous grey warehouses loomed over him. This couldn't be right.

Breathless, he slumped against the gate. *Phone. Check the address.* He hung the suit carriers on the gate's top rail, then fumbled in his inside pocket. Damp fingers smudged his phone's screen as he scrolled through his emails. Bingo. Unit 3B, Alfred's Way, Barking. Definitely the right place. But a *Runway Rivals* audition—on an industrial estate?

Equipment whined from inside the warehouse on his left. The rest stood silent. Breeze blocks on a summer's day.

He reached for his suit carriers, and his phone slid out of his clammy hand. He made a grab for it, but it dropped on a corner, spun away, and landed face down on a mangled metal bracket. The dull crack of splintered glass. He swiped the blank screen, hoping for the best, and pain jagged along his fingertip. Blood smeared the glass. *Great.*

Careful not to get blood on his suit, he eased his phone back into his pocket and rubbed his eyes. Still sore from yesterday afternoon, yesterday evening, and this morning.

His scalp prickled. None of the warehouses bore numbers. If he sweated much more, the hair he'd been careful to gel and scrape back would loosen and curl. Not the look he wanted.

At the end of the first row of units, he caught the waft of fried onions. Burger van. Sure enough, between the warehouses in the second row, five men in shapeless, dirty orange overalls queued for food.

Kit pushed back his shoulders and approached. "Excuse us, lads. Where's three B?"

The last two men in the queue broke off their conversation, then looked down at him. One, pale face except for a bright red forehead, cackled. "What's this, bring your kid to work day?"

Here we go. "I'm twenty."

The other, cracked tooth and a buzz cut, laughed along. "Bit far from home, ain't you?"

There wasn't time for this. "Three B?"

Paleface jabbed a thumb over his shoulder. "Nancy boys been mincing into that one all morning."

"Thanks, lads."

Two units up, someone had taped a *Runway Rivals* logo on a crooked aluminium door.

Kit struggled through the entrance, grateful for the empty foyer's cool air. A white corridor stretched ahead of him, cracked mint linoleum scattering the floor.

A frizzy-haired brunette lass sitting behind a makeshift desk gulped down the last of her Diet Coke and leapt to her feet. A plaster perched over her left eyebrow. Five foot five. She wasn't tall, but she had a few inches on him. Her desk—a folding wallpaper table positioned across the empty corridor—bore half a pencil, a creased piece of paper, and two name tags.

She grabbed the pencil and paper. "Name?"

"Redman. Kit Redman."

"Very James Bond. You're two five oh nine." She waved her hand across the two tags. No names. Numbers. "I'll match your number with your name."

Kit picked up the tag. "Thanks, umm—?"

"Layla. I'm a production assistant." She fiddled with her hair, trying to force it behind her pink ears. It sprang back. "I'm new."

Kit jostled his suit carriers over one arm and offered her his hand. "Nice to meet you, pet. Hope you settle in soon."

Her ears reddened. She took his hand and shook it. "That's nice of you. If I'm honest, I'm all over the place. The other contestants have been a bit, you know."

"Distracted?"

"One girl threw me her overcoat and asked for a ticket. Does this look like a cloakroom?" Layla stepped around her desk and looked him over. "Check you out in your suit. Very smart, but you must be boiling. It's more like July than late May."

He held out his sleeve arm to give her a better look at the material. "You like it? It's tweed. We call it 'old gold puppy tooth' at work." Layla blinked back at him. "I'm a tailor," he said. "I wear a suit all day." *Tailor* stretched the truth. He was a trainee fitter, but he didn't have time to get into the difference. He'd explain it on his way out. "I work on Savile Row."

"Savile Row as in bespoke suits? In Mayfair?" Layla pushed out her bottom lip and bobbed her head. "I'm impressed. And you're a Geordie?"

"Newcastle, born and bred." Her opinion of him would go

one of two ways: cheeky Northern chappy or gobby party animal.

"I love the Geordie accent. My boyfriend Carl hates it, but yours is lovely and soothing."

The lass had taste, he'd give her that.

Layla pointed to a door at the end of the corridor. "Through there. Do you want a hand with your stuff?"

"I'm fine, thanks."

She took his badge and pinned it to his jacket. "Two five oh nine. Look for the table with the same number." She hesitated. "Are you okay? You look like you've been crying."

"Hayfever."

"Your nose isn't running."

He ducked away, snatched the pocket square from his breast pocket, then pretended to wipe his nose. "Not much. Tablets must have kicked in."

"Your eyes are red raw, you poor thing. I might have some eyedrops in my bag, if I can find it. I'll run them over to you. Good luck."

Kit paused at the door, pushing his shoulders back to release the tension. This was it. Beyond that door was his chance to be a part of the biggest reality TV show in the country. *This is for you, Grandpa.* Kit pushed the door. Nothing. Pushed again. Still nothing. Was it stuck?

"You're supposed to pull," Layla called out, tapping the plaster over her eyebrow.

Kit battled through the door. With his free hand, he covered his eyes and peeped through his fingers. Lights—so many lights—hung from gantries three times his height. Men with shoulder-mounted TV cameras on their shoulders cruised through a sea of bodies clad in black. Surely these people couldn't all be crew? Through gaps in the churning bodies, rows of white tables stretched ahead.

Two five oh nine.

He stepped forward but hesitated at the edge of bodies. This, hanging back at the edge of crowds, made him late today. Five Tube trains came and went before he worked up the courage to push forward and get on, apologising all the way. Two years living in London, jostled on the Underground and pushed from side to side on pavements. On the busiest days, he walked in the road, as close to the pavement as possible.

Two five oh nine.

Kit's table waited. His audition waited. If he kept stalling, he'd never make it.

He ran through his reason for being here: series seven of *Runway Rivals*, the hit fashion design reality show created by Nancy Shearsmith and Brian Foster.

Nancy, founder and editor of *Shear Style* magazine, acted as executive producer and head judge. She'd taken down so many designers—both on and off the show—*Scorch* magazine dubbed her "The Jewelled Assassin". The tabloids settled for "Shear Scorn".

Media mogul Brian owned and ran Bacchus Broadcasting, the show's production company. Tall, greying, and beefy, Brian once performed in gay porn under the name Bobby Bacchus. No one knew why he disappeared from the entertainment industry, but when he returned, he founded Bacchus. *Scorch* dubbed him "The Silver Fux" until he sued them for half a million and donated the money to a homeless charity.

No one pushed Nancy or Brian around.

Kit took a step forward. *They're only people.*

If he made it through the audition, he'd join fifteen other contestants and compete in weekly challenges. If he made it to the final two, he'd have twelve weeks to complete twenty-five pieces for London Fashion Week. Based on that collection, the judges picked a winner. If he won the show, he'd have one hundred thousand pounds, the exposure to launch his career, and hands-on mentoring from Nancy.

Kit took another step forward. One more and the swarm of bodies would suck him in.

Runway Rivals. Tears, drama, conflict. There'd been blood, too, when that lass from series three sewed through her little finger, then puked on her machine. Memes scattered the web: Nancy rolling her eyes, contestants sobbing, and that puke.

Runway Rivals, TV's biggest reality hit.

Terror slammed Kit back and something hard cracked against the back of his head. A TV camera toppled from a man's shoulder. *No, no, no.* Kit dropped his suit carriers, catching the lens end, staggering under its weight until the man grabbed the camera's body, then hoisted it back into place.

Kit rubbed the back of his head, then picked up his suit carriers. "Sorry, man. I hope it's not busted."

"You all right?" the cameraman said, downturned mouth showing no sign of concern. "Hope so. The last thing I need's getting blamed for hurting one of you lot."

Five foot seven—shouldn't a cameraman be taller?—thirty-six-inch chest, thirty-four-inch waist, twenty-nine-inch inside leg, and miserable as sin.

The cameraman swung back to his subject. A young lass with a blunt brown bob. She wore a suede dress the same colour as her hair. She faced the crowd so her measurements didn't come easy. An eight?

She turned to the camera. No, a six. "So this is it, the last day of auditions, and the atmosphere is buzzing."

"Kit?" An older woman approached him, clipboard in hand, black blouse and jeans, early fifties, size sixteen. Her smile creased her eyes the same way as his grandpa's. "Kit Redman?"

"Am I late?" Kit's fingers worried around the handles of his suit carriers. "I'm useless on the Tube."

"Don't worry. We're running late, surprise, surprise, and

you're not the last to arrive." She gave his shoulder a quick squeeze. He appreciated the gesture. Most women mothered him because he looked like a child, not a twenty-year-old man. "Are your models on the way?"

What the—? "Models?"

"For your audition." Her smile fell. "Loads of people haven't brought them. We hoped to have enough models for everyone, but they've all buggered off to Miami Fashion Week."

Models? Kit had watched all the behind-the-scenes videos, read all the contestants' interviews. Never, ever had they mentioned models at the auditions. Clothes on a rail. That was it. Just clothes on a rail. What had he missed? His scalp prickled again. Much more of this and his hair would be as frizzy as Layla's. "Models are... new."

The woman ran a chewed ballpoint pen down the list of names on her clipboard. "We're mixing up the format this series. Keeping things fresh. We wanted the designers to show their work on live models because, despite the judges knowing a good design right off the hanger, viewers don't. It was all in your invitation email."

"It had a lot of attachments."

"I can't seem to find your name."

A belt of anxiety tightened across Kit's chest. "My best friend Hannah got me to apply at the last minute. I didn't expect to make it here."

The woman flipped over the paper. "Where's your name?"

Swapping his suit carriers from hand to hand, Kit wiped his palms on his jacket. "And work's mad busy, so I might have skimmed a few documents."

"Stupid girl. Here you are."

Kit tugged at his collar. Air warm as breath puffed under his chin. "That's why I haven't got any models, but I can model this suit myself." He lifted one shoulder to offer a better view of his hand-stitched lapel, the perfect width for his frame. "Will that do?"

She scribbled something and gave his lapel a cursory glance. "I don't see why not. Let me show you to your table. The place is more like a war zone than a studio, but we had to find somewhere larger to meet demand."

He should have prepared. At this rate, he'd have no chance. "Doesn't sound good."

"We're swamped this year, especially after all the turmoil of series five and six." She pinned her clipboard under her arms and jostled her way through the mob, pointing out areas of interest. "Hair and makeup. It's up to you if you want your makeup done, although a lot of chaps don't. If I were you, I'd get some foundation or you'll look greasy on camera. Viewers don't go for greasy. Makes you seem untrustworthy. Spare models loiter at the water fountain over there by catering. Some stand outside the emergency exit for a smoke." Her voice dropped. "Don't drink the coffee—"

"I drink tea."

"—it's so strong it'll turn you into a jabbering wreck, especially if you're already nervous. Are you nervous?"

Heat built in Kit's belly. "A bit."

"Viewers don't want nervous. It makes them nervous. What are you nervous about?"

Was she kidding? So much rode on this. Ever since he was a kid, he'd dreamed of designing and making clothes, and he'd made a promise to Grandpa and Hannah to audition. He couldn't let them down. If he didn't get through, didn't win, there weren't any other dreams to chase.

The woman stopped at a table and tapped a label stuck to the corner. "Two five oh nine. Put your pieces on the rail with your number on it." A battered metal frame stood to one side. Four wheels, one bent. Someone had scrawled his number on a tag and tied it to one end of the rail. "Only five pieces." The chewed end of the ballpoint pen slipped into her mouth as she rose on tiptoe. "There are steamers somewhere."

Another change? "It used to be nine pieces," Kit said. "I've got three three-piece suits."

A pained smile worked its way onto her face. "It's five o'clock now. We don't have any male models, so you'll have to model. Three jackets, perhaps, and two of anything else?"

"But the only one my size is the one I'm wearing."

"The changes to the number of pieces was—"

He knew the answer. "In the attachments."

She hugged the clipboard to her chest. "You're not very organised, Kit. Wear your suit and show them something else." She pointed to a set of double doors at the back of the room. "The audition room is through those doors. When you're called, head over there, then wait for one of us to take you in. It'll be me or Layla." She paused as if she'd forgotten something. "Did I tell you my name? It's Pamela. I'm on the production team."

Kit recognised that name from last-minute revision with Hannah. "You're Pamela Patton. You're the *head* of the production team."

Her smile returned. "And you're already my favourite. If you need anything, let me know." She looked closer at Kit's face. "Are you okay? Your eyes are very pink."

"Hayfever."

"Then that's a definite on the makeup front." She patted the side of his face. "I've got a marvellous feeling about you. Despite your lack of prep, you might pull this off. Get yourself together, and good luck." She left him alone, the churning throng swallowing her body as she walked away.

Alone at his table, Kit slipped each suit from its carrier: the mustard tweed with a gold-and-soft-blue over-check; the blue, three season flannel; and the women's white linen with flared trousers.

Grandpa Redman would have been proud. He'd started work in Savile Row when he was fifteen, learning his craft from those before him. Every school holiday, Kit and his older brother Greg stayed at their grandparents' house in north London. Whenever Grandpa sewed at home, he pulled up a stool for Kit to watch. While Greg played video games, Kit witnessed Grandpa's hand-cranked sewing machine whirr into action. Fabric glided under the foot until, piece by piece, clothes came to life under the tapping needle. Two days later, Kit asked to try. He started with the basics—a t-shirt for his teddy bear. By the end of the summer holidays, he'd made himself a waistcoat. To celebrate, Grandma bought Kit an ice cream from the corner shop. Greg had a sausage roll.

From time to time, Kit used a machine but had to hand sew at work. He proved to be adept with a needle and thread, developing a perfect backstitch. His boss, David Stitchworthy, once accused him of using a machine but fell silent when Kit produced another uniform row of hand-sewn stitches before his eyes.

Kit placed each suit on his table and smoothed them down. The linen needed a steam. The tweed and flannel survived the journey in perfect condition.

A lass in a pink, heavily beaded jacket strode out of the crowd, a shock of colour emerging from the black sea. Five eleven, thirty-three-inch chest, twenty-five-inch waist.

She sidestepped him and stood at his table, her yellow-green eyes on his work. "How super. Did you cobble these together all on your own?"

The hair on his neck bristled. *Posh cow. Cobbled?* "That's the point, right?"

She clapped, her wide eyes taking on none of the brilliant, white smile looming over him. "And you're northern? How delightful. Six series, and I don't think they've ever had someone like you on the show." Her eyes flicked back to his suits. "You're bound to get cast for being a Northerner alone." She had to be a contestant to be trying to psyche him out. When she thrust her hand out and he jumped back with a yelp, she shrieked with laughter. "Aren't you the funniest little thing. I'm Emilia Winchmore." She paused. Should he know her? "I'm not surprised you don't have a clue. I expect the newspapers in your neck of the woods are bursting with grim stories about raging unemployment and destitute children. Perhaps someone in the know will fill you in vis-à-vis my standing in the Chelsea set." Emilia walked away.

Kit cleared his throat. "Let's see your stuff, then."

Slow as an iceberg, she turned, left eye twitching. "I beg your pardon?"

"You've seen my stuff. Let's see yours."

"As you wish."

Although Emilia glided gracefully through the room, her ponytail whipped like an angry tiger's tail. People darted out of her way.

Her table groaned under piles of clothes: jewel-toned silk charmeuse blouses; vibrant beaded dresses, primary colour panels on nude mesh; off-white corded lace culottes; and a mint-green tulle ballgown with a jacquard bodice. So much expensive fabric. It was all Kit could do not to throw himself on the lot and nuzzle into it.

Her eyes gleamed. "Voila. Daywear, evening-wear, bridal wear."

His hand hovered over the pieces. "Can I?"

"Yes, you *may*."

Kit picked up a pair of narrow legged trousers.

Emilia let out a casual sigh. "My only problem will be choosing what to take in."

Kit smirked when he examined the garment's puckered seams. "You've got more problems than that, pet. These are machine made, and your thread tension's too tight. If you'd loosened it a little and adjusted to a larger stitch length, it wouldn't look so... cobbled together."

Quick as a viper, Emilia snatched back the trousers. "How insightful. Thank heavens I used a fabric of the highest quality. And I think you'll find I pressed the seams flat, so the puckering is barely visible."

Amateur. "The point of the show's winning enough money to launch your own line."

David Stitchworthy's words rang in Kit's ears: "The discerning customer expects quality."

Emilia tossed the trousers back onto her table. "I'll hire the very best pattern cutters and seamstresses. Perhaps you'd like to apply for a position at my *atelier* when it opens, subject to police record checks." She stepped up to him, making the most of her height advantage. "I wouldn't want the wrong sort of person working beneath me."

Kit did his best not to take her down with a few choice words.

Pamela marched past with a lad carrying two bags in tow. "Don't drink the coffee," she said. "It's super strong and will turn you into a jabbering wreck—"

The lad noticed Emilia. He scowled, then stopped in his tracks.

"—especially if you're already nervous." Pamela slowed when she registered she'd lost him. "Is everything all right?"

"What are you doing here?" The lad spoke in Emilia's same clipped accent.

Emilia backed away from him and into her table. Her hand went to the side of her neck, and when she spoke, she stuttered. "The same as you, I expect."

The lad looked her over, neck forward, eyes narrow. Kit looked him over, too. Six two, forty-inch chest, thirty-inch waist, thirty-four inside leg. Bleach blonde hair, fake tan. Handsome face, nothing fussy. Two faint lines across his brow and a cleft chin. Like everyone except Emilia, he dressed in black: leather jacket, polo neck, jeans and boots. The lad was nothing special until he looked at Kit and smiled. Sharkskin grey eyes and brilliant teeth. Before the urge to run kicked in, Kit smiled back.

Pamela cleared her throat. "Good luck, Barker." She didn't pat his face before she left.

Who the hell called their kid Barker?

Those grey eyes locked back onto Emilia. "Are you being a bitch to this chap?" Emilia's mouth worked, but nothing came out. "Or should I ask how *much* of a bitch are you being?"

Her eye twitched. She said nothing.

Barker transferred a bag to his other hand, then put his free arm around Kit's shoulder. "Thought as much." With a gentle pull, he guided Kit away. "Pamela said my table's next to yours. You must be Kit."

"Guilty." Kit kicked himself for an answer as dull as Barker's smile was white. Lad must have had his teeth done. Had to be a London thing. No one in Newcastle had teeth that white except those spray-tanned gym bunnies on *Geordie Shore*.

Barker scanned the room as they weaved through the crowd. "Where are you taking me?"

Kit slowed. "You want me to take you somewhere?"

Barker's speech slowed, the lines on his brow deepening. "To find our tables."

"Right."

"What did you think I meant?"

"Nothing, man." Face throbbing with embarrassment, Kit found his bearings. "That way."

Barker hoisted his bags onto one shoulder, then took his hand off Kit's back. He strolled to match Kit's stride. "Have you come straight from work?"

"Just got here. Dead stressful."

They arrived at their tables, and Barker dumped his bags.

"Please tell me I'm not contestant two thousand five hundred and ten."

"Don't think so. We're row twenty-five. I'm nine and you're ten."

"Thank Christ for that. Where do we change?"

Kit tugged on the hem of his jacket. "I don't need to change."

"But you're wearing a suit."

Hands raised, Kit stepped back. "I'm a Savile Row tailor. There's nowt wrong with what I'm wearing."

Barker grimaced. "The thing is, there are Savile Row suits and there are designer suits. You—" Barker rested his hands on his table and eased off one of his boots with the toe of the other "—you look like a banker. A moderately successful banker, but a banker. *Runway Rivals* is looking for fashion designers. Who else do you see in a suit?"

A sea of black t-shirts, blouses, and sweatshirts. "No one, but Gunter always wears suits."

Kit idolised Gunter Lyffe, the show's undisputed breakout star. Impeccably dressed, well spoken, and kind, Bacchus had hired him from the London University of Creative Arts—LUCA—as a mentor to the designers during the challenges.

Barker clicked his fingers in front of Kit's face. "Earth to Kit. Gunter is not a designer. He's not even a judge. See that caterer over there? He looks cooler than you, and he's dressed like a penguin."

A teenager yawned behind a table groaning with plates of yellowing sandwiches and scattered coffee cups. Five nine, thirty-two-inch chest, twenty-eight-inch waist. Black satin bow tie—pre-tied—crisp white cotton shirt, and a black wool, slim-fit waistcoat.

A shiver ran down Kit's spine. He rubbed the back of his neck in contemplation. Mounds of luxury fabrics on Emilia's table, Barker's sleek outfit, Pamela's concerns about Kit's preparation. His fashion design career wouldn't be getting off the ground today. He toyed with the mustard suit's right sleeve. He'd put one hundred and six hours into it, and all for nothing. "Maybe I should go."

Barker eased off his other boot, then put them both on the table. "Nonsense. What's your shoe size?"

"Eight?"

Barker paused. "That's big for—"

"The 'funniest little thing'?"

"Is that what Emilia called you? I'm not sure funny's the word. Intense, perhaps." Barker bent to unlace Kit's shoes. "Kick these off. I take an eleven. If you wear my socks and yours, my boots might fit."

Kit tried to jerk his foot away. "I'm not wearing your hacky socks."

Barker gripped Kit's foot behind the ankle, then took off the shoe. Barker stood, shoe in hand, and squinted at him over a wry smile. "'Hacky'? What does that even mean? You can wear my jeans, too, but they'll be long on you. We'll tuck them into the boots."

In another time and place, and if Kit had three or four drinks, he might work up the courage to get his clothes off in front of Barker, but not in front of all these people. "I can't be stripping off here, man."

Ignoring him, Barker picked up one of his bags. "I'd already planned on changing into my Versace jeans and Gaultier jacket. If you're embarrassed, which you need not be, get changed behind that rail over there. It's stuffed with clothes. I'll keep a lookout." When Kit didn't move, Barker sighed. "I'm only doing this to help you, Kit."

Something about Barker puzzled Kit. Why would someone like him, a competitor, want to help? Kit wasn't important; he was background. What would Barker get out of this?

Kit ran his thumb along the texture of his sleeve. "Why did you see off that Emilia?"

"Because if you'd punched her in the face, it'd go against you." Barker unzipped his leather jacket. "*Runway Rivals* loves a bit of drama but not that kind."

"I wouldn't have punched her."

That wry smile again. "Wouldn't you? I've seen her push people to the edge. What do you say to getting behind that rail and letting me help you look the part?"

Arms crossed, Kit studied Barker's face. "How do you know her?"

"She went to my school."

Kit shuffled his feet, leaving sweaty silhouettes on the polished concrete floor. "Why're you helping me?"

Without looking up, Barker unbuttoned his jeans. "I enjoy being surrounded by pretty things."

Pretty? Kit burst out laughing. No one ever called him that. He made sure no one was looking, then slid behind the rail. *Please, God, don't let this rail's owner audition next.* "There's still nowt wrong with this suit." The skinny jeans Barker slung over the rail didn't change Kit's mind. "Skinny jeans and a suit jacket? I'll look well odd."

"I'm not finished with you yet."

Kit flushed at the warmth of Barker's jeans. "Can people see you?"

"Of course," Barker said.

"You're naked?"

Barker tutted. "I'm not an exhibitionist. Leave your waistcoat on and pass me your jacket."

Kit hesitated to pass his clothing over the rail, but Barker reached over and took it from him. *Fine.* Kit eased his way into Barker's jeans. They sort of fitted, baggy around the thigh, but like Barker said, the boots would swallow the excess material flapping past Kit's toes.

When Kit stepped out from behind the rail, Barker loitered between their tables, dressed only in his polo neck and underwear. Shoulders of a gymnast, damn him, and the thighs of a sprinter.

Two lads and a lass skulked behind Barker's left shoulder, each one checking him out. When Barker noticed them, he glared until they moved on.

He turned his attention back to Kit. "How do you feel?"

"Like a kid wearing his dad's clothes."

"Older brother, thank you very much. Turn around for me."

Kit swung his arms and curved up his toes. *Keep your cool. It's not you who's standing in your pants.* When fitting customers, the best of them did as they were told. He turned around.

Barker hummed in approval. "Not too bad a fit on the waist and, ah, very nice elsewhere. Let's get these bad boys on you." Barker turned Kit back, then rolled up the jeans to form thick cuffs around Kit's feet, sliding his own socks over the cuffs. "That should do it." He met Kit's eyes, his face creasing with amusement. "You look like you're about to keel over. Relax. I know what looks good."

"Are you a stylist or a model or something?"

Barker gestured around them. "Design show, remember? Besides, could you imagine me on the cover of a magazine?"

Break out the Photoshop, erase the freckles, and smooth the brow. Barker's eyes would do the rest. Sharkskin grey, drawing people to the magazine racks for a closer look.

"I'm a fashion design student," Barker said. "For one more day, at least."

"They're kicking you out?"

Not looking up, Barker tied the bootlaces. "My anger issues have come up occasionally but, no. I graduate tomorrow, then I win this show and start my label." He stood, took hold of Kit's tie, and coaxed him closer.

17

Nice hands, but he'd gnawed away his right thumbnail, exposing raw pink flesh underneath. Not so confident after all.

Barker's voice dropped. "So don't be better than me, okay?" If Barker had smiled, Kit might pass it off as a joke. He didn't.

"You really want this."

Barker's smile drifted back. "I never joke about the truth. Let's lose the tie, shall we?" His fingers worked around the knot.

Where should Kit look? Shoulder? Cheek? That cleft chin? Anywhere but at Barker's mouth would do.

Kit's head swam at Barker's acrid smell: intense, powdery deodorant and a whiff of… smoke? Coal tar? Designer clothes and cheap toiletries didn't go together.

Barker's bottom lip pressed upward and his chin pitted. "Tricky bugger, this knot. It's not a Windsor."

Kit gasped for air. "Grantchester. Want me to do it?"

"No need. I have it." A moment later, Barker whipped the tie away and dropped it onto Kit's table. "One last touch, and you're set. Don't be mad, all right?"

"Mad at—?" Barker held a ragged-edged, chocolate brown piece of viscose. Kit recognised it at once. He snatched the lining—his suit's lining—from Barker's hand. *No, no, no.* "What have you done?"

"I've improvised. You need a bandana and this lining goes beautifully with your waistcoat. But you knew that, didn't you? You had the superb taste to use it."

Kit held the fabric to his chest and stumbled backwards, legs weak. "You've ruined my suit."

"Chin up." Barker stepped forward and steadied Kit so he could undo the top two buttons of Kit's shirt. He gave him a pinched smile and took his voice up an octave to imitate Emilia. "Just because you're a Northerner, it doesn't mean you have to look like one."

"You heard her?"

Barker rolled down Kit's collar, then tugged the lining from his clenched fists. "No. Educated guess. A month after joining my school, they voted her head bitch." He folded the fabric into a rough triangle and drew it around Kit's neck. "By the faculty."

"That explains it."

Barker's hands moved carefully at Kit's neck. Little zaps of excitement ran through Kit every time Barker's knuckles touched his skin. "Explains what?"

"You talk the same. Posh."

"You can thank Charterhouse for that."

Kit didn't know what Charterhouse was, but it sounded impressive. He'd google it later.

Barker stood back. "Emilia and I couldn't be more different. She's new money." He folded Kit's collar up and into place. "Perfect. Let's go find a mirror."

Barker took Kit's hand, then led him through the crowd. How Pamela, Emilia, and Barker navigated through this many people, Kit didn't understand. People stepped aside for Barker, their heads turning as he passed. Emilia scared people; Barker dazzled them.

Barker found a mirror propped up against a pillar. He stepped between Kit and his reflection. "One last thing." He removed Kit's gold cufflinks, then rolled up Kit's sleeves. "Okay. Look again."

A Victorian barrow boy stared back at Kit. All he needed was a flat cap. Just as he'd feared, his slicked-back hair had softened, loose curls rolling back from his forehead, blurring his short back and sides. He rubbed his jawline with the back of his fingers. *Should have shaved again at lunchtime.* At least his eyes had calmed.

The proud smile faded from Barker's face. "You don't like it?"

"It's not that." Kit examined his reflection from different angles. "It's nothing like what I'd pick."

Barker's eyebrows threatened to collide. "So you like it?"

Kit liked Barker's uncertainty as much as the fresh look. "It's proper canny, man."

"Another Geordie turn of phrase. I'll take that as a yes, judging by the soppy grin on your face. Now, may I please finish getting ready? I'm practically naked and destiny calls."

This time, Barker left Kit to find his own way back to their tables. Kit watched him go. Gymnast's shoulders, sprinter's thighs, and a footballer's backside.

Emilia charged out of the crowd and strode past Kit. Three models trailed her, each one tottering on five-inch platform shoes. She flung open the set of doors leading to her audition.

Pamela sidled up to him, checked her clipboard. "She was supposed to wait for one of us. I've no idea where Layla is."

"She said she'd lost her handbag. Maybe she's looking for it?"

"Not long until you're in there," Pamela said. "Do you have all of your pieces on your rail, or are you still playing dress-up?"

He gave her a brief bow. "On my way, boss."

"'Boss'? I like that. You seem to have hit it off with Barker. Such a relief that apple fell far from the proverbial tree. Now get a move on."

With no idea who the 'proverbial tree' was, Kit found his way back to his suits. Barker's table stood unattended. Kit needed something to distract him from his growing nerves. He found a spare steamer and smoothed the white linen suit. Now he'd had a makeover, he was down to the three suits he'd brought with him. He split the jackets, waistcoats, and trousers to fill the rail. Unless someone noticed he had over five garments, he'd see how things went during the audition and pick his pieces accordingly.

As Kit checked out the competition, the woman in the brown suede dress approached, microphone in hand. The cameraman he'd backed into followed behind her.

She held out her hand. "Kit? I'm Tabitha Frost, fashion vlogger, influencer, and presenter of *Coming Undone*." Kit vaguely remembered people talking about *Coming Undone*, the *Runway Rivals* after-show. But he hadn't watched it. There had only been so much time to absorb the information Hannah gave him. Because of that, she'd concentrated solely on the main show. Tabitha ploughed on. "The sister show to *Runway Rivals*? Series five was so popular the producers decided a behind-the-scenes show would be—"

"Didn't catch it." It came out blunter than Kit would have liked. "Sorry, pet."

Tabitha waved away his apology. "That's okay. I hadn't found my feet in the first series, so I'm sort of pleased you didn't. Can I nab you for a quick interview?"

As the camera swung up in his direction, he covered his face with a hand. "I've not got makeup on. Pamela said viewers don't like greasy."

Barker returned. He'd been to makeup and found somewhere to get changed. The makeup covered his freckles and softened the lines across his brow. Blusher contoured his face. They'd reduced him to standard-issue handsome. Kit preferred the freckles.

Barker's clothes—blue and white striped denim blazer, jeans, and plimsolls—changed him from brooding biker to Monaco chic.

When Barker noticed the camera, he cleared his throat. Tabitha and the cameraman both swung round. Barker swaggered over to one of his bags and made a show of pulling out a silk, buttercup-yellow dress, but the fabric ripped at the left shoulder seam. As Barker cried out, the dress slipped from its hanger to land at his feet.

Tabitha's voice dropped to a whisper. "Oh, no."

The glare of attention hurled Barker into action. He plucked the dress from the floor to shield it with his body. "It's okay."

Kit darted forward. "Let's have a look. I can—"

Snatching the dress away from Kit's outstretched hand, Barker hunched over it, voice ragged. "Don't."

"I'm only trying to help."

But Barker wasn't listening. His hands twisted the dress, threatening to rip the neckline, too. "I can't—I can't fix this."

Kit put one hand on Barker's back and spoke under his breath. "I can. Just give it to us."

Pamela's voice cut through the throng of people who'd heard Barker's cry and gathered around his table. "Five minutes, Kit. Let's have your rail."

Barker's eyes glistened as they met Kit's, voice thinning to a whisper. "It's ruined, you idiot. What could you do in five minutes?"

Kit covered one of Barker's hands with his. "There's time. Please, just let us have a look."

"Kit," Pamela called again. "Rail, please."

two
. . .

BARKER COULDN'T BELIEVE IT. As soon as the shoulder seam shredded, so did his chance of being cast.

The dress was his statement piece and the centre of his graduation show. He'd spent days trying to get the drape right, manipulating a toile fabric on a dress form, pinning and unpinning, looking at it from every angle until satisfied. The torture of transferring the fabric to paper, creating the pattern, checking the measurements, smoothing the curves. The horror of constructing the finished garment, cutting yards of silk, sobbing when it all went wrong. The rest of his student loan went on the second, third and fourth attempt. Three months later, he had nothing to show for it. His tutor Sybille bought him the fabric for his fifth attempt and sat with him for two weeks, coaching him through every stitch. When he finished, he sobbed again. This time into the crook of Sybille's neck.

This dress wasn't just for his graduation show; he'd designed it to secure his place on *Runway Rivals*.

He had to get on the show and win. He needed the money, and he needed the platform to launch his label. All the money he'd wasted—Prada sneakers he lost the first night, bottles of

Cristal and Patrón for the entire bar, the go-go boy he flew to Paris for dinner. And all on social media, his business card to the world. All except the go-go boy.

Everything changed when the money dried up.

Kit held out an upturned hand. Spittle bubbled through Barker's teeth. "Don't be soft, man," Kit said, turning to Tabitha, who still gawked at the torn dress. "Can you give us a minute, pet?"

The camera swung to the side as the cameraman strained to get a better angle on the dress. Barker swung his body around to block the man's shot. He had to pull himself together.

Kit advanced on Tabitha with outspread arms. "We need to concentrate and get this repaired. Would you mind?"

Mute, Tabitha gestured for the cameraman to turn away.

Kit retrieved a travel-sized sewing kit from his bag. "It's all right, man."

Shame settled on Barker, pushing down his head and shoulders. He'd called Kit an idiot on camera, but the chap hadn't shied away from him—he wanted to help. Barker's fingers relaxed. "I'm sorry."

Kit eased the dress from Barker's hands. His fragrance—star anise and pine needles—washed over Barker, bringing an odd sense of calm.

Pamela's voice rose above the chatter. "Three minutes, Kit."

Kit didn't look up from his examination of the damage. "Three minutes won't do it."

Barker squeezed him on the shoulder. "I'll be back in two." He didn't understand what Kit could do, even with a few extra minutes, but he had to give it a shot.

Pamela stood by the doors to the audition room, frustration staining her neck pink. She waved her clipboard at Barker as he approached. "He's not getting changed again, is he? You can tell him there's no time for makeup, and I warned him about looking greasy."

Barker held up his hands. "I can only imagine how stressful this job is, Pamela. Am I right?"

"You've no idea. This is the fifth day of auditions. Everyone's exhausted." She used her clipboard to point out a group of lighting technicians sagging under the weight of an enormous lamp. One tripped over a cable, and the entire thing crashed to the floor, glass exploding in a wide arc.

Both she and Barker ducked, hands over their faces.

Exhausted meant dangerous. As one bulb went out forever, another went on in Barker's head. "What time did you start?"

Pamela checked her watch. "Six o'clock, and we didn't finish yesterday until one o'clock this morning. Most of us haven't had more than four hours sleep." She scribbled on her clipboard. "Will you please get Kit?"

Barker hooked one finger over the edge of her clipboard and pressed down. "How about a cup of that super-strong coffee?"

"There's no time."

"Tell that to the government."

She stared at him as though he'd lost his mind. "What?"

"Regulations entitle any worker to a twenty-minute break if they've worked for six hours. You started at six this morning, and it's now two in the afternoon." He gave her his most sympathetic smile, then raised his voice. "These people deserve a break, Pamela. *You* deserve a break. It's not only the law—it's the right thing to do."

After some hesitation, during which the crew—drawn in close by Barker's suggestion—all looked at Pamela with pleading eyes, she tucked her pen behind her ear and bellowed to the room. "Twenty minute break, everyone."

Barker ran his hands through his hair. "Super. Milk and sugar?"

When Barker returned to his table with two cups of coffee, Kit hunched over the dress, deep in concentration. Barker

25

placed the cups well away from the dress and watched Kit work, curious how someone might mend something as bad as that horrific mess of frayed edges.

Nauseated, Barker looked away. "I appreciate this, especially after the way I spoke to you in front of Tabitha, on camera." No response. "I was upset. That dress is my best piece by far, but that's no excuse. I hope you can forgive me."

Kit's head stayed down as he snipped away the torn edges of Barker's dress with a pair of fabric shears.

Barker pressed on. "What with the audition today, I guess things got on top of me."

The shears clunked against the table. Kit threaded a needle. Unsure of what to say next, Barker sat in silence and took his coffee, making sure it stayed well away from Kit.

Kit sewed, hands quick and careful. Barker couldn't take his eyes off the delicate fingers whipping a needle as thin as a hair from edge to edge of the trimmed edges. Calloused skin thickened Kit's thumb, index and middle fingers. Not so delicate after all. A spot of dried blood stained his index finger.

Barker sipped his coffee. "What happened?"

Kit stopped sewing and glanced up at him, eyes refocusing. "To what?"

"Your finger. You're not using it."

"Smashed my phone. Don't want to get blood on this."

Kit went back to his work, his needle creating rows of thread between the edges to replace the fabric he'd cut away. Fifteen minutes later, he finished.

Barker leaned in. Kit hadn't only created rows of thread—he woven in decorative sections.

Kit knotted and snipped the last thread. "It's not exactly couture. It's darned. Sort of."

His olive green eyes darkened when they met Barker's. "I helped you because you helped me, but if you call me an idiot again, I'll make that tear look like a loose thread."

The angry energy blazing in Kit's eyes made Barker want to quench it with a kiss of thanks, but he had no idea if Kit was gay. For a short chap, Kit's dark, slicked back hair, heavy features, and early afternoon stubble conjured the word dashing.

Barker blinked. "I, uh, got you a coffee."

"I don't like coffee."

"I promise," Barker said, "I'm not a massive cock."

The corner of Kit's mouth twitched before setting back into a grim line. "Massive cocks have their place, I guess." He hopped off the stool, then drew himself up to his full height, which wasn't much. "Thanks for the makeover. Good luck with your audition."

By the time Barker opened his mouth to speak, Kit wheeled his rail toward the double doors.

Emilia sidled up to Barker's side. "You have a knack of making friends in low places, Barker. Perhaps you're more like your father than you care to admit."

If she wanted to be a bitch, he'd give as good as he got. "How did your audition go, Emilia? Did you suck enough cock to get through to the next round?"

"That's more your forte." She inspected her nail varnish. "Besides, Gunter bats for your team, as you well know."

Barker sniffed the air between them. "Ah, so that explains the whiff of minge."

Emilia's face collapsed in disgust. "You're so vile. I wouldn't go down on Nancy Shearsmith for a million pounds, let alone one hundred thousand."

Barker hooked the yellow dress onto a hanger and placed it on his rail. "We all have our price, Emilia. How about two million?"

"And some of us charge less than others, or so I'm told." Emilia looked around, checked to see if anyone listened, then smirked back at him. "I appear to be done." She flicked her hair across his face as she turned her back on him. "See you tomorrow."

"Tomorrow?"

"At your graduation show, silly. Where else?"

"Why would you be at my graduation show?"

"Daddy's considering whether to become a patron of the university, so he wants to check the standards."

As she walked away, Barker's fists clenched.

One day, Emilia, you'll get what's coming to you.

three

. . .

KIT STOOD by the double doors, making sure his back was to the room, and closed his eyes. "This is for you, Grandpa."

Mending Barker's dress was the right thing to do, despite him calling Kit an idiot. He'd done Kit a favour with the makeover, and the distraction gave Kit less time to panic.

Yesterday morning, he'd had plenty of time to panic. As soon as he woke up, he sent Hannah a text, asking her to meet him at the coffee shop outside her office.

Kit bought her a single-shot, skinny, raspberry mochaccino —light on the foam, heavy on the sprinkles—and a breakfast tea for himself.

Hannah stood over two teenagers sitting at the table she and Kit always used. Once they surrendered and moved on, she wiped down the table with a clean paper napkin.

She sat, squinted at the foam and sprinkles, took a sip. "How's it going with the telly thing tomorrow?"

Kit took off his jacket and sat opposite her. "That's not until Thursday."

"Tomorrow is Thursday."

Hannah was such a kidder, like the time she convinced him

the clocks had gone forward and he turned up at work an hour early.

Kit fished the tea bag out of his cup. "Howay, man. Thought you had me going, I bet."

"Nope." Hannah thrust her phone in front of his face. "Today's Wednesday. See?"

Kit twisted to his sides, digging his hands into his pockets until he found his phone. Hannah might have messed with the date on hers. She hadn't. *Shite*. He scrambled up out of his seat. "I have to make a call."

On his way out of the coffee shop, Kit stepped around a lass with a cardboard tray of cups. He held the door open for her while he dialled Maureen from the theatre group.

Maureen answered, voice thick with sleep. "Hello? Kit? Is everything all right?"

The lass with the cardboard tray passed him. "Thank you so much."

Kit gave her a strained smile. "No worries, pet. Maureen? You know you said you'd give us the costumes I made for the show? For my audition? I got my dates mixed up. I need them tomorrow."

"It's dress rehearsal."

Double shite. "I could have them back for the evening."

At Maureen's end, a kettle rumbled, and china clinked. "Dress rehearsal's in the afternoon, ahead of technical rehearsal in the evening."

This couldn't be happening. Not now. "Please, Maureen, just a couple."

"I'm sorry, Kit. I just can't."

Maureen was right. Taking the costumes, as good as they were—the female leads squealed with excitement when they saw them—would let the theatre group down. He couldn't do that.

Back at his and Hannah's table, he sat with his head in his hands.

"I'm not ready. I can't have any of the costumes I made for the play. I don't have any womenswear. All I have are the suits David let me make in my spare time. I can't go, not like that."

Hannah blew on her drink. "You bloody can. You'll be great even if you're not prepared. Do you remember what you're going to say when you get in there?"

Kit recited his lines. "Always wanted to be a designer since I learned how to draw."

"Check."

"Being on the show will give me a chance to show them my potential."

"Check. And?"

"Um—"

"Come on, Kit. We've been over this, like, a million times. Whatever...?"

"Whatever happens, being in the room with you has been the highlight of my life." He took a swig of his drink. "And it still sounds naff."

"I've done my research and, based on my findings, the lot who trot out the banalities get picked for the show."

Hannah had to be right. She worked for Bacchus Broadcasting and watched every *Runway Rivals* audition tape as part of her mission to secure Kit a place on the show. If he'd been more organised, her work might not have gone to waste.

Kit caught her hand over the table. "And I appreciate it, pet, but naff is naff."

And here Kit stood, at the double doors leading to the *Runway Rivals* audition room, eyes closed.

Pamela's voice boomed. "Shall we get started?"

When he didn't move, Layla appeared at his side, took his rail, then pushed against the doors leading to his audition.

"I'm sorry," Layla said. "I can't find my bag anywhere. Hope your sniffles don't ruin your audition. How are you?"

"Yeah, good. I'm good."

She stopped, then placed her hands on his shoulders. "They wouldn't have put you through to this stage if you didn't have a decent chance of getting through, so get on in there and show them what you're made of. It isn't just what you've made, okay?" Kit nodded. "Once you're in, head for the *Rivals* logo on the floor and wait. Gunter's running the auditions this year, so you're in excellent hands."

Kit gasped, spine rigid. "Gunter's in there?" A few of Nancy's *Shear Style* gang usually ran the auditions, not Gunter.

Layla gripped him. "Don't worry. He's always lovely."

"Thanks, pet. I appreciate it."

Kit took the rail, then stepped into the audition room, heart ramming against his rib-cage. White light pummelled his eyeballs. He stumbled, blinded.

Gunter's smooth, familiar voice called out to him. "It's all right. Take all the time you need."

Squinting through the blazing light, Kit's eyes took a moment to adjust. A huge, curved desk confronted him. Behind it, two seats, one occupied. Kit took his position on the *Runway Rivals* logo—this year, a shade of aqua leaning towards green.

Gunter picked up a piece of paper. "Kit, is it?"

For the first time since he'd arrived, excitement pumped through Kit. He idolised Gunter Lyffe. As mentor to the contestants, Gunter demanded the best of the designers but made allowances for the pressures of the competition. Since the show began, Gunter developed the look of a greying badger. Now, at fifty-one, the white hair at his temples bolted back through salt and pepper hair. Rectangular, matt black glasses framed deep-set, sage green eyes. His smile had lost volume over the years; its gentle encouragement hadn't. Orderly stubble blurred his sharp jawline. Judging by the soft shoulder construction of his jacket, he worked out but didn't flaunt it.

Gunter scanned the paper. "What brings you here today?"

Kit's voice rose, high and tight. "Ever since I could draw, I wanted to be a designer."

A thin-limbed, jewel-encrusted insect of a woman emerged from the shadows behind Gunter. "I swear to God, if I hear that phrase one more time I'll lobotomise myself with my own Louboutins."

Nancy Shearsmith, in all her desiccated glory.

Pamela stepped out from behind a monitor. "For pity's sake, Nancy, you've just had a break. Can't you play nice?"

Nancy stepped up to take her seat. Kit's mind swam with additional confusion. Nancy didn't take part in the audition process, either. Head judge during each series, yes, but she never lowered herself to auditions.

"So." Nancy stretched out the word as she checked a piece of paper. "What's your, God help me, story?"

Shiteshiteshite. Rehearsed lines wouldn't work on Shear Scorn. *What do I say now?* Kit held up a hand and retrieved the mustard jacket from his rail.

"I was just a bairn when I started, uh, making clothes. My grandpa is—was a tailor. He taught me everything I know. When I, uh, turned eighteen, I moved down south and—"

Nancy's hands rose, palms up, and beckoned for Kit to pass her the jacket, ready to receive it as though it were a newborn. Stumbling in Barker's huge, unfamiliar boots, Kit gave it to her.

She placed the jacket on the desk, lifted the lapels, examined the buttonholes, outside pockets, lining. "You say you made this?"

"Of course. I mean, yeah. I mean, yes. It's—"

She pinched her first two fingers and a thumb to cut him off, then conferred with Gunter. "Hand stitched. Hand stitched very well. Fabric's a good weight. The lining could be jauntier."

Gunter took the jacket. "Oh, yes. This is beautiful work. You really made this all by yourself?"

"Yes, sir. It's my job. I work at Stitchworthy on Savile Row."

Pamela spoke from the darkness. "No advertising, Kit. Say that again, but without your employer's name."

Nancy leaned forward, pinning him to the spot with sudden focus. "Stitchworthy? As in David Stitchworthy?"

Kit opened his mouth to speak.

Pamela cut him off with a wave of her clipboard. "Let's go again."

Grateful for the pause, Kit pushed his shoulders back and gathered his thoughts. *Just tell them the truth.* "It's my job. I work on Savile Row."

Nancy gestured to his rail. "If you've watched the show before, which I'm sure you have, you'll know that almost all challenges are for womenswear."

"We only have one menswear challenge per series," Gunter added.

Nancy paused for effect. "What else do you have to show us?"

I'm going home. All I have are suits. Kit pulled his rail over to the desk, then took the three white linen pieces making up the women's suit. It was still a suit, but the shawl collar set well with the curves of a woman's body. He'd shortened the sleeves to expose bracelets or a watch. The two-button jacket balanced the silhouette of a tall woman. Boot-cut trousers favoured a high heel. Not quite couture, but more than bespoke.

Nancy checked stitches, turned out pockets, and pinched hems before she handed the pieces to Gunter. She locked her fingers together and studied Kit. Tension strained her voice. "This is what I'm struggling with. The designer standing in front of me looks current. But you're not reflected in these clothes. You and your designs don't add up. What am I missing?"

"I would have brought some other designs, but the theatre group wouldn't let me borrow them."

Nancy made a point of raising one eyebrow and tilting her head. "I'm sorry. Did you say 'theatre group'?"

I shouldn't have let that beautiful bastard make me over. "Yes, I make costumes for—"

Nancy gave him a quick, disgusted snort. "'Costumes'? We don't want 'costumes'." She scoured her papers. "Is he dead, this grandfather of yours?"

Don't. Please don't.

Gunter leaned towards her, voice low, cautious. "Nancy."

"Are you on—I can barely bring myself to say it—a journey?" Nancy stressed the last word to emphasise the reality show cliché. "Who," she checked her paper again, "is Kit Redman?"

What should he say? That Barker made him over? That Kit let him do it because he doubted himself? That the only reason he turned up was because he'd made a promise to Grandpa and Hannah?

Nancy rolled her eyes. "Come on. I haven't got all day."

Barker's advice hadn't worked. Kit yanked off the bandana, then unbuttoned his jeans. Pamela stepped forward as though to intervene, but Nancy stopped her with a flashing hand.

Kit spoke, calm and focused. "You're right, Miss Shearsmith. This isn't me." He unlaced and discarded Barker's boots and socks, then pulled down his jeans. When Gunter chuckled, Kit's heart sank. He'd worn his lucky pants—a genie's lamp printed over the crotch and the legend: Keep Rubbing, You Might Get Your Wish.

Kit huffed. *Great.* "I'm a Northern lad whose grandpa taught him the beauty of well-made clothes." He folded the jeans, then placed them neatly on top of the boots and socks.

Nancy and Gunter watched him intently as he went to the rail and took down the suit trousers and jacket he'd arrived in. "I moved to London where I knew I could make suits with the best tailors in the world. And I do." He slipped into the trousers and pulled on the jacket with the torn lining. Without his shoes, he'd be shorter than ever. *Fuck it.* "I'm not only doing this to honour my grandpa's memory, but he's in every stitch I make, like his hand's guiding mine." It might have been the glare of the lights, but Gunter's eyes sparkled.

Nancy's satisfied sigh gave Kit hope. "I see you, Mister Redman. Now tell us so we're clear. Who are you?"

Kit's hands clenched for a moment before the tension melted away from his limbs. "I'm Kit Redman, and I make the world's finest suits."

For a moment, the room fell still. The boom of Gunter's laugh made everyone jump.

Nancy spoke, her tone even. "Thank you, Mister Redman. You've been honest if nothing else. Do you have anything else to add before we move onto the test?"

Coldness trickled down Kit's spine. "There's a test?"

Nancy's languid smile made the back of his throat ache. "It's something new this year to weed out those—how shall I put it?—*short* on talent."

The crew wheeled out nine three-dimensional models of a woman's torso—a dress form—and positioned them in a semi-circle behind Kit.

Gunter picked up a laminated card and measuring tape, then walked into the semicircle. Six foot, forty-inch chest, thirty-two-inch waist, thirty-two-inch inside leg. Spearmint flecks in those sage green eyes. "Your challenge is to size these dress forms according to this chart, then place them in order. The smallest size should go on the left as you're looking at them now and work up to the largest on the right. Clear?"

"I guess so."

"Excellent. You have five minutes." Gunter leaned in. "Take your *time*." He winked at Kit, handed him the laminated card and measuring tape, then went back to his seat.

Kit examined the card. It listed each dress size from eight to twenty with all their qualifying measurements. Taking each dress form's measurements, Kit checked them against the list. Nothing matched. Could he dispense with the tape and make a judgement on each one? As he walked down the line, he changed their positions, but when he stood back, they didn't increase in volume as he expected. Two dress forms seemed close to a size twelve. He measured them again, but each had at least one measurement that didn't correspond—a waistline here, a hip circumference there. Hannah complained the same size from one shop wouldn't fit from another. Was that it? Was it a trick question? Kit scowled at the forms. The men who came to Stitchworthy didn't conform to off-the-peg sizes. Sizes were a guide, and nothing fitted a man like a bespoke suit. The same had to be true for women, but there was something else: Gunter had whispered about Kit taking his *time*. What did time have to do with dress sizes?

Unless…

Draping the measuring tape around his neck, Kit examined the dress forms, walking around each one, examining their materials. Some were in better shape than others. One had an ornate, carved wooden stand. Another stainless steel. And another, plastic. *Take your time.* That must be it.

Gunter called out. "One minute."

Kit grabbed the dress forms, rearranging them, using nothing but the painful memories of all the theatre group's terrible musicals. He picked at one dress form, surprised when his fingernail scraped the surface. Wax? Victorian? Papier mâché covered another, pages of sheet music. Slim silhouette, flattened chest… Thirties? The one with the Bakelite stand and cinched waist… Fifties? As Gunter called time, Kit hauled the last form into place.

Nancy scowled at Kit. "Interesting. Care to explain?"

"They're all twelves."

Gunter and Nancy exchanged glances. "How so?"

Kit's muscles tightened in readiness. "That one's wax, late Victorian. The slim one's Twenties. The third's Thirties—the sheet music's dated. The Bakelite one? At first I thought it might be Fifties, but I think it's Forties. The rest go decade by decade. The Seventies one has an Abba sticker on the stand."

Gunter beamed. "Very interesting. Very interesting indeed."

"Frankly," Nancy added, "I'm in shock."

If the look on her face was shock, her bloodstream had to be two parts Botox.

Kit squared his shoulders. "Am I right?"

"Let's hope so," Nancy said. "Because I have very little confidence you're the designer we're looking for. I'm not sure you're a designer at all."

Come on, Nancy. Please. "But, like, you've seen what I can do."

Nancy's voice rose to imitate his. "And I'm not convinced that that's enough, 'like'." If Kit worked at *Shear Style*, talking back to Nancy would have got him the sack. "Now unless you have something else to show us, I suggest—"

"Find us a model, and I'll show you."

"I have no such intention of finding you anything. Procuring models was your job."

Gunter patted the folded stack of Kit's clothes at his side. "Show us what?"

"That women's suit on your desk. The white one. You look at that suit on a model and tell me I can't design."

Nancy considered this for a long time, looking first at Gunter, who nodded with enthusiasm, and to Pamela, who checked her watch then nodded. "Very well. Find yourself a model and come back later. Pamela will see if we can fit you in."

Kit exhaled, deliberately hiding the sudden release of tension throughout his body. "Thank you, Miss Shearsmith. Mister Lyffe."

When he stepped out of the audition room, holding Barker's clothes and boots, the bustle of the main room felt like open ground.

Barker hovered by the double doors with his rail. "How did it—" The next word died on his lips when he saw his clothes in Kit's hands.

Kit handed Barker his clothes. "It's not over. Nancy's in there."

The doors swung open. Pamela. When she spotted them together, she huffed. "You've still got our tape measure, Kit."

"Sorry, Pamela. Force of habit." Kit pulled the tape over his head, then handed it to her.

Pamela beckoned for Barker to follow her. "Come on. You're up."

Kit patted Barker's arm. "Good luck, man." Then hurried toward three models dawdling by the water cooler. Five foot eight. *She won't do*. Five foot nine. *Too busty*. Five foot ten. *Too scrawny*. None of them would fit his suit. Pamela said something about models smoking outside. Kit pushed through the fire exit and out into the late May evening.

Three girls stood chatting under the partial shade of a fire escape. One caught his eye. Five foot eleven, thirty-one-inch chest—hardly a bust—twenty-four-inch waist, thirty-three-inch hips, so a size four. Light brown hair coiled over her shoulder in a scruffy plait, the biggest pair of wooden-framed glasses he'd ever seen. Perfect.

Kit approached her. "Excuse us, pet. Could you help us?"

She beamed at him. "Why aye, man." Thick, genuine Geordie accent. "You need a tab?"

The relief of finding another Geordie felt like coming in from the cold. "No, but I could do with a favour."

She stubbed out her cigarette on the fire escape. "I'm no good at sewing, pet, if that's what you mean."

"It's not."

After tiptoeing to a nearby skip to dispose of the crushed cigarette butt, she rubbed her hands together. "What's your name?"

"Kit. Yours?"

"Alex." They shook hands. "So, Kit, if you didn't mean sewing, what did you mean?"

four
. . .

WAITING outside the audition room as Kit hurried away, acid burned in Barker's chest. He fumbled in his blazer for his indigestion tablets. Nothing. *Fuckfuckfuck*. They must still be in his leather jacket.

Barker's five models joined him. The tallest, Deja, wore the buttercup yellow dress, her ebony skin lending maximum contrast. It was a wonder a swarm of bees hadn't burst through the fire exit and ravaged her. Kit's intricate darning made the dress all the better.

Judging by the way Kit rocketed out of the room, his audition couldn't have gone well. And what did he mean by it not being over?

Pamela held open one of the double doors to allow a frizzy-haired brunette girl to pass. The girl pulled a rail of mustard, blue and white garments behind her. Kit's suits.

Pamela tapped her clipboard. "Ready, Barker?"

Barker swallowed the bubble of acid burning his throat, then turned to his models. "Ready, girls? Good. Let's blow their bloody socks off." Pamela held the door open, and the girls filed through.

Barker paused when he reached Pamela, then lowered his voice, doing his best to cover his nerves. "How bad was it? You know, for Kit?"

"Difficult to say. He might have won Gunter over, but Nancy gave him a hard time." Pamela fished in her pocket, then handed him a tatty, half-tube of indigestion tablets. "These were under your table."

Desperate for relief, Barker tore a strip of foil and paper from the packet. Ulcerated oesophagus, the doctor had said. Barker would be grateful if the tablet softened the acid on the back of his tongue. He pulverised it with his molars—chalk with a hint of bile—and swallowed. *Good enough.*

Pamela caught his arm, pulling him into motion. "Now get your arse in gear. Those girls can't walk forever. They're living on Evian and a packet of Bensons."

Barker strode into the audition room, head high, shoulders back. He hit the *Runways Rivals* logo and—bam!—enormous smile. "Nancy, Gunter. What a lovely surprise. All we're missing is Bruna."

Gunter returned Barker's smile. "She's out of town on a shoot, I'm afraid. You'll have to make do with us."

Nancy scowled over her notes. "Who's out of town? Oh… her."

During series five, Nancy and the show's host, Bruna Bannister, locked horns in a spectacular, on-camera argument about whether to vote off a middling contestant. Nancy suddenly accused Bruna of marrying billionaire Robert Bannister so she could afford to hire someone "to dig gold on your behalf". Bruna, who'd arrived late to set and fluffed her introductions, fled the set in tears. The following morning, the papers reported Robert had been diagnosed with terminal skin cancer. *Shear Style* hastily put together a full page apology and hurried it into publication before Robert died. Series six's ratings soared, with viewers glued to the two women's frosty exchanges for later dissection online.

Gunter gave Nancy a brief scowl. "Play nice." He turned his attention back to Barker. "Would you like to talk us through your collection? Mister…?"

And so it began. "Wareham. I'm Barker Wareham."

"I see." Gunter adjusted his glasses. "Might you be the son of Ludo Wareham?"

Barker cleared his throat. "This collection is inspired by lush vegetation reclaiming the wasteland of urban decay." His first model stepped forward, wearing the knee-length, rust-coloured leather dress. Leaf-shaped cut-outs spiralled down from the neckline, skimming the model's left nipple, then curling around the base of her spine to settle across her right thigh.

Gunter leaned forward, eyes narrowed, scanning the dress as the model walked towards the desk, turned, then walked back. He plucked up his pen to write on his papers.

Barker's second model followed, wearing a bodice and flared skirt. Embroidered foliage piled up from the skirt's hem to the bodice's bust. "It's nature's destruction of construction, if you will."

Nancy sat back, folded her arms, then turned her head to Gunter. "McQueen. Spring nineteen ninety-nine."

Pain shot down from Barker's throat to his chest. *Shouldn't have worn this jacket. It's too hot.*

The third model stepped forward. She wore an asymmetric, steel grey dress in heavy satin. Barker spent a week folding and pin-tucking the dress's purple, leg-of-mutton sleeve into a blooming flower.

Nancy's jewelled fingers closed around a pen, then she made notes. Had she just nodded?

"The yellow dress symbolises the life-giving golden orb of the sun nourishing the Earth."

Head held high, Deja stepped forward, walking at speed so the silk flowed behind her. Each whipping flash of fabric a solar flare licking the darkness.

"Heavens." Gunter glanced sideways at Nancy. "That's the most poetic introduction to a collection I've ever heard."

"Yawn." Nancy pointed at the model in the yellow dress. "You. Come over here." Nancy stepped down from the desk, jewellery exploding with kaleidoscopic colour under the lights. The Harry Winston pieces clutching her throat and wrists must have totalled half a million. Barker could have bought two Lamborghinis with that, or an apartment in Venice. One ring priced at forty-five thousand. Barker's mother owned the same one. She always wore it for Sunday lunch.

Nancy's eyes roamed over every seam and hem of the dress. "Turn for me," she said to Deja. "Slowly."

Deja did as she was told.

Nancy reeled off her observations like a dentist during a checkup. "Proportions are fresh. Uneven hem. Well-placed cutout on the ribcage, although a poor finish on the edge. Fits well. Right shoulder seam slightly puckered." Her eyes flicked to him, then she pointed at the left shoulder seam where the open latticework of Kit's repair clung to Deja's shoulder. "Who did this?" He opened his mouth to speak, but she cut him off. "And don't tell me it was you. This work is conspicuous by its skill."

To prepare for his audition, Barker trawled the internet for every article Nancy wrote as a journalist, and every interview she granted as fashion editor of *Vogue*. She stopped giving interviews after the launch of *Shear Style*, but her editorial column served as a reminder that her opinion defined the course of British fashion. Everyone listened to Nancy Shearsmith, and Nancy didn't do bullshit.

"It tore while I was taking it out of its cover." Might it harm his chances if he admitted the truth? He wouldn't lie. Dishonesty ruined his life once. If the truth did the same, so be it. "A fellow contestant helped me."

Gunter joined Nancy to examine the repair. He checked the time. "They spent all morning on this when they could have prepared their own work? I don't understand."

"It—uh—only took him twenty minutes." This wasn't how Barker expected this to go. His construction needed work—his tutors always badgered him to spend more time honing his skills—but fashion houses weren't one-man bands. Every *atelier* housed a small army of pattern cutters and seamstresses. Barker's tutors conceded his collection would stun the audience. Why focus on one tiny detail?

Gunter ran a finger over the repaired shoulder. "Twenty minutes? Who could do that?"

Still examining the repaired shoulder, Nancy clicked her tongue. "This is Mister Redman's work."

"Redman?" Barker said, struggling to get the word out from his burning throat. "Do you mean Kit?" *This isn't Kit's bloody audition. It's mine.*

Nancy took her seat at the judges' desk. "This is what I'm struggling with. You can design—there's no question of that—but you'll be making your own garments day after day. I'm concerned your poor construction skills will end up being a hindrance."

Barker wasn't about to let his chances slip away. "I can keep up."

"Can you? Could you have repaired that damage in twenty minutes?"

"I—I don't know."

Nancy crossed her arms, then rested them on the desk. "I assume you watch the show?"

"Every episode."

"Then you'll have seen many designers go home because they couldn't do their designs justice in terms of construction."

"If you give me a chance." Barker hurried to Gunter, who stood with Deja. "I'll work twice as hard on my construction before filming, I promise. I won't let you down."

"Only twice as hard, Mister Wareham?" Nancy said. "I don't know. If I had a laboratory, I'd mix your DNA with Mister Redman's. But you? On your own?"

Barker strode to the desk, hands clasped together. "Please, Miss Shearsmith. Please."

Gunter stepped forward, an index finger raised. "If I may?" Nancy indicated for him to go on. "I'm inclined to agree. Every challenge has a strict deadline, and we won't only be seeing your designs on the catwalk. We'll look at them in detail before we make our ultimate decision about who goes home. This could be your undoing." He turned Deja until she faced sideways. He pointed at a separating side seam. "Literally your undoing."

Nancy slumped back in her chair. "Good grief."

Barker paced between Nancy and Gunter, hands held at his chest. "Come to my graduation show at LUCA in two days. Please. You'll see my entire collection."

Gunter gave a polite cough. "That's inappropriate."

"Please."

On the desk, a phone buzzed. Nancy picked up the phone, jabbed the screen with the finger, then brought it to her ear. She blinked slowly at Gunter as she listened. "All right." She hung up, settling her gaze on Barker. "I'll think about it." No one moved. "So we're done, yes?"

Gunter rocked on his heels. "We finish with the test, Nancy."

Sweat trickled down Barker's spine. "There's a test?"

five
. . .

KIT MARCHED into his second audition, slowing when the glare of lights hit him. He opened his mouth to speak. Nothing came out but a strangled squeak.

Alex stepped around him and whispered. "I'll get the show going, pet."

Kit took one step to the side. *Look relaxed.* He put a hand on his hip. *Too camp.* He settled on his weight on his left leg, right leg out to the side.

Alex strutted around the room. Kit's last-minute adjustments to the suit stressed her waspish waist and flattened what little bust she had. Her refusal to wear anything underneath the waistcoat paid off. Perfect Seventies vibe. *Looks amazing.* The suit came alive on her body and after one loop of the studio, Alex oozed out of the jacket and draped it across her right shoulder.

Nancy's eyes fixed on the waistcoats's vintage brown and orange satin back. "Talk me through this."

Alex, now on her second loop, neared Kit's spot. "Boho," she mouthed to him as she passed.

Ten minutes earlier, Alex had slid her legs—a giraffe would

have killed for them—into the white linen trousers. "You've got to speak their language, pet. It's the only way."

Boho. Kit sputtered to life. "It's boho-chic meets trust fund with a Seventies vibe." He'd become used to people coaching him for the show. If they could do the same for his love life, he'd be golden.

Nancy's focus sharpened. "The shoes are all wrong. It needs a high, stacked heel."

"Told you," mouthed Alex again, winking at him. She turned on the spot, shrugged the jacket onto her arms and hit a pose: three-quarter profile, jacket hanging off her shoulders, thumbs in her trouser pockets, weight on her right leg. *Lass is a pro.*

"A pussy-bow blouse might work," Gunter offered. "Or a tie?"

Nancy's eyes narrowed as she ran a finger under her chin. "Only if you lost the waistcoat. But an oversized tie—very wide—with a ruffled shirt." Her eyes settled on Kit. "If you'd made this up in an embossed, metallic fabric—"

Gunter sat back, gazing upward, a faraway look in his eyes. "Gucci green."

Nancy gave him a sideways sigh. "—you'd be going through with flying colours."

A thrill rose in Kit's chest. "So you like it?"

"I didn't say that." Nancy rose to her feet. "Time's up, Mister Redman. We have given you more than a fair chance."

Gunter thanked Kit for his time. Nancy abandoned the room without a word.

With no sight of Layla or Pamela, Alex led Kit out of the audition room and into the main space. One of the crew propped open the fire exit so another could wheel out a trolley heaving with coils of tightly wrapped cables. Fresh air swept through the open door, cooling Kit's face and neck. The storm of people moved on, leaving a handful of pale, sagging crew and sobbing contestants.

Kit returned to his table with a skipping Alex in tow. Barker's table stood empty.

Alex swung the jacket off her shoulders then handed it to Kit, chattering all the while. "I've never been that close to Nancy before. From the front row at shows and stuff, like, but never that close." When Alex unbuttoned the waistcoat, Kit looked away. "Did you smell her?" she said. "I heard she has her own scent. Pays thousands for it, like. No one else has it. Reminds us a bit of Poison, you know, the way it lingers behind her, but she smells amazing. I was tempted to rub up against her like those perfume strips you used to get in magazines." Sliding the waistcoat off, she handed it to Kit, then slipped on the blouse she wore when they first met. "She's like the sexiest headmistress in the world."

Kit grinned up at her in surprise. "You think?"

With a shy smile, Alex may as well have been a child. "I've always liked older women." She stepped out of the suit trousers, then back into her own. "Good luck, pet. I hope they pick you. They'd be mad not to." She handed him a little blue card.

He turned it over in his hand. Silver lettering on the front, black and white headshot printed on the back. "Nice."

Alex gave him a quick hug and a kiss goodbye. "Give us a shout if you make it to Fashion Week."

In long swinging strides, Alex left through the fire exit.

Pamela wandered over to where Kit stood. "Well, you had quite the time today. How're you doing?"

Kit packed his suit carriers. "I've never been so stressed in my life. When I first saw Nancy, I nearly passed out. The second time was worse. How do you deal with her every day?"

"She doesn't have much to do with us, to be honest. She's not a—"

"People person?"

"Assuming she's an actual person. But I shouldn't be talking about her like that, especially not to you. You might sell your exposé to the papers."

"Don't worry about that." Kit picked up his shears. A vibrant yellow thread from Barker's dress still clung to them. "I've already signed the NDA."

Pamela slapped her temple with her palm. "Do you have your inspirational object? I forgot to ask you for it earlier."

That was one attachment he *had* read. Kit put down his shears, then pulled a tattered leather photograph album out of his bag. He handed it to her. "Here you go. It's all my grandpa's work. He took a picture of every suit he ever made."

Pamela cradled the album in her arms, patting the front. "Thank you for this. We'll take excellent care of it and return it after filming, no matter which way things go. We might need to ask you back for a bit of voiceover, you know, talking about how it inspires you. If it wasn't such a last-minute idea, we'd have had Tabitha interview you about it earlier."

Kit placed the shears into his carry case, then put the case into his bag. The relief at not being interviewed by Tabitha before his audition lightened his tone. "No probs. It's daft anyway."

Pamela blinked. "The idea?"

"No, the album. I'm sure the others had much better things."

"It's lovely." Her eyes rested on Barker's table. "I hope you don't mind me mentioning it, but Tabitha told me how Barker spoke to you when you offered to mend his dress."

Kit picked up his bag. "So?"

"Before he went in, he asked me how your audition went."

"Measuring up the competition, I bet."

Behind the Seams

Pamela stared at Barker's empty table for a moment. "Perhaps."

Kit shook her hand. "Thanks for being so kind, like. It was nice to have someone on my side."

"Nonsense. The crew's all rooting for you. You've been no trouble at all."

"Not even keeping you late with my second audition? You must have wanted to gan yem."

Pamela paused, as though processing what he'd said. "That means 'go home,' right? I'm sorry. It's been ages since I've chatted with a Geordie. You haven't kept us at all. Barker's audition was very short."

Kit rubbed his eyes. Had Barker messed things up? "Good short?"

Pamela shook her head, then leaned down to whisper. "Not a word to anyone, but he flunked the test in record time. Barely seconds into it, he just gave up and stormed out."

"I didn't see him come out of the room."

"He used the judges' exit."

Why would Barker, especially after all the drama about his dress, throw away his chances? Kit picked up his suit carriers. "Who's the 'proverbial tree'?"

"I'm sorry?"

"Earlier on, you said something about Barker falling far from the 'proverbial tree'. Who did you mean?"

Pamela hugged the photograph album. "His father's in prison."

Kit's mouth went dry. "What for?"

Pamela glanced at her watch. "Crikey. Look at the time. I'm sorry, I have to go to a production wrap-up." She hurried to the double doors, shouldered them open, then disappeared into the audition room.

Kit made his way out of the main space, back into the long corridor that led outside. He gave his numbered badge back to

Layla, who sat slumped over her desk in tears, surrounded by badges and scribbled pages. A shabby brown leather satchel slumped next to her.

Layla looked up from the mess. "I found my bag. Do you still want the eyedrops?"

Kit jostled his bag and suit carriers to free a hand, then squeezed her shoulder. "No, pet. I think you need them more than me."

He backed through the industrial unit's front door. Fuzzy, early evening heat swelled from the tarmac. Kit started in the entrance gate's direction.

A scraggly line of men queued at the burger van where Kit had asked for directions. Barker, back in black, stood chatting to a good-looking, mixed-race lad. When Barker saw Kit, he broke out of the queue and jogged over to join him. He'd washed off his makeup, and his faint freckles were back.

Barker slowed as though he was cautious. "Kit. Hey. You okay? How did it go?"

Kit ducked his head and kept walking. *You're not blushing. He just caught you off-guard.* "Proper canny, like."

"Is that good?" Barker walked sideways, bending his legs so he could catch Kit's eye. Barker rooted in his jacket pocket, then brought out a packet of cigarettes and a lighter. "I'll assume it is. So how did they come to call you back in?" He lit a cigarette, took a long drag. "Because they said I couldn't sew for shit."

Kit stopped walking, Barker's honesty catching him off guard. "But they liked your designs, right?"

"Well, yeah. I'm a talented designer." Barker looked Kit up and down. "Why did you change clothes?"

"They wanted to see my clothes on a model."

Barker's cigarette might have fallen out of his mouth if it hadn't stuck to his bottom lip. "Really?"

"Yeah."

Barker took another drag. "Don't bullshit me, Kit."

Kit dumped his bag and suit carriers onto the warm tarmac. He dug his hands into his pockets and rocked on his heels. "I—uh—didn't feel comfortable."

Barker kicked at the ground, voice soft. "You looked good, though."

"Yeah, well, Nancy called me out for faking it. Saw right through it."

"And that's why I got a chest full of boots?"

"Did I—? I was in a hurry—"

Plucking the cigarette out of his mouth, Barker half-turned away, his free hand gripping the elbow of his other arm. "I deserved it for interfering. I couldn't even tell you why I did it, but it doesn't matter. It won't happen again."

Again with the honesty. Kit struggled to work this lad out. Barker's face came alive when it moved. His sleek, espresso brown eyebrows shouldn't look right against his blonde, highlighted hair, but they set off his grey eyes, and his nose pointed to lips that—

Kit shoved his hands deeper into his pockets—fighting the impulse to put a thumb in the dimple in Barker's chin and pull him in for a kiss.

Barker's free hand carved through his hair. He gave Kit a brief smile. "It won't happen again."

Tugging on his jacket, Kit shook off the temptation to kiss him. Lads like Barker had a way of making you feel like the most important person in the room before they turned on you.

Barker frowned at him. "Are you listening to me?"

He's so gorgeous. I want to be that ciggy. Was it worth another shot? "I'm listening. I was wondering if…"

The frown disappeared as Barker's eyebrows rose, expectant. "What?"

"If you'd…" Tall, handsome, champion smile, and dripping

in designer gear. No way a lad like Barker would be interested in him.

Barker looked back over his shoulder. The mixed-race lad stood by Barker's bags. "Would you like to go for a drink?"

Did he just ask—? Kit checked his watch. Six thirty. "Bit early, isn't it?"

"For what?"

"Trying to get me drunk."

Barker looked up, down, sideways. "That's not what I meant," he drawled. "I meant a coffee. For a chat. To get to know you better." He turned towards the burger van. The mixed-race lad smiled back at him.

Kit's heart sank. "Or you could go with your better option."

Kit ducked to pick up his stuff. Barker took him gently by the shoulders and pulled him back up. "You can't be serious." He stepped out of the way so Kit had an unobstructed view of the lad. "What's he wearing?"

Six foot, forty-two-inch chest, thirty-two-inch waist, thirty-two-inch inside leg. Broad shoulders in need of careful measurement. Not bad looking. Long wavy hair piled on top of his head in a messy bun. "Floral shirt with an olive green yoke."

"And the designer?"

Kit pictured the last set of runway videos he'd watched online. "I don't recognise it."

"That shirt is from Gaultier's last ever season."

"So?"

"What did I wear for my audition?"

"A Gaultier jacket."

"Based on that evidence, who might be my favourite designer?"

"Jean Paul Gaultier. But you wore Versace jeans."

Groaning, Barker rolled his eyes. "For this exercise they

don't count. What about that chap must have caught my attention?"

Kit turned to face Barker, then sighed. "The lad's shirt."

Barker beamed. "Lovely. Now can we go for that drink? After what we've been through, we could both do with a friend."

Great. Barker just wanted a friend. Kit broke eye contact, then picked up his bag and suit carriers. "That's grand."

Barker jogged back to the burger van, gathered his bags over his shoulders, then said something to the mixed-race lad who looked down at his shirt. Laughing, the lad gave Barker the thumbs-up.

Kit shifted his weight from foot to foot. Did Barker walk as fast as other Londoners?

Barker returned, running his hands up and down his bags' straps. "So where are we going? Your place or mine?"

six

BARKER MADE sure he kept a pace Kit could manage, and it made a pleasant change not to hurtle from one place to another.

"How long have you lived in London?" Barker asked after nearly losing Kit to an overzealous ticket barrier.

"Two years, just over."

Kit hesitated to get on the train when they changed at West Ham. Barker hauled him through a gap between two overweight American tourists, then guided him to a seat.

Kit slumped, taking quick breaths. "Yeah. Two years."

"Right."

Kit's shoulders sagged. "I know I'm pathetic. I plan and I plan my routes, but if anything goes wrong, I'm lost. I'm late, more often than not."

"You're the best seamster I've ever met. You can't be good at everything."

Kit screwed up his face. "Is seamster a word?"

Barker chuckled. *He's adorable.* "You prefer seamstress?"

"I prefer tailor."

"Either way, you're the best."

57

Kit's shy smile met his. "Thanks."

The little pop-up café Barker picked didn't have the views of the river he preferred, but it was cheap for London. Why would he want to look at the river when Kit sat opposite, all cute and awkward?

The café weathered the early evening crowds on the Southbank. Nothing more than a wooden booth with seating outside, its jewel-coloured tablecloths and illustrated chalkboards defied the National Theatre towering over it, brutal concrete against a china blue sky.

Barker insisted on paying for his coffee and Kit's tea. At London prices, he wouldn't be taking a cab to wherever he secured a bed for the night.

Wanting to talk about the auditions, Barker only held back to watch Kit load his tea with three sugars.

Barker pushed aside the sugar biscuit tucked into his saucer. He'd eat it later. "How do you stay so slim?"

Kit ate his biscuit straight away, grinding the pale disc to dust, thumbing sandy crumbs from his rounded bottom lip. "Work's busy, so I live on the odd protein bar. The gym helps. How do you do it?"

You can't lie to him. "I can only afford to eat once a day. Twice, if I'm lucky."

"Hilarious. You're dressed from head to toe in designer gear. You must be able to afford a meal a minute."

If only he knew. "How did you do? At the audition? Might we be rubbing up against each other on the show?" Barker paused. "If you'll pardon the expression."

"God knows. Nancy gave me a right grilling about whether I could design at all. It was my fault, not being prepared, but I reckon I aced the test. You?"

"I think I mentioned they said I couldn't sew for shit, right? The sizing challenge could have gone better."

Kit sipped his tea, olive eyes looking at Barker over the rim of his cup. One eyebrow twitched. "How did you line them up?"

Bugger. "Oh, you know, left to right."

"I know that, man. But in what order?"

Barker looked out at the river, a slab of steady brown. A rubbish barge floated past the party boats moored to the riverbank opposite. "I don't remember."

The little sod smiled. "Right."

Barker tapped his biscuit on the side of his cup, watching the edge crumble, piling sandy rubble in the bowl of his teaspoon. "Maybe talking about our auditions isn't such a splendid idea."

"Okay. Why did you ask me for a drink?"

Because I'm lonely. Might you be, too? "Why did you accept?"

Kit rubbed his face. "You answer a lot of my questions with questions."

Barker stopped tapping his biscuit when he'd reduced it to the size of a large coin. Kit had smarts. "Is that a problem?"

"You did it again."

Barker tucked the biscuit between his index and middle finger, then rolled it through his fingers. "I was trying to be funny."

Kit stirred his tea. "That's a good trick." He sipped, added more sugar. "But not such a good diversion."

Here we go. Don't screw it up. Barker lowered the biscuit. It jittered against the saucer until he let go. "I think we have a lot in common."

Kit studied Barker's face. "We don't, but you seem like a decent lad."

"I am a decent lad," Barker said too quickly. "Decent. And we have things in common. We both love fashion. We both make great clothes. Nancy Shearsmith both put us through the wringer…"

Tipping back his head, Kit groaned. "Can we please not talk about Nancy? I want to forget today."

"Okay, okay. What would you prefer to talk about? Politics? Religion? The socioeconomic development of Bangladesh?"

"You're nuts, man."

Barker licked his tip of his index finger, pushed it into the crumbs in his saucer, then sucked it clean. "Nuts have their place, I guess."

"Are you flirting with me, Mister…?"

Hesitation froze Barker for a second. "Wareham. My last name's Wareham."

Kit's gaze bridged the space between them. He bit the edge of a smile. "Kit Wareham has a nice ring to it."

So he is gay. Anticipation charged every nerve in Barker's body. Matching wedding suits, meaningful looks across a reception crowded with their friends, that enormous bed in the honeymoon suite. *Fuck.* Leaning back in his chair, Barker held up his hands. "Slow down Mister Redman." He grinned at Kit's sudden frown. "Nancy told me your surname."

"Oh, right. Well, I was joshing with you about the Kit Wareham thing. I'm cool with a little flirting."

Barker ran the finger he'd sucked up and down the edge of his cup. "How about a lot of flirting?"

Kit scowled in the river's direction. "Bit early."

"Man trouble?"

"More like lack of man trouble."

"Well, that's another thing we have in common." Barker raised his coffee cup. "A toast to the lack of men."

Kit's thick eyebrows pinched together. "I'm not drinking to that. There's plenty of lads. They're all twats."

Barker forced a laugh. "I only meant it to be a joke."

Jaw set tight, Kit drained his cup. "I've been in two relationships, both after I'd moved to London. They didn't last more than two months."

How could anyone finish things with Kit? Barker edged his seat forward. "What happened?"

"When I met the first lad, I was pulling some long nights at Stitchworthy. He had a lot of time to fill."

"And…?"

"He found another lad who filled more than just his time."

"Sounds familiar. Welcome to London."

Kit dropped his cup into its saucer with a clatter. "It's not funny."

"Who said I was trying to be funny? And the second?"

"It was Christmas just gone. He lost his phone. I called it so we could find it."

"And?"

"I got to his phone first…" Kit trailed off, head down. "He'd saved my number as 'Stuart Little'."

Barker leaned forward, reaching out to take Kit's hand.

Kit drew his own hand back, then fiddled with his spoon. After a brief silence, Kit rubbed his eyes. "Want another drink? My shout."

The fire behind Kit's eyes challenged Barker to say no.

"I'd love one."

Kit froze, his gaze cooling. "Really?"

Anything to keep you here. "Yes, really."

Kit threw a handful of change into his saucer before loading his second cup of tea with sugar. "So, what is it with you and that Emilia lass?"

The mere thought of Emilia drained Barker's energy. "As soon as she joined my school, she pursued me."

"Haddaway, man. You're gay." Kit hesitated, frowning for a moment. "You are, right?"

Barker nodded, savouring the moment.

Kit tapped his spoon on the table, grinning. "Is that why she's so nasty to you?"

"No."

Frowning, Kit sat forward as though expecting Barker to elaborate.

"Something like that," Barker said.

Emilia dismissed his reluctance for coyness. It wasn't until she'd caught him creeping out of a man's hotel room the morning after a charity ball, clutching a fistful of money, that her humiliation turned to spiteful resentment. She outed Barker to his father Ludo, taking great delight in the man's wrath at the Wareham bloodline ending with his only son.

Kit checked his watch. "Oh, shite. I have to go. I have a fitting with a client."

"Are you joking?" Barker said. "It's gone seven."

Kit shot to his feet, then snatched up his bag and suit carriers. "I don't joke about work. The guy works himself into the ground. Doesn't take lunch. Works weekends. When he's free, we're free."

"This isn't some excuse, is it?"

"If you get through, I'll be rooting for you. See you, Barker." Kit paused. "How do I get to Oxford Circus?"

"Bakerloo line, four stops." Barker stood, looked around for a napkin. He couldn't let Kit go like this. "Can I get your number?"

"Phone's busted." Kit shifted his weight, fumbling with his bag. "I'll find you, okay? How many Barker Warehams can there be?"

Christ, no. Don't look me up.

Kit hurried away toward Waterloo station. Barker raised his hand in a feeble wave. Kit didn't look back to see it. In a second, he disappeared into the crush of tourists.

Barker tipped the change from Kit's saucer into his hand, then set off to find a payphone.

seven

. . .

THE FOLLOWING EVENING, Kit stood outside Hannah's front door, bag and suit carriers piled around his feet on the sun-warmed steps. Music played in the distance, accompanied by children laughing. Kit knocked on the door twice.

When Hannah answered, she almost dropped her toast. "What are you doing here?"

A single tear slid down Kit's cheek, then the determined dam he'd built crumbled.

Hannah leapt forward to hug him, gentle arms giving him space to breathe between the howls bursting from his throat.

Kit hid his pain all the way through his audition, then again today. No more. He sobbed into her shoulder, clutched at her hoodie.

She rocked him. "What's wrong?"

"Grandpa's dead, Han. He's dead."

"Oh, God. When?"

A smallest lull let Kit pull away, blinking with tears, wiping his nose. "Two nights ago."

Hannah pulled him back into her arms. "I'm so sorry. He loved you so much."

The pain didn't come in waves; it came in one gigantic, city-shattering tsunami. Kit didn't care who heard it. Grandpa Redman was dead, and something in Kit died along with him.

Hannah didn't let him go until his sobs tapered off. "Go inside, mate. I'll get your stuff."

An old pine table dominated the kitchen. Dented by pans and stained with tea, it stood solid and dependable. It made the kitchen the place to be.

Kit pulled up a chair to sit with his head in his hands. Hannah brought in his bag and suit carriers, setting them in the hallway, then crossed the kitchen to a large roll of quilted paper towel.

Tearing off sheet after sheet, she sighed. "Judging by the fact you're wearing a suit, I'm guessing you went into work today. What did they say?" She handed him the paper towel.

Kit pressed the sheets hard against his eyes. If he pressed hard enough, he might hold back his feelings. "Didn't tell them."

Hannah sat beside him. "Please tell me you didn't go to that audition."

Kit peeked at her from behind the paper towel, then dabbed the crumbs away from the corner of her mouth. "Please tell me you're not eating toast for your tea."

"I'm being serious, Kit."

"I didn't want to let you down. Or Grandpa."

Eyes squeezed shut, Hannah pushed herself up. "I can't believe you went because you promised us. Christ, Kit. You're so decent I could spit." She went to the kettle. "And if by 'tea' you mean dinner, then yes, I'm eating toast. And how very dare you question the nutritional value of burnt bread."

Kit crushed the paper towel into a ball, but kept it in one hand. "I'm questioning why I don't have burnt bread of my own."

Hannah's large, angry eyes considered him from beneath her thick blonde fringe. "It'll cost you."

"How much?"

"The dish on your au-*dish*-on."

Sighing, Kit rolled the ball of paper from hand to hand. "I signed an NDA. My lips are sealed."

Hannah's eyes twinkled as she leant back on the kitchen counter. "As sealed as my bread bin? Such a shame. A plate of *nothing* smeared with butter and marmalade won't have the same effect as a thick, golden slice of yeasty goodness."

"Fine. I'll tell you everything as long as I can have a crust. I'll make the tea." Kit filled the peeling, enamelled kettle and put it on to boil. "Are you going to tell the CIA withholding toast is more effective than waterboarding?"

"And lose my competitive advantage?" Taking the bread out of the bread bin next to the geriatric toaster, Hannah nudged him out of the way to get to the cutlery drawer and grab a knife. "But you'd better talk. Have you been there all this time? It's been two days."

"No, thank God. I had to get back for a fitting with that hedge fund manager."

"The evil one with the big watch?"

"He argued with all of his measurements, so by the time I finished it wasn't worth going home. I slept at the shop, worked today, and here I am."

"Bonkers. What was the talent like?"

"None. Today was quiet."

"Not work. The audition."

"There was this one lad. Proper gorgeous."

Hannah collapsed on the kitchen counter, forehead on folded arms, voice muffled. "How could you do that?"

Kit gave her a sideways glance, then opened the cupboard over the kettle. "What?"

"First, that's not the talent I was asking about—I meant the design talent—and second, you massively failed the Bechdel Test."

"I thought the Bechdel Test was about women not talking about men. Have you got any mugs that aren't chipped?"

"Detail, detail, but, yeah, I suppose you're right." She straightened up enough to dump four thick slices of white bread into the toaster. "The good mugs are at the back."

Kit reached into the back, then rummaged around until he found two Bacchus Broadcasting mugs. "And you don't even like boys."

Hannah sputtered, mouth gaping. "Yes, I do. I like boys. Some of my best friends are boys."

Kit didn't have to fake his laugh. The easy banter with Hannah dulled the fuzz of pain sitting in the back of his mind. "Thanks."

"But the test, Kit, the test. It doesn't require that one or both of the women involved in the discussion about said man has to fancy said man."

"You sure about that?"

"No, but I'll google it later. Can we please get back to how your audition went?"

"Everything was different." Kit popped the cork lids off the pristine, white porcelain caddies standing by the kettle. "These are new." He threw a tea bag into each mug, then spooned out sugar. "Gunter was there. And Nancy."

Hannah slammed the butter knife on the counter, covered her mouth. "Shut your stinking northern cake-hole."

"It's true. They were. Gunter was lovely."

Hannah bowed sagely. "As expected."

"But Nancy was panto evil, and not entertainingly, neither."

Popping toast punctuated Hannah's awed silence.

By the time they finished eating at the table—including a

second round—Kit had filled Hannah in on every detail of the audition. Almost.

Hannah unzipped her hoodie, revealing a yellow t-shirt emblazoned with an enormous red star. "Did they give you any idea how well you did?"

Kit pushed his plate away. "There's no way I'm in. No chance. Is that a *Simon Galaxy* shirt?"

Hannah pulled on the hem of the t-shirt, looking down at it. "Yeah. Got it free at work. You can't be sure about the audition, though. It sounds like Gunter was helping you. He wouldn't have given you that clue about time unless he wanted you in."

"Maybe, although I doubt he has much clout. It's not like he's a judge, and he's nice to everyone, isn't he? I mean that's his thing."

Hannah bobbed her head from side to side. "His thing might be to be genuinely genuine."

Considering this, Kit drained the last of his tea.

Hannah's eyes narrowed. "So how about that guy? The gorgeous one?"

Kit slumped over his mug. "It was so embarrassing. He was so slick, and I was so not slick, and he got me to put on his jeans and stuff."

"Hold the phone," Hannah said, thumping her hands on the kitchen table. "He did what now?"

"I know, I know. He said I didn't look like a proper designer, so he pulled off his jeans and boots in front of everyone and—" Kit looked out of the window, sipping tea that no longer existed, faking nonchalance. "—got me to put them on."

"Is that, uh, some gay mating ritual?"

"He's not interested, pet."

"Don't be so sure. If he wasn't interested, he wouldn't find an excuse to strip off in front of you, especially if you're competing. More toast?"

Kit pushed his plate towards her. "So I'm wearing his black jeans and boots…"

Hannah picked up the plates, put them back on the counter, then loaded the toaster with four more slices of bread. "Black jeans and boots. What colour was his top?"

"Black. And his jacket."

"Ugh."

"What?"

Hannah leaned against the kitchen counter, arms crossed. "Does any of that sound familiar?"

Kit's ex, Ryan—Stuart-fucking-Little Ryan—wore black all the time.

Kit mashed his hands against his cheeks. "Don't."

"Was this guy posh?" Hannah asked.

"Barker?"

Dissolving into laughter, Hannah clutched at her chest with one hand and beat the kitchen counter with the other. "His name's Barker?"

Kit flinched. "Yeah."

Hannah ripped off a sheet of paper towel to dab away a tear rolling down her cheek. "Oh, mate. Bet he's got a name like 'Barker Plummington the Third' and lives in Chelsea or something. You've got a type."

Kit's limbs sank. She might have been right. Ryan lived in Chelsea. He might know Emilia.

The third round of toast popped, and they ate it in silence.

"How did you leave things with him?" Hannah asked when she finished.

Kit wiped his mouth with the back of his hand. "At top speed."

"Didn't you give him your number?"

"I was so stressed about getting back to work, I forgot. It's not like he asked or anything. Nothing would happen anyway. We're proper opposites."

Behind the Seams

"Might be awks if you both get through."

"Never gonna happen. How's your Comic Con outfit coming on?" Kit edged forward in his chair. "Can I see it?"

Hannah gave him a cautious smile. "Pretty well and no you can't. I know it's mad having a bestie who can do this kind of thing with his eyes shut, but I want to do this on my ownsome."

"Go on, pet. Give us a little look. Please."

"Ugh. Okay." Hannah went upstairs to her room, her comfort trailing behind her.

Kit's grief snuck up on him, playing back the hospital's phonecall and the news Grandpa had gone. He went to the sink, then splashed cool water on his face. It wouldn't be fair on Hannah to come downstairs and find him sobbing again.

Her costume needed careful manoeuvring to get in through the kitchen door.

Kit had no idea what it was other than some lizard mixed in with a robot, a bodysuit printed with scales visible under a silver skeleton. "Looks good," he said, helping her to get it propped up against a kitchen chair. "That skeleton—is it painted foam?"

"Yes, and it's an exoskeleton. It's an Evocore."

Kit examined the bodysuit's seams, then knelt by one leg and ran his eyes along its stitches. "Is that hot glue?"

Hannah hovered at his side, rubbing her arms as though she was cold. "Maybe."

Standing, Kit put his hands on his hips. "It'll give out, eventually. Two backstitches and you're sorted."

Hannah crouched, scooped up the leg, then hugged it against her chest. "I know you mean well, but you took over my last two costumes and didn't even know you were doing it."

Kit stretched his fingers, lowering his voice. "Did I?"

"You're about to do it now."

"I'm only trying to help."

"I know, but it's my project. If I mess it up, that's on me."

"Fair enough. I'm still not sure what an Evo-whatsit even is, let alone what it should look like."

Kit's phone rang in his breast pocket. They both jumped.

Kit didn't move.

Hannah released her costume's leg. It landed with a whomp. "Answer it."

"It can't be the production company. It's too late."

Her gaze darted to his chest, eyes bright. "Might not be too late for them. Answer it."

Kit pulled the phone from his breast pocket with his thumb and index finger, as though it might bite him. He winced, unable to see the caller's name through his smashed screen. Could it be someone from Bacchus? "I can't have made it for them to ring so fast."

Hannah licked her lips. "Or you're straight through, but you won't know unless you—take—the—bloody—call."

Kit's stomach tingled as he pressed the button to answer.

"Hi, Kat. It's Layla."

"It's Kit."

"Sorry. The judges decided that your collection—" Layla spoke slowly as though finding it hard to read someone's writing. "—lacked enough visual flair to differentiate yourself from the designers who have already made it through."

Tension ebbed from Kit's body, loosening his muscles, hanging his head over the phone. "Oh, okay. I appreciate you letting us know so fast."

"I'm sorry, Kat."

"Kit."

"You must get that a lot." Layla hung up.

Hannah ruffled his hair, then wiped her hands on her hoodie. "That bloody Brylcreem. Your pillows must be rank."

She made a fourth round of toast. "I've got a new *Super Mario* game if you fancy it?"

But Kit had had his arse kicked enough these past few days. He gathered up his bags, wished Hannah goodnight, then left for his grandparent's house in north London.

Kit dreaded walking into a house Grandpa would never see again, but all he wanted was his bed and peace and time alone. Grandpa had died, and *Runway Rivals* didn't want Kit, but at least he had a job he loved and a friend in Hannah.

That might be enough.

eight
...

THE FRENZY of Barker's *Runway Rivals* audition paled in comparison with the panic at his graduation show. He'd arrived late, ghosting through a backstage area crammed with twenty-somethings high on everything from caffeine pills to cocaine. Three years of study at the prestigious London University of Creative Arts, better known as LUCA, carried a weight of expectation. The pre-show atmosphere suffocated; the careers of several high-profile artists and designers had launched based on LUCA's graduation show.

"Mister Wareham," Sybille Fitzpatrick said as she spotted Barker putting down his bags. "You'd better have a bloody good reason for walking in here at this hour." As usual, Sybille wore layers of blazing colours with an equally bright shawl pinned at one shoulder with an oversized, vintage brass brooch inset with emerald, sapphire and amethyst glass. Three short knitting needles adorned with pompoms skewered her piled white hair into a chignon. "If it wasn't for the fact the catwalk show's ordered alphabetically by surname, I'd have cut your collection."

"My collection?" Barker said, unfazed by his course

leader's threat. Thanks to his father Ludo, the Wareham name became so infamous it drew in the curious and guaranteed column inches.

And Sybille knew it.

Barker yawned. "The same collection that Nancy Shearsmith herself described as 'poetic'?" He knew full well that Gunter said the word, albeit about Barker's introduction, but the word had been bandied about in Nancy's presence, and she hadn't objected.

Sybille's mouth dropped open. "Poetic, you say? Yes—well —I take it your audition went smoothly?"

"So smoothly. So, so smoothly."

"Right. Well. Jolly good. There's your rail. I put your models into hair and makeup lest they died of boredom. All nine of them need to wear what I trust is in the bags at your feet and please tell me those philistines at that television show didn't trash them."

"On the contrary. One's much improved." Kit's image appeared, backstitched into Barker's thoughts.

A shriek of horror went up somewhere behind Sybille. She looked back, craning her neck to identify the source of the anxious wailing, then produced an envelope from deep in her shawl. "Here are your guest tickets." Another yowl. "Go on," she said, looking back at him and waving the envelope at him with increasing speed.

"I don't have any guests."

"What about your parents?"

Every nearby student turned to stare. Everyone knew not to mention Barker's parents.

Sybille gawped at them in confusion until the proverbial penny dropped. "I'm sorry, Barker," she stammered. "I wasn't thinking." She shrank back in expectation of one of his regular meltdowns. She'd seen plenty of those over the years, usually following the infamous portfolio reviews during which students were often told their work was beyond saving—and promptly destroyed—but Barker's meltdowns were the stuff of legend.

With fear writ large in every face, an electric bolt of shame buzzed through him. "Perhaps," he said, trying to control his inner monster, "someone else might put them to better use."

"Yes, yes," Sybille agreed. "Lovely idea." Without hesitation, she thrust herself into the backstage crowd.

Once his models came back from hair and makeup, Barker talked them through their running order before taking a stroll around the deserted exhibition hall to calm his nerves. Two shows in three days.

Life at university started well enough. Invigorated to be doing something he loved other than what his father expected of him, Barker spent his first year pushing his creative boundaries. Sybille described his work as "dangerously avant-garde" —which he later found out was code for unwearable—before working with him to rein his style back into something a future-focused woman would want to wear yet still catch the eye of a fashion editor.

During the summer break before his final year, Barker stayed at his family's Miami house. One morning, as he got ready to pick his mother up from the airport, he received a call from the *Daily Mail* asking him to comment on his father Ludo's arrest. Barker's hands shook so violently it took several jabs at his phone to hang up. He raced to check the news websites.

By the time he arrived at the airport to meet his mother, he had a packed suitcase and bought tickets for them both to fly straight back to London.

To bolster the family's finances from the ravages of inheritance tax, Ludo Wareham masterminded the largest, most complex financial fraud ever conducted in the UK. To make matters worse, when the police raided Wareham Manor, officers found Ludo—who used his marriage to debutante-turned-supermodel Romilly Prescott to bolster his public image—balls-deep in a decidedly un-super catalogue model.

Ludo's trial began during Barker's second semester of his final year. With the family bank accounts frozen and Barker's trust fund spent, he found himself in the unfamiliar position of applying for a student loan, using Romilly as a guarantor. The adjustment to a paltry student income proved difficult, and Barker developed an unhealthy relationship with credit. His debt mounted slowly as reassurances from Ludo's lawyer dripped through. If the family money was soon to be unfrozen Barker's purchases would barely have time to accrue interest before he paid them off. An evening of drinks for his many friends would be fine, and that new Marc Jacobs collection wouldn't hurt, either. By the time it was clear the money would be locked up for the foreseeable future, Barker's spending was as much for comfort as it was to impress. He maxed out his credit cards. The banks declined extra credit. When his drink parties dried up, so did his social circles. Barker ended up with one friend from school: Caspian Kendall, captain of the hockey team and all-round rogue.

While Barker developed an unhealthy relationship with money, Romilly did the same with prescription drugs. As the pressure of the trial increased, both mother and son pushed their relationships to the extreme.

Ludo lied on the stand, and his defence crumbled. A guilty verdict, a fine of five million pounds, and a prison sentence of one hundred and ten years left Barker and Romilly fending for themselves.

Barker pawned his possessions, falling into a cycle of selling last season's clothes to buy this season's. Romilly fell into a mental health unit. Barker lashed out at the paparazzi and ended up in all the papers. Romilly lashed out at her wrists and ended up back in France with her elderly parents.

Unable to cope with their daughter's self-destructive behaviour, they booked Romilly into the best interventional psychiatry clinic money could buy. Appalled with Barker's behaviour, any possibility of financial aid for him fell off the table.

When the Inland Revenue seized both Wareham Manor and the Miami house, Barker had nowhere to go.

The only thing he possessed was privacy regarding his sexuality—Emilia only outed him to Ludo—and pride in finishing his degree course. Finishing his debt would be another matter. He applied to *Runway Rivals* for the money, but his design talent made him an ideal candidate for the show. If he worked as hard as Sybille drove him, he had a good chance of winning the show, and the one hundred thousand pound prize would clear his debts.

If Barker didn't win the show but secured investment, he'd clear his debts and launch his own label. He wasn't ready to deal with the shame of declaring himself bankrupt. Like his father, Barker made some stupid choices where money was concerned. Unlike his father, Barker would do everything in his power to put them right.

Sybille's voice echoed through the exhibition space. "Barker? There was a call for you. Girl called Layla. She's calling back after the show."

Barker vaguely recalled the name, but "Layla" might be a bailiff. He made his way backstage where he'd blend in with the crowd.

Emilia materialised at his side, sheathed in a gold sequined, plunge-neck minidress. Alexandre Vauthier. Very nice.

"Sneaking off, Barker?" She clicked her fingers at a passing girl. "Cortado."

The girl sniggered. "If you want a drink, the tea urn's right there."

With a theatrical sigh, Emilia shoved the girl aside then

approached a table bearing a stack of white plastic cups and two stainless steel thermal jugs. Emilia attempted to pour coffee from the jug. Nothing came out.

"For God's sake, Emilia, you're supposed to push the button on top. Even your little brother would know that."

Emilia poured a coffee, then slunk back to his side, watching the backstage hubbub. "Remember when you used to have a butler for that sort of thing, when the only baggage you had was luggage?"

"Things change when you least expect it, Emilia."

"Like the bed you sleep in."

He dropped his voice. "It wasn't like that, and you know it."

"Creeping out of some deviant's bedroom with a pair of Tom Ford loafers in one hand and a fistful of fifties in the other? Screams 'whore' to me."

"The chap gave it to me at the fundraiser."

"I'm sure he did, and no doubt you took it with enthusiasm —and the money."

"I'm not my father."

"Just as well. Speaking of which, where did you sleep last night? I'd have offered you my Hampstead flat, but then I thought, 'no'."

Barker picked lint from his sleeve, feigning an airy yawn. "I hear your uncle's light on his feet. Perhaps he has a bed we can use."

Emilia's self-control evaporated into a hiss of rage. "Stay away from my family, you revolting creature."

Barker pouted. "What and lose a potential source of income? You might be new money, Emilia, but it's coming in thick and fast."

"Does that mean you've yet to pawn those loafers? I'd get on that quick smart. I wouldn't want to trip over you in some doorway." She sipped her coffee. "Or perhaps I would."

"Go to hell, Emilia."

"Talking to you is hell enough, thank you." Emilia sauntered away, pushing aside anyone who got in her way. How times changed. At school, Emilia used to do that to get to him.

Backstage stress levels reached fever pitch.

"Did you hear who's rocked up?" said a student whose hair smelled of crayons. "Only Nancy-bloody-Shearsmith."

Sybille turned this season's shade of green, then wormed her way through the excited throng to Barker's side. "Is this your doing?"

"As much as I'd like to say I engineered this as a thank you for all the time you've invested in me, I'm as surprised as you."

"Hell's bells, what could she want? We gave up inviting her years ago. Did you mention LUCA during your portfolio review?"

With no intention of confessing he'd begged Nancy to come to the show, Barker rubbed the back of his neck. "Possibly, Sybille. They wanted to know a bit of background."

Playing with her hair, Sybille looked around. "That's 'Miss Fitzpatrick' when we're around the student body."

"Noted, but I noted LUCA on my application."

Sybille climbed up onto the back of the catwalk, careful to remain unseen by the guests spilling into the seating area. "Good God." Sybille turned religious when she panicked. "She's got Osred East with her—and they're sitting in the chancellor's and vice chancellor's seats. What are we going to do?"

As *Shear Style*'s fashion director, Osred East served as one of the few leading men in women's fashion publishing. There were plenty of them running fashion houses, working as buyers and creative directors, but Osred's appointment to *Shear Style* caused ripples throughout the industry. In his early thirties, many dismissed him as something of a trophy employee, hired by Nancy as a symbol of her ability to emasculate up-and-coming men, but Barker noticed a gradual shift in the magazine's editorial spreads. They still carried the aspirational weight readers came to expect from *Shear Style,* but Osred infused them with growing innovation. The women who bought *Vogue* suddenly carried copies of *Shear Style*, too. Despite their detractors, Nancy Shearsmith knew talent when she saw it, and no one conceived a shot like Osred.

Barker hoped Nancy saw talent in him. "Give me ten minutes, Miss Fitzpatrick," he said, "and three glasses of Moët."

Barker manipulated Pamela into delaying Kit's audition by twenty minutes. He'd do the same for a little face time with Nancy as he sorted out her seating.

If there was one thing Barker could still buy it was time.

nine

. . .

ANGER CHURNED in Kit's guts, hot as lava.

"What were you playing at?" he roared at his mum Zosima, "letting a bunch of workmen take Grandpa's machine?"

A fifty-one-year-old woman, Zosima's neglected body wore the features of an eighty-year-old. The washed-out black rinse rusted the limp grey framing her aged face. Years of scowling peaked and trenched her forehead, shadowing disdainful eyes the same shade as Kit's. At rest, her expression showed no sign of joy. Instead, her narrow lips told of her regular displeasure.

Zosima's Italian accent thickened. "You visit from London. You never take it. Was in the way."

"Of what? You haven't been upstairs in three years."

"I can now. They put in stairlift. That bloody council's fault. Been waiting for downstairs wet room for—"

"And since when do you give a monkey's about what's used and what's not?" He pointed at the mountains of hacky laundry, unused gadgets and unopened mail piled around where she sat in the middle of the lounge in a shabby, high-backed chair. "You've not binned a copy of the *Daily Mail* since Da left."

Zosima waved a hand around her. What little daylight struggled through net curtains thick with grime, slumped on towers of unread newspapers. "Might be something important there I need."

"That's what I bought you all them scrapbooks for, Mam. Cut out what you want and bin the rest."

"Do I look like I've got time for scrapbooking? I've got things to do, *piccolo*."

Calling Kit "little one," didn't help his mood. "Like what? Monitoring the bastard neighbours that keep parking across your drive? The drive you don't use? That drive?"

Her lips pursed. "There's your brother. He needs his mama to look out for him."

"By texting him every five minutes and panicking when he doesn't text back? Greg told me you called the police when you couldn't get hold of him for forty minutes. Said you told them he was depressed about turning twenty-five. That he'd been drinking heavily."

"That wasn't a lie."

"He only had a hangover, Mam."

"That's not point. Point is—"

"The point is, why did you think it was okay to let people you didn't know take Grandpa's machine? My machine? He gave it to me."

"You have one at his house."

"That's his." Kit couldn't bring himself to use the past tense. Grandpa died nine days ago. Kit came to Newcastle for comfort. He didn't get it from Zosima. "I wanted the one he gave me."

Zosima fell silent. But it wouldn't wash with him today.

"Come on, Mam. Why d'you do it?"

When the wailing started, Kit lost any chance of getting an answer. The few gasped words she dotted in between the cries of anguish were a defence mechanism he'd seen her use a thousand times, especially when asked by medical professionals why she, a dangerously overweight woman with a history of heart attacks and strokes, had been frying sausages the last time she fell.

Kit wanted Mam back: Mam who rallied when her husband left; Mam who worked in town all week and still had energy to cook and clean all weekend; Mam who lived her life. That's who he wanted, not this bloated impostor, skin as mottled as her thinking, body as neglected as her manners.

Kit pressed on. This time might be different. "Why give away my machine?"

The wailing stopped. The shouting followed. "Don't talk to me like that, fucking runt. He wasn't your real *nonno*. Your *nonna* said he no give her the sex. Bet he wanted boy like you. Bet he touched you."

Kit dug his fingernails into his palms, focusing on the pain. "Mam."

"Bet you liked it, *puttana*. Run back home and let the mens fuck you for money."

Kit bolted out of the house, angry at her for what she'd said, angry at honouring his duty to drop in on her. Time after time it ended with her vile abuse.

With the sewing machine gone, Pamela better send his grandpa's album back soon.

Greg waited for Kit in his battered Ford Focus. "Don't tell me—lots of shouting and bawling?"

"Got that right."

Firing up the car, Greg took the cigarette tucked behind his ear, then lit it. "Same old, same old. Let's get home." He wound down the window four inches, then pulled away, turning left out of the road and toward Byker.

Bricklaying moulded Greg's body. He shared Kit's curls, but their resemblance ended there. Greg had Da's features: a blue-eyed buzzard with piercing eyes and a narrow nose with a hump and hook. Days working in the cold northern mist weathered his skin. He bound his brown hair in a short ponytail. "Soph's made us a Sunday roast."

"It's Saturday."

Greg blew smoke into the gap of the open window, then took a hand off the steering wheel to ruffle Kit's hair. "Her roast's canny good, like. Why wait 'til Sunday?" Greg swore, rubbing his hand on his jeans. "What's that shite you've got in your hair, man?"

Kit flipped down the passenger visor to check his reflection, teasing his hair back into place. "Brylcreem. Grandpa used to wear it."

"Well, wash it out before you go to bed. Soph'll go mad with that on the pillows."

"I'm not staying over, man."

"Are you daft? Dinner, shower, sleep. You must be proper paggered."

Growing up, Greg poked fun at Kit all day long, but at school switched to big brother mode, shutting down Kit's bullies. He walked Kit to and from school every day, so everyone saw he had Kit's back. Once they got indoors, the teasing started again. Greg—friend and enemy all in one.

Sunday afternoon, when Kit got home to a bare fridge, he walked to the corner shop for bacon, bread, and a pint of milk. Barker's yellow dress blazed on the cover of an independent, short-run fashion magazine. Although Kit refused to buy it on principle, he couldn't resist flicking through the pages until he stopped at a photograph of Barker handing a glass of bubbly to Nancy and that Osred fella from *Shear Style*. They'd attended Barker's graduation show. The milk practically curdled in Kit's hand. If Barker squirmed his way onto *Runway Rivals* like that, Kit swore he'd never watch it again.

He'd savaged half a bacon butty when Greg called, breathless. "Have you heard from Mam?" Greg said. "She's proper bad, like. Phoned the police in a panic this morning, saying she needed help blocking her chimney because a swarm of bees was coming for her."

"What bees?"

"That's what the police asked her. African bees, she said. Read about it in—"

"The *Daily Mail*. So what's going on?"

"They've taken her, man. Locked her up in a mental health unit."

Worry thumped in Kit's chest, but none in his heart. "You're joking? I can come back if you need—"

"Get away with you, man. You've got Grandpa's funeral to arrange. Besides, it's a bloody party round our house. They've confiscated Mam's phone and put her under observation. This afternoon's the first time me and Soph watched a movie all the way through in years. Right, gotta go."

"Did you know the workmen who—?" But Greg hung up. When the phone rang again, Kit answered at once. "Do you know who took Grandpa's machine?"

"Um," a young woman said. "Is that Kit?"

"Aye." He looked at the number but didn't recognise it. "Who's this?"

"It's Layla from the *Runway Rivals* production team. I'm sorry to interrupt your Sunday afternoon, but there's been a horrible mistake."

"It's all right, pet. We already spoke. I know I'm not on the show."

"That's not exactly true. Because of an administrative error —" She paused. "I messed up, Kit. I'm so sorry. I mixed up your details with someone else's. A girl called Katherine."

"Katherine?"

"Yes—'Call me Kat.'—Katherine."

"So…?"

"She didn't get through. Are you still there?"

The half a bacon butty he'd demolished was in danger of making a reappearance.

"Kit," Layla said. "You're our final contestant."

"You're funning, right?"

Her voice faltered. "I'm sorry?"

"Are you being serious?"

"Filming starts first week in July. I'll get the details out to you tomorrow."

"Hold on, pet." How could he throw this chance away? "I can't accept."

"Have you lost your mind?" Hannah said as she opened her door. "I read your text literally just now."

Kit held his arms out wide before clamping them over his head. "How can I go on the telly while my mam's in the looney bin?"

Hannah stood back, pointing to the kitchen. "In."

Kit shuffled past her. "I'm not here for a lecture, mind."

"Well, you're getting one." She followed him into the room. "Sit. Good. Now—"

"How's your costume going?"

"Horribly. I'm using hot glue for pretty much everything and don't change the subject."

"Why don't you let me help?"

"Because it's my thing, like this show is your thing. It is your thing, isn't it?"

Kit's fingers carved through his hair, keeping them there to hold his head from bursting with uncertainty. "Yeah. No."

Groaning, Hannah picked up the kettle. "I'll need something more directional. What's stopping you? It's not like you and your mum are close."

He looked at her for a long time. "It's complicated. Fear?"

"And that's perfectly valid. Fear of—?"

"I don't know."

"You know," Hannah whispered. "You don't want to say it, because saying it takes its power away." She filled the kettle and put it on to boil. "To get over the profundity of what I said, I'm making tea, and there's a definite chance of toast. Are you in?"

Kit drummed his fingers on the table, mouth flooding with saliva. "Is it thick sliced and white?"

"Isn't it always?"

He gave her a thumbs-up. "I'm in."

"And the show?"

"Still can't decide." The energy drained out of him and he slumped back in his chair. "I'm afraid of finding out I'm not good enough. I know I'm good at making suits. David's trained me harder than Grandpa ever did. But as a designer? What if it turns out I'm a one-trick pony?"

"What about all the costumes you make for that ungrateful lot at your theatre group? Surely that has to count for something."

"It's mostly period stuff. They don't want to see that. How many times have they criticised something for being too costumey?"

"Eighty-six. What's the worst that could happen? Getting kicked off in week one?"

"No way. Getting kicked off the round before the final. It'd be so close I could taste it."

"Say you get kicked off. What happens?"

Kit picked at the table, lifting a splinter, then pushing it back down. "David said that if I left Stitchworthy, I couldn't have my job back."

Tilting her chin down, Hannah frowned. "Bit harsh."

"And I've just spunked half a month's wages on a new

phone. City's not the same since the crash last year. We've had a bit of a rush on recently, but that's all from the old boys, and there's not enough of the old boys to keep us going for much longer. He'd be relieved if I resigned, because he's too soft to sack any of us. But I want to be a designer. I want my label."

"Making suits?"

Kit shifted in his seat, a jitter in his belly. "Making collections that get people talking, that look great on the runway, that people love to wear."

Hannah took the seat next to him, then put a hand on his thigh. "Go on the show. If you lose, keep going. One telly show shouldn't define you as a person."

Kit's thigh drummed under Hannah's touch, unable to settle. "I can't do it. I can't."

David Stitchworthy — "Actual name. I have the birth certificate to prove it." — hired Kit as soon as he mentioned Grandpa Redman.

"He made my wedding suit," David said, "and I show it to all my staff to strive for the same quality."

All of David's staff turned out to be two Greek men in their fifties: Lefkos and Renos, or "Left and Right" as David sometimes called them when his memory slipped.

Lefkos took Kit's decision to stay at Stitchworthy well, Renos less so.

"What you doing wanting to go on the TV?" Lefkos said. "You don't need all that. People poking in your life. You wanna be designer? You go to school, learn it proper."

"It's filmed at the London University of Creative Arts," Kit said. "It is a school. The best school. Have you seen my shears? I can't find them anywhere."

"Humph. They don't teach you. You have camera in your face when you trying to measure. You get legs all akimbo."

Renos waved Lefkos away, then threw a meaty arm around Kit's shoulders. "Don't argue with tailors, my friend. They carry scissors. You do what you need. Don't hide your dreams for nobody." He jabbed a fat finger in Kit's chest. "What's inside you, let it out or you go crazy."

Kit was sure Renos's finger would leave a bruise. "You talk like you have dreams."

"I do." The big Greek sighed. "I did. I give up on them. Too late for me, so the advice I give you is advice I wanted when I was young man. Go after your dreams before they get away from you. We not long on this earth." Renos dropped his head. "Your *papou*. Sorry, Kit. Funeral soon?"

Kit blinked up at Renos. "Next week. Thanks, man. I miss him. Have you seen my shears?"

David jogged down the steps to the cutting room, his thick, silver white moustache hiding his top lip. "Kit. Barty's in for his shooting suits fitting. Renos, keep an eye on him, will you?"

"Barty or Kit, Mister David?"

Their boss chuckled. "Thirty-three years and you're still calling me 'Mister David'."

"And you still saying the S at end of my name."

"Point taken. Barty knows what he's doing. Oh, and Kit, come and see me when you're done."

Barty Ribblestone, Lord of Puckeridge, was his usual enthusiastic self. "Kit, my boy. You've graduated to a cutter, eh? Very impressed."

Barty's waistcoat corseted his belly. Nothing corseted his personality, so much more than the jolly cliché. With five daughters, four of whom lived with him at Belgae Hall, Kit suspected Barty came in for the company more than clothing.

Kit dipped his chin. "Thank you, Lord Puckeridge."

A flush crept along Barty's cheeks, turning them as crimson

as his bulbous nose. "Come, now. Let's not have all that nonsense."

Kit glanced at Renos for guidance. "Okay, Mister Ribblestone?"

Barty drummed his hands on his paunch. "You know you can call be Barty when David's not around."

Kit gave him a brief bow. "Thank you, Barty. Let's get started, shall we?" Kit helped Barty into his basted suit and stepped back to observe. "Neck is nice, shoulders look good."

Barty worked his shoulders, rolling each one, shrugging. "Shouldn't we draw them in?"

"They'll be too restrictive. We might give you a little more ease in the back. It's a little tight."

"They need letting out every shooting season. You get to eat what you shoot."

Renos didn't look up from his notebook. "You must be good shot."

Barty hooked his thumbs into his waistcoat pockets. "Shooting's the sport of kings."

"Waist is nice," Kit said. "Length looks good."

Renos signalled his agreement with a tiny nod.

Kit continued. "Let's try to find a bit of cuff." He tugged Barty's shirt sleeves, so they showed past his jacket sleeves.

Barty hesitated. "Do you know, Kit? My grandson Bartholomew—Barty the Third—reminds me of you. Lovely little boy. Very gentle. Always smiling despite the ribbing he gets at school."

Lovely little boy. "I take it he's short?" Kit said.

Barty pulled at his collar, smile weak. "Yes, now you come to mention it."

"Hold old is he?"

"Nine."

"There's still time. I kept growing until my thirteenth birthday."

"And he loves going through my clothes. Stays with us every school holiday. Empties my wardrobe. Pores over everything. Even caught the rascal unpicking a dinner jacket last summer."

Kit walked around Barty. "I'd lengthen the jacket sleeves so you only have, say, between a quarter and half an inch of cuff showing." With a pinch of the back of the shoulder, Kit lifted the crown of the sleeve. "This needs to come up. It'll give you a cleaner line in the back so it's not bunching up."

Barty's laugh burst like a pipe. "Good, isn't he?"

Renos rubbed his chin. "Makes me sick," he said, voice kind. "When I was twenty, I could not even thread needle. This one best tailor, finisher, cutter I ever come across—for his age."

"Let's move to the front." Kit moved to face Barty. "Lapels look good for your width. Chest has a little of drape. I'd leave that." Kit stepped back. "Okay, how is it?"

Barty turned in front of the mirror, examining the jacket from different angles, then patted his belly. His lidded look of satisfaction said it all. "Very comfortable."

"And you're having one in tweed?"

"For formal shoots."

"And the other in moleskin for…?"

"The informal."

"Very good. Give us four weeks, sir, and we'll see you for your next fitting."

"Most excellent," Barty said as Renos stepped forward to help him out of the jacket.

At that moment, Kit had no desire to be anywhere other than Stitchworthy. "You should bring him in."

Barty's brows knitted. "Bring who in?"

"Barty the Third. I was only a few years younger than him when Grandpa introduced me to sewing. I'd be happy to give him the tour."

Barty beamed. "Renos?"

"Sir?"

"You tell David he needs to give Kit a raise."

Kit didn't get a raise. When he went to see David after Barty's fitting, David let him go.

"I'm so sorry, old chap, but you know how business is. We don't have enough work in the pipeline to keep you on."

Horror shredding Kit from the inside, legs threatening to give way, he grabbed a chair for support. Breathing heavier than he ever had, the room blurred around him. *First Grandpa, now this.* His mouth sagged open. No sound. Spittle dripped from behind his teeth, then onto his lap. *Not this.* When his sobs forced their way out, they wracked his entire body.

David put a tentative hand on Kit's shoulder. "Kit…"

Kit launched himself into David's arms, pressing in, seeking comfort.

After an awkward pause, David's body relaxed. He squeezed Kit back. "Go on home. I'll pay you for the next two months and have your things sent on to you."

A week later, a parcel of Kit's equipment arrived, including a long velvet pouch embroidered with Kit's initials. Inside the pouch were the shears Kit used for the last two years. David had them engraved. The inscription read: *Leave Elegance to the Tailor*.

ten
. . .

THE FIRST MONDAY IN JULY, Kit arrived at LUCA, warm afternoon sun welcoming him to his first day on *Runway Rivals*. A guilty Layla took his luggage, then issued his security pass.

"I'm still mortified about what happened," she said. "Wait in the studio and have a look around. If you've never been in a proper studio before, it's amazing."

Kit tried and failed to read the names on her list. Only eight names when there should have been sixteen. "Where's everyone else?"

Layla drew a line through his name. "One of you's already in. You're both early. I'm sure the others will get here soon enough. Who'd be late for something like this?"

In the studio, technicians busied around what used to be LUCA's exhibition space. For inspiration, Kit had been to exhibitions here twice. Now, as it had for the previous six series, it housed the *Runway Rivals* set. He'd watched every episode of the show and seen its black gloss catwalk so many times. Now, up close, Kit couldn't process the real and surreal all at once.

Of all the people in the studio, Kit's eyes snagged on one:

Barker. He wore a black, collarless leather jacket, skinny jeans, and suede boots, and leaned motionless against the left wall, with his back to Kit. If Barker heard him coming in, he didn't turn his head.

Kit shaded along the studio walls until he reached Barker's side. The scents of clean skin and leather washed over him, a world away from the cheap audition fragrance. "All right?"

Sharkskin eyes flicked to him. "You made it."

"Aye. You, too."

A lengthy pause, during which the sullen cameraman from the audition noticed them and began filming.

Barker dropped his voice. "I'm glad you're here."

"You are? Why?"

When Barker turned to face him, the full weight of his attention rooted Kit to the spot. As the camera drew close, Barker leaned in, his even breath warming Kit's cheek. "Because I'm going to crush you."

Kit's mind stuttered. Before he could take in what Barker said, Pamela burst in, clipboard in hand, six excited people trailing her. Emilia swept past Pamela, chin high. *Shite.* And that lad from the burger van queue, the one in the Gaultier shirt. Layla brought up the rear.

Pamela called out. "Barker. Kit. There you are. Okay, everyone. Let's run through some logistics because we're almost ready."

Because I'm going to crush you.

"As you look at the runway from here, you'll sit in the two rows on the right. There will be no judges when the first challenge is set, but there will be cameras to get coverage on your reactions to seeing Bruna for the first time and cameras on Bruna herself."

I'm going to crush you.

"Because there will be a reaction, yes?" No one spoke. "Yes?"

"Yes," Kit said, mind jarring.

The other designers echoed him, obedient as schoolchildren.

"Thank you, Kit. Let's get you seated and do some camera checks before you go into hair and makeup. If any of you want to get changed, that'll be the time to do it. Gents, you'll sit at the back, so in order that's Barker, Aden, Patrick, and Kit. Ladies at the front: Fay, Izzy, Mukta, and Emilia."

"Oh," Emilia said, airily. "I shouldn't sit in front of Kit, what with him being so short. He'd look even more ridiculous, assuming one could see him at all."

Looking up from her clipboard, Pamela gave Emilia the once-over. "Yes, I suppose we should do what we can to minimise that ungainly height of yours." Someone sniggered, and Emilia's neck pinked. "Let's all sit in order of height, so that's the boys unchanged. Girls, you sit as Emilia, Fay, Izzy, and Mukta." Everyone shuffled into place and sat.

Barker said something to Emilia, who turned to look at Kit, then laughed.

Crush you.

Pamela continued. "These are your set positions. As we eliminate each designer, you will move to occupy the seat to your right, should it become vacant. Understood? Lovely. Talk amongst yourselves while the cameramen do their thing." She retreated into the shadows.

Mukta, a Muslim girl with eyes the colour of old copper, stood the same height as Kit. An intricately patterned orange scarf complemented her long, blue, tunic. She spoke first. "I cannot cope with this stress. All I want is food."

"I know, right?" Fay said, fat pushing against her dress as she spoke across Izzy. "They say the camera puts six pounds on you. I already done that on the journey in."

Patrick, the lad from the burger van queue, turned out to be Irish. He graduated from Saint Martins, but apart from the shy smiles didn't have much to say until Mukta dragged the facts out of him.

Aden, a redheaded lad from Grimsby—Emilia grimaced at the mention of the place—self-taught through watching online videos.

Izzy, a dazzling black forty-something, worked in lifestyle and fashion publishing for years, but an addiction to TV reality shows forced her into applying. "I can't believe I'm even in the room. Nancy was vicious about my collection."

Mukta had an Open University degree in textile design and was now studying for a PhD in anthropology and sociology. No one understood her research even after she dumbed it down three times.

Fay, a thirty-two-year-old mother of three, was glad to be out of the house. "Sometimes I hide in the airing cupboard to get away from my kids. That's bad, ain't it?" She shifted her gaze to Emilia and Barker. "What about you two?"

His tone flat, Barker shook his head. "I don't have children."

Emilia pulled a face of disdain and straightened her skirt. "I think I speak for Barker when I say it's better that we all maintain a professional distance."

With a sweet smile, Izzy raised her eyebrows. "That won't be a problem."

Pamela stepped back into the light to bundle them all off to hair and makeup. Only Emilia changed clothes. She emerged from a temporary dressing room in a fitted red dress.

"Blimey," Mukta whispered to Kit. "That dress costs a fortune."

It wasn't long before Pamela returned. "Are we all ready? Splendid. Let's get you all sitting in your assigned places. When Bruna walks onto the runway, I want lots of excitement, okay? There'll be cameras on you the entire time, so pay attention to what she's saying. The cameras will distract you at first, but I promise you'll be used to them in no time. Good luck, everyone." As soon as she led them back to their seats, she stepped back and two pedestal-mounted cameras swooped in.

When the *Runway Rivals* theme tune shook the studio, tears welled in Kit's eyes, and he swallowed a sob.

The first glimpse he got of Bruna was her perfect pair of legs.

Well into her fifties, ex-ballroom dancer Bruna publicly denounced plastic surgery and embraced a strict vegan diet and exercise regime of vacuum suit yoga, treadmill biking, and weighted pole dancing. "Hello, designers. I want to welcome all of you to the runway. We have many surprises for you." Izzy and Fay exchanged a quick look. "First impressions are everything."

Gunter appeared on the catwalk, immaculate in a navy suit, and carrying a velvet bag. He cleared his throat. "We want you to make each other an outfit based purely on your first impressions." Collective gasps and chest clutches went up from all the girls and Patrick. "But there's a twist. The only materials you'll be using are the ones you're wearing right now." Barker swore loudly. Gunter grimaced. "You have eight hours to complete this challenge."

"Cut," Pamela called from between the cameras. "Let's do that reaction again, but make it bigger, and keep the swearing to a minimum. This will be a tough series, so we need to restrict the number of fucks, and we're only allowed one cunt."

Aden and Fay dissolved into tears of laughter. Emilia silenced them with a glare.

Barker jumped to his feet. "This jacket is Balmain, and you expect me to cut it up? You've lost your minds."

Mukta whispered to Kit. "That's a two-and-a-half-grand jacket."

Gunter looked down at Barker, his handsome face unreadable. "If you can dress you partner with the other garments you're wearing, you may save your jacket. If not, you'll lose the challenge."

Jaw working furiously, Barker lowered himself back into his seat. Kit spotted a fire exit. He didn't intend on being around if—make that *when*—Barker blew up.

Bruna drew names from Gunter's velvet bag, pairing Emilia with Izzy, and Fay with Mukta. Kit relaxed, unsure what he'd have done with a woman's suit jacket other than make it smaller. Barker paired with Aden, and Kit with Patrick.

"May I swap?" Barker said as Bruna and Gunter turned to walk away.

Pamela weighed in. "No, you may not. Layla will show you the way to the workroom."

"But—"

"Can I suggest," Pamela said, voice cold, "you do as you're told and follow Layla to the workroom?"

"*May*," Emilia muttered under her breath.

"Thanks a lot, mate," Aden said to Barker's retreating back, then glared at Patrick and Kit. "What's so special about these two?"

Emilia slithered past. "Barker's clothes will go further on someone as tiny as Kit. Come along, boys. There's a challenge for me to win, and I want a decent fight."

Bacchus Broadcasting converted a third-floor workroom into the famous *Runway Rivals* workroom. Smaller than it looked on TV, the walls bore painted diamonds in cool, calming blues. A false wall covered the actual windows, but frosted plastic-covered light panels gave the illusion of daylight.

"To control the lights for filming," Layla said.

Every two metres, a mirror leant against a wall.

Eight gigantic tables, set out in two rows of four, stood in the centre of the room. The four on the left had a dress form each while the four on the right had tailor's dummies.

Eager to get underway, Kit grabbed the second row's far-right table. Barker took the one in front. Great. All Kit had to look at was the back of Barker's stupid neck.

Patrick picked the table next to Kit. "Makes sense if we're working together."

Emilia complained loudly while they changed into white jumpsuits behind privacy screens. But it was the rigid set of Barker's jaw that said it all.

Crush.

"Look at this," Emilia said to Fay, grabbing handfuls of loose jumpsuit fabric. "It's hardly Roland Mouret, is it? How am I expected to look good on camera?"

Fay's jumpsuit clung to the rolls of her belly. "We're all in the same boat, babe."

"True," Emilia said, turning her back on Fay to check her reflection in a mirror. "Better to look like a milk lolly than a blancmange." Her gaze fell on Kit. "Or a mini marshmallow."

Fay grumbled to herself. "Bitch."

Two men with shoulder-mounted cameras backed into the room, followed by Gunter. Curious about the lack of a boom mic, Kit looked up. Dozens of tiny microphones hung from the ceiling.

Gunter rubbed his hands together. "This is it, designers. Your first challenge is the most personal we've ever set. You'll have eight hours over two days to rework your own clothes to make over your partner. Make it your own." He made one circuit of the room, then left.

Patrick turned to Kit, all smiles. "Ready to measure me up?"

"I don't need to. Six foot, forty-two-inch chest, thirty-two-inch waist, thirty-two-inch inside leg."

Patrick's face fell. "And there was me looking forward to the Savile Row experience."

"The only thing I wasn't certain of was your shoulder measurements. If you want me to, I'll double-check the rest."

"That's grand."

Kit retrieved a measuring tape from the equipment supplied by the show. "Ready?"

The Irishman held his arms out. "As I'll ever be."

Measuring a new client was always tricky, and no different with Patrick. Invading someone's personal space, even though they expected it, called for careful placement of hands to avoid embarrassment and never, ever saying someone's measurements aloud. Kit always finished with the inside leg. Some tailors liked to get it out of the way first, but he preferred to put his clients at ease before that awkward moment when he knelt in front of them. "On which side do you dress?"

Patrick grinned at him. "You say that? Uh—" His hand went to his crotch and squeezed. "Left."

"How do you know what I do?" Kit said, placing the tape against the top of Patrick's right thigh, running it down to the ankle. He noted the measurement.

"Saw your name on Layla's list at the audition, and your social media's all public. You should do something about that."

"Why look me up when you didn't know I'd be on the show?"

"Layla can't keep her trap shut. Told me all about the Kit-Kat fiasco when I called her with some questions about the contract. Can't keep her legs shut, either. Fay reckons she's banging that cameraman."

"Which one?"

"The miserable dryshite. What she'd see in him is anyone's guess."

Patrick's shoulders measured fifty-one inches, only eleven inches shorter than Kit stood.

Patrick brandished his measuring tape. "Your turn." He brushed Kit's crotch when measuring his inside leg. Neither of them acknowledged their embarrassment. They returned to their tables, then sketched.

Mukta wandered over, cameraman in tow, on the pretence of borrowing a seam ripper. "Does that Barker have a problem with you?" she whispered. "He watched you measure Patrick. Gave the pair of you the proper evils."

Kit signalled Barker's direction, where he measured Aden exactly as Kit measured Patrick. "Guess he was learning how to do it properly."

Chuckling, Mukta took the seam ripper. "I didn't have you down as a bitch."

"I prefer 'bastard'. Besides," he tipped his head in Emilia's direction, "'bitch' is taken."

Emilia snapped at Fay. Mukta clamped a hand over her mouth to stop from laughing. "Works for me, love." Winking at him, she went back to her table.

When Kit turned back, Barker met his eye, brow furrowed. *What's his problem?* Pushing back the urge to ask—and surprised he still gave a shit—Kit looked away and got on with sketching.

Patrick attended Saint Martins, where he'd been encouraged to experiment. If Kit played with texture and volume, it might convey Patrick's schooling. Apart from that, Patrick was Irish and, at first, shy. And he worked out. When Kit measured him, each press of tape met muscle. Kit could play on the tension between Patrick's shyness and physical appearance. For someone who didn't seek attention, Patrick sure as hell had a body that'd demand it if he didn't cover up. Kit sketched a smart jacket, then scribbled it out. Force of habit. Some workout gear and a sleeveless hoodie might work? Maybe an oversized hood so it hid Patrick's face? Kit sketched twists in the fabric, giving it the texture of a Francis Bacon painting. *Francis Bacon was born in Ireland, right?* Kit wouldn't mention the artist's name unless questioned. For now, he'd call it "painterly". Fingers crossed.

The clothes Patrick wore for the first day of filming: indigo jeans; white shirt; and a pale blue blazer didn't scream sportswear. At Kit's audition, Barker tore the lining out of Kit's jacket. Kit turned Patrick's blazer inside out. The lining might work for a vest, although there might not be enough to make shorts. Making shorts from his jeans was too obvious, but the denim would give Kit the stiffness he needed in the oversized hood.

Kit rolled out a length of pattern paper, then drafted Patrick's basic block. When he finished, the others were as engrossed in their work as he'd been in his.

Only Patrick looked back at him, face slack. "You drew that so fast. You're amazing."

Kit rummaged in his sewing kit for a pair of shears, wishing his own pair twinkled up at him. *Leave elegance to the tailor.* Now was not the time for elegance.

With unfamiliar shears in his hand, Kit made his first cut.

eleven

. . .

THREE ROOMS OPENED along the wall to the right of Kit's table: a brightly lit sewing room furnished with eight, flatbed, industrial sewing machines; a room filled with perspex shelves of shoes and accessories in this season's colours; and a tiny, orange breakout area with a sink, kettle, fridge, and standing table large enough for four.

Ready to begin construction, Kit approached the sewing room, his stride uneven. What if he couldn't get the machine to work? What if he messed up his design? What if he sewed through his thumb? A cameraman swooped in at Kit's shoulder, ready to capture the series's first sewing footage.

No sooner had Kit sat at the machine closest to the door, than Fay stuck her head in, wide eyed. "Oh, my God, babes. I'm still scratching my head back here. What you making?"

"A gym kit and a hoodie. But *painterly*." Nobody ever asked for *painterly* at Stitchworthy.

"Sounds posh for our Paddy, but if I had a body like his, I'd want to show it off in a gym kit. Do us a favour and make it snug." She pinched her fat again. "But not like this sodding jumpsuit." She wandered back to her table.

The sewing machines might as well have been spaceships compared to the ones at Stitchworthy, let alone Grandpa's. Kit placed his fabric on the table. Under the table, a foot pedal and a pad attached to a vertical bar. The machine itself — a chunk of beige metal with five dials — supported a digital display.

Shite. Kit tapped a loose fist against his lips. The cameraman edged closer. Looking past the lens shoved in his face, Kit caught Izzy's eye.

She offered him a slight smile, then put down her work. In a dozen strides, she entered to workroom, then pulled up a chair to sit at Kit's side. Voice soft, she tapped the pad. "Knee lift. Push it to your right, it'll raise the presser foot. The pedal does what you'd expect." Her hands moved across the machine. "Foot presser regulator, hand lifter, thread take-up spring, reverse stitch lever." She sat back, eyes on the pedal. "This machine's top speed's something like three to four thousand stitches a minute."

Kit's eyes darted from dial to lever to display. *There's no time to hand stitch this.* "I don't think I'm gonna—"

Izzy nudged his knee with hers. "You've got this." She toed the pedal. "A light touch on the front runs it a low speed. Press harder for top speed. Press the back of the pedal for thread trimming."

"How do I stop it?"

Izzy glanced at the camera trained on her. "You, uh, stop pressing the pedal. You good?"

Mute, Kit squeezed his eyes shut. He nodded.

"Excellent stuff." Izzy went back to her table.

Using a fabric off-cut, Kit practiced a run. The machine took off, taking him by surprise. He yanked his fingers away when the fabric shot under the needle. Things might have been easier without the camera shoved in his face, but Kit had to get control or he'd lose what little confidence he had. In twenty minutes, he produced five parallel stitches of different lengths, and the same for zigzag stitches, overlock, blind hem, and a buttonhole. In another ten minutes, he worked out freehand stitches for texture work.

Over the next two hours, the others drifted in, each taking a seat as far apart from the others as possible. Barker entered last, hesitant steps across the threshold, uneasy glances. His eyes fell on the one free table, right next to Kit. When Barker's eyes met Kit's they exchanged too-quick smiles.

Flushed, Barker unzipped several inches of his jumpsuit, rolled up his sleeves, then took a seat. No wonder he'd unzipped—sweat beaded along his hairline.

From the corner of Kit's eye, it was hard to make out what he'd designed, although it didn't seem a world away from what Barker had worn. And there was Barker's upper chest, firm muscle scattered with dark, damp hair. Sweating all over? Apart from his underwear, Barker should have been naked, but a tattoo crept across Barker's collarbone. From where he sat, Kit couldn't make out more than a scrawled edge of ink.

Barker sewed. Seconds later, his lower thread tangled. He stopped, cut it away, continued. The thread tangled again. He slipped back the bobbin case, fished out a tangle, then threw it on the floor. The third time, he didn't move at all.

As soon as Kit had the urge to ask if he was okay, Barker raised the presser foot, waggled the needle, put it back, then sighed. When he tried the foot pedal again, the machine made an ominous, shuddering hum then did nothing. Barker swore under his breath until he caught Kit's eye.

"A little help?" Barker said it so softly no one turned around.

Kit overlocked an edge of fabric at top speed. "Sorry. Busy."

"Watching me mess things up, I suppose?"

"If this is you crushing the rest of us, we're in real trouble." Kit went back to work.

The afternoon stretched into evening. Designers and

cameramen drifted in and out of the sewing room. Three hours after the challenge started, Kit took his mandatory, twenty-minute break in the kitchen along with Aden and Mukta.

"How's it going?" Aden asked as he crushed a bag of salt and vinegar crisps, then poured the contents into a ham roll. "You two seem like you've got it going on." He tore off some roll, then stuffed it into his mouth.

Mukta rubbed her eyes. "No idea. I didn't expect anything like this. They've never set a makeover challenge before, right? What're they playing at?"

Aden swallowed, then wiped his mouth. "I heard one cameraman complaining they're having to film a lot more of our day. And they were whispering about a house."

"House?" Kit said. "For us?"

"Can't be," Mukta said. "They always stick the designers in a hotel."

Aden's mouth twitched. "No. They *usually* stick the designers in a hotel. We're staying in a house in Hadley Wood. I reckon that's why there's only eight of us. They're going to try to get under our skin. I bet they film us for twenty-four hours and make us share rooms like they do on *Big Brother*."

Mukta turned to Kit. "Can I share with you?"

Another piece of Aden's roll stopped on its way to his open mouth. "Oh, thanks. You lot are staring to make me paranoid. Why does no one want anything to do with me?"

"Poor baby." Mukta threw her arms around him. "I'm sorry for hurting your widdle feelings. I'll share with you."

Aden wriggled out of her arms, trying not to laugh. "Get off me, woman. I don't want you now."

When they fell back out into the workroom, giggling, cameramen followed them to their tables.

Mukta put her hands on her hips, feigning annoyance. "Why aren't there any camera*women* on this show?"

Gunter strolled into the workroom—navy, soft wool suit,

notched lapels, lilac shirt and tie. "Designers," he called, "let's have you all back at your stations. I can't wait to see what you're working on."

Those still in the sewing room hurried out and put what they'd made on their dress forms or dummies.

Gunter's gaze swept the room. "I'll talk to you all in pairs. Emilia and Izzy, let's start with you."

Izzy opened her mouth to speak.

Emilia cut her off. "Despite my reservations in destroying my vintage Zandra Rhodes—a personal favourite of my collection—I'm designing Izzy a mini cape dress, using my dress's lining for the cape." She watched the rest of the group as though expecting wild applause.

Gunter winced. "As I understand it, you're turning a dress into another dress?"

Emilia's eye twitched. "It will be sensational."

"Izzy," Gunter said. "Let's see what you have in store for Emilia."

Izzy pushed up the sleeves of her jumpsuit. "I've designed Emilia a bodice and ruffled skirt."

Fingers clasped loosely at his waist, Gunter took calm breaths. "I like the way you've built out the bust and hips. It adds volume to Emilia's—how shall I put it?—*boyish* frame." Emilia opened her mouth to speak. Gunter walked away, calling over his shoulder. "You're playing it safe, Emilia. It's time to punch things up."

"Don't encourage her," Patrick grumbled.

Gunter moved on to Fay and Mukta, who waited for him at Fay's table.

Bobbing on her toes, Fay licked her lips. "All right, babes?"

Mukta elbowed her in the ribs. "Hello, Mister Lyffe."

Gunter winked at them both. "Gunter, please. I'm eager to see what you have to show me."

Fay launched into action. "I'm making Mukta a well delicate cocktail dress out of my wrapped trousers."

Arms folded across his chest, Gunter lifted his chin. "It's very organic."

"We don't buy organic," Fay said. "I ain't paying over the odds so some chicken gets extra legroom."

Gunter's mouth slackened.

Mukta cut in. "I'm making Fay an off-the-shoulder, three tiered prairie dress, and a handbag made from my boots."

Glancing sideways at Fay, Gunter moved to Mukta's design. "This is very retro and very young. It's a lot to mesh."

Mukta put an arm around her dress form. "I can do it."

Gunter drew back. "Very well. Kit and Patrick?"

Patrick surprised Kit with sudden confidence. "I'm combining my jumper and shirt to make Kit a suit jacket."

Gunter hooked a finger over his chin. "If you've spent time with Kit, you'll know he practically lives in a suit jacket. Why put him in the same old thing?"

"I'll admit it's like what he usually wears, but this challenge is based on first impressions."

"And what is he wearing under his jacket," Gunter asked, "if you're using your shirt to make it?" When Patrick couldn't answer, Gunter turned to Kit. "Are you prepared to walk the runway shirtless, Kit?"

Kit fiddled with the zip of his jumpsuit. Was it big enough to swallow him up? *It's not like you won't have a jacket on, and you trimmed your chest hair this morning.* "I suppose I could."

Gunter beamed. "Very good. I like your chutzpah. And what are you designing, Kit?" Kit stood back so Gunter could see his table. "Oh, you've been busy," Gunter said. "Talk me through this."

Kit ran Gunter through his process, conscious of Patrick and the others inching closer as he spoke. "It's sportswear meets Saint Martins. I'm going for a relaxed gym kit, combining panels of my blazer and its lining to give flexibility where it's needed without sacrificing structure and support." Gunter inclined his head. Kit continued. "But Patrick's from an art school known for producing great painters, and he comes over as shy, so I'm adding a large textured hood so he can pull it up when he doesn't want to engage."

Picking up the unfinished hoodie, Gunter examined the hood. "Is this denim? It looks like brush strokes." Gunter's voice cracked. "You've sewn into it so it looks painted."

Somewhere out of sight, Mukta—the textile designer—made an appreciative sound.

Setting down the hoodie, Gunter sucked air in over his teeth. "I'm concerned about time. Will you finish?"

"How long have we been working for?"

"Three hours."

"So that's one more hour today and another four tomorrow?"

"Correct."

"I can finish it, no problem."

Patrick leaned in to examine the hood. "It's hatchet."

Kit's pulse picked up. "Is that good?"

The Irishman patted him on the back. "You teach me Geordie slang, I'll teach you some Irish."

Aden's assessment didn't go so well. "Barker doesn't say much, so I haven't got a lot to go on."

After one glance at a mutinous Barker, Gunter's focus settled back on Aden. "This isn't an ice-breaker. You need to consider how your first impression of Barker might translate into a garment."

"Three inch spikes?" Aden muttered.

Gunter shook his head in dismay and moved on to Barker. "Talk me through what you're making."

"Aden said he was from Grimsby—"

"Vile," Emilia called from the other side of the room, head in her work, tacking her dress's cape to its neckline.

Barker gave her the same flat look he'd given Kit. *I'm going to crush you.* "But all I know about Grimsby is the fish."

"Do you have fishing connections?" Gunter asked Aden.

Aden shook his head. "I prefer a battered sausage."

Fay's head snapped around. "I'll batter your sausage, babe." Mukta glared at her, and Fay fell silent.

Barker continued. "My biker jacket has a sheen, so..." A camera closed in on his face. "So I..." He spread his hands on the table and dipped his head, jaw muscles tightening. "I..." Turning away from the camera, he chewed the side of his thumb.

Stepping into Barker's space, Gunter opened his mouth to speak, then paused as if collecting his thoughts. "Doubting our ideas is part of the process."

"What if you don't have any ideas?"

For a split second, Kit expected Barker to lash out. *It's ruined, you idiot.* Now he seemed... crushed.

Gunter squeezed Barker's shoulder, his voice light. "You need to let go of whatever's going on. Get out of your head. It's holding you back, but there's time to fix it." Barker didn't reply. Gunter turned to Aden. "Make him talk."

"Sure," Aden said.

Gunter addressed the room. "Do you all appreciate what's happening here? You're on *Runway Rivals*. It's exciting. Have fun. There'll be plenty of time for stress later. Designers, you have one hour." And he was gone.

Activity blurred the rest of their working time. Gunter's concerns about Kit finishing his fabric treatment in time were justified. Kit finished the body of the hoodie, but the texture work on the hood would take at least another two hours. That left him two hours at most to make the shorts and vest, assuming they stopped the clock for fittings.

At eight o'clock, a baggy-eyed Pamela shambled into the room and told them to stop working. "Time to take you to your new home, everyone. Stop working and collect any personal items you need. You can't take any equipment home. Not so much as a safety pin. Your bags are already at your destination." She stood back as they filed past.

Kit tapped Izzy on the shoulder. "Your tape's still round you neck."

Izzy looked down at the white plastic. "You're such a sweetheart." She took it off, then put it back on her table before catching up with the Mukta and Fay.

Exhaustion sapped the last of Kit's energy. He shuffled out behind the others, the tips of his shoes occasionally catching the floor.

Aden hung back with him. "You auditioned with Barker, right? What was he like? He's finally talking, but he's still as mardy as his bum."

Kit managed a shrug. "He was proper lovely at first—styled me up and stuff—then lost it when his dress ripped. I know it's important, like, but his reaction was way over the top. He's got something else going on."

"Well, yeah," Aden said. "All that stuff with his dad."

"What about his dad? Is he sick, like?"

Barker walked ahead. If the lad had personal problems, how many allowances could Kit make for his sudden change in behaviour?

Aden shook his head. "Patrick told me they locked his dad up for some fraud thing. Got a prison sentence and a massive fine."

"Probably why he didn't want to cut up his jacket," Izzy said, who'd eavesdropped. "Can't afford a new one."

Kit fell silent as they descended the stairs. What happened to Barker sounded awful, but that didn't give him the right to take it out on everyone else.

Two black BMWs hummed outside on the pavement. Izzy and Mukta whisked Kit away from Aden and hauled him into the car Fay had already claimed.

Mukta closed the door behind them, then swore. "How stressful was that?"

"At least you're not working with Emilia," Izzy said, eyes rolling.

Mukta chuckled. "More like the Snow Queen." She turned to Kit. "Why's she so mean to you?"

With a yawn, Kit bobbed his head. "She was at my audition, but we didn't have a row. She was a proper bitch from the off. Hates us because I'm Northern."

"And that Barker," Fay said. "I swear down he gave you the proper evils," Fay said. "What did he say to you earlier, in the studio? He was whispering to you when we were walking in with Pam."

"He said he would crush us."

All three women laughed in surprise.

"All of us?" Mukta said. "Or just you?"

"All of us. Even at his audition he said all he wants is to win."

Fay hissed. "Posh twat. I mean, we all want to win, but we don't have to be wankers to do it."

Forty-five minutes later, they swept through the gates of a massive house in Hadley Wood.

"We're not staying here, are we?" Fay said, looking up, her wide eyes filling with tears.

The red brick house stood as wide as the terrace Kit grew up in. Eight windows spanned the first floor, and four columns supported a sandstone entryway leading to a gloss-black door you could drive a bus through.

Emilia led the way into the house, striding past the

cameramen who stood on the doorstep. White wood panelled hallway, grey marble floor, six doorways leading off. In the centre, their luggage waited.

Barker skulked at the back of the group while they explored the house.

Upstairs, they counted six bedrooms. The master suite—pale gold tones, black floor, and a mahogany sleigh bed—led to an en suite bathroom as big as the bedroom. Of the five other rooms, painted French grey, ammonite, blush pink, powder blue, and cabbage white respectively, two also had en suites. Two bedrooms had twin beds. Every bedroom had white shutters.

Downstairs, two lounges, a study, a games room, a gym, and an orangery. In the middle of the orangery lounged a dining table for ten, leather chairs for all.

In the main lounge, two deep, green-blue sofas held their own against deep mustard walls. Double French doors led to the garden.

A motion sensor sat high in one corner of every room, upstairs and down.

Patrick whistled when he walked into the kitchen. "Jeez man, it's the size of Cork."

Cool white walls contrasted with the industrial grey cabinets.

Sighing with appreciation, Izzy ran her hand over the long, stone-topped island that ended in a circular, wooden worktop. "I've always wanted a handmade kitchen," she said. "This is smoked oak."

"That island's bigger than my Mini," Mukta said to Aden, who watched Izzy roaming around the rest of the room, a cameraman tracking her every move.

Fay peered into the fridge. Everyone but Barker and Emilia laughed when she squeals of excitement. "Bubbly! Who's up for getting stuck in?"

"Ugh," Emilia said, screwing up her face. "What sort of pleb gets 'stuck in' to Champagne?"

"Oh, shut your face," Fay snapped. "You're such a jumped-up cow. I haven't had a glass of fizz since I married my Kev, and that was three years ago."

Izzy frowned. "But your eldest is seven."

Fay hunted through four cabinets until she found one for glassware. She pulled out eight glasses and poured. "Kev's not their dad. Their dad pissed off with his best mate's girlfriend. His best mate was Kev."

"Classy," Emilia muttered.

Fay exaggerated a sigh. She faced Emilia. "You got a problem with me, babe?"

"Do you have to tell us all the tawdry details?"

"What does 'tawdry' mean?" Fay asked Izzy.

Izzy sipped her Champagne. "Vulgar."

For a moment, Fay's chin trembled, then she waved a dismissive hand in Emilia's direction. "Oh, piss off, you icy bitch." Then, as if nothing had happened, Fay propped herself against the kitchen island and returned her attention to the rest of the group. "Anyway, I tried dating apps, but all the blokes on there wanted a shag."

"Nothing wrong with that," Aden said, draining his glass, then holding it out for a refill.

"Yeah, but I'd got to where I just wanted someone to watch Netflix with who'd play with my tits."

Kit frowned. "And Kev…?"

"Liked my tits."

After they stopped crying with laughter and made a dent in the Champagne, Mukta suggested they get on and choose their rooms. With six rooms and eight designers, it took negotiation.

Emilia, difficult as ever, stood ready, chin high. "I won't share with anyone but Barker. We went to school together."

Barker gulped the last of his Champagne. "Not going to happen."

When no one else offered to share with him, Barker sneered at each of them but passed over Kit. "Fine," he said. "I'm off to bed." And he promptly snatched up his suitcase and disappeared upstairs.

"Now you know how I felt," Aden called after him.

A door slammed.

Emilia speeded upstairs, as fast as her gigantic suitcase allowed.

Kit should have hit the sack himself, but his excitement over the house kept him going, and he wanted to get to know the others.

"That leaves four rooms and six of us," Izzy said. "I'm happy to share with anyone who doesn't snore."

Fay raised her hand. "Like a diesel engine. Even my kids complain, and they sleep through Fireworks Night."

"Mammy says I could sleep through the apocalypse," Patrick said. "Might work."

"My Kev wouldn't want me sleeping with a fella, babe. Unless you were… you know."

All eyes turned to Patrick, who blushed. "You'd be safe with me, girl."

"Ooh," Mukta's black eyes glittered. "Maybe you and Kit should share."

"That'd be grand," Patrick blurted.

"No, no, no," Izzy said. "It's *Runway Rivals*, not *Desert Island Dicks*."

Fay sighed. "I love that show. All them fit blokes getting it on."

Aden raised his empty glass. "I auditioned for that."

Izzy handed Aden a bottle of Champagne. "Are you gay?"

"No, but I'll play hard to get." He threw up his hands. "So no one want to share with me?"

"I'll share with you," Kit said.

"You could sound a little more enthusiastic. Anyway, I'm not sure I want to bunk up with Barker's boy."

A cheer went up from the girls.

"He looks at you like he wants to stick you, babe," Fay said.

Mukta made two fists and thrust her hips forward. "And not necessarily with a knife."

"Haddaway, man," Kit said, scowling over his glass. "Barker'd be lucky to have us, but I want thrilling, not killing."

Aden opened the bottle of Champagne Izzy gave him. "A toast to us, the series seven designers of *Runway Rivals*." Glasses rang together and everyone drank. "Even though it's a bloody catwalk."

"'*Catwalk Contenders*' isn't sexy enough," Mukta said.

Fay giggled. "That Gunter's a bit of all right, and did you see that cameraman—the miserable one—did you see his arms?"

"Bigger than Pat's arms?" Mukta said. "Can we call you Pat?"

Blushing, Patrick gave them a brief nod.

Fay yawned, putting down her glass. "I'm gonna crash, bitches. What time's our call tomorrow? Six thirty?"

"Bugger," Izzy said, yawning too. "So that's Fay and Pat sharing, and Aden and Kit, so Mukta and I get our own rooms? Sweet."

Aden wrinkled his freckled nose. "'Sweet'? Bit old for that, aren't you?"

Izzy flicked her hair before flouncing along the hallway, giving him the finger over her shoulder as she went to get her suitcase. "I'm going to pretend you didn't say that. Besides, I'm down with the kids."

Emilia's voice ricocheted through the house. "Will you kindly keep the noise to a minimum? Some of us are trying to get some sleep."

"That's us told," Kit said. "You lot go ahead. I'll lock up. Aden? Leave the door open so I know which room we're in."

"Sure thing, fella. I'll take your bag up."

"We'll leave you to it, mate," said one cameraman before giving all but one of the others permission to leave. "You mind seeing us out before turning off all the lights, finishing with the hallway? Makes for a nice shot from outside."

The other cameraman cleared his throat.

"What?" the first cameraman said. "Pamela said we need to make sure we capture 'the story'. The other cameras will do the rest."

"Huh?" Kit said, peering at them both.

The second cameraman widened his eyes at the first, who squinted at the corner of the room. "Forgot about all that."

Kit's eyes followed his. On closer inspection, the motion sensor—a white cylinder mounted on a bracket—encased a lens surrounded by LED bulbs. They weren't motion sensors; they were cameras.

The first cameraman showed Kit the central lighting control under the stairs, then both men left. Kit switched everything off, locked the front door, then turned off the hall lights. He stood at the bottom of the stairs. As great as it was being with a friendly bunch of people, he needed a moment alone. When he climbed the stairs, his legs grew heavier with each step, every muscle giving in to gravity. He headed for the only open doorway.

Still dressed, Aden sprawled on the bed farthest from the door, his massive feet hanging over the end. "Is this okay? My room at home's cold, and I've gotten used to it. This—" He tapped the powder blue paint above his bedside table. "—is an exterior wall, so it's nice and cool. And I scored us a room with its own bathroom. Sweet, eh?"

"'Sweet'? Bit old for that, aren't you?"

"Joker. Any problem with me having a shower? I reek

worse than Barker's attitude." He peeled off his jumpsuit and socks.

They should have cast Aden for *Desert Island Dicks*. The eye-popping bulge in his underwear would have been TV gold. Being straight must have scuppered his chances.

"Yeah, yeah," Kit said. "I could do with a shower myself. I'll find another."

twelve

...

TO AVOID EMILIA, Barker shut himself in the first bedroom he stumbled upon, only to find it didn't have its own bathroom.

After stripping off his jumpsuit and retrieving his washbag, Barker grabbed a folded towel from the bed. He hitched it around his waist, then padded out onto the landing in search of a bathroom, wishing he'd paid attention when the group explored their new home. Grateful to find a sticky note scrawled with the word 'bog'—had to be Aden—he slipped in, then locked the door.

'Bog' didn't do the room justice. Icy tiles skated across the floor, twinkling mosaic tiles formed a wall of frost behind a wall-mounted vanity unit, and a secretive bathtub hid behind frosted glass panels. Crystal light fittings splintered across the ceiling, stark winter branches veiling a glacial hideaway. *Wouldn't want to use this on a chilly morning.*

Barker hung his towel on the back of a ghost chair, then inspected the bathtub. A long letterbox fireplace ran along its side, providing a slither of glorious heat to the room. Above the bath, a faux night sky offered a soothing blanket of stars.

Too tired to risk falling asleep in gallons of sultry water, Barker cranked up the shower. He pulled off his socks and underwear, binned his contact lenses, then stepped under the pounding spray.

What a disaster. The makeover challenge gave him no choice but to sacrifice a brand new jacket. And to waste it on that insufferable ginger idiot? It only added insult to injury.

He should never have agreed to the deal Nancy offered him, but she'd caught him off guard with her proposal when he approached her and Osred before his graduation show.

"I've pleaded with the producers not to do this to you," Nancy told him between sips of Moët, "but they want a brooding bad boy on the show."

"But that's not who I am," Barker said, looking from her to Osred and back again. "I'm a designer. The show's about fashion, not us. It's not *Big Brother*."

"You're preaching to the choir, I'm afraid," Nancy said. "But this is television and all about the ratings." She handed her empty glass to Osred, then took his. "If you're not up to a little roleplay, I understand."

"Should be easy," Osred said, looking him over. "After all, you grew up with the biggest bad boy of them all."

A muscle jumped in Barker's cheek. If Nancy hadn't been standing next to Osred, Barker might have punched him. "I'm not my father."

Nancy smiled. "You don't have to be, Barker. You just have to act like it. Besides, you have nothing left to lose."

And so Barker accepted. The other contestants meant nothing to him, but… Kit? He liked Kit.

In the *Runway Rivals* workroom, Barker only took the table in front of Kit, so Kit wouldn't be in his eye-line. It seemed like a good idea but he couldn't ignore Kit's accent. It turned every sentence into a melody hummed on a fine morning. Barker's eyes wandered to Kit at the sewing machine, to Izzy helping

Kit, to Kit smiling to himself as he worked. Then Kit helping Mukta with a buttonhole, Kit showing Izzy a better way to ruffle fabric, Kit talking Aden through the nightmare of turning out welted pockets.

Kit, Kit, Kit. The chap was everywhere.

If anyone called Barker out for his behaviour, it would be Kit. The chap had it tough enough with Emilia on his case. He didn't need Barker needling him, too. Just the thought of that sweet, handsome face falling when recounting the story of his ex. *Stuart Little.* Barker didn't want to be another story.

"Because I'm going to crush you," Barker said to himself. A stupid thing to have said. And then to ask Kit for help? Fool.

Barker washed his hair and body. Even if he kept up the series villain act, he still had to pull out all the stops to win the show. If he won—he had to—he'd seek Kit out, go heavy on the charm, then turn things around, see where they went.

He rinsed off, towelled himself dry, then wiped down the cubicle and mirror. Drawn face, eyes as baggy as the jumpsuits. Even his reflection looked exhausted. He fished out his glasses case, pushed on his Oakley frames, fastened the towel around his waist, then opened the bathroom door.

Someone lurched into him, knocking Barker's wash-bag out of his hand and throwing him off-balance. Barker caught the edge of the door to stop himself from falling backward. His wash-bag skidded under the chair.

The person who crashed into him toppled too, arms flailing, catching the doorframe in time to stay upright. Black hair, black brows, black stubble.

"Kit?"

Kit eyebrows dropped along with his jaw. "Barker?"

It was only a matter of time before the others saw Barker with his glasses on, but Kit got there first. Barker snatched them off all the same.

"You look different," Kit said. He pointed at Barker's shoulder tattoo. "And what's that?"

Barker's eyes flicked to each corner of the landing ceiling until he spotted a camera. They'd rigged the entire place. He forced a scowl. "That's none of your damn business."

"Your hair looks darker."

"Obviously. It's wet."

"How stupid of us." Kit waved his hands through the cloud of steam billowing onto the landing. "Suppose you used all the hot water?"

Barker tried a sneer, but wasn't convinced it worked with his heart crashing into his ribs. "What can I say? I'm cold blooded." The production company wouldn't have put cameras in the bathrooms, would they? If he pulled Kit in, then shut the door...

Kit stepped back, stretching out his arm. "I'll let you get back to the privacy of your own bedroom."

For a moment, Barker didn't know what to do with Kit's dismissal. People weren't in the habit of dismissing Barker, but he retrieved his wash-bag, went to his room, and opened the door. Kit muttered something under his breath.

As soon as Barker dumped his wash-bag on the bedside table, he whipped off his towel and threw it over the radiator.

What can I say? I'm cold blooded. Another horrible thing to have said. He should have told Nancy Shearsmith to shove her offer up her puckered Gucci arse and never agreed to this ridiculous charade.

When he eventually slid into bed, the luxury of percale cotton sheets took him home to all the nights his mother tucked him in.

"Goodnight, my darling," Romilly said. "Close your eyes and dream of puppy dogs."

Usually, Barker did.

Behind the Seams

He pulled the pillows from the other side of the bed and used them as bolsters to curl himself around, praying sleep took him soon. Except Kit was across the landing, and possibly naked. When Kit finished in the bathroom, he'd go to another room, climb into another bed. Did he have his own room? Please, God, don't let him share with Patrick. Barker worked out, but he couldn't match Patrick's physique.

If things were different, Kit would come to Barker's room, climb into Barker's bed and talk to him in his soft Geordie accent until Barker fell asleep.

Why risk ruining everything and wait until the show finished before finding an opportunity to repair things between them? Despite what he'd promised Nancy? Win the show and get the guy. Could he do both?

Barker excelled at breaking things. Repairing them? Not so much. He'd tried to mend his relationship with Emilia, but she'd taken it wrong. There were plenty of straight men who were convinced that all lesbians needed was a talented man to turn them straight. Emilia thought the same about Barker. He'd like to see the back of her, but needed to keep her sweet. He wasn't prepared for her outing him on TV. The papers exhausted stories about his father and the fallout of his crimes. All they needed was something juicy on Barker and they'd bury him. Coming out to a friend was one thing. Coming out on TV was something else entirely, and he'd had all the attention he could handle. *Runway Rivals* was a necessary evil.

The bathroom door opened and closed. For a moment, Barker hoped Kit stood outside his bedroom, about to knock, but his footsteps died away and a different door opened.

Groaning into his pillow, Barker willed himself to sleep, to stop his mind from wandering. His mother had trouble sleeping. How was she coping in a clinic night after night? The last time they'd spoken, he told her it might be the last time for weeks but couldn't tell her the reason. She took it well enough. He promised to visit her as soon as the show finished.

For him, the show could be over tomorrow. One designer was going home, and it mustn't be him.

thirteen

...

IF ONE DESIGNER was going home, Kit would make sure it wasn't him.

Showered and fed, he hurried downstairs and boiled the kettle by six o'clock. Izzy joined him first, fresh-faced and wearing a sherbert orange jumpsuit.

Kit looked at her over the rim of his mug. "Didn't think you'd be wearing that after yesterday. Looks good with your skin tone."

Izzy smiled as she did a little spin. "If they're keeping us in prison, I may as well look the part. As long as I don't look like a chocolate orange. I don't, do I?"

The others drifted in one by one, bleary-eyed and thirsty for caffeine, then dragged themselves off to the lounge.

Kit made another mug of tea.

Izzy smothered toast with butter and jam. "I know I shouldn't, but I eat when I'm nervous. I'm convinced Emilia will throw me under the bus by saying she loathes her makeover. I wouldn't put it past her to say she was allergic to cotton or something equally ridiculous. Who's going home?"

Kit stole half a slice of toast from Izzy's plate. "Too early to call. We've got four hours left. Any of us could pull it out of the bag in that time."

Izzy smirked. "Even Barker?"

"You've not seen the best of him yet. His stuff's amazing; he can design, all right, but he can't sew for shit."

The doorbell rang. Fay shuffled off to answer it, followed by Mukta. A moment later, Barker, wearing a skintight black singlet and shorts, stood at the kitchen sink, pouring himself a glass of water. Fay and Mukta trailed in after him. All three women fell silent, watching sweat run down the back of his neck, shoulders, and arms. Ignoring the sight of Barker's wet body—he'd seen it last night—Kit put his mug and Izzy's plate in the dishwasher.

Izzy recovered first. "You'd better mind your time, Barker. Pickup's in—" She checked her watch. "—ten minutes."

Barker tossed his glass in the sink, smacked his lips, then gave her a cocky smile. "I'll see you in nine."

No sooner was he bounding up the stairs than Fay turned to their little group. "Did you see the arse on him? He could blunt Nancy's diamonds with that."

"She'd have to get her hand near it," Mukta said, "unless someone took her arm off first."

They all looked sideways at Kit, who put Barker's glass in the dishwasher and said nothing.

Nine minutes later, Barker whipped past Mukta and grabbed the seat next to Kit. Handsome as ever, Barker wore a black Gucci sweater with red and green trim at the neck, cuffs, and hem, paired with distressed black jeans. Not as much product in his hair, it sat lighter and looser on his scalp. His familiar leather scent washed over Kit, who turned to the window and concentrated on counting the railings separating the driveway from the world beyond. No one should look that good in nine minutes, especially not out of the corner of an eye.

The leather scent intensified. "Kit, we need to talk. Off camera."

Kit pointed to the camera mounted under the car's rearview mirror, then turned back to the window, his excitement fogging it in seconds.

When they arrived at LUCA, Barker sprang out of the car, bounded past an open-mouthed Pamela, then went inside.

Patrick caught up with Kit. "What's the craic?"

"I guess I'm feeling the pressure."

"C'mere to me," Patrick said, throwing his arm around Kit's shoulders. "It's a grand old day for showing these tools who's boss. You'll be up to ninety before you know it."

"Ninety?"

"Flat out."

By the time they got to the workroom, Barker stood at his table, slashing his precious jacket into strips.

When Barker headed for the sewing room, Mukta raised her eyebrows at Fay. "Someone's muse is back."

Emilia butted in. "For some of us, it never leaves." She turned her attention to Izzy's dress form. The bodice she'd made for Emilia glistened under the workroom lights, tiny silver beads hand-stitched along each perfect seam. "It's not looking any better, is it?"

Izzy caught Kit's eye. "Told you," she mouthed.

Gunter's visit took on an unsettling urgency as he pushed them to make sure they finished their garments in time. "You owe it to yourselves," he said, rounding them up in a group. "You're all talented designers and based on the potential I've seen, I don't want to see any of you eliminated."

"Unless you use your Lyffe Line," Aden said.

Gunter cocked his head. "It's too early for that. One of you will go home today. Whatever you're making, let's make fashion."

Cameras swung around, capturing the contestants' reactions to Gunter's catchphrase. Kit and Izzy lost their cool and clapped. Patrick joined in.

No one spoke after Gunter left, all racing to finish, although Mukta's excited squeaks grew louder as time slipped away.

Barker emerged from the sewing room. He'd woven strips of his jacket lining, t-shirt, and jeans to make a three quarter length jumpsuit with a copper zipper fastening. When Aden tried it on, the zipper brought out the red in his hair.

"Thought you'd got it arseways," Aden said, admiring his reflection, "but you pulled it off."

Fay appreciated Aden's beefy calves. "I never knew I was a leg woman, Ade, but you've got me bubbling."

"Vile," Emilia said.

With a huff, Fay made a face at Emilia. "Not as vile as your dress."

"How dare you? This dress is Temperley."

"Temperley? No, babe. *Permanently*."

To everyone's relief, they had the full four hours to finish up before Pamela gathered them together.

"Because you are the models, things will work a little differently. The stylists will meet you together in your pairs. Please dress in what your fellow designers made for you. If you're not already in your runway outfit, get changed now, and be back here in five minutes."

The jacket Patrick made for Kit was too big in the chest and too small in the upper arm, but not so much that Kit couldn't squeeze into it.

"Aww, feck," Patrick said. "I might get away with it if you don't bend your arms."

Patrick slipped into his sportswear and hoodie. "Fits like a glove, son." He dropped into some pushups. "To bring out my triceps," he said. "You know, for the camera."

Fay giggled. "Turns out Pat's not so shy. Gave me a right eyeful while we were going to bed last night."

She'd have been more impressed with the eyeful Aden gave Kit.

Emilia looked over, face like a cat's arse. "Yuck. Who'd want a lump like her drooling over them?"

"I heard that, and if you weren't wearing something Izzy made you, I'd punch your lights out, you rancid old slapper."

Turning to the nearest cameraman, Emilia demanded the footage be kept. "She threatened me with assault. I'll need it as evidence."

"It's only a threat if I *don't* do it," Fay said before going to get changed.

Backstage, Kit's nerves threatened to get the best of him. Pacing the floor, he eyed the exits. What if he tripped? What if he fell off the catwalk?

He'd spent so long working on his design it hadn't sunk in he'd be on a catwalk—on camera—in clothes he hadn't made. It was one thing having his clothes judged, but being judged as a model…? Bad enough to be insecure as a designer, but competing with Barker's face and Patrick's body? Patrick's physique made Kit look like a weed, and Barker had to be the most beautiful lad in London. Just as well it wasn't an underwear show, or he'd have Aden's knob to compete with, too. Being well-hung wasn't at the top of Kit's list of boyfriend requirements, but Aden's knob made his look like a light switch.

The crew did a sound test, then the *Runway Rivals* theme music thrummed in Kit's chest. Only Emilia and Izzy remained calm and confident—like they belonged. Barker looked straight back at Kit, but his expression was impossible to read. *Kit, we need to talk. Off camera.*

Pamela joined them backstage. "Don't panic, everyone. This will be a dry run to get you used to the light and sound levels. None of the judges are here, but Gunter will watch from the studio floor. Take four lengths of the runway, so that's two trips up and back. Stay here after your run. No wandering off unless you need to pee. After you've all taken your turn we'll bring the judges in and you can go again."

The music came up, and they were off. Emilia went first, then Izzy, Fay, Mukta, Barker, Aden, Patrick, and Kit.

The moment Kit stepped onto the catwalk, the lights blazed brighter and the music boomed louder than he expected. *Just do it.* He screwed his eyes up against the lights and set off. *Look confident.* He tried a swagger. *Not that confident. Try sexy.* He tried a slink, a black panther on black marble. *Not bad.* He skittered to a halt. If the crew hadn't marked the catwalk edge's with white tape, he would have slunk off the end. How would he do this in front of Bruna, Nancy, and the guest judge? Patrick's hard work deserved better. Kit turned, tugged down on the hem of his jacket, then glided back like a waiter in a five-star restaurant.

"You took forever," Emilia said when he returned, "but you do only have little legs."

Barker rounded on her. "For Christ's sake, Bitchwhore, shut up. It's tough enough without having to deal with the likes of you, too."

Emilia's mouth twisted, then she turned her face away.

"'Bitchwhore'?" Mukta roared with laughter. "The best Fay and I came up with was 'Reptilia'."

Pamela returned, all smiles. "Very good. You'll be pleased to know we're ahead of schedule because you're all naturals. We'll use your practice runs instead of asking you to walk again."

Relief lightened the dread sinking in Kit's stomach.

"We'll bring the judges in and get on with it," Pamela said. "No need to wait for Bruna to do her intro. We'll film that later. Let's get you on, get you judged, and get you home. You look fantastic, but you must be shattered. I'll warn you now—when one of you is eliminated, there will be tears."

When the music rose again, excitement crackled through them.

Izzy peeked around the corner of the catwalk's backdrop, then grabbed Aden, pulling him to her. "Guess what? The guest judge is Vonnie Valero."

Aden's mouth dropped open. "As in Minted Sting's Vonnie Valero?"

"Who?" Fay asked.

"The rock band," Izzy said, her eyes gleaming. "They're massive."

"Me and my Kev only listen to Hip Hop."

"They're the best band in the world," Aden whispered, as though trying not to break a spell. "Thank God I'm wearing this."

Barker might have smiled to himself, but Kit noticed. Nothing beat Barker's smile.

When Pamela called them back on stage, they stood in the same order they'd walked.

Bruna, magnificent as always, perched on the edge of her stool in a red, beaded dress.

"Vintage Bob Mackie," Mukta whispered along the line. "Cost her at least a grand."

Pamela's hand went up. "Let's go again. Concentrate, Mukta."

"Izzy," Bruna said, "tell us about your design."

Izzy gestured to Emilia. "There's no denying that Emilia's first impression is that of a lady, so I wanted to—"

Nancy, sitting on Bruna's right, interrupted. "Make her look like a man?"

Things didn't improve.

To Emilia: "You've made a sow's ear out of a silk purse."

To Fay: "You've put a Muslim woman in a dress that could get her killed."

To Mukta: "Emilia could have saved herself some time and used your sow's ear."

To Barker: "This is reminiscent of junior school basket weaving."

To Aden: "Ludo Wareham might be a disgrace, but that doesn't mean his son should dress as one."

Barker's hands curled into fists.

Again, Pamela's hand went up. "Too personal. Let's go again."

Nancy's face set hard. "I have to question the level of taste in this design."

To Patrick: "Congratulations, Mister Harrington. You're the first man to crossbreed a Hobbit and a venetian blind."

And to Kit: "He's overdeveloped *and* overexposed."

Vonnie Valero sat on Nancy's right. A tartan goth with crimson hair and black lipstick, she looked over her shoulder as though she wanted to be somewhere else.

Bruna took Nancy to task. "Might I remind you, Nancy, that we're here to judge the clothes and not the people in them?"

Nancy's laser-sharp gaze moved to Bruna. "I'm judging the designers and the clothes they made. If part of that judgement includes how well the design fits the model's body I will mention it."

Bruna stepped off her stool and waved her cue cards in Nancy's face. "You called Fay fat and Kit a Hobbit."

Nancy looked around, her mouth open in disbelief. "What utter nonsense. If you're going to be so easily offended, Bruno, I suggest you distance yourself from the fashion world. You've already made an excellent start with that dress."

"Bruna. My name is Bruna."

Gunter hauled Pamela out of the shadows. "Do something."

Pamela beamed as if all was well. "Let's take ten, shall we?

There's a, uh, a problem. Yes, a problem with camera two, so we need to reset. Designers, there are refreshments backstage."

As they trooped off the catwalk, Fay peeled away in tears and ran to the toilet with Mukta and Izzy in hot pursuit. Emilia headed for the water fountain at the far end of the corridor.

The boys turned right into the backstage area for the refreshments. Aden and Patrick wasted no time tucking into the waiting trays of food.

Kit made tea.

Barker loitered at his side. "Hot water for me. I'll make myself a green tea."

Kit poured the water, then handed him a cup. "How very sophisticated."

"I don't like the taste, but it burns calories."

"Dyed hair—" Kit started.

"It's not dyed."

"—contact lenses, early morning runs, and now tea that burns calories. Maybe you weren't born perfect."

Barker clicked his fingers to get Aden's and Patrick's attention, then pointed to their drinks. "In your opinion," he said to Kit, "who's on their way out?"

Kit folded his arms. "Are you trying to have a conversation with me?"

A camera swung in their direction.

"Answer the question," Barker said, voice rising. "You must have an opinion."

Kit eyed the approaching camera, scratching at his cheek. "I guess it's anyone's game, although Fay's and Aden's," he whispered, "are the weakest."

"I suppose I'll be blamed for Aden's design. He'll say it was all down to me." Barker paused until the camera reached them. "What's he like to sleep with?"

Kit swallowed. So Barker was playing to the camera. "Do you mean what's he like to share a room with?"

"If that's what you're calling it," Barker said with a smug grin.

Bring it on, Barker. "He's got a massive knob. If you want to swap rooms and get a better look, that's fine by me." Kit snatched up a tea bag, dropped it into Barker's mug, and did his best to keep his voice from shaking. "As knobs go, his is almost as big as you."

fourteen

. . .

BARKER FUMED. That bloody cameraman interrupted his conversation with Kit, forcing Barker to goad Kit about something. Sure enough, that something was Aden. Then Kit got the better of him and made him look like a fool.

And the cameras at the house weren't just up on the ceiling. Tiny lenses peered from clocks, picture frames, and even a plug socket. He'd even found one in the bathroom, set into the starry sky over the bath.

When he checked his contract with Bacchus Broadcasting, it stated they could film everything. *Everything*. All the sodding time.

Everyone loved Kit. The group gravitated towards him all the time, not just in the workroom. When he made tea, they were there. When he wandered outside—more cameras—they followed. Pamela mothered him. The girls adopted him as one of their own, drawing him aside for quiet conversations that ended in tears of laughter.

Kit wasn't defenceless; he held his own with Barker and Emilia. When anyone engaged with Kit, he came alive as if he'd hovered at the edge of a party all night until someone dragged him into their group.

Judging by the smile on Patrick's face when Kit measured him, and the way he lingered over fitting clothes to Kit's body, Patrick wanted him.

Aden, all swagger and banter, flirted with everyone but Barker and Patrick. With Kit, Aden couldn't keep his hands to himself. An arm around Kit's shoulder or a hand on Kit's back if he reached around him for something. Barker wanted to find a hammer and mash Aden's fingers.

Only a moment ago, Kit snatched up a tea bag and dropped it into Barker's mug of boiling water. "As knobs go, it's almost as big as you."

Kit strode out of the room. Seconds later, someone hammered on a door. "Fay! Get your arse out that netty."

Following Aden and Patrick, Barker hurried out into the corridor. Izzy and Mukta flanked Kit, both open-mouthed at his frenzied yelling.

Kit beat the door with his fist. "Don't make us tell you again, pet."

Fay's tear-stained face peeked around the bathroom door.

Panting, Kit raised a finger in Fay's face. "Nancy Shearsmith wouldn't know a real woman if she saw one. Your body's had three bairns, and you've spent your life grafting for what you have. She's spent the best part of thirty years knocking about with girls so skinny they'd look fat if they put in a tampon. Don't be listening to gobshites like that, pet. You've more love and compassion in your little finger than any fake—" He glared at Barker. "—doylem."

Good God. The fire in Kit's eyes, the pumping of his chest, the clench of his fists. Could Barker rouse that reaction from Kit in bed? He'd try if he got the chance.

Fay emerged from the toilet, her eyes red and puffy. "Doylem?"

"Idiot," Patrick translated, hopping from foot to foot. "Can I get in there for a slash?"

The girls—all except Izzy, who still loitered by the water fountain—ushered Fay towards the tea urn. Kit made her a sweet cup she had time to drink before getting her makeup fixed.

Ten minutes passed before Pamela reappeared to drag them back on set.

Nancy's stool stood empty.

"Sadly," Bruna said. "One of you will be going home. If I call your name, please step forward."

Gritting his teeth, Barker swallowed hard to keep rising acid from flooding his throat.

Nancy had criticised everyone's designs. Wherever she was, she'd have cast her vote. Assuming she'd given everyone the lowest possible score, it was down to Bruna and this Vonnie Valero woman.

"Emilia," Bruna announced. "Fay. Aden. Patrick." Patrick swore under his breath. "You're all safe, but please step back and stay on the runway."

Fay punched the air. "Get in."

"Izzy, Mukta, Barker, and Kit. Two of you have the highest scores, and two of you have the lowest. Izzy, tell us about your dress."

Izzy cleared her throat and turned to Emilia who smirked then hunched her shoulders to make the bodice look as ill-fitting and uncomfortable as possible. "Well, Emilia is tall and slim, so I tried to give her more volume around the bust to accentuate her femininity."

"You don't look very comfortable," Bruna said to Emilia. "Is this the sort of dress you'd—?"

"No," Emilia said at once. "Accentuating one's bosom is positively vulgar."

Izzy's skin darkened.

Vonnie spoke up. "I thought this dress looked amazing and easily something I'd wear to a summer party. Well done, Izzy."

Bruna looked down the line to Barker. "Tell us about your design."

Had he placed high or low? What he said might change their minds. "Inspired by the cultural heritage of Aden's home town of Grimsby, I wove material together as a nod to the fishing baskets and nets of the industry. The copper zip emphasises Aden's natural colouring."

Emilia stepped forward. "May I say that Barker reworked his design, so what you're seeing today was created in four hours this morning. That needs to be taken into consideration."

Vonnie exchanged looks with Bruna. "Whoa. Looks like you've got yourself a cheerleader there, Barker."

Bruna nodded, humming in agreement. "Now to you, Mukta. Tell us about your design."

"Fay's a brilliant woman, and we all love her." Emilia cleared her throat in an obvious wish to differ. Mukta continued. "So I wanted to give her something she could wear on a rare night out away from the kids and let her hair down. I played with texture and, well, that's about it."

Bruna smiled. "Thank you, Mukta. You captured Fay's fun personality, although you drew attention to parts of her that most women don't want noticed."

"Are you saying I've got a fat arse?" Fay said, her throat deep pink.

"No, no," Bruna said, sitting forward. "But a different would have accentuated your amazing curves."

Fay's expression blanked. "I led six hundred people on a cry-in when our McDonalds's closed."

Bruna's mouthed worked in silence. When she recovered, she looked back down the line. "Kit, tell us about your design."

A camera rolled up to Kit, who shied away from its lens. "I was interested that Patrick's clothes didn't draw attention to his body. I'm used to covering men's bodies—" Aden sniggered. "—so I pushed myself to make him something that showed off all the hours he's put in at the gym."

Bruna nodded at Vonnie. "I like that."

But Kit hadn't finished. "Also, he graduated from Saint Martins. I sewed into the hood to give the impression of brush strokes. Patrick's coming out of his shell, but he's still shy, so I made the hood big so he can retreat into it."

"Would Patrick wear this, being so shy?" Bruna asked.

"It's not something I'd buy for myself," Patrick said. "But I love it. I want to keep it if Kit lets me."

Bruna eyebrows twitched. "I'll let you talk about that later. Designers, we have decided."

The long, dramatic pause Barker saw on TV flashed by compared to the endless time before Bruna spoke again.

"Kit, you are the winner of this week's challenge."

Barker turned away, squeezing his eyes shut, holding back the lightning swell of tears.

Bruna and Vonnie applauded.

"You identified something unique about Patrick," Bruna said. "You made something that pushed him out of his comfort zone and looks great on him."

Barker recovered and started along the line to shake Kit's hand, but Patrick pulled Kit in for a bear hug. A pang of jealousy stopped Barker in his tracks. Everyone else congratulated Kit, whose mouth fell open, tears streaming down his cheeks.

When everyone returned to their positions, Bruna smiled up at Barker. "You are the runner-up, Barker. Although you lost time on your first design, you realised your mistake and produced something with a solid concept. However, there were some concerns with your finishing. If they had been better, you could have been this week's winner."

Barker wasn't in the bottom two. For the cameras, he punched the air like Fay and did a little victory dance. No one rushed forward to congratulate him, but he didn't care. If Bacchus wanted cocky, he'd given it to them.

Bruna waited until he finished his jig. "I take it you're very pleased with yourself. That means Izzy and Mukta are in the bottom two. Izzy, your design could have been magnificent if you'd given us a little more artistry, but it fell flat on the runway. Mukta, your design also showed real promise, but ultimately it came out looking poorly made. And so the designer leaving tonight is…" Another excruciating pause. "Mukta."

The others leapt forward, smothering a stunned Mukta. Even Emilia joined in. Barker hung back and patted Mukta back from arm's length. By the glint in his eyes, Kit wasn't impressed when Barker patted him by accident.

Fuck it. Barker dove into the group. With a hand on the back of Kit's neck, Barker pulled their foreheads together. Kit's fresh scent—orange, almond, vanilla—made Barker draw him closer still.

"Well done," Barker whispered. "Truly."

It wasn't until Aden prised them apart that Barker stepped back to enjoy his runner-up placement.

He might be in with a chance.

fifteen

. . .

BACK IN THE WORKROOM, the contestants changed clothes, then gathered in LUCA's reception area.

On their way out to the cars, Barker tried to catch up with Kit, but the three girls bundled the chap away, leaving Barker stuck with Emilia, Aden and Patrick in a car he didn't recognise.

"I find it impossible to believe they picked that little runt's design over yours," Emilia complained from the back where she sat next to Patrick.

Barker, sitting in the front with Aden, didn't spot a camera. He tapped the driver on the shoulder. "Why are we in a different car?"

"The other one's in the garage, mate. Bloody BMWs. More trouble than they're worth."

We're not on camera. Barker flung a scowl at Emilia. "Don't call Kit a runt. His work is fantastic, and it's not like I'm going home. I'm runner up."

Patrick's mouth made an O. "Who are you and what have you done with Barker?"

Emilia remained undeterred. "I shall be having choice

words with that Bruna. They obviously got shot of Nancy so they could have their own way."

Patrick threw up his hands. "For God's sake, you lickarse, will you give it a rest? That geebag tore us all to shreds. If it was up to her, we'd all be going home and they'd be getting in eight new designers. Like the man says, it's not like he's going home."

Chastised, Emilia shrank back into her seat.

Patrick squinted out of the side window. "So what's the plan for tonight? It's only four. We could go out for dinner. What do you say?"

Aden shook his head. "We're on lockdown, fella. It's press day tomorrow, yeah?"

Unease crawled over Barker's skin. "Press day? So soon? We don't air for weeks."

"If they're filming us twenty-four seven," Aden said, "there could be a nightly show and a live feed overnight. Either way, they're not letting us out unless it's their idea and there's a shitload of cameras on us."

Patrick rocked his head from side to side. "Doesn't mean we can't have a craic back at the house though, does it?"

Aden gave him a wink. "What kind of craic did you have in mind?"

"Repulsive," Emilia said with a sniff. "And watching you lot get tipsy isn't top of my to-do list."

Aden did his best to impersonate her. "'Tipsy'? Getting rat-arsed never sounded so posh. Say it again."

Back at the house, Izzy discovered a replenished stock of Champagne. She cracked open a bottle, pouring everyone a glass. Emilia, subdued by Patrick, orbited the conversation but said little.

Mukta, gracious in her defeat, sat next to Kit on the living room sofas. She held his hand. "It's going to be weird doing press tomorrow when I already know I'm going home. I hope I don't give it away by bursting into tears."

Barker sat on the opposite sofa. "You'll be all right once you're home with your family. Everything will get better. Besides, you'll still be designing for Fashion Week."

"What?"

Barker felt sure what he said next wouldn't be broadcast. "If they're taking you to press day, they don't want anyone to know who's eliminated. We'll all get to design a collection."

Fay put her empty glass on the coffee table and sat forward. "How d'you know?"

"I found an obscure interview with Brian Foster online about the original concept for the show. What's happening to us now is like that."

"They never said nothing."

Izzy swirled her glass. "That doesn't mean it won't happen. They've changed almost everything else so far."

Emilia's gaze rested on Barker. "And made a considerable investment in doing so. This house, security, filming everything backstage. That takes resources. They won't risk mismanaging a show they're trying to make bigger and better."

Aden looked up. "Are we being filmed now?"

With a sneer, Emilia pulled her glass to her chest. "'Film'? How very kitsch. It's all digital these days."

Barker and Kit spoke as one. "The motions sensors are cameras."

Kit's quick look at him made Barker's face burn.

Aden leapt to his feet. "What else is a camera? They need different angles, right? They've got those rat runs around the house on *Big Brother*. Can't do that here."

Barker stayed quiet. *You'll find out in your own time.*

After their second glass of Champagne, during which everyone debated how many other cameras there might be, Aden and Izzy set off to cook dinner. Emilia and Mukta retreated to their rooms, Patrick challenged Fay to a game of pool, and Barker wandered outside for a cigarette.

To his surprise, Kit, who'd said he'd play the winner of the pool game, joined him on the patio of limestone cream tiles. An ornate iron patio table with matching chairs sat off to the left.

Face to the lowering sun, Kit hummed. "Nice to be outside." He closed his eyes, long lashes holding Barker's attention.

"What're your roots?" Barker said.

Kit touched his hairline. "I don't dye my hair. That's your thing."

"It's not dyed, and you know what I meant."

Eyes closing again, Kit half smiled. "Roman."

"Seriously. We've all got a little Roman in us."

Kit gave him a quizzical look. "Mam's family came over from Rome, and I don't want to know how many Romans have been in you." Kit's implication wasn't as unkind as Barker expected.

"Yet it was you who accused me of having knobs on the brain."

Kit undid his top three shirt buttons. "You surprised us earlier. Didn't expect you to congratulate us."

Damn. Barker hoped no one caught it on camera. "You don't give me any credit." It was hard to hold Kit's gaze when the pink cotton shirt hugging his body demanded attention. Barker let his gaze fall to Kit's thick chest, then lower still. Would his hands fit around Kit's waist?

"Maybe I don't." Kit's bicep popped when he ran a hand through his hair. "Today's done my head in. I knew it'd be stressful, like, but I never expected this."

Fay cheered from inside the house. "Get in."

Desperation peppered Patrick's response. "Best of three."

Barker pulled a chair away from the patio table, then carried it to a raised flowerbed heaving with showy gardenias.

He sat, lit a cigarette. "It won't be long until we know who's in the final. Once tomorrow's out of the way, we'll have two more days for the next challenge. If we get the weekend off, that's another two challenges next week, so the final two are determined in the last challenge in the first part of the week after that. That's only two-and-a-half weeks. It's too short."

"Two-and-a-half weeks with you and Emilia's long enough."

Ouch. Barker took a drag of his cigarette. "Maybe there are another eight designers in another house and they'll suddenly throw them in the mix."

Kit pulled up a chair, but not as close as Barker wanted.

Barker flicked ash into a flower bed. "And another you and me sitting outside."

"Two of you? I'd rather die." Kit's mouth set into an awkward smile. "Sorry. That was a bit too harsh."

Barker's agreement with Nancy faltered. "I guess I deserved it."

"Really, Barker. It was supposed to be, I don't know, funny." Kit stood. "I'm going to go back in. It all goes to shit when we talk."

Barker raised a hand to catch Kit's, but too great a distance separated them. "So we keep trying. That's how you learned to sew, right? You can't have popped out of your mother with a silver thimble on your finger."

Kit's head cast between the house and Barker before he took a seat, hand crossed over his knees. "I suppose. But just when we're getting along, it all goes—"

"To shit."

"We have loads in common, but there's something getting in the way."

Ash dropped from Barker's cigarette, crumbling when it met the limestone. "What does friendship mean to you?"

Kit looked across the garden. Barker gaze followed his.

Around the perimeter, ivy scaled brick walls. A straight smooth path, flanked by low box hedges, led to a sky blue summer house. The smart, manicured lawn pooled around a huge weeping willow rippling in a soft breeze. Twisted wicker teepees supported pale yellow jasmine and deep orange honeysuckle, splashes of colour against the falling night.

"Friendship's going out," Kit said. "Having a laugh, talking things over when you've got a problem. You know, the stuff you do with all your marras."

Barker flicked his ash, the cinders barely visible in the twilight. "'Marras'? Is that Italian for 'friends'?"

Kit shook his head. "No, it's Geordie."

"After my father... Do you know about him?"

Loosening his fingers, Kit planted his feet and leaned forward. "Aden told us some stuff about fraud. Is it true?"

Barker made a mental note to thank big-mouth Aden later. "After his arrest things fell apart." *Careful, Barker.* "To be fair, they were falling apart before that."

"How?"

Cupping his hand over his mouth, Barker whispered in Kit's ear. "Someone outed me to my father. The news didn't go down well because he, along with his best friend Walter Winchmore, had an unspoken agreement Emilia and I would—you know."

Kit shivered. "You're saying our Emilia was supposed to be your wife?"

"Things rarely work out as expected." Barker stubbed his cigarette out on the side of the raised bed, then dropped the butt into his empty glass.

"What happened?" Kit said.

"The usual stuff. The money ran out and so did my so-called friends. Old money sticks together. New money hangs on. By the time I joined LUCA, I learned I could purchase friends. I was one year into my studies when Emilia, who'd taken a year off, joined the year below me."

"And now she's here." Kit looked up at the darkening sky. "That's mental."

"Daddy's doing, I'm sure. She's good enough, but she lacks flair. Now she's here, I have to keep her sweet." He gave Kit's knee a friendly punch, so Kit looked back down. "What are you thinking?"

"How I'd feel if everyone wanted to be with me for my money or avoid me because I didn't have any."

"And?"

Kit's eyes bored into Barker's. "It'd mess with my head."

I want to kiss him. "If we pare things back with honesty, we find what's real."

Kit's eyes, soft as a favourite t-shirt washed too many times, said he understood. Parents let you down. "Da—we don't call them 'Dad'—left when I was a bairn. I have these broken bits of memories. Nothing much to go on, mind. Grandpa Redman refused to have anything to do with Da once he left, but he looked after us. Mam seemed okay at first, but slowly she hoarded stuff and got paranoid about the neighbours. Now she's living in a house that's more landfill than anything. I tried getting her to a counsellor, but she's having none of it. My brother—"

"You have a brother?"

"Aye. You surprised? You got a brother?"

"My mother lost what would have been my little sister. She didn't fall pregnant again." Kit started to speak, but Barker stopped him with a raised palm. "No pity required. Go on."

"Oh, right. Well, I'm sorry, anyway. My brother Greg and his girlfriend Sophie kept an eye on her after Grandma died and I moved in with Grandpa, although..." Kit picked at his knee.

Barker placed a hand over Kit's to stop him grazing the fabric. "What?"

Kit looked at a camera mounted on the wall above their heads, then lowered his voice. "She had a fall a few weeks back. When the crew arrived she was babbling on about bees and the workings she'd cast not protecting her."

"Workings?"

"Something to do with the power of the universe or angels or some other shite she used to avoid getting on and doing stuff herself. Doctors decided she couldn't look after herself properly and took her in for observation. She's in a mental health unit."

"And you feel bad for being here."

They both fell into a silence. Barker looked out to the garden. Night swallowed everything.

"What's on your mind, Barker?"

"That people are shit."

With a groan, Kit fell back against his chair. "I should feel bad. I didn't realise the mess she was in until it was too late."

Barker screwed up his eyes, trying to make out the willow tree. "I know that feeling."

"You do? How?"

"Another time."

"Is it to do with your mam?"

Too much, too soon. "I said another time."

"Right." Kit rubbed the back of his neck. "Are we going to be friends now?"

Barker stood, caught Kit by the hand, then pulled him up. If it wasn't for the cameras, he'd have kissed him on the spot. "Haven't you been listening to anything I've said? Friendship means nothing, and people are shit."

"What you said... I thought you meant friendship means everything if you're honest."

Before Barker could respond, Izzy stuck her head out of the patio doors.

When she spotted them, she stepped onto the limestone slabs, then closed the doors behind her. "I didn't mean to interrupt anything. That is, assuming this particular... anything is the type of anything that is in fact an actual, you know... something."

Barker shook Kit's hand out of his, and the night air turned cold without it. "You're babbling, Izzy." He pushed Kit forward with a gentle shove. "After you, champion. You must have worked up an appetite with all that winning."

sixteen

. . .

KIT SANK into the leather chair at the head of the table.

Embarrassed that Barker had his hands on him, let alone the way they squeezed his shoulders and neck, he waited for the others to react. Only Mukta gave them a second glance.

Izzy corralled everyone to dinner in the orangery, and Barker sat on Kit's right.

"What are you playing at, man?" Kit said to Barker.

Shaking out his napkin, Barker gestured for Kit to do the same. "The winner should sit at the head of the table and the runner-up on his right. It's the proper thing to do." When Emilia approached, Barker pointed her to the opposite end of the table.

Kit shook out his napkin, then laid it across his lap. "What about Mukta? She lost. You going to make her eat in the other room?"

"Of course not. She can sit on your left."

Naturally, Emilia disagreed. "If Kit is the host, the principal guest sits on his right and the second sits on his left."

"All right. Kit, where would you like us to sit?"

The expectancy on Barker's and Emilia's faces flustered Kit, who fiddled with the napkin on his lap. *Why me? Ask someone else.* "Here's fine. No need to make a fuss as long as we're all together."

"There's your answer, Emilia."

Izzy and Aden brought in plates of spaghetti and bowls of steaming sauces. Fay lumbered in after them, arms laden with seven bottles of red wine.

Izzy tied up her hair, then wiped the back of her neck with her napkin. "Okay. Three bowls of sauce. Bolognese for the meat-eaters, arrabbiata for lovers of all things spicy, and alfredo for—"

Fay turned down her mouth. "There's this guy at our local Italian. Proper creepy, yeah? Reckon he wants his penne in my cunnelloni."

Sighing theatrically, Emilia rolled her eyes. "It's cannelloni, you fool."

Fay gave her the finger. "It was a joke, you dullard."

Kit couldn't help but roar with laughter at the look of shock on Emilia's face. He slapped his left hand on the table, then made an L shape on his forehead with the right. "*Sfigato!*"

Laughing along, Barker reached for the Bolognese sauce. "Well said." Raising one eyebrow, Barker smirked down the table at Emilia. "*Sfigato* means 'loser'."

Barker spoke Italian?

Patrick pointed at Aden's mouth. "You've got some sauce on your lips there, pal. Hope you haven't been double-dipping, because I don't want a dose of the shits."

Aden wiped the sauce off his mouth with the back of his hand, then swore at the unused napkin laying at his side. "Where the fuck do you think my mouth's been, Paddy?"

The sauce's colour matched the shade of Izzy's lipstick. No wonder she'd tied her hair up to cool off.

"Careful," Mukta said. "You're only allowed so many F-bombs and one C-bomb. Use them wisely."

Following Aden's lead, everyone helped themselves to the pasta sauces, passing bowls to one another. Fay refilled everyone's glasses.

Families eating Italian style. Exactly what Kit needed to relax into after a stressful day.

"I know," murmured Barker so only Kit could hear.

Barker's mood changed. He blazed his way throughout the meal, cracking jokes and telling stories.

Since their conversation on the patio, Barker's sullen attitude lurched to the other extreme. He cracked jokes about scrapes he got into while travelling the world with his friend Caspian and told stories about the famous faces he rubbed shoulders with at parties.

When Kit convinced himself Barker would make it all about him, Barker drew everyone in with beckoning waves, encouraging them to share stories of their own. Best of all, he took Kit's arm or squeezed his leg when he turned to ask him a question or laugh at his jokes.

Emilia glared at Kit over the rim of her glass. Izzy winked at him over the rim of hers.

"That," Barker said as he placed his knife and fork on his plate, "was spot on. Compliments to the chefs." Izzy and Aden soaked up the following wave of thanks from everyone else. Barker stood. "I'll wash up. It's the least I can do after such a fine meal."

Kit helped gather everyone's plates, then followed Barker into the kitchen.

If someone had said a tsunami ripped through the kitchen that evening, Kit would have believed them. Pots and pans littered every surface from range cooker to the smoked oak counter. Wooden spoons drowned, face down, in puddles of sauce. A gloopy colander took cover in the sink.

The colour drained from Barker's face. "What the actual

fuck? This is why I'm a firm believer that if one prepares the meal, one also does the dishes. It reduces the volume."

Kit rolled up his sleeves and sorted the washing into piles. "This is nothing. Imagine these times a hundred and you've got Mam's house. Glasses first, so the water'll leave them clear."

Barker joined him, Kit catching his leather scent every time Barker reached across for a plate to wash. Was this what gave people a fetish for bondage gear?

"So where does the name Kit come from?" Barker asked. "It sounds Greek."

"Why Greek?"

"Like Kitsopanidis."

"No. It's short for Cristoforo. It's Italian. Roman, remember?"

"Wouldn't the short for that be Cris?"

"Could be, I suppose, but it's Kit. What about Barker?"

"Father wanted to call me Barclay, but my mother refused. When he fainted in the delivery room, she called me what she wanted. I googled it once. It's an old American term for someone who uses a glib sales pitch to attract people."

It worked on me. "Is that what you were doing?"

Barker turned on the hot water. It pounded into the sink, fuzzing mist up from the basin. "What do you mean?"

"It's—you were so charming—and so sudden, like." Kit rubbed his thumb along the edge of the worktop. "Was that the real you?"

Barker tested the temperature of the water with his hands, then gave them a flick. He turned to face Kit, hands gripping the edge of the sink behind him. He dipped his head. "That depends," he said, dropping his voice to a baritone hum and giving Kit a sideways glance. "Do you prefer the bad boy?"

I prefer to flick sauce over your shirt so you have to take it off. "Can't say I did."

"Earlier, when we were outside, was the realest I've been with anyone in a long time."

Kit dipped his head, Barker's honesty juddering his thoughts.

"Talking about friendship," Barker said. "Or lack of it."

Their eyes met.

"I liked that Barker," Kit said.

Barker plugged the sink. "Where's the washing-up liquid?"

Kit found it in the tall cupboard next to the fridge. Barker put too much liquid in the water, then battled the rising bubbles.

"You only need a bit," Kit said. "Next time, put it in with the running water."

Barker grunted through a tight-lipped smile. "You think there'll be a next time?"

They worked at a good pace, Barker scrubbing each plate as though he and they had unfinished business, then handing off to Kit who dried and stacked.

When Barker wiped the sink, he did it with the same flourish he'd used when ripping the yellow dress from its cover. This time, nothing got damaged. "If the competition goes horribly wrong, I suppose I could work in a kitchen. How about another glass of wine to celebrate our first team effort?"

Kit didn't care about wine. His eyes drifted up Barker's chest to the patch of tattooed skin on Barker's neck. "What's this?"

Barker tugged up his shirt, then dipped his chin. "Another time."

"Not that again. What is it?"

"What does it look like?"

The random criss-cross of furious, intersecting lines weren't a pattern Kit recognised. "Like someone's been at you with a marker."

"Then we'll go with that."

Kit went up on his tiptoes to get a better look.

Barker ducked away, voice urgent. "What are you doing?"

"I was—"

"Friends, Kit. *Friends*."

The word did nothing to help Kit, whose brain knotted like cheap thread. "You thought I was going to kiss you?" Anger flared in his chest. "I don't even know who you are."

Barker's eyes messaged fear and frustration. "Ditto."

Kit backed away. Things took a wrong turn. They always did. "What do you want, Barker? Do you even know?"

No answer.

"Do you get off on people begging you to be nice for five minutes?"

Still no answer.

Kit threw his tea towel onto the counter. "You know what? You can celebrate our first team effort on your own."

He stalked upstairs. So much for all that winning.

seventeen

. . .

KIT CHECKED HIS WATCH. Five-thirty. A ladder of morning sun peeked through the shutters. No Aden. Had he got up early or not come to bed at all?

If Kit got a move on, he could be ready in twenty minutes. That gave him ten minutes for a cuppa before pickup. If he had time to catch up with Izzy, all the better.

True to form, Izzy waited for him in the kitchen, pushing a mug of tea across the kitchen counter when he took a seat. "Barker drank himself stupid after you went to bed. You wouldn't know anything about that, would you?"

Kit cupped the mug in his hands. "Aden wasn't in our room when I woke up this morning. Wouldn't know anything about that, would you?"

She looked out of the window, throat bobbing. "No idea."

"Not even a little one? Or, you know, a big one?"

Izzy swilled the rest of her coffee, then put the mug into the dishwasher. "I intended on giving you a lecture about you and Barker, but under the present circumstances I can't."

"Me and Barker. You reckon there's something going on because we did a shit load of washing-up last night?"

Izzy pointed to where she'd put her mug, eyebrows raised above quizzical eyes. "We have a dishwasher."

Kit couldn't do anything but smile. "There was a lot of washing up."

She grinned. "It looked like a foam party in here. One of you wiped the sink down, but everywhere else...? I spent a good ten minutes trying to wash it all away." She gestured for Kit to drink up. "Do you think he's on the up and up?"

"He's playing some sort of game," Kit said, gulping down half his tea.

Izzy lips tightened. "That's what I'm worried about. He came on strong last night."

"Are we talking about Barker?"

"God, no. Sorry. I'd moved on to Aden. He's a lot younger than me."

If Kit grew to half as cool as Izzy he'd be proud. "You're a strong woman, pet. Any lad of any age would be lucky to have you. I'm an excellent judge of character."

Izzy's hand flew to her mouth, but she couldn't hide the smile crinkling her eyes. "I can't believe you said that."

"Not of men," Kit said. He finished his tea. "But I have good vibes about you."

Izzy watched the morning sun creep onto the edge of the kitchen counter. "He's convinced himself there are more cameras, and they're all concealed. When he woke up this morning, he blew a kiss at the smoke alarm."

Smiling, Kit swilled his mug as though some tea remained. "So he slept in your room."

"Yeah, well, he fell asleep before anything happened. How was it with Barker?"

"He didn't come to my room."

Patrick trotted into the kitchen with Fay in tow. "Who's a bastard for not waking us up?"

Fay paused. "You okay, Iz? You look pale."

Patrick reached over Izzy's head to get a mug. "How can you tell?"

"That's well racialist, Pat," Fay said, glaring at him.

Patrick flicked on the kettle. "Bollocks. We're both black."

"No, babe, you're mixed race. Izzy's proper black. Like Naomi Campbell black."

Patrick nudged Izzy. "Now who's the racist?"

Fay continued. "My nan was racialist. She had a dog called Nig—"

Kit jumped to his feet. "Fay, stop. Don't say it."

Covering his face with his hands, Patrick groaned. "Please don't tell me she was about to say—"

"Jesus," Fay said. "What's the problem?"

"Do you want to explain it to her," Izzy said to Patrick, "or shall I?"

Patrick slumped against the kitchen counter. "I can't. I'm exhausted with explaining it to white people."

Kit held out his hands. "I guess we're all nervous about today."

When the rest of the contestants appeared, Kit avoided eye contact with Barker. The black circles skulking under Barker's eyes deepened their grey. Once sharkskin, now a sunken wreck.

Mukta sank into a seat at the counter. "I'm dreading this."

Barker grunted. "I bet I get the *Daily Mail*. They printed a story about my father every week since his arrest."

This was the first time Barker alluded to his father in front of the group. Everyone fell silent until Aden went into the hallway and called back to Izzy.

"Babe, have you seen my trainers?"

Patrick's mouth fell open before springing into a wide grin. "'Babe'?"

All eyes turned to Izzy.

Emilia, hair swept into the tightest ponytail she'd worn to date, cocked her head and peered out of the window. "The cars are here." And to Barker: "What have you been doing? You look dreadful."

Izzy widened her eyes at Kit. "And so it begins."

Emilia hauled Barker off to a car with her.

Kit sat in the other, with Aden and Izzy. Patrick climbed in next to him.

In the front row, Aden and Izzy giggled together, Izzy putting her head on Aden's shoulder.

Patrick whispered to Kit. "Didn't see that coming. Do you think they've done it? From what I've heard about him, she'd need help walking. Have you seen it?"

Everyone's obsession with Aden's knob verged on the unhealthy. Given the chance, Kit would take Barker — the nice version — any day of the week. He fancied Barker taking him, too.

A camera waited for them on the pavement outside LUCA, this time accompanied by Tabitha Frost.

"So here we are with the designers." She held a microphone out to Emilia, who oozed out of her car. "How's it going, guys?"

Emilia stood with Tabitha as though they were best friends. "Tabs! So lovely to see you again. The level of talent is extremely high this year, even at the shorter—sorry, Kit—lower end of the scale."

Fay muttered loud enough for the other designers to hear. "My level of rage is extremely high. All I want to do is smash Bitchwhore's face in."

A warm hand pressed against Kit's lower back.

Barker's voice rumbled with sleep. "Do you have your answers and anecdotes prepared?"

Even messed up, Barker's perfection annoyed Kit. "I hear you celebrated pretty hard after I went to bed."

"We'll be asked the same questions again and again. 'What are you trying to say with your fashion?' 'What is Nancy Shearsmith like?' 'Who's your biggest threat?'"

The heat of Barker's touch warmed Kit's spine. "I guess you're well rehearsed. No comment, no comment, and no comment."

"Wrong on all counts," Barker said. "I'll say the future, like the past, is all about glamour; Nancy is a vision and a wonder; and my biggest threat is Kit Redman."

The compliment flashed annoyance. Kit shook off Barker's hand. "Play your mind games with someone else."

Barker watched Kit walk towards LUCA's entrance.

Mukta looked over her shoulder at Barker and gave him a brief smile. "He's your biggest threat?"

Barker moved to her side, dropping his voice. "He is. How're you?"

"Awful. All I want is to go home."

"It'll be over before you know it, I promise. Keep your wits about you. They'll try to twist whatever you say to get the angle they want. Don't give them anything. Now let's get in there and *not* give the people what they want."

Once Tabitha coaxed a soundbite from each contestant, Layla scampered out of LUCA and beckoned the group to follow her inside.

Kit stood inside the doors, joining the group and positioning himself until he walked at Barker's side. "Which Barker will the press be getting?"

Pleasure flushed through Barker. Despite being mad at him, Kit persevered. "The charming one."

"Can't say I've ever met him."

Layla led the designers along a narrow corridor barely wide enough for two people to walk side by side, let alone a camera. One cameraman walked backward in front of the group. Another brought up the rear. Barker and Kit walked in the middle. Now might be his chance.

Barker yanked Kit through the first open door they reached, Aden crying out in surprise, then slammed the door behind them.

Once inside, Kit struggled out of Barker's grip. "Get off us, man."

"Shut up," Barker said in a low hiss. "All of this, of me, is an act. I made a deal with—"

Pamela barged into the room. "What the bloody hell's going on?"

Without looking at her, Barker held up a hand to keep her at bay. "Give me a second."

"I'll do no such thing. Out here now. You'll be separated for the rest of the day."

Barker shouldered past her, punching the doorframe above her head, revelling in the pain shooting from his knuckles to his elbow.

Get that on camera, you bastards.

An intensive hour of media training did nothing to settle the questions churning in Kit's head, nor did the tray of bacon sandwiches made how he liked them: rashers burnt to a crunch and thick white bread dripping with butter.

The novelty of being interviewed by national newspapers lost its sparkle after the unexpected moment with Barker. Despite each journalist asking the same questions, Kit couldn't relax. Judging by the lack of eye contact, most journalists didn't want to be there. Kit didn't understand. A show as big as *Runway Rivals*, and no one came across as bothered?

The woman from the *Guardian* complained the loudest. "I got a first in law from Oxford, and I've spent fifteen minutes with a contestant who defined injustice as buying recycled toilet paper and unexpectedly goosing herself when it split."

Had to be Fay. Had to be.

Celebrity gossip magazine *Scorch* proved tricky. After five minutes of harmless banter, the chirpy male journalist pumped Kit for information on Barker. "I know it's still early days," the journalist said, "but is it tough having someone like that in the house?"

You've no idea. "Like who?"

The journalist leafed through his notebook. "I overheard Emilia telling the *Daily Mail* Barker's already been vile to everyone and that, last night, he got trashed."

"She's one to talk."

"Really? Emilia doesn't seem the type to get smashed."

"No, but she's plenty vile to us."

The journalist tapped his notebook. "We saw that in last night's show."

'Last night's show'? They were on telly already? A gasp swelled Kit's lungs. "What?"

"Nightly shows. First one went out yesterday."

Aden had been right. *Runway Rivals* had turned into *Big Brother*. "Oh."

The journalist sat forward, running the tip of his pencil along the notebook's spiral hinge. "You're anxious, Kit. Is there anything particular we should look for tonight?"

Kit jumped when Pamela stuck her head around the door. "Time's up, I'm afraid. Ready for Emilia?"

The journalist smirked back at Kit. "The Winchmore girl? Oh, yes. I have questions for her."

"Are you all right, Kit?" Pamela said. "You look as if you're about to pass out."

The press behaved exactly as Barker expected, or perhaps the journalists were wretched because that's what he expected.

Only one, a bright-eyed woman from *Stylist* magazine who kept her questions strictly to his work ethic, design background and influences, got more than two words out of him.

True to form, the *Daily Mail* went straight in with questions about his father, hinted they suspected his mother's admission to a psychiatry clinic, then suggested he gave them something meaty or they'd make something up. When Barker threatened to ram the journalist's notebook so far down their throat it would puncture their "fucking kidneys," Pamela swooped in and called time to the proceedings.

But the *Scorch* interview? Horrific.

"What were you thinking?" Barker roared at Emilia the moment he saw her waiting on the pavement for their cars. His initial shock gave way to cold fury. "Do you know the damage you've done talking to *Scorch*?"

Emilia, already pale, drew back from where she stood with Izzy and Fay. "I'm sorry. They tricked me."

Fay screwed up her eyes. "Tricked her into what?"

Jabbing a finger at Emilia, Barker glowered at Fay. "She hinted I fucked Kit."

Emilia's eye twitched. "Poppycock. I didn't mention names."

Rounding on her, Barker moved closer. "You didn't have to. The *Guardian* told me Bacchus edited the show to make it look like something's going on with me and Kit. You practically confirmed it."

Fay rubbed her brow. "But you're gay."

Barker's hands flew to his temples. When he threw them

Behind the Seams

down, they made fists at his sides. "That doesn't mean I want to come out on national fucking television. The show's supposed to be about fashion, not who we sleep with."

"Come on, Barker," Izzy said. "*Scorch* could have done it to any of us."

"Shut up, Izzy. This is between me and her."

Aden broke off from where he stood with Patrick and Mukta. "Don't talk to her like that."

Without looking, Barker pushed him out of the way. Stumbling back, Aden swore. When he regained his balance, he faced off with Barker. One cameraman dumped his equipment, then braced his arms around Barker's chest to hold him back.

Pamela sprinted from the building, then pushed her way between Aden and Barker. "Stop this nonsense at once."

Aden, tall enough to reach over her, shoved Barker's shoulder. "Keep your hands to yourself, yeah?"

Snarling, Barker fixed Aden with a stare. "Sound advice from someone who's been shagging Izzy, you ginger prick."

Izzy's gaped at Aden and Kit. "What did you tell them?"

Kit shook his head. "I didn't say nothing, pet."

The icy burn of Barker's anger threatened to engulf him. "You've been gunning for me," he said to Emilia. "Ever since you realised I didn't want you." He should reign himself in before he made it worse, but he couldn't stop. His words crashed out. "I've tolerated you for years and this is what I get?"

With her hands up, Emilia looked around as though someone might step in. A cameraman moved closer to get his shot. "I told you." A sly smile crept across her lips. "She tricked me."

"Tricked you? You're as sharp as they come, Emilia. You've haunted me ever since you joined Charterhouse, picking and picking at me, and now you're taking it out on Kit because you're convinced I want him."

165

Emilia sauntered forward. "And you don't?"

The cold in his belly erupted, the acid in his throat turning it to fireworks. "I don't. I'm only here to win."

Kit stepped in, jaw tight, eyes glittering. "I might not speak proper nice like you and your pathetic hanger-on, but at least I know who I am. Get on with your act but leave me out of it, you fake bastard." He snapped at Emilia. "Both of you."

Desperate sparks short-circuited Barker's mind. *It shouldn't have gone like this.*

Emilia's voice, thin as a scalpel, cut through the heavy atmosphere. "Barker…"

The moment Barker sagged, Pamela blundered into action. "Enough. Everyone, please go to your cars. Mukta and Barker will leave in their own vehicles. I'm afraid it's time to say goodbye to Mukta."

The others said their goodbyes and left.

Barker stood alone with Mukta. "What have I done?"

She looked after the departing cars, lips pulled into a sad smile. "They'll be okay. You all will."

Punching his forehead with a fist, Barker groaned. "Why do I get so angry?"

Mukta shaded over to him, putting a hand on his back. "It'd be nice not to feel anything at all, wouldn't it?"

Unable to speak, hollowness threatened to engulf him.

"Barker…" She hesitated. "I don't know you, but you seem messed up. If you like Kit, and he likes you, maybe—"

"I do, but it's only been three days."

Her eyes twinkled. "Four, if you include your audition, and you've had a month to think about each other."

Her car pulled up. Barker held out a trembling hand. "It was nice to meet you."

Mukta pushed his hand aside and hugged him. The edges of his hollowness warmed. "Be kind to yourself," she said. "And be kind to Kit. I couldn't have knitted you a better fella."

Rising on her tiptoes, she kissed Barker's cheek. "See you at Fashion Week."

Barker waved her off.

"Mister Wareham," Pamela called from where she stood halfway between him and the building. "I need to speak with you. Alone."

eighteen
. . .

IN THE STUDIO, Kit spotted the missing chair from the front row. Everyone took their seats.

Fay sniffed. "I know you lot didn't know Mukta for long, but we was next to each other at our audition. I'm gonna miss her."

After yesterday's spat, Kit wasn't sure he'd miss Barker.

Izzy put an arm around Fay's shoulder. "She was good fun on her last night. That must have been hard. It would have been interesting to see what she came up with next."

Patrick leaned forward. "It'll only get worse. On the bright side, if it's me next, Fay'll get a room to herself."

"She could now," Izzy said, "if you moved into Mukta's room."

With a cackle, Fay turned to slap Patrick across the thigh. "You silly sod."

"Why can't you move?" he said to Fay.

"I'd miss looking at that hot bod of yours, babe. My Kev hasn't been to the gym since we got married." She patted her belly. "Not like I can complain. Glass houses and all that."

Pamela loomed out of the darkness. "Right, you lot.

Yesterday was a shambles, but we've had conversations." She looked meaningfully at Barker. "So let's crack on. Bruna's in the wings."

Music. Cameras. Bruna striding along the catwalk in a baseball uniform so tight the fabric strained against her breasts.

Kit legs spasmed, willing him to get onto the stage and let Bruna's shirt out at the side-seams.

Emilia gasped, then screwed up her face in disgust.

Bruna noticed, and her smile faltered. "Can we do that again? I stumbled."

"You did?" Pamela asked, looking to the camera crew for confirmation. "I didn't see you stumble."

Kit put his arm in the air. "She did."

Bruna gave him a tiny nod of thanks. "I'd like to go again."

Emilia didn't gasp, but she still made the face.

Bruna rose above it. "Good morning, designers. Behind every talented designer is a skilled team. From pattern cutters to seamstresses, everyone has a unique set of skills. For today's challenge, you will form two teams and produce three sporty looks for today's woman. That's three looks for each team. We will choose team leaders at random."

A member of the crew scurried onto the catwalk, then handed Bruna a velvet bag.

Even as Bruna stepped down from catwalk and offered the bag to Emilia, Kit knew the smug cow would be a team leader. His certainty didn't stop his stomach turning over when she pulled out a token embossed with the letters TL. The bag moved down the girls' row, then up the boys' row with no one drawing another team leader token. Barker face drained of colour when the bag landed in his hands. He reached into the bag as though snakes writhed at the bottom, then drew out the team leader token. His head turned in Kit's direction. Kit looked away, studying his lap.

"Team leaders, please join me on the runway. Emilia,

because you drew the first token, you get to choose your first team member, followed by Barker, until you've picked everyone."

Fay's shoulders slumped, then she folded her arms. "Anyone else getting netball flashbacks?"

Emilia took time making her first choice, ensuring the cameras caught every affected reaction to the contestants. She saved a smirk for Kit.

"I was captain of the lacrosse squad at Charterhouse," she said. "I'll take Patrick because he's also an athlete."

Dread in his eyes, Patrick stood. "Even though I walk through the valley…" He climbed onto the catwalk to stand behind Emilia.

Bruna beamed at Barker. "Your turn."

"Izzy," Barker said without hesitation.

Izzy didn't move. "Me?"

"Izzy," Barker said again, his voice tight-leashed.

Before Izzy stood, Emilia picked Aden, so both climbed up together.

Barker didn't look Kit in the eye. His gaze drifted over his seat as though it stood empty. "Fay."

"What do we do now?" Emilia asked Bruna. "If I take Kit the teams will be uneven."

"That's the advantage of being the first team leader. You have an additional team member."

"Emilia," Patrick said. "You're talking like you don't want him."

Emilia looked over her shoulder. "I don't."

"Are you mental? You should have picked him first. The lad drafts patterns like a pro, and he sews up a storm. We'll crush them."

Barker winced.

Looking over to the closest camera, Emilia scoffed. "If Barker wanted him, he would have snapped him up."

Kit looked into the darkness at the back of the room. Would Emilia ever get off his case?

Bruna signalled for Patrick and Emilia to stop. "We will weight your overall scores to reflect the team sizes. Kit joins Emilia's team. Please make your way to the workroom where Gunter will give you more information. Good luck, designers."

In the workroom, seven remaining tables stood in two distinct groups.

Had Mukta packed away her own things? Kit left Stitchworthy empty-handed. At least David spared him that humiliation.

Gunter stood in the centre, impressive in a suit of ash grey, Guanashina cloth.

He looks like he's stepped out of Stitchworthy.

"Hello, designers," Gunter said. "Bruna's set your challenge, now I will give you some specifics. Your task is to create a capsule sportswear wardrobe for your model. You'll be sending three accessible looks down the runway, but each piece should mix and match to form other looks. The winning team will have their line carried by Marco Blue's new label."

Fay beamed. "Shut up. *The* Marco Blue?"

Marco, the least talented member of the defunct boy band Abstraction, supplied the abs, the distraction, and not much else. After the band disbanded, his talented co-stars carved out solo music careers. Marco studied business and surprised everyone by building a formidable fitness empire. Not bad for someone who, when asked to describe his favourite Christmas wrapping, replied: "I don't think spitting lyrics about money and bitches is very festive."

Gunter chuckled at Fay's reaction. "Marco will join the judges for the runway show. You'll have two full days for this challenge and a budget of five hundred pounds. You'll have two hours before we head to Cloth for your fabric purchases. Use your time wisely."

Emilia drew herself up to her full height. "Right, Team Winchmore, let's get to work. I want each of you to spend an hour sketching before presenting your ideas back to me and the rest of the team for consideration. I will, however, make the ultimate decision. Once we've established the designs, we'll assign tasks for production. Questions?" Aden opened his mouth to speak. "No? Off you go."

Kit trudged to his table, choosing to stand with his back to the other team. He should be past caring, but his face burned with embarrassment at not being picked at all. He only had himself to blame—he'd taken Barker and Emilia down on camera.

Patrick nudged him. "You okay?"

Aden looked up from his sketch pad. "Why wouldn't he be okay?"

With a click of his tongue against the back of his teeth, Patrick shook his head. "No one picked him."

Kit did his best to give Patrick a smile of reassurance, but it sat uncomfortably on his face. "I'm fine, lads." He stared at his sketchpad.

Voice gentle, Barker drew Izzy and Fay into a group design session. "What kind of woman buys from Marco Blue? What sports does she play? What does she need to wear for those sports? We need her background."

Kit never played sport. He did an hour in the gym every day, and that was it. *One suit in tweed for Barty's formal shoots and another in moleskin for the informal.* Kit sketched a shooting suit, then moved on to experiment with cut and proportion. What best suited the female body? When the hour was up, he had twelve pages of designs.

Emilia thumped the table to get their attention. "Let's go alphabetically. I'll go first."

Patrick pointed at Aden. "Umm?"

"Alphabetically after me, the team leader."

Her designs were so good Kit could spit. A solid mix of layered clothing designed for multiple disciplines, all rendered in black and charcoal grey. She'd even placed colour blocks down the centre front to trick the eye into seeing a slimmer silhouette.

Aden's, mainstream and predictable, included chevrons and stripes. "To show motion, even when standing still."

Emilia's fingers tapped on his sketches. "I'm not convinced your chevron placement would flatter a woman. Let's see what you've come up with, Patrick."

"But Kit's next."

"Yes, yes. We'll get to him. Continue."

"I've gone for a unisex design, using a mesh base you can attach padded panels to, depending on the sport you're playing."

Kit loved it. "That's amazing. I never would have thought of that."

Patrick ducked his head, then gave him a playful punch.

Aden guffawed. "If you sat in that for long, your arse'd look like a tennis racket."

Emilia had a faraway look in her eyes. "Or a waffle."

"Like you've ever eaten a waffle," Fay called out.

Emilia bristled. "There wouldn't be any left if you were present, you lump."

Fay threw down her pencil. "Men like something to grab hold off."

"I doubt that very much."

Stepping into the centre of the room, Fay clicked her fingers at Aden. "Come on, Ade. Would you rather stick your knob in a tube of Twiglets or a doughnut?"

"Krispy Kreme's chocolate dreamcake all the way."

Emilia turned away from Fay's triumphant cackle. She didn't look at Kit when she spoke. "You're up, Kat."

Bitch. He raised his voice. "It's Kit. My name's Kit. You know it is."

"So sorry. Off you go."

"I started with a shooting jacket before—"

Emilia put both hands to her forehead. "Did you say shooting?"

"Yes, but—"

Her hands moved to her chest. "No, no, no. This is unacceptable. I won't be a part of anything that promotes the senseless killing of innocent animals."

Patrick chimed in. "It's not senseless if it's culling, though, right?"

Emilia's voice rose. Cameras swivelled to point at her. "It's nonnegotiable. I will not be a party to this."

Aden waved his hand to catch her attention. "What about clay pigeon shooting?"

She shook her head and folded her arms. "We'll go with my designs. Kit will be in charge of production under my close supervision."

Funny how someone who didn't want him on their team knew exactly how to use him to their advantage.

Patrick threw up his hands. "Whoa, whoa, whoa. What about our designs?"

"I explained I'd make the last decision. No one protested." She scowled at them. "It's too late to start now."

Aden called out to the other team, who watched the exchange with the same focus as the cameras. "Can I come and join your team? Bitchwhore's living up to half her name."

Fay waved him away. "Nah, you're good. We're enjoying our bitch-and-whore-free status."

Emilia laughed. "I'd like to take your word on that, but if I'm only being a bitch, we all know that leaves someone to be the whore. Isn't that right, Aden?"

He gave her a black look. "You're out of order, Emilia."

"As are you. I've made my decision."

Kit caught Barker's eye. *You put me here.* Barker ducked his head, leafing through a sketchbook.

Patrick sauntered off towards the kitchen area. "That's grand. We've got nearly an hour before we go to Cloth. I'm making a brew. It won't be Irish, but it'll have to do."

Aden took Kit by the arm. "Come on, Kit. You love a brew and you can talk us through sewing stretch fabric."

As they passed Izzy, she gave Kit's hand a quick squeeze. "You got this."

Barker coughed. "Come on, Izzy. I need you to focus."

Once the boys resigned themselves to Emilia's designs, Kit split the work. "We'll only have half an hour when we get to Cloth, so head straight for the mesh, neoprene, and micro fibre. If they have the right colours in something waterproof, get that too."

Patrick closed his eyes, repeating the list. "But no fleece."

"Yeah. We good?"

Aden and Patrick spoke as one. "Yes, boss."

Kit sighed. "Don't call me that in front of Emilia or we're all in trouble."

"We're already in trouble," Aden said. "If we don't win, we'll have a one in three chance of being thrown under the bus."

He had a point. Kit piled sugar into his tea. "If that happens, we all know who's getting run over."

nineteen

. . .

BARKER WAS grateful things with Kit took a nosedive.

They both needed to concentrate on the challenge and divert everyone's attention. Let Aden and Izzy be the series 'showmance'. Shooting would end soon, leaving Barker to explain everything to Kit. God willing, Kit would forgive him.

Yesterday had almost been too much to bear. First his grilling from the press and second the horrific scene in front of everyone.

Worst of all, the conversation with Pamela. She'd pulled him into a classroom scattered with tables. Figurative sculptures dotted each one. Fine dust coated everything, and the muddy chemical scent of clay and plasticine starched the air.

Pamela tossed her clipboard onto a table, scuffing up rolling, powdered clouds, then reached into her pocket. "You'll need these." She drew out a tube of antacids, then held them out.

Barker grabbed the packet as though it were a life raft. "Thanks, Pamela. I—"

"Don't thank me yet."

Whatever she'd say next wouldn't be good. Cautious, Barker thumbed the packet in his hand. "I don't understand."

Pamela took a deep breath, eyes locked on his. "You're off the show."

Fear roiled in Barker's guts. "It was just an argument. It's not like—"

"Not like you hit him? I'm not convinced. If Carl hadn't—"

"Carl?"

"The cameraman who restrained you. If he hadn't, you would have hit Aden. Don't tell me otherwise."

Pamela's certainty scared him. This couldn't be happening. He'd talk her around.

But her gaze didn't waver. Her feet didn't shuffle. She'd decided. "I have to do what's best for everyone."

The clouds she'd raised when throwing down her clipboard diffused along with any sense of hope.

Without hope to quell his fear, Barker only had anger. "Are you fucking serious?"

"Barker." Pamela's voice remained cool.

Barker's grip on the tube of antacids snapped it in two. He'd never argued with his fists before; his words packed all the punch he needed.

Pamela's eyes moved from the broken tube to meet his. "I'll step away and give you time to cool down. If you want to talk instead of shout, I'm all ears."

Barker wanted a fight, but Pamela wouldn't give him one. She picked up her clipboard, tapped the edge against the table, then left the room.

Barker stayed quiet, waiting for the storm in his chest to abate, but he couldn't help sparring with himself. Pamela's footsteps echoed in the corridor outside. As each echo lessened, so did his fury.

He remained still, blinking in unison with each step of an

alternative plan. Then he strolled out of the classroom and called down the corridor. "I've done everything you wanted."

Pamela turned on her heels, eyebrows pinched into a frown. "Sorry?"

"The deal Nancy delivered on your behalf. A spot on the show for the bad boy."

Pamela's frown deepened as she stuck her hands on her hips. "What on earth are you talking about?"

Barker didn't need to be told Nancy had played them both —he read the confusion on Pamela's face faster than a one word note.

Pamela advanced on him, each step less hesitant than the one before. "What exactly did Nancy say?"

"That unless I gave them—you—what you wanted, I wouldn't be cast."

With a quick look over her shoulder, Pamela beckoned him back into the classroom. "Is that why you've been such an insufferable little prick?"

"Obviously."

Pamela would be on his side in no time.

Her face fell. "You stupid, stupid arse." She held the clipboard across her chest, smearing powdered clay across her top. "I can assure you Nancy had no authority to make you such an offer, but I still can't let you stay. Even if you were playing a part, you physically threatened a fellow designer."

A lump formed in the back of Barker's throat. "Please, Pamela. I need this."

She shook her head. "I'm sorry, Barker. You brought this on yourself."

He rubbed the back of his neck with a shaking hand. "Don't do this to me."

Pamela's eyes softened. "Put yourself in my position."

Barker's hand moved from the back of his neck to his trembling lips. He bit into his thumb so hard, blood seeped across his tongue. "What about mine?"

"There's more to life than *Runway Rivals*."

The pain in Barker's thumb faded. He bit harder. This couldn't be happening.

Pamela eyes widened as blood ran down Barker's chin. "Oh, God." She rummaged in her pocket, pulled out a tissue. "Give me your hand." Wrapping the tissue around his thumb, she stared up at him. "What's got into you?"

Desperation pushed past his control. He sobbed once, then wrapped his free arm across his chest to keep from shaking.

Pamela hurried him to a chair at the nearest table. "Sit, sit. Give me those." She tugged the antacids from his fist. "Listen, I'm going to refer you to the psychological consultant. You—"

Barker ploughed his fingers into his hair. "I'm not crazy. I'm poor." He took her hand. If he stopped shaking, relief might sink in. He'd told no one about his situation.

Pamela crouched in front of him, then pulled his hands into his lap. His hair collapsed over his brow. "What do you mean?"

Ragged gasps staggered his explanation. "Burned through my trust fund. Racked up thousands. Debt. Nothing now. Please. Have to win this. Please."

Pamela brushed aside his hair. "Even if I let you stay, you might not win."

"I can. I have to. And Kit…"

"What about him?"

"I can't leave him. Emilia will eat him alive."

"Is that all?"

Barker tears dropped onto the floor, mixing with clay dust to form pallid discs of misery. "What?"

Pamela smiled, tilted her head. "Don't you think I watch all the footage with the editors? We could air a half-hour montage just of you watching him with your heart in your eyes."

Barker's laugh surprised him. "Is it that obvious?"

She patted his hand. "Every girl in Production wants someone to look at them like that. Most of the boys, too."

"Please, Pamela. Let me stay. I'll do anything."

Pamela bit her lip, then slapped the broken halves of the antacids in his hand. "All right. Fuck it. Stay."

Barker threw his arms around her neck, fresh sobs wracking his body.

Pamela hugged him back, one hand in his hair. "But if you pull a stunt like that again, I swear I'll castrate you with Emilia's shears."

***

In the workroom, Barker and the girls completed their designs and fabric choices. With five minutes to spare, the girls went to the loo. Barker got a drink of water from the kitchen, throat still thick from yesterday's sobs.

Gunter whisked them away to Cloth. Emilia's team dashed inside before Barker's team climbed out of their car.

Izzy cringed. "We haven't estimated how much we need of each fabric."

Shit. "We've got five hundred quid," Barker said. "Let's get three yards of everything we like the look of until we hit our limit."

Fay let her head fall back and whined. "What about fastenings and shit?"

"Okay. Let's get that first and double back for the fabric. That a plan?"

Cloth was the biggest fabric shop he'd ever been in. Tucked into a narrow Tudor building, its rabbit warren of stacked fabric rolls covered five floors and proved harder to navigate than it looked on TV.

Barker gave Fay and Izzy half the budget each, tasking them with finding the best fabrics they could afford.

Fay brandished her money. "What are you going to do?"

Barker scanned the rolls of fabric standing against every wall. "I'll cover every inch of this place in case something jumps out at me."

"What," Fay said. "Like Aden's willy?"

Laughing, Izzy slapped her on the arm.

Once Gunter and his two camera people, one a woman—Mukta would have been pleased—captured enough coverage of Barker's team, they moved on to Emilia's.

Barker ducked his head to clear the top floor's low ceilings and navigate from room to room. Vintage fabrics, everything from felt to lace, hugged the walls. More a museum than a shop, Barker forced himself to move on rather than linger over each delicate roll, none of which suited the challenge. He rounded a corner and found Kit alone.

Barker bumped his head on a ceiling joist in surprise. "Oh."

Kit's eyes narrowed. "What're you doing up here? Something to say?"

Barker couldn't will his lips to move.

"Good," Kit said. "I wanted you to shut your mouth. Keep up the good work."

"Mukta told me to be kind to you."

"So go away."

"The kindest thing is the truth."

"I'm not interested."

Barker rooted his feet and drew in a breath. This could go either way. "I made a deal with Nancy. I'd get a spot on the show if I agreed to play the bad boy. I was stupid and weak and I feel wretched for being a shit. It got in the way of you and me."

Kit rested his head on a roll of lace, then closed his eyes. "I've never been so unhappy in my life."

"What?" Barker took a step towards Kit, who didn't move.

"My Grandpa died the night before our audition. The

theatre group wouldn't let me bring any dresses. When I got the call to say I'd got through, I turned it down."

"Why?"

"I tried to palm if off on my mam going into hospital, but I know I don't have it. I don't fit in with people like you. Then I lost my job and didn't have a choice but to come here."

"Kit…"

"All I want is to go home." Kit faced him, distraught.

Barker couldn't help but gather him up in his arms. "You won our first challenge, and you fit in. Everyone loves you."

Kit sobbed into Barker's chest. "Emilia doesn't. She doesn't love anyone except you."

"If that's love," Barker said. "I'm worried."

Kit pulled back enough to put one hand on Barker's chest. "I put a lot on you, and you don't deserve it."

Barker held Kit tighter and dropped a kiss on the top of his head. "I'll take it. You're feisty and funny and talented."

"Ten minutes, designers," Gunter called from downstairs.

Emilia's voice followed. "Where the bloody hell is Kit?"

Kit wiped his eyes. "I have to go. She'll use any reason to get rid of us."

"Do you want me to talk to her?"

"I can handle her if it kicks off." He gave Barker a quick hug. "Now help your team. The last time I saw Fay, she was fingering some polyester."

Making sportswear turned out to be tougher than it looked. If it hadn't been for Stitchworthy agreeing to produce long johns for Barty, Kit might have thrown in the towel.

"Bloody hells," fellow tailor Lefkos had said the previous year when the two-ply fabric for Barty's long johns kept snagging in his machine. "I'm gonna kick this shit into next week."

Renos snatched it out of his hand and used the overlocker instead. "Why you make it hard on yourself?"

With their frustration fresh in Kit's mind, he produced sample after sample until Emilia gave him a curt nod of approval.

With that, Kit trained Aden and Patrick, asking them for samples of their own.

Aden handed over his ninth effort. "Well?"

"You haven't threaded the tail of threads back through the stitching. It'll come undone."

"Are you joking?"

Barker didn't look up from where he stood over his pattern pieces. "Kit doesn't joke about work."

It took all afternoon before Kit approved the boys' samples.

Gunter arrived for his mid-afternoon check in, resplendent in a royal blue Italian wool suit, and rapping his knuckles on Team Winchmore's empty dress form. "You might have all day tomorrow, but your model is due in an hour. You have nothing to fit."

Emilia pushed Kit aside. "We'll take her measurements."

Gunter pointed to the plastic briefing folder sticking out from under a pile of fabric. "You have them."

Kit got nothing but a steely glare when Emilia looked to him for backup. Gunter needed reassurance. The entire team did.

"We'll have something to fit," Kit said.

Gunter pursed his lips. "You're going to draft, cut and make something for a fitting in an hour?"

"I can do it."

The others helped where they could. Aden pinned fabric on to the dress form, sculpting the basic shapes, then Kit drafted them onto pattern paper.

Patrick watched. "I've never seen someone work so fast. You're amazing."

Kit used French curves to make final adjustments. "Ready."

They all steered clear of him when his shears came out. He was grateful for the focus it required. The conversation with Barker at Cloth changed things. If Kit kept his mind on sewing, he'd figure things out.

With thirty seconds to spare, he finished a crop top and a pair of shorts.

Emilia cut acid orange fabric to tack on to the base garments during the fitting.

Gunter strode in, arms held wide. "Designers, please give a warm welcome to your models."

The first model who walked in had worn Barker's yellow dress at his audition. The second, Alex. Kit scampered towards her, arms open for a hug, but she headed for Barker's team.

Alex gave him a little wave. "Sorry, pet. I'll catch you later, if there's time."

Team Winchmore's model Deja, a statuesque black girl with blue-grey eyes, sported an impressive six pack.

"She's an absolute stunner," Patrick whispered to Kit. "Do you suppose she'd be having any brothers?"

Aden leaned in. "Not unless you'd be having them first."

With a jab of his shoulder, Patrick shoved him back. "Be off with you, you clown."

Emilia watched Deja walk up and down the workroom. "Let's go with the charcoal fabric for the base garments. It'll look softer with her skin tone than black, and it'll echo those amazing eyes. Put your hand down, Kit. I'm well aware you'll need to adjust the shorts for that—"

Aden chimed in. "Spectacular arse? Magnificent booty?"

Fay looked over. "Izzy's in the room, yeah?"

With a huff, Emilia planted her hands on her hips. "I was going to say well-developed glutes, but each to their own, I suppose." She pinned on the orange fabric, made a few adjustments, then asked Deja to walk again. "That's it. Chaps?"

Alex laughed at a joke Izzy made, then fell against her, one hand on her shoulder. Barker looked on, not getting the joke, but smiling anyway.

Kit wanted to kiss that smile more than anything. If it wasn't for this damned competition, he could have. But if it wasn't for this competition, he wouldn't have met Barker.

What would Hannah think of Barker? She'd have an opinion. Kit hoped it'd be a good one.

Emilia's voice snapped Kit back into focus. "What do you think?" she said.

Even in bare feet, Deja towered over him. "Perfect," Kit said. "Come on, let's make fashion."

Patrick flinched. "I'm sure you can't say that. That's Gunter's thing, right?"

Gunter stepped out from behind a cameraman. "Indeed." He'd been so quiet Kit forgot he was there. "But if you'd like to adopt it as your battle cry, you have my permission."

Aden gathered the team into a circle and counted down from three to one before all four of them shouted Gunter's catchphrase in unison. They gave each other high fives, although Emilia missed Kit's hand. Whether on purpose, he didn't care. He had a collection to make.

twenty

. . .

DESPITE THE EXHAUSTION weighing him down, Barker wanted to talk with Kit, but as soon as they walked through the front door Kit retired to his room.

Barker changed clothes—grey Ralph Lauren shirt and black Fendi jeans. On his way down to dinner, he paused outside Kit's door. Kit had a rough day. Might he want to talk it through? With Barker? He rapped twice on the door. "Kit? Are you all right?"

No movement.

Barker placed a hand flat on the door. "Would you like something to eat? I can bring supper up to you."

No answer.

"If you need to talk, you know where I am." Barker wandered to the top of the stairs, then gave Kit's door one last look before heading downstairs.

Fay and Patrick made dinner. At the table, the group's conversation stuck to the challenge.

Aden jabbed a carrot with his fork. "I can't believe you didn't pick Kit first, Emilia. He's dynamite."

"What would you have done if he'd referred to you as a 'pathetic hanger-on'?"

"Swallowed my pride and picked the best seamstress—is that even the right word?"

Barker pushed a lump of mashed potato around his plate. "It's 'seamster', but he prefers 'tailor'."

"Why not 'designer'?"

Izzy put down her knife and fork, then leaned back. "Because he doesn't believe it."

Good God, she's astute.

Fay pushed out her bottom lip. "Don't he? What do you reckon, Barker?"

"You'd have to ask him."

"I will, and I'll tell him it's a load of bollocks."

Emilia clucked. "Why must you use that foul language?"

"Here we go," Fay said. "Little Miss Perfect. Why do you have to stick your bony little nose into everyone else's conversation?"

"Because I have every right to my opinion."

Fay's knuckles turned white as her fingers tightened around her cutlery. "No one gives a shit about your opinion. The only opinion that matters is Nancy's. She's running the show, not you."

"That's fortunate considering she doesn't like your work. What was it, again? Something about your design being so bad it would get Mukta killed?"

Patrick put a hand on Fay's shoulder. "Stall the ball, you two. It's too late in the day for drama. What say we turn in?"

Fay dropped her cutlery, but didn't take her eyes off Emilia. "Good idea, babe. Let's go."

Grateful for another fight quashed, Barker cleared the table. "I assume no one wants a nightcap."

The others traipsed upstairs while he loaded the dishwasher.

In the main lounge, Barker turned off the lights and sat alone. He flicked on the TV. Nothing but static. He turned it off. A minute later, he flicked it back on.

"What're you doing up?" Kit stood in the doorway. "My bad. Didn't realise you were down here."

Barker stretched, taking Kit in. White t-shirt, snug boxer shorts, unshaven chin, and a full mouth. "It's not a problem. Can't you sleep?"

Kit took a few tentative steps into the room. "Hungry."

Barker stood. "I'll make you something."

Folding his arms across his chest, Kit gave him a shy smile. "I can do it. I only want tea and toast."

Already on his feet, Barker shushed him. "I've got this. I'm no chef, but like you said, it's only tea and toast."

Kit threw himself into the corner of the sofa. "Thanks."

"I'll bring it in."

Barker prepared two slices of toast as if making them for royalty, buttering edge to edge, then cutting them into four triangles. The same attention went into the tea, adding an estimate of the sugar Kit loaded into his cup the first day they met.

The word 'hungry' hadn't prepared Barker for the way Kit attacked the toast. He tore through the first slice in seconds, then did the same with the second.

"Needed that." Kit put his plate on the floor, then his mug on top. "Why didn't you go to bed?"

"I can't switch off. You missed another skirmish between Fay and Emilia. At one point I thought Fay might hit her."

Kit pulled his knees up to his chest. "She's a bit of a charva, but her heart's in the right place."

Barker slipped his hands under his thighs to stop himself from stroking the black hair feathering down Kit's shins. "Perhaps. Are you any better?"

Fingers interlaced, Kit pushed his palms above his head

until his arms straightened, then yawned. "Could do with a cuddle."

Barker's throat tightened. *Runway Rivals* would be sure to broadcast that. "Um."

Kit's expression changed, mouth open, eyes wide. "I didn't mean…"

"I'd oblige, but…" Barker raised his chin to the camera above.

Kit's head fell back. "I'm so sick of being watched." He stared at the ceiling, stretching out one leg. Barker trembled when Kit's foot touched his thigh. Kit snatched it back, his head snapping upright. "Sorry."

Barker reached out, beckoning for Kit to stretch again. "It's fine. More than fine."

But Kit pulled his legs back, digging his toes down between the sofa cushions. "My feet are cold."

Barker pulled out one of Kit's feet, then gave it a gentle squeeze. Soft skin and a touch of delicate hair on the curved crown. How might the rest of him feel? "They aren't cold at all."

Kit froze. Fear? Excitement? "Barker…"

Barker moved his hand up to squeeze the back of Kit's firm calf. "Yes?"

"Take off your shoes and socks."

Barker blinked at Kit. "I beg your pardon?" He hadn't bargained for Kit having a foot fetish. *Fuck*.

"Don't be talking back to us," Kit said, slow but insistent. "Do it."

Barker hesitated.

Face impassive, Kit tutted. "I won't be sniffing them. Get your arse in gear and take them off."

Barker did as he was told, his eyes never far from Kit's.

Kit held out a hand. "Pass us your socks." As soon as he

had them, Kit hopped up onto the back of an armchair, then covered the camera with a sock.

"What are you—?"

"Any others?"

"What?"

Sighing, Kit climbed down from the chair. "Are there any other cameras in this room?"

Barker's thoughts rushed. What did Kit want to do in this room?

Kit snapped his fingers in Barker's face. "Earth to Barker."

"Um, no. None."

"Back in a minute." Kit disappeared with the other sock, padding upstairs.

When he returned, he pulled Barker to his feet. What Kit lacked in height, he made up for in strength.

Dragging Barker out through French doors, Kit pointed up at the camera high above them. He'd covered it with the other sock.

Head down, he pulled Barker along the path leading to the summerhouse, then around to the back of the building. "No cameras here."

The air could have suffocated Barker, but Kit's scent muted the honeysuckle flooding the garden.

Alone at last.

Kit nudged Barker backwards until the wooden cladding pressed against Barker's back. Still warm from the sun, each plank's slatted pressure loosened Barker's muscles. Kit's hands moved to Barker's waist, their gentle weight anchoring both men together. Barker stood in silence, bathing in Kit's presence, drowning under his touch. When his hands ventured to Kit's hips, Barker eased his thumbs under the hem of his t-shirt, stroking upward until skin met skin.

Kit ran hot. Every time Barker's thumbs moved, Kit's

breath shook. His voice, barely a whisper, wavered. "Take me to your room?"

Leaving one hand on Kit's waist, Barker cupped the back of Kit's head with the other, then nuzzled their foreheads together. "The first time I wanted to kiss you? Putting on your bandana before your audition. You were so nervous." Barker moved the hand on Kit's waist to the small of his back, smiling when dimples cupped his fingertips. One day, Barker would kiss those dimples.

Kit's back arched. He pulled back as much as Barker allowed. "I don't usually. I mean this—I—"

"When I was in the studio on the first day, I thought I could keep up the act I'd promised Nancy, then you showed up."

"And?"

Barker's fingers curled into Kit's hair. "Then I wanted to win you *and* the show."

Kit's back arched again, exposing his neck. His breath quickened. Barker dropped a kiss onto Kit's throat, faint as a whisper. Kit trembled, angling his head to the side, moving his lips closer to Barker's. Their breath mingled.

After all the hours Barker spent watching Kit, he thought he knew everything about his lips, but nothing prepared him for feeling them against his. Released from the torment of anticipation, Barker opened his mouth.

Kit rose on his toes, deepening the kiss, reaching for the top button of Barker's shirt.

Smiling, Barker caught Kit's wrist. "We can't."

Kit's fingers splayed across Barker's chest, coaxing shivers, and Barker wished they could sink to the floor and escape everything but each other. Kit's hands moved down Barker's body to the top button of his jeans.

Again, Barker caught Kit's hands. "Not here. Not like this." It could be like that. They could undress each other right here in the warm summer evening. Kiss. Taste. Release. They could do all those things, but Barker wanted something more. "Kit."

"I don't care." Kit tugged at Barker's jeans.

Barker raised Kit's hands to his mouth, then kissed them. "I do, and so will you when it's on television and the internet forever."

Moonlight glinted in Kit's eyes. "Let's find a place to stay the night."

"Let's wait awhile. Get to know each other." Barker kissed him again, lingering in Heaven. "We deserve that."

"Please," Kit said, hands in loose fists bumping Barker's chest. "Nothing has to happen."

If they were in the same bed, Barker wouldn't be able to control himself. Kit stripped naked. Kit tumbled onto the bed. Kit's thighs pressed each side of Barker's waist. Kit, Kit, Kit.

"We both know something would."

Kit dropped his hands, looked away. "Guess we'd better turn in." He led Barker back to the house, head hung low. Halfway across the patio, Kit glowered at the sock-covered camera. "Wait. I've a plan."

When they slunk back inside, the house stood silent. If anyone monitored the cameras overnight, they'd have raised the alarm by now.

Kit pulled Barker close. "Go to your room and wait for me."

Barker fidgeted with the chewed edge of his thumb. "Kit, I—"

Kit gave him a cocky smile. "Just go to bed."

In his room, Barker unbuttoned his shirt, then hesitated. If he undressed, it might give Kit the wrong impression. The papers already used the words 'showmance' and 'fauxmance' for reality show relationships. Barker didn't want that. He buttoned his shirt before lying on his bed.

Should he investigate? Footsteps on the stairs stopped him

from getting up. A door opened, but not Barker's. The door closed. Footsteps grew closer, softened, then Barker's door opened.

Kit slid in through the gap, wearing a pair of jeans. He closed the door behind him, crossed to the window, then drew back the curtains. Moonlight pooled around him until he stepped out of it and sat cross-legged at the top of the bed. "My plan is this, sitting with you, in the middle of the night, with no one listening or watching."

The light on Barker's bedroom camera no longer blinked on and off. It stayed off. "Have you cut the power?"

Kit shrugged, nonchalant. "Some cameramen showed me how to use the central lighting system. The fuse box was next to it."

"Surely someone will notice?"

"The lad from *Scorch* mentioned a nightly show, not a livestream. I don't reckon they'll check the camera feed until five or six when we're getting up."

"I hope you're right."

Kit edged closer. Barker pushed against his chest to stop him.

Kit sat back. "Go on. I'm cold."

"Honestly?"

"Honestly. You talk like you're not used to people being honest with you."

"They're not."

Kit pulled Barker up onto his feet. "I honestly want to get to know you better, so relax." Kit ran a thumb down the tattooed side of Barker's neck. "Are you ever going to tell me what this is?" Barker shied away. Kit patted his shoulder, lingering on his upper arm. "Despite all your carrying on, you're sewn up tight. Who is the real Barker Wareham?"

Barker crossed to the window. "That's a big question."

"What's the big answer?"

"Where to begin? I'm twenty-three. I did a year at art school before I got into LUCA, and—"

Kit gave Barker's arm a brief tug. "I'm not bothered about your CV. What was your life like as a kid? If you could change one thing about your past, what would it be? That stuff."

"Only one?"

"That's the stuff I want to know."

Barker paused, then walked Kit to the bed. He lay down, pulling Kit down to lie at his side. Kit rested an arm and his head on Barker's chest.

Barker played with Kit's hair. "One of my earliest memories is being on holiday with my mother and father."

Kit gestured for him to go on, and pleasure swelled in Barker's chest.

"We'd moored up in Puerto Banús. It was one of those warm, sticky nights. Hundreds of people walked the length of the marina, looking at all the yachts, including ours."

"Fancy," Kit said, drawing out the word.

Barker squeezed Kit's head against his chest. "Stop taking the piss."

"Okay."

"I was old enough to appreciate some people might want what we had. That night, when my father was out at dinner with clients, my mother took me out into the town. We walked through streets lined with luxury boutiques, but she wasn't interested in a single window. Deeper into town she stopped opposite a house. Shutters open, a family sat around the table, passing around bowls of food and laughing as they ate. 'That,' my mother said, 'is what happiness looks like. Never forget.'"

Kit raised his head, smile pleased. "That's why you perked up when we had our first group dinner."

Barker kissed Kit's forehead. "I remember that family to this day. I think that's the root of my problem. My family never had that. My father wanted the perfect family, but he didn't understand his role in it. He sent me to the best schools, I achieved the highest grades—"

The hand on his chest patted twice. "And there was us thinking you were just a pretty face."

Barker covered Kit's hand with his. "I learned the piano. I played tennis, cricket, polo. I did all the things expected of me, and I assumed the reward was a family like the one in Spain. It never happened. I was grateful for what I had, but that family's moment? It never came." He stroked Kit's hand. "What about you?"

Kit hesitated. "Da left home in the autumn. Mam always hated the nights drawing in, even before he left. She had to get out, so she'd take me and Greg with her. We walked miles to the next town where all the rich folk lived. She'd stand at the end of their drives and say, 'I bet they're happy,' and I'd say, 'I'm happy with you,' and she'd smile. I thought it meant she was happy with me, too. It ate away at her that Da left her with two young bairn. She worked for a bank in Newcastle. Long hours. Greg used to walk us home, maybe make some tea. When Mam got home, she'd tidy and clean and fall asleep in front of the news. She never dated anyone. When the holidays came round, I couldn't wait to see Grandpa in London. He'd make me toast, and if it were the weekend, we'd watch cartoons in the morning. He'd take me to the shops and teach me about making clothes. It was magic."

"Would they like each other, our mothers?"

"Mam's past liking anyone. She's too far gone. Do you?"

"When they were younger, perhaps. My mother would have liked a normal job. She needed something of her own."

Could this be the moment Barker waited for? Shutters open to the night, being with the one he — Could he love Kit? So soon?

Kit shifted position, dropping his arm to Barker's waist and hooking a leg over Barker's. "Are you afraid of anything?"

"Of coming apart at the seams."

Kit's voice dropped to a whisper. "I like what I've seen of your stuffing."

Barker rolled Kit onto his back, then kissed him, savouring the heat curling in his mouth.

Kit contemplated him. "What was that for?"

"For not taking my shit when I lost it at the audition, for mending my dress and making it better, for not taking my shit later, for calling me out for being fake, and for recognising when I wasn't."

Kit grinned. "One kiss for all that? I mean, I know you're broke and all—"

Barker kissed him again, tongue wandering deeper, skimming the line between gentle and sexual. The seam of tension in his stomach unpicked itself. "I've plenty of kisses to spend."

He worked his hands under Kit's t-shirt, moving over his stomach. Stubble peppered Kit's abs, thickening in the cleft running between his chest and up to his throat.

Kit unbuttoned Barker's shirt and, this time, Barker allowed it.

"I'll let you know when you're paid up," Kit said, tracing the edge of Barker's tattoo with thoughtful fingertips. "But you owe me big time."

As the night drew on, Barker's debt showed no sign of being settled.

twenty-one
...

BARKER WASN'T sure what time they fell asleep, but he awoke with a full night's alertness.

Still dressed, his limbs tangled with Kit's. Kit slept, face jammed in Barker's neck, breathing heavily, brushing Barker's skin with unconscious kisses. Kit wasn't perfect, which made him all the more perfect. He stroked Kit's face until a sliver of green peeped out at him.

"Wake up, sleepyhead," Barker whispered. "We've got fashion to make."

Kit rubbed his eyes, breathed into his palm, then sniffed. "How could you kiss me, man? I can taste my breath."

"Because I—" Barker couldn't say it after one night. "Because it's not that bad."

Rolling onto his back, Kit stretched. "I don't want to make fashion. Fashion hates me."

Barker climbed over him, kissing him on the way. "You need reacquainting. Come on."

"What time is it? Has someone put the power back on?"

"No idea." Barker flicked the light switch, but nothing

happened. "We're safe. Let's see if we can smuggle you back to you room without being spotted."

"Wait," Kit said as he nudged him up against the door, then obliterated everything with a kiss demanding closed shutters and locked door.

"Last night," Barker said. "I don't usually… connect with people."

Kit's thumb, soft and warm, slipped under Barker's t-shirt, then circled his navel. Barker powered up, energy crackling from his belly to his groin.

"Did I push things too hard last night?" Kit said. "It's been a while."

Barker traced Kit's jawline with the back of his fingers. "Under the conditions, I'd say you did admirably. If it puts your mind at ease, it's been a long time for me, too. That's exactly why I don't want to rush things."

Biting his lip, Kit pressed his forehead against Barker's chest. "I was worried you'd say that."

The rest of the day blurred. No one spoke to anyone outside their team; everyone focussed on completing their pieces. Even discussion within the teams stayed brief. Barker marvelled at Fay's commitment. She worked harder than anyone.

Gunter made his last rounds of the day. "This is a quiet workroom. I like it. It means you're contemplative."

Contemplation muted the journey home. Two electricians worked under the stairs.

Barker approached. "Hello, chaps. What are you doing?"

"'Chaps'?" The electricians sniggered to each other. "Finishing up, mate. Someone dicked around with the power last night, so we've put the camera system on a different circuit with a tamper-proof fusebox."

Bastards.

Striding past, Emilia flicked her ponytail. "Thank Heaven for that. I didn't appreciate having a cold shower this morning."

"I'm surprised the Snow Queen noticed," Fay called after her.

A sombre mood settled over dinner. With the cameras back in operation, Barker and Kit scarcely made eye contact lest they give themselves away.

Kit volunteered to clean up the kitchen. "Wanna help?" he said to Barker.

They washed up in silence, only touching when Barker stroked Kit's hand under the bubbles.

Later, in bed, alone—torture. Moonlight framed the closed curtains, silvering the memory of last night's magic. Kissing a man for hours until you both fell asleep? Other men lasted little more than an encounter, their lives mysteries compared to their bodies. Mysteries were unknown problems, question marks. Back then, Barker hadn't looked for answers.

When the camera light in the corner of Barker's room winked off, anticipation halted his breath, but it winked on a second later. Defeat smothered his body, then sleep.

If Barker slept that night, his reflection didn't agree. With eyes too dry for contact lenses, he dressed, scraped back his hair, then slipped on his glasses.

The sombre mood over last night's dinner paled compared to the silence in the hallway where the contestants stood waiting for their cars.

Barker darted in front of Emilia to sit in the back of a car with Kit. Their legs touched, the warmth of Kit's thigh both soothing and exciting. He'd only kissed Kit's mouth, face and neck. One day he'd kiss that thigh and the rest of him. One day.

The moment Barker stepped onto the studio floor, negative energy crackled through everyone. Bruna, Nancy, and Marco perched on their stools as the contestants took their seats.

Whispering, Patrick jerked his head towards Nancy. "That's not the look of love."

Nancy glared at Pamela's back as the producer retreated into the dark. Whatever Pamela said, Nancy hadn't liked it.

Deja and Alex took turns parading up and down the catwalk. Each model tried to change into fresh pieces of the capsule wardrobes while the other walked, but neither succeeded. Filming halted repeatedly. No one spoke during the gaps. Every time Alex and Deja travelled the catwalk, Nancy's razor-sharp eyes raked the looks, time slowing until the liquid black platform may as well have been a tar pit.

Six series of *Runway Rivals* taught Barker if Nancy didn't take notes, it was a dangerous sign. The fashion maven sat with a stack of notecards firmly in her lap, covered by jewel-encrusted fingers glinting under the studio lights. His foolish decision to skip breakfast meant a familiar burn grew in his chest. He flexed his fingers, then dipped his hand into the breast pocket of his teal Hermès blazer. Removing an indigestion tablet from the tube, he slipped it under his tongue.

When modelling finished, Bruna and Marco applauded either side of a poker-faced Nancy.

The contestants climbed onto the catwalk and the critique kicked off.

Bruna spoke her mind as always, careful to sandwich critical observation between praise. "Emilia, your collection's colour choice compliments Deja's skin tone. How might it have worked on the other team's model, Alex?"

A flash of scornful disbelief flashed across Emilia's face before she hurried to replace it with an eager smile. "The cut would make the most of Alex's less-developed physique. I'd expect a fashion conscious woman to select a colour best suited to her." She couldn't help herself. "And as I'm no doubt you're aware, Bruna, fabrics are manufactured in a range of colours."

Nancy dropped her head, shoulders heaving.

Marco made a point of praising Deja's six pack before getting to business. "It's well sporty."

At first glance, Marco was too perfect, but his high-pitched voice undid his masculine bone structure.

Bruna gaped at Marco as if he'd gifted the room with the secrets of the universe.

Head still bowed, Nancy produced a silk Tom Ford pocket square, then dabbed her eyes.

Bruna tore her gaze away from Marco. "Barker. Your collection seems safe in comparison. What—?"

Nancy jumped off her stool, pushing aside a cameraman who'd swung in for a reaction shot from Barker. "For pity's sake. It's *all* safe. These designers are safe." Although she stood below them on the studio floor, her presence loomed. "You're the fresh blood. I want fashion-forward. 'Well sporty' is fine for our mainstream guest here, but—"

Marco's throat coloured, "Who are you calling mainstream? I'm pansexual."

She waved him silent. "Oh, please. Your fetish for cookware doesn't make you interesting."

"It does. *Scorch* magazine did a whole spread on it."

Spinning on her heel, Nancy waved her empty notecards at Marco. "More like you spread yourself for them, you talentless little oik."

Pamela's voice blasted from the dark. "Nancy."

Nancy hadn't finished. She gave each contestant a thorough inspection. "Look at you. You're on television, representing the future of British fashion, and two of you are wearing high street jeans. Only this young man—" A bejewelled finger pointed at Barker, who'd matched his teal blazer with a vintage Gaultier t-shirt and tailored black trousers. "—

made an effort." She stopped in front of them, folding her arms. "All of you," she waved a hand along the line, "have shown nothing but disrespect for the fashion industry. If I had my way, I'd cast new designers, designers *I* picked, and start all over again. One of you will win today, and one of you will go home, but you should all be ashamed of yourselves."

When Nancy sat, Bruna looked back into the darkness until Pamela nodded for her to continue. "Emilia, who should leave the—?"

"Kit. He contributed nothing to the design process, and his designs were in such poor taste I found them upsetting."

Bruna looked from Emilia to Kit. "Kit? What did you design?"

With a dramatic shudder, Emilia looked up as though blinking away a tear. "A suit for, and I can barely bring myself to say it, shooting defenceless animals."

It was all Barker could do not to give her a genuine reason to cry.

Nancy's hands flew up. "Another suit, Mister Redman? Will you ever desist from flogging your one-trick pony?"

A muscle worked in Kit's jaw. "If you remember, Nancy, I designed Patrick sportswear for the first challenge—and won. The shooting jacket was a starting point. Emilia wasn't interested in the destination. Shooting weekends don't have to mean dead animals."

Another flash of jewellery. "I'm not interested in a debate on the morality of hunting. We'll leave that to the die-hards. What I am interested in is the fact, yet again, you fell back to suits."

"I made seventy percent of this collection."

"This isn't a competition to find the best *première tailleur ateliers*, it's finding the best designer."

Kit raised his voice. "That's all she gave me to do."

Barker watched Nancy's body sag. "Because," she said. "Emilia judged your designs to be poor."

Colour rose in Kit's face. "She didn't even look at my designs. That doesn't mean they weren't sound."

Nancy paced. "'Sound' doesn't strike me as something new and exciting. If the best you can hope for is for your collection to be considered 'sound' perhaps you might be better suited to designing for the high street or a catalogue."

"If I may," Izzy said, "from my admittedly limited experience working on *Horse & Hound*, there is a demand for luxury, high-end sportswear. I don't think many women consider going to a Savile Row tailor for a sports jacket, so bringing that level of quality to a mainstream garment seems pretty... sound to me." She took a step back when Nancy eyed her and would have toppled back onto the contestants' seating if Aden hadn't caught her.

Bruna stepped in. "Barker, who should go home?"

Barker's body stiffened, adrenaline rushing through his body. "What?"

"I said—"

"Sorry. I heard you. It's... why are you asking me?"

"As the leader of the rival team, I assumed you'd paid attention to what they were doing."

Fear travelled through Barker's veins but never made it to his face. "I suppose so. Yes."

"From what you saw, who should go home?"

Everyone turned to look at him, Nancy's expectation weighing heaviest. Dread needled through Barker's skin, threading its way down his spine. His stomach filled with wadding; his mind unravelled. "Not Kit," he said automatically, and the fear of losing him unpicked the dread at once. "Not him."

"No surprise there," whispered Aden, loud enough for Barker to hear.

Decision made. "Aden should go home," Barker said. "He took the longest to pick up garment construction."

Nancy sat. "I keep telling you this is not a sewing competition."

"I understand that, but his designs weren't used either, so he lacks the basic skills required for this competition. If you can't come up with an excellent design or put in a zip, what's left?"

Nancy smirked. "An interesting viewpoint."

"Kit," Bruna said, "who should we eliminate today?"

"No one. Everyone worked hard. Even though my designs weren't used, I trained other members of the team."

Nancy pulled a face. "Not well enough for Aden to put in a zip."

Kit's voice grew stronger. "We produced an excellent range of garments based on excellent designs."

"So someone from the other team should go?" Bruna said.

"That's what not I'm saying."

"That's what I've always struggled with," Nancy wailed. "What is it you're trying to say with your fashion? What is your voice?"

Bruna moved things along. "Thank you, designers. If you'd like to wait backstage, we'll—"

Gunter strolled onto the set. "I'd like to say something, if I may."

A flash of irritation shadowed Bruna's face, but she signalled for him to go on.

He straightened a tie that didn't need straightening. "There has been some talk about the roles you've played in this challenge and the importance of excellent design. I want to impress upon you, whatever the judges decide today, the value people with Kit's skill-set bring to our industry. Never underestimate them because without them even the best designs fail. In an argument between a designer and a tailor, the tailor will always win. Do you know why?"

Kit spoke, deadpan. "Because the tailor's carrying scissors."

Gunter gave Kit a little bow of agreement. "This is a competition, and you're all here to win, but in real life bringing out the best in those around you reaps far greater rewards."

"Thank you, Gunter," Bruna said. "Designers. Please wait backstage while we make our decision."

Barker trudged into the holding room. Kit cupped a mug of tea to his chest, whispering with Izzy.

Aden sidled up to Barker with a sneer. "Thanks for the vote, *Barkington the Turd*. Do you reckon Kit's telling Izzy how shit you are in bed?"

"Nothing happened."

"Why? Couldn't you get it up?" Aden sniggered. "Guess you lost more than your trust fund."

"Why don't you piss off?" Barker turned away to find a camera shoved in his face. With that clip, they'd play up his bad boy image, but he didn't care.

Winning the show and winning Kit was all that mattered.

twenty-two
・・・

KIT MADE himself busy mashing a tea bag against the side of his mug.

Izzy joined him at the rumbling water urn. She took a mug. "Who do you think's getting their marching orders? I can't believe you kept your cool while Bitchwhore and Nancy gunned for you."

Grunting, Kit tossed his tea bag into the bin. "I see we've graduated from 'Snow Queen' to 'Bitchwhore'." He supped his tea, burning his top lip. "I'm not sinking to her level." He handed Izzy a spoon. "Thanks for sticking up for us, pet."

Izzy's gaze snapped to Barker. "Wasn't only me. Barker came to your defence." Barker snarled something at Aden, then walked away. "Our men really don't get on, do they?"

The corners of Kit's lips fought a smile and lost. He looked down, willing away mischievous thoughts. "He doesn't get on with anyone."

Izzy spooned coffee into her mug, then filled it with water. "So he is your man? He's looking like he wants to talk. Everything okay?"

"I thought the toughest thing about this show was proving I'm a talented designer. Turns out—"

"It's horribly complicated?" She gave him a gentle smile. "Sounds about right. I wish I could give you some sage advice, but I've had three long-term relationships, and they all ended up being bloody nightmares in their own special way."

Barker made his excuses to Izzy and squeezed between them on the pretence of making a tea.

He looked pointedly at Izzy. "May I have a word, Kit?"

Examining Barker's face, Izzy tossed her spoon onto the table. "I'll be off, shall I?"

Once they were alone, Barker inclined his head. "Everything all right? We've barely spoken today."

"I'm knackered, is all. Promise." *And I'm rock-hard whenever you're near me.* Kit watched Barker make a green tea. "How're you?"

"I can't stop thinking about how cruel it is to be thrown together *and* kept apart."

"Tell me about it. If my lips weren't still tingling, I'd have believed last night was a dream."

"A wet dream?" Barker asked, digging a hand into his pocket to rearrange his privates.

Kit elbowed him in the ribs, wishing the hand was his. "Don't. I can't be going on telly with a stiffy."

"You could if you were on *Desert Island Dicks*."

"Why is everyone obsessed with that show?"

"Fay watches it because it's gay men, so her husband can't complain, and Izzy watches it because she's obsessed with all things reality. Aden's too obsessed with his own dick to care whether he was on an island."

Curiosity struck Kit. "What was that between you just now?"

"Friendly banter," Barker said, his tone light.

Kit wished he had a biscuit to dunk in his tea. "Thanks for

speaking up when Emilia was throwing us under the bus. You didn't have to."

Barker looked at him in horror. "Yes, I bloody did. I've only had you for five days."

Five days? Was that all? If Kit felt tired, Barker looked ready to keel over. "You look like shite, man. Get your arse back into makeup or you'll be proper gutted when you see yourself on telly."

Barker voice cracked as he fished his tea bag out of his mug. "I don't want you to go, Kit." The tea bag trembled on Barker's spoon before it dropped it into the bin.

Kit gave him another nudge in the ribs. "I know, but we'd end up battling it out in the final and you won't want us to win."

Barker's finger ran down Kit's arm. "Don't say that."

"You're right. This is no time to be joshing with you. Go get some concealer under your eyes."

As Barker walked away, guilt pestered Kit for making light of him wanting to win. Considering Barker's honesty about his problems, he didn't deserve stupid jokes.

As soon as Barker returned from makeup, no trace of tiredness under his eyes, Layla called them all back in.

When Bruna announced Emilia as the overall winner, Kit could have screamed. There was no way the judges would ignore her opinion on who to send home. He was done for.

Bruna stretched out the next announcement. She looked at each of them. "Fay. You're out."

Fay grabbed Kit's arm. "What the fuck?"

"Cut," Pamela called. "Let's do that again. No swearing please."

"Fay. You're out."

"Are you fucking kidding me?"

Emilia stepped forward and tried to peel Fay's hand off Kit. "You heard the woman. Go home."

Fay's hand tightened on Kit's arm. "I'm not ready to go home. My kids are shits."

Bruna stood and put her cue cards on her stool. "I'm sorry, Fay. The judges' decision is irrevocable."

Emilia burst into applause, congratulating the judges for making the right decision. "I wouldn't want to go home to your dreadful children, either, but—"

"Piss off, Bitchwhore." Fay's grip on Kit tightened, buckling his knees from the pain.

Barker reached for Fay. "You're hurting him."

She slapped his hand away. "Don't touch me, you fucking toff."

Everyone in the studio gasped when Fay slapped him with her free hand. Barker spun away.

Cameras zoomed in from all sides.

Emilia lunged for Fay, grabbed her by the hair, then yanked her forward.

Kit pulled Barker's arm over his shoulder for support. Together they staggered down the steps and away. Every movement of Kit's arm lanced pain into his hand, and spots of colour dazzled his sight.

Crew stormed the catwalk, separating the shrieking women until three burly security men raced in and dragged Fay towards the exit.

A shellshocked Marco tried to steady himself against Nancy until she shook him off.

She swore so fiercely everyone flinched.

Aden cupped his mouth with his hands. "Hey, Pamela. That'll be your 'cunt'."

Pamela yelled back. "Backstage, all of you. Now."

In the time it took for Kit and Barker to get backstage, angry welts swelled Barker's left cheek. He wasn't any less handsome for it.

Barker helped Kit into a seat, then rolled up his sleeve.

Deep bruises bloomed on Kit's bicep. "Are you okay, sweetheart?"

"Proper knacks, like."

"Hurts?"

"Yeah, sorry. Your face…"

Barker caught Kit's hand before it touched his swollen cheek. "I'll be fine."

"Thanks for the save."

Barker snatched the biggest mug, then dropped in a tea bag. "They should invest in a proper teapot."

"I said thank you."

As he poured boiling water into the mug, Barker gave him a grim smile. "You should thank Emilia. She got there first."

As if summoned, Emilia swept into the room with the other contestants in tow. When she gathered Barker's face in her hands, she ignored his cry of pain. "My poor darling." She plucked the mug out of his hand, then tossed it on the table. Tea spilled over the edge. "No time for that. You need to see a first-aider."

"It's nothing," Barker said as she hurried him out of the room, calling for Pamela.

Patrick whistled when he sat next to Kit and gave his arm the once-over. "Fay made a holy show of herself, so she did. Didn't think she had it in her."

Aden leered. "Maybe if you'd put it in her, she wouldn't have been so angry."

Izzy glared at them both, then knelt in front of Kit to check his arm.

He examined it, too. It burned as though an invisible flame licked his skin. "Looks worse than it is." The commotion in the studio faded away. "What's going on?"

"Pamela's reading Fay the riot act. Layla's taking witness statements. Fay must have wanted to win more than she let on."

"Or smack Emilia."

"How's Barker?"

If Emilia hadn't beaten him to it, Kit would have wrapped Barker in a blanket of care. "He's seeing a first-aider."

Patrick folded his hands in his lap. "Why didn't Barker take you?"

"Emilia. Happened kinda fast."

"Didn't have her down as an equaliser," Patrick said.

Aden grunted. "Only for show, I bet. Coffees all round?"

Izzy helped him. They made drinks for Barker and Emilia in case they reappeared.

Patrick patted Kit's thigh, leaving his hand for comfort. "I reckon we should get langered tonight."

Kit closed his eyes, pain stealing a portion of his thoughts. "You're on. Let's get proper mortal."

It wasn't until Pamela whisked Kit away, ushered him into a production office, gave him a cuddle, and asked if he wanted to press charges, that he burst into tears.

"Is Barker pressing charges?" he said between sobs.

"Would it make a difference? He's decided not to, despite Emilia's efforts to the contrary. Let's hope Fay doesn't press charges against Emilia." Pamela passed him a tissue. He blew his nose. "Still, it makes you wonder, doesn't it?"

"What's that, like?"

"How much some people want to win."

twenty-three

• • •

TRAILED BY EMILIA, Barker marched back through the studio to the cars. He could run away. Take Kit and go—where? Newcastle? One hundred thousand pounds might free him from debt, but the price? Unwanted press attention and enough complications to screw up their flourishing relationship.

Pamela caught up with them before they climbed into a car with Patrick. Her eyes shone with gentle concern. "If your swelling hasn't gone down by tomorrow morning, I'll ask the crew and Tabitha to keep you out of shots and interviews. The press has gotten wind of trouble."

Barker's mouth ran dry.

"Already?" Emilia said.

"I know, I know. A shot of Barker's face will only add fuel to the fire."

"Or they'll make something up," Barker said, stomach turning over. "Like I bumped into one of my father's investors." He leaned against the car. "But isn't a fire what you all wanted for your ratings?"

Emilia flung her arms around his neck. "Don't say that, darling."

Pamela watched Emilia with surprise before mouthing the word 'darling' at Barker, her frown a question mark.

Barker extricated himself from Emilia's embrace, thanked Pamela, then climbed into the car.

Patrick looked back. "It's all clear. The others have just gone, Fay's been taken away, and Layla's gone ahead to pack Fay's bags. There shouldn't be a round two."

Emilia plucked at her floral Chloé blouse. "Shouldn't you be with Kit? This would be the perfect opportunity to wheedle your way into his affections."

Patrick looked sideways at them both. "Is that why you're all over this one here?"

Her hand snuck into Barker's. "Not at all. I'm taking care of my childhood friend."

Barker freed his hand from hers. "It's only a slapped cheek."

They sat in silence until the car pulled away. Barker wanted to be in the same car as Kit, feeling the warmth of his body pressed into his. Barker's face smarted, but the welts would shrink soon enough. Kit's arm could have bruises for weeks. Fay was stronger than she looked. Restraining rowdy toddlers must do that to a person.

In time, the cars swung into the driveway. The Teletubbies on Fay's suitcase peered out from the front step.

Emilia hissed as she walked past the garish luggage. "Vile."

Inside, marbled pink balloons hung in the air, choking the entrance and the hallway leading to the kitchen. Lidded foil trays covered every countertop. Outside on the patio, half barrels of ice heaved with beer bottles, cider, and rosé wine. In the centre of the patio where the table and chairs once stood, a gas-fired barbecue as big as a car shimmered the surrounding air.

Hands on his head, Aden took in the decorations. "There's nothing to celebrate."

Emilia's self satisfaction made Barker's heart sink. "*Au contraire*," she said. "It's my birthday. They're regaling me with a party so you can celebrate *avec moi*."

Patrick pluck a beer from the barrel closest to him. "I'll be waking up with the fear tomorrow."

"Hangover," Kit explained to a puzzled Izzy.

"You okay?" Barker mouthed to him, desperate to kiss away his pain.

Kit gave him the thumbs up. When the doorbell rang, he went to answer it. Barker followed.

Emilia beat them both to the door. She lifted a flat, wide box out of Layla's hands. "For me? That's so thoughtful. Look, Barker, a gift for my birthday!" She slammed the door in Layla's face. "I'll put this upstairs while you fire up the barbecue. I know how you men get that caveman instinct for cooking outside."

Kit peered at the box. "Don't you want to open it now?"

"Oh, no. I'll open it in my room. Be a darling for a change and help the men."

Can't you leave him alone for a change? "He is a man," Barker said.

When Emilia disappeared upstairs, Barker checked the others were all outside, caught Kit by the hand, then led him to the kitchen. "Are you sure you're all right?"

"Yeah, yeah—I…" Kit ran his thumb along the edge of the worktop and looked away. "It shocked me more than anything." His tanned skin glowed in the early evening light. Stubble darkened his jaw. He shoved his hands into his pockets. "Still am."

With a lengthy sigh, Barker raked his fingers through his hair. He dropped his voice, hoping the noise outside masked his words from the cameras. "I wish I could tell you how I feel without being recorded."

Taking a step closer, Kit dropped his voice, too. "You don't remember, do you? You called me sweetheart."

No sound, despite everyone gathered a few feet away on the patio. Barker saw them talking, but the air seemed to have been sucked out of the surrounding space. "On camera?"

Aden marched in, oblivious. "I know it's Bitchwhore's birthday, but please tell me all these boxes aren't full of dead babies for her to eat."

Barker recovered. "It's for all of us. They sent her a present."

Kit thrust a thumb towards the hallway. "She's taken it upstairs."

"Upstairs? Let's hope it's a dildo. Might chill her the fuck out."

Kit groaned. "Let's hope it's not immunity for the next challenge. There's nothing I'd like more than to wave her off—"

Aden's hand clamped to the back of his neck. "A cliff?"

"Down a pothole." Kit gave Barker's arm a quick squeeze as he pulled two trays off the counter. "Either would do. Who'll be head chef? Something tells me you'd like the job."

Aden rubbed his hands together. "Well, if no one else wants it."

"Go for it," Barker said. Anything to get rid of the fool.

Patrick joined them, rummaging through the kitchen cabinets. "I'll make a marinade."

Kit picked up a foil tray. "Great. Grab some food, Barker, and help us set up for the chef."

Tapping his nose, Barker frowned. "Me?"

"He's only got little legs," Aden said, not unkindly. "If you don't help him, it'll be dark by the time he brings it all out."

As soon as they were outside, Kit drew Barker out of earshot. "Can I be honest?"

Dread crept over Barker, like a lamb headed for slaughter. "Honesty. Always." Shoving his hands into his pockets, he scuffed the patio with his shoe. Once he rearranged his face into something he hoped looked nonchalant, he met Kit's solemn gaze.

Kit pressed his finger against Barker's lips. "I like you more than anyone I've ever met."

"You bastard," Barker said. "I thought you were going to finish it."

Barker hadn't attended a barbecue in years. The occasional country wedding featured a hog roast, but they were the gentleman farmer variety and fully catered. This was the genuine thing.

Aden shook chicken breasts in a bag of spices dark as rust, then sauntered out of the kitchen towards the barbecue, waving the bag at Patrick to shoo him away.

"A marinade won't work, mate."

"It's fine," Patrick said. "Never had a problem before."

Aden said, gesturing to the smokeless barbecue shimmering in a haze of heat. "But this is gas."

"So?"

"You marinade with coal," Aden said, words slow as if addressing a child, "and rub with gas."

"Have you lost your mind, you clown? You're not even making sense right now." Patrick waved a plastic bag of chicken floating in milky green fluid.

"Look," Aden said. "Do you want me to take over? I know what I'm doing."

Patrick blocked him with his elbow. "I know what I'm doing. Get yourself a beer and leave me be."

Aden snatched a beer from a barrel, then threw himself on a sun lounger, cradling his bag of chicken. "Thicko."

"Another glorious day in the corps," Izzy said at Barker's side, making him and Kit jump. She offered them a glass of

Champagne. "Are you mentally prepared for an evening dedicated to the celebration of Emilia's gift to the world?"

"What's that?" they said together.

"Herself."

As they laughed, Emilia appeared behind them. She'd changed into silver flapper dress, each strand of beads sparkling in the sunlight. "Well, this is pleasant, isn't it? I'll admit that it's a far cry from what I'd normally do. Last year, I had a huge bash at a secret bar in London, but I suppose I'm catering to the masses this year."

Izzy groaned. "You're not catering to anyone. This isn't your house, and you didn't buy the food or drink."

"What was the present?" Kit asked.

"I'm wearing it right now." She twirled, beads swishing as she moved.

Izzy's mouth twisted into a wicked smile. "Hmm. Spanx?"

Patrick spread the chicken breasts over the barbecue and grimaced. "That's messed up. What kind of perv sends a contestant on their show underwear?"

Chin high, Emilia swished her ponytail. "No, you pleb. This dress. Layla promised me a good edit, so I guess I needed a wonderful dress to go with it." She teetered towards the kitchen. "I'll open another bottle of Champers." She disappeared into the house.

Izzy sighed. "Is it a fix? I always thought that smug cow from series two was a shoo-in right from the first episode."

"If it is," Aden said from his sun lounger, "we need to drink this place dry. Who's with me?"

twenty-four

• • •

AS SOON AS Kit opened his eyes to his dimly lit room, his hangover took its revenge, and the gentle knock on his door might as well be a sledgehammer.

Izzy stuck her head in. "Come on, lazybones." The bags under her drooping eyes told him she felt as bad as him. "It might be a Sunday, but a fresh challenge awaits."

Kit managed a moan before retreating under the duvet. "Already? You're joking us, man."

"I wish I was. Up you get." When he gave her another groan, she left him alone.

He liked Izzy, but she could do with a slap for — Oh, God. Fay. Kit explored the arm she'd grabbed. His hand recoiled. The pain wasn't as sharp as the day before, but his bicep throbbed, stiff and sore.

He squinted at the rest of his body. An early morning hard-on squinted back. He accepted his horny hangovers. He could deal with throbbing there. It was the throbbing in his head he could do without.

In the bathroom, he splashed water on his face. *If only I could splash it on my brain.* Waves of nausea added to his misery.

At this rate, the only way he'd make it downstairs would be step by step.

On his arse, bumpety-bump.

A long shower later, he tucked a towel around his waist, then shuffled out of the bathroom.

Izzy stood by his bed, holding up a black sweater. "Thought you'd appreciate this."

"Why?" Kit rubbed his arm, sharp-edged bruises protesting. He took the sweater and pulled it on. "Cashmere? Nice." He checked the fit in his bathroom mirror. "Oh…"

Izzy recognised the worry on his face and smiled. "It has a low neck, but you'll like what it does to show off your body."

"I'm no Patrick," he said, heading for the bathroom mirror. Izzy was right. The sweater clung to Kit's physique, the deep v-neck showcasing his upper chest. He'd suffered thousands of incline bench presses to develop the cleft between his upper pecs. His chest hair, clipped before he arrived six days ago, matched his stubble.

"Very nice," Izzy said. "Few people can pull off black but once Barker sees you in that he'll want to."

Kit looked to the ceiling and grinned. "Howay, man." He looked toward the door, then whispered. "Did me and Barker…?"

"Nothing happened. At least not in the front of everyone. Even if you'd wanted to, I doubt you'd have succeeded."

"Huh?"

"You were wasted."

"What about Barker?"

"Merry but not drunk. Bitchwhore was all over him, much to his irritation."

Kit huffed. "He wants to play things cool because of the cameras."

Izzy's eyes widened. "He does? I'd like to see him try. He

looks at you like…" She paused. "There's something I keep meaning to tell you."

"About you and Aden?"

Izzy's face stiffened for a second, her eyes flicking to the camera, then she forced a weak smile. "That power cut saved my embarrassment on national television."

"So that was when you first—?"

"But I keep panicking it's only a showmance for him."

"And for you?"

She avoided his gaze. "He's a great stress reliever."

"That's it?"

Hands in her hair, Izzy sat on the edge of Aden's bed. "He's annoying. This morning, I caught him waving his willy at a vase." She cuffed Kit's head when he laughed. "It's true. The sex is great, though. Either he's naturally good or he's bringing his A game because he's convinced millions of people are watching on livestream."

"Aren't you worried they are?"

"I've got that covered. I put the M into MILF."

"Mother?"

"Mummy. I wrap myself in sheets before I let him anywhere near me. Seriously though, I'm too old for him. I'm forty-two and he's…?"

"Twenty-six."

Izzy toppled over onto the bed and covered her eyes. "I've been shagging someone whose mother was in labour while I was sitting my GCSEs."

Kit pulled her into a cashmere hug. "Don't. Any fella would want to be with a canny lass like you. You're a hundred times better than Naomi Campbell."

Emilia's screech echoed around the house. "The cars are here."

Kit slipped his jeans on under his towel, then he and Izzy hurried downstairs.

twenty-five

...

THE MAY FAIR Hotel's foyer disquieted Barker. He'd identified with its casual luxury once, but no more. Ebony woods, sandy marble floors, bright leather couches, and black velvet chairs—he'd taken it for granted. Now, he couldn't even afford a room.

His hangover lurched and gurgled in his stomach. He'd run out of indigestion tablets again and made a mental note to ask Layla for some as soon as filming stopped.

Please, God, let the filming stop.

This morning, the moment Kit appeared in the kitchen wearing a black v-neck sweater, Barker thought of nothing except kissing his way from Kit's chest, to Kit's throat, and on to Kit's stubbled chin. And as for his delicious mouth…

Barker made damn sure he took the same car as Kit, weaving through the group, throwing an arm around Kit's shoulder, then holding him tight to his side. Izzy and Aden joined them.

No sooner had the car pulled away than Kit snuggled up to Barker and fell asleep, head bobbing against his Barker's chest.

Fifteen minutes into the journey, Izzy sat forward and scanned the view. "This isn't the way to LUCA."

Covering his face, Barker groaned. "Don't let it be another press day. Don't let it be another press day. Don't let it be another—"

Aden shushed him. "If it was, we'd all be fucked. Present company included."

"We haven't done that," Barker said. *You ginger prick.*

Aden raised his eyebrows. "You haven't? You need to get your game on, Barks. I bet Kit's a firecracker between the sheets."

Izzy slapped Aden's arm. "Focus. Where're they taking us?"

Kit raised his head, one hand on his forehead to shield his eyes from the morning sun. "Why don't you ask the driver?"

The driver looked into the rearview mirror. "We're going to a London landmark."

Aden groaned. "I bet it's a sodding, bloody, dull, bloody bridge."

Their destination blindsided them all. The May Fair, one of London's most prestigious hotels.

Wood, leather, and marble.

The last social engagement of Barker's old life took place in this very hotel. Thanks to the free bar, he'd nearly missed his flight to Miami the following day. No matter how much he wracked his faltering memory, the party's reason evaded him. A vague memory of girls wafting scented strips of embossed cardboard—a fragrance launch.

Gunter met the contestants in the lobby, resplendent in a black wool Gucci suit. "Welcome to The May Fair, designers." His voice cracked on the last word. Holding a fist to his upper chest, he cleared his throat before resuming. "Fashion is about reinvention. The May Fair served as high society's playground in the twenties, a magnet for film industry moguls in the fifties, and reinvented itself again for the noughties. It truly is a hotel like no other. As the official hotel of London Fashion Week, the two finalists will stay here the night before their shows."

A ripple of excitement spread through the remaining six contestants. Bruna stepped out from behind a pillar in a floral and snake-print silk midi dress, also by Gucci. "But we're not here to show you the future. We want you to design it. The May Fair is a fortress of secrets, staffed by employees with unrivalled standards of discretion."

Something else waved at Barker the night of the fragrance launch, and it hadn't been a strip of cardboard.

A short line of hotel staff walked in from each side of the lobby. They flanked Bruna and Gunter.

"Your next challenge," Gunter said, "is to reinvent one of these uniforms." He pointed to each member of the line. "Bar, porter, kitchen, waiting, reception, and housekeeping. Questions?" No one spoke, but Emilia's thunderous expression said it all.

"You have a budget of one hundred and fifty pounds," Bruna said, "and an hour to sketch before Gunter takes you to Cloth."

As soon as the cameras dropped away, Emilia marched up to Gunter. "I'd prefer to design for the hotel's clientele, not the help. It's hardly testing us, is it? We've only had a makeover challenge and a sportswear challenge. When are we going to get to show off?"

Gunter showed his teeth in something like a smile. "You're already showing off, Miss Winchmore, and in the most spectacular style."

To Barker's right, Izzy stifled a laugh. Aden's attempt wasn't as successful.

Emilia turned on him. "Shut up. I've had too little sleep as it is thanks to you and your trollop."

Barker stepped between them. "Let's not get into another brawl, shall we?"

Aden looked him over. "I seem to remember you going for me in the same situation."

"Granted, but a fight in The May Fair's reception won't do our reputations any favours. Emilia, you owe Aden and Izzy an apology."

"Why?" Emilia bridled. "I'm not the one who jumped into bed with someone I barely know."

Holding Aden back with one hand, Barker met Emilia's blazing eyes. "St. Barts."

She blinked at him. "I beg your pardon?"

"St. Barts. You remember. The winter after we graduated from Charterhouse?"

Eye twitching, Emilia shifted her weight onto one leg. Her eye "I don't understand what you're talking about."

"Really? Because I seem to remember a Creole deckhand taking your fancy."

Emilia's look of confusion melted away to horror. "How did you—? No one knew."

"He filmed you *in flagrante delicto*. I caught him showing it to the rest of the crew."

"He…?" Emilia trailed off as she turned, too slow, moving robotically to a chair, then sinking into it. "If it ever gets out—"

"It's all right, Emilia."

Her voice shredded to a whisper. "I'll be ruined."

Barker tried again. "I said it's all right."

Emilia's entire body shook. "Ruined!"

Bruna, Gunter, Pamela, and Layla all looked over.

Barker crouched at Emilia's feet, then put his hand on her knee, a token of reassurance. "I had a quiet word with the captain and the footage was deleted." For the camera that flew in, Barker stood and sighed. "May we please get on and sketch?"

Layla distributed sketch pads and pencils, and everyone got to work. Furtive glances found Emilia, who still slumped in her chair.

Barker pretended to consider the coloured veins threaded through the marble floor while trying to listen in on Bruna whispering to a round-shouldered Gunter. Kit wandered off to the other side of reception, studying a chandelier.

Someone tapped Barker's shoulder. He turned to see a handsome black face, black eyes tinged with deep forest green.

"Hello, stranger. Remember me?"

A welcome rush of memories—laughter in the room they shared, thrashing the competition at tennis, plotting revenge on teachers.

"Caspian! What are you doing here?"

"I'm checking out. There was a thing here last night. You know how it is. So, how're things?"

"Good."

Pamela strode across the lobby towards them.

"I'm on this television show…"

"Can I help you?" Pamela said to Caspian as she joined them.

Caspian unleashed the smile that dropped hundreds of knickers and a generous handful of boxer shorts. "Caspian Kendall. Barker and I went to school together."

A smile broke through Pamela's pinched lips. "We're in the middle of filming and pushed for time. Will you be long?"

Caspian gave her a long, appreciative look from head to toe. "You could tempt me to stick around. What time do you get off?"

The insinuation destroyed Pamela's composure. "Our schedule is very tight."

Caspian raised a perfect eyebrow. "I'm sure it is. What say I wait for you in the bar after I've finished talking to my friend?

I need a Bloody Mary to take the edge off last night's adventures."

Mute, Pamela wandered away.

"Same old Caspian," Barker said. "Still charming the ladies."

Caspian chuckled and rocked on his heels. "The older ones have their advantages."

"I doubt Pamela's particularly flush."

Caspian's smile vanished. "And you?"

Averting his eyes, Barker exhaled. "I'm coping."

Eyes darting to the bar, Caspian touched Barker's arm. "I owe you an apology, Barker. When everything with your father happened, I should have been there for you—especially after what you did for my family."

"I'm sorry I couldn't do more."

"Let's not have any of that nonsense." Caspian held Barker by the shoulders. "If there's anything I can do to help you in return, anything at all, say the word."

Barker eyed Kit. "Actually, there is."

twenty-six

. . .

THE MAY FAIR'S lobby loomed over Kit, but compared to the black stranger taking Barker by the shoulders, he was microscopic.

Six three, forty-two-inch chest, twenty-nine-inch waist, thirty-five-inch inside leg.

Barker gave the stranger a lingering handshake, and all of Kit's insecurities flooded back. When Barker threw Kit a mischievous grin and beckoned him over, Kit didn't move. Standing next to this unfamiliar man would only make him look smaller. Thirteen inches smaller. Barker waved again.

Pamela wasn't around, and cameras pointed elsewhere, so he slunk over to Barker and the towering stranger.

"All right?" Kit said.

Straight away, the stranger shook Kit's hand. "Caspian. It's a pleasure to meet you. I haven't watched the show, but Barker's been telling me all about you."

Barker's smile had the twist of a child determined to keep a secret but desperate to set it free. "Caspian's going to help us."

The way he said it bombarded Kit with random possibilities, none of which made sense. "Help us do what?"

Caspian shoved something into Barker's hand, his voice low. "There's an exit door behind me. Skirt around the back of the building and there's less chance of being seen. Hurry, though—it's pouring outside."

It was?

Barker took Kit by the hand, pulling him towards the exit. "Come on."

Kit pulled back. "Where?"

"Caspian booked a late checkout, but he's leaving now. He said we can have his room." Barker squeezed Kit's hand. "Don't you remember?"

Kit's memories parted to reveal a declaration of love for his colleagues at Stitchworthy, before bursting into tears and falling asleep. But there had been something else. "When the others weren't looking," he drawled, memories creeping back to mind. "I dragged you back behind that summerhouse…"

"And…?" Barker's eyes flashed.

The lobby spun. "I said I wanted you," Kit whispered, sudden heat radiating through his pores.

The corners of Barker's mouth held the slightest curve. "In vino veritas."

"I don't know what that means."

Barker's eyebrows rose above quizzical, joyful eyes. "It means that when you're drunk, you speak your hidden desires."

Too bad the wine dried up. "Three words translates into all that?"

Barker grinned. "Not literally, no. I'll understand if you'd rather not." His smile faded. "I was hoping—you might—want to…" He trailed off, looking back at Caspian.

Caspian smiled, head cocked. "I didn't need to hear that, did I? I'll head for the bar and let you chaps discuss this alone."

"Thanks, old friend. I owe you."

"It's the least I can do," Caspian said, saluting them both, then steering himself towards the bar.

Once they stood alone, Kit kept his distance from Barker. The possibility of finally having him only made him pull back. "What about the show? You need the money. You made that deal with Nancy. You'll—we'll—lose our places."

Barker's smile faded. "I'm sick of it. All of it. Don't you want to?"

Layla wandered over. "Have you seen Pamela?"

Barker sent her off in the wrong direction, then called after her. "Kit's not well. When you find her, can you ask her to call a doctor?"

"Huh?" Kit said.

"Alibi," Barker said to Kit. "Well?"

It was stupid to be scared, but Kit couldn't help it. Sometimes, he could be brave, like facing off against Nancy, and other times he could be reckless, like cutting the power at the house. Right now, he didn't know which Kit he was. His chest rose and fell, desperate to keep time with his racing heart.

"If we were anywhere but here, I'd say yes. I'm hanging, but I'm horny, and you're so, so gorgeous."

Barker's frame slumped, hands in his pockets. "But? Be honest."

"You said you wanted it to be special. I want to be important. When I'm with you, my head spins." Kit looked back at the others. "I came here to prove that I'm a designer. I'm not, but you are. Whatever happens, I promise I'll help you win." He couldn't look Barker in the eye. "Because I'd be lucky to win you."

"The first time I met you," Barker said, his voice gentle, "I've never met anybody like you. You're honest and principled, and I need that in my life. What I've said and what I've done haven't always added up, and I've been looking for a quick solution to my debt. I shouldn't be doing that with you."

Barker worried his bottom lip. "But you can't wear a top like that and not expect me to want to tear if off you."

"Hashtag, me too."

Barker put his face in his hands. "That came out so, so wrong."

Kit said nothing, tempted to take Barker up on his offer. Barker lifted his face to his, and the trap of Kit's desire snapped shut. "I want to," Kit managed. "But there's no time."

"It's all under control. Caspian will hit the fire alarm in the gents' toilet, then let the staff know he's okay. That way, they won't go looking in his room."

"What about the prize money?"

Barker's chest moved deep and even. "I'll find another way. Besides, I won't last five minutes once I get your clothes off."

It took an eternity for a camera to sweep past them. Barker's hand moved in his. He looked up into grey, expectant eyes.

A fire alarm screeched through the lobby.

"Well," Barker shouted above the din. "What are we waiting for?"

They were outside in less than ten seconds. The rain fell in sheets, bouncing from every surface as they hurried along the side of the building, storm drains bubbling with run-off.

When they rounded the corner, Kit slowed to a stop. His hand slipped out of Barker's who, without Kit's weight behind him, staggered forward and collided with a man in a navy trench coat, huddled under an awning, fumbling with a gold-plated lighter and an unlit cigarette. As the lighter fell from the man's hand, Barker froze, but Kit leapt forward to snatch it from the air. He placed it back into the man's hand, who shook so violently Kit held it tight.

Kit studied the man's face. "Gunter—?"

"Oh, shit," Barker said. "What on earth's the matter?"

Gunter clutched Kit's hand to his chest. "I'm fine, boys."

His hair clung to his skull, skin so grey his blood must have tried escaping the rain. "Where are you going?"

Barker didn't hesitate. "Exploring. Seeing as the fire alarm's gone off, we hoped there might be something interesting out here. You know, architecture and all that."

Gunter eyed them both, movements as robotic as his voice. "Where are your sketchbooks?"

The only thing Barker held was Caspian's room key. "Um…"

Kit took the key, then gave it to Gunter. "We weren't exploring."

Barker shook his head. "Kit…"

Looking up at Barker, Kit nodded. "Honesty. Always." He took his hand off Gunter's chest. "We wanted to be alone."

"Alone?" Gunter's eyes narrowed, examining them both. "I wasn't aware that things had progressed."

"Progressed?" Kit said. "From what?"

Gunter swallowed. "From the way you look at each other."

A taxi hissed over the wet road, stopping behind them. A couple flung open the doors, laughing at the shocking downpour.

Barker's hair, swept up and back that morning, collapsed and clung to his forehead. "It's that obvious?"

Gunter's gaze followed the couple as they rushed inside the hotel. He pulled Kit and Barker under the awning's protection, then held up the key. "Is it worth risking your place on the show? As young people building a relationship, is this what you deserve?"

Barker looked away, fists clenching and unclenching, shoulders rolling forward. Fear bubbled up in Kit's chest.

"Well?" Gunter said, voice hard. "Is it?"

. . .

Kit relaxed when Barker agreed they deserved better, but he gave Kit the next best thing: the heady thrill of a rain-soaked kiss.

As soon as the ashen Gunter pocketed their key and sent them on their way, they'd no sooner rounded the corner when Barker yanked Kit into a doorway and crushed his mouth with his.

"If I can't have you the way I want you," Barker said, "I need this at the very least." His breath clouded between them before cool air ebbed it away. One arm hooked around Kit's waist and Barker lifted him off his feet.

"Barker—"

"Please, Kit. Please."

Barker put one hand against the wall above Kit's head and kissed him again, a wave of warmth in the rain-flicked air. Pressed against him, Barker's body heat soaked through Kit's wet clothes.

They can't kick us off the show for this. We'll get a warning. Kit wrapped his legs around Barker. "They'll never miss us."

The hot, wet kisses continued until Kit's thoughts ran into each other like so many raindrops.

"What the hell were you doing, taking yourself off like that?" Pamela said as Kit entered the hotel foyer with Barker in tow. "Look at you. You're drenched."

Barker slipped a hand around Kit's waist. "So, so sorry, Pamela. I took Kit outside for some fresh air. One minute he was fine and the next—bam!—out cold when the fire alarm went off. As a fully qualified first-aider, I—"

"Do you honestly expect—?"

"I instinctively acted on my training. Thank goodness I was here, especially as you'd gone missing."

Desperate not to laugh, Kit stared at the ceiling as Caspian approached.

Setting her face to casual indifference, Pamela glanced at Caspian, but a furious blush betrayed her desire. "Yes, well, you should have informed me immediately so I could arrange things. I shouldn't have to find out from Layla." She stepped closer, signalling for the ever-present cameramen to turn away. "Now you listen to me. This job's difficult enough with the collected egos of the judges, let alone the likes of you. And speaking of you, Mister Wareham, I'm assuming you're here to salvage what little good standing your family has—"

Barker coloured up. "Now hang on."

"—so if you want a decent edit that doesn't make you look like you're cut from the same cloth as your father, if you'll pardon the pun, I suggest you get your urges back under control. This is *Runway Rivals*, not—"

"*Desert Island Dicks*. I know, I know."

Aden strolled up just as Pamela retreated.

"What're you grinning at?" Barker said.

Waving his sketchbook, Aden laughed. "Fifteen minutes of sketch time and what have you got to show for it?"

Kit tutted. Aden didn't need to know. There was no way they'd been outside for that long. Five minutes, tops.

"Shame," Aden said. "You can do a lot in fifteen minutes."

Willing Barker to keep his cool, Kit stepped between them. "For you, maybe, but Barker's more of a long-distance runner."

Aden retreated to other three contestants, then whispered something before they all looked over.

Izzy's expression said it all: *What have you done?*

twenty-seven
. . .

FOLLOWING ten minutes of production team deliberation, Bruna told other contestants to wait in the car.

Layla issued Kit and Barker with a sketchpad and pencil each. "Fifteen minutes, guys."

Pamela trotted back to the bar to be soothed by Caspian, who brandished a crystal gin glass.

Five minutes later, a man stormed into the lobby and all hell broke loose.

"Christ," Barker said, "that's—"

"Brian Foster," Kit finished.

Kit gaped as Brian—head of Bacchus Broadcasting—summoned Layla with a hooked finger.

Tanned skin, defined chin, and a firm jaw curving around a neck corded with muscle. A mid grey jumper over a blue shirt stressed Brian's build—bold thighs, striking arms, and a prominent chest.

Kit's ability to size a man with one look dissolved into fuzz. He didn't have to picture that body. He'd seen it—all of it—plastered across the internet.

Brian Foster, the gay porn sensation formerly known as

Bobby Bacchus, disappeared from the industry as suddenly as he'd arrived. He fell in love and cleaned up his act. Years later, he returned to the entertainment industry, founding a models' union dedicated to eradicating the casual exploitation of its members. From there, he built Bacchus Broadcasting, its name acknowledging his beginnings in the adult entertainment industry. A string of hit shows established his power in broadcast media.

"What the bloody hell's going on?" Brian shouted at Layla, who looked over at Kit and Barker.

"Is he here to sack us?" Kit said.

Brian clicked his fingers. "Layla! Pam's late for a meeting. She should have been in my office an hour ago."

Layla's expression resembled a smile, teeth bared, sparks in her eyes, but her left hand spread like a pale starfish around her thigh while her right brushed a strand of tight curls from her face. "She's addressing a scheduling issue. A designer fell ill during filming."

Brian followed her gaze to Kit, his ice-blue eyes turning Kit's insides to frost.

In three paces he dwarfed them, a pillar of muscle. "You don't look ill."

Kit wanted to slide his hand into Barker's for confidence. "Not now." The stillness of Brian's unmoving gaze saw the lie in Kit's. "I'm better now."

Brian's blue eyes turned on Barker, storm clouds before lightning hit. "And you?"

Barker opened his mouth to speak but snapped it shut when Pamela skidded out of the bar. Unable to gain traction on the marble, she would have stumbled into Brian had he not grabbed her by the arms.

Kit didn't need to see the look on Brian's face; the twitch in Pamela's legs as she fought the urge to turn and run did that. Her jaw locked tight, the Caspian-induced flush draining from her skin. In seconds, she turned the colour of a body dredged from ice water.

"My office," Brian said. "Twenty minutes, including time to find Gunter." He spoke over his shoulder, his voice unexpectedly low and husky. "Go back to the house, lads. If the others are as exhausted as the pair of you look, we're working you too hard."

Pamela made a squeak. "But the schedule…"

"Fuck the schedule. We have a responsibility to the contestants. No one's collapsing on one of my shows."

To Kit's relief, Brian declared The May Fair challenge void.

Despite complaints from Aden — "I had winning designs." — it meant the chance to turn in early with a bleary-eyed Barker.

"You look how I feel," Kit said, lying on Barker's bed.

Lying next to him, Barker rubbed his eyes, barely able to speak. "I'm fine."

Kit prodded his arm. "Honesty. Always."

Barker wrapped an arm around him, then pulled him close. Kit sank into Barker, the lingering worry about his future finally melting away. He hugged Barker back, wanting the moment to last forever. Barker said there'd been something familiar about Kit, but there was something familiar about Barker, too. The way Barker's body moved with the loose grace of a gymnast, the leathery scent of his aftershave. Even the long, simple rhythm of his heartbeat. Kit knew them all from quiet moments of fantasy, and this was the first time he had a man's body, a man who wanted him in return, pressed against his own.

Barker fell asleep, body relaxed, breath steady. Kit followed slowly, then all at once.

· · ·

Bruna, magnificent in a black suit nipped in at her waist with a single button, addressed the contestants. "Hello, designers, and welcome to your second week." *Is that all it's been?* "The key to elegance is simplicity, and the reason suiting has endured for so long. This challenge, some of you are built for, and some of you might dread."

All eyes turned to Kit, who prickled with confidence. He had this.

Bruna continued. "You're to make a suit for one of the best-dressed men in the industry—none other than our own Gunter Lyffe."

Gunter joined Bruna on the catwalk. Blue, single-breasted, Gucci suit with notched lapels, and slim leg trousers. Kit couldn't have made better, but he'd have to to win the challenge.

"Gunter," Bruna said. "It's over to you."

"Thank you, Bruna. Now, designers, first impressions are everything. I believe a good suit is the foundation of any man's impression on the world around him." He bowed to Izzy and Emilia. "Or any woman. A suit makes a statement. It affords the wearer respect in the corporate world and credibility on the red carpet. Some might argue it's psychological protection. They were called suits of armour for a reason. Your challenge is to design and make a suit for me to wear to my very first Met Gala. You'll have five hundred pounds and two full days for this challenge."

Kit had the skills he needed to win, but hundreds of hours went into his suits. What could he manage in a few days? Details would be key. Would Cloth stock the fabrics he used—used to use—at Stitchworthy? Flannel? Cashmere? Worsted?

When the cameras stopped, Aden stood boot-faced. "What's the point of us even trying? Kit'll wipe the floor with us."

Barker's hand settled on Kit's lower back, where the others

couldn't see it. Its heat seeped into Kit's flesh like the slow strokes down his back he'd awoken to that morning, driving him crazy, stopping, then doing it all over again until he begged for Barker for a kiss.

Emilia rounded on Aden. "Speak for yourself. I have no intention of anybody wiping the floor with me. Any fool can make a suit. The key is to design something fresh."

Gunter helped Bruna down the steps at the back of the catwalk, then they joined the contestants.

"This might come across as unfair," Gunter said, "especially after yesterday's disruption, but you must remember this is a design competition. It bears repeating we take your construction skills into account, but that doesn't mean Kit will be safe. You each have a unique approach."

"And remember," Bruna added, "the Met Gala has a different theme every year, coinciding with the exhibition that follows. Choose a theme that plays to your strengths."

Pamela waved the contestants over, pinking when she caught Barker's eye. "Sorry, all, but the traffic in town's appalling today, so we need to get you over to Cloth now. You'll have an hour to sketch once you arrive, then thirty minutes to buy everything you need."

Kit and Barker sat in the back of a car with Izzy and Patrick. Aden, still pissed off with yesterday's challenge cancellation, took the other car with Emilia.

No one spoke, making Barker's hand on Kit's leg seem like a scream. With everything that had happened, Kit would struggle to concentrate on this challenge, but he was determined to ensure Barker's success. Kit didn't break his promises. Barker's construction skills were his weak point, and everyone knew it. Kit would coach him. If it came to it, he'd make Barker's suit himself.

Cloth was empty as usual but the press must have published its interviews because a group of fans waited for

Gunter, copies of his latest style book clasped in eager hands. Gunter greeted them with the same gentle friendliness he gave the contestants.

How much effort did it take to be so nice? And the cost? Maybe the distraught man huddled under The May Fair's awning was the real Gunter Lyffe.

No one spoke during design time. The scrawl of pencil on paper soothed Kit, the crown of his head tingling, and the same sensation rippling through his entire body.

Kit needed ideas. Next year's Met Gala theme wouldn't be announced until October. This year's theme was *Camp: Notes on Fashion*. It stood to reason next year's theme might be the other end of the spectrum. Butch, perhaps? Gunter compared modern suits to suits of armour. Who wore armour? Kit made a brief list of the images popping into his head: modern Kevlar, medieval knights, chain mail, Roman helmets, Grecian breastplates. The Met Gala might embrace a Grecian theme. Grecian armour, a breastplate and a back piece fastened with straps and buckles over the shoulder-seams and side-seams. It could work. And bronze… A bronze pinstripe?

Kit sketched, played with the details, adjusted the proportion of the lapels, then did away with them. He altered the cut of the jacket, waistcoat, and trousers—tight torso, loose at the hips. Gold buttons for the jacket sleeve buttons suggested ancient coins. Once he had something he liked and pushed the boundaries of the suits Gunter wore, he turned his attention to the colours.

Gunter rarely wore anything other than brown or navy. Coaxing him into another colour would be fun. The Met Gala turned out amazing and not-so-amazing looks over the years, and Kit keened to steer Gunter away from outlandish fabrics. No florals, no brocade, and no mesh. *The key to elegance is simplicity.* Gunter deserved simple elegance.

Kit reached the fabric selection stage, deciding to sew a

bronze pinstripe into a plain oxblood fabric, when Pamela came and found him, her mouth pulled tight.

"I need you to come with me," she said.

"Why?"

"I need you to come with me now."

"Has something happened? It's not my mam, is it?"

Barker appeared, Izzy at his side. "What's going on? Look, if this is this about yesterday…"

Pamela spoke again, slow and clipped. "I need Kit to come with me right now."

Barker handed his sketchbook to Izzy. "I'll come, too."

Pamela shook her head. "You'll do nothing of the sort. Kit. With me. Now."

Kit assumed they'd return to LUCA, but the car headed in the opposite direction. Silence, tightness in Pamela's jaw and shoulders. Kit's belly did the same.

After an hour of crawling London traffic, they pulled up outside a building Kit didn't recognise. Behind the huge glass facade, stood a golden statue of a naked man rising from sculpted brass vine-leaves, a goblet held high in a silent toast. A crown of grapes circled his head. Bacchus.

Bacchus Broadcasting?

Pamela reported to reception, then ushered Kit into a private lift. The sudden acceleration flipped his stomach. When the lift stopped, Pamela escorted him into a dark-panelled hallway leading to a vast office with panoramic views over London. Behind an imposing desk crafted in the same dark wood as the hallway sat Brian Foster: three piece suit, gigantic watch, more intimidating than ever.

Whatever happened next, it wouldn't be good.

"Kit," Brian said, his voice heavy. "I'm sorry to drag you away so abruptly. Please take a seat."

Kit sat in a deep red leather chair. "What's going on?" His

feet barely touched the floor. To Brian, he must seem like a child.

Brian ran his hands through his greying blonde hair before he leaned forward. "You know how I got into the entertainment industry, don't you?"

"Uh, yes—?"

"So can you imagine the people I dealt with?"

There were all the people Brian had—

"Not the ones I fucked," Brian added as though he'd read Kit's mind. "The ones off camera."

The only person who sprang to mind was the old boy who owned the Full Throttle porn studio where Brian debuted. Not long after Brian disappeared from porn, the old boy had gone to prison.

"Alfie—?"

"That's it. Alfie Collins. Got done for handing around underage lads at his house parties. There was a lot more than that going on, but that was the only evidence the police had."

Where's this going?

Brian continued. "I built this company on a foundation of hard work and unshakable ethics. Bacchus takes pride in not sinking to the level of its more unscrupulous competitors. We maintain a zero tolerance policy for cheating the system. Any system."

Hoping to steer the subject away from yesterday, Kit tried misdirection. "Is this about cutting the power the other night? Because I'm sorry about that."

"No, you're not, but that's not it." Brian pulled open a drawer, then lifted something out. "It's about this." He dumped a thick tome on the desk. Familiar, tattered leather. *Grandpa's photograph album?*

"I don't get it," Kit said. "You called me away from a challenge to give that back?"

Shoulders heaving, Brian grunted. "A fellow contestant informed us this album might be of special interest."

"Who? Why?"

"That's not the point."

Kit's thoughts pulled in opposite directions. *This is a joke. This is serious.* "Why would my photograph album interest you?"

"Because it interested them when they discovered its contents."

Any remnants of certainty blew away with Brian's icy stare and the blizzard of confusion it brought. "I'm lost."

Brian slid the album towards Kit. "See for yourself."

Kit looked to Pamela for an explanation, but got nothing in return save for an awkward grimace. He pulled the album off the desk, opened the cover, then turned the pages. The same as always: cream pages, opaque glassine interleaves, each photograph a customer dressed in a suit made by Kit's grandpa. "I still don't get it. What's wrong?"

Brian pushed back from his desk. "A photographer once told me there's a story behind every photograph. What's behind yours?"

"My grandpa made these suits. I guess there's a story behind each one of them and the client wearing it." Glue of impatience stuck to Kit. "What's your point?"

"It would seem you took that view literally, Kit. Look closer."

Kit turned the album upright on his lap. With his fingernail, he eased open the cardboard layers of the first page, being careful not to damage them. Behind the first photograph hid gossamer-thin, folded paper. Kit pulled it out, then opened it. A sketch—not a drawing of the suit in the photograph—but a sketch of a hoodie and shorts. Not exactly what Kit made for the first challenge, but the basic shape. Kit's blood caught fire. He checked more photographs and found more drawings. More sportswear, dresses, menswear, kids wear. "I don't—it can't be. These aren't mine." Soon, his hands clutched a dozen sketches, crumpling them as if trying to quell his confusion.

Pamela spoke at last. "The rules state the possession of any reference material, whether they be design books or pattern books is prohibited."

"You broke the rules," Brian said, his voice flat.

Kit's heart sank, but his anger flared. "You don't—? I didn't know these were there."

Brian crossed his legs, one ankle over one knee. Doubt radiated from him. "Am I expected to believe you?"

"I've had this album for two minutes. You've had it since my audition." Pamela didn't move, didn't look at him. "You took it away at my audition. This is the first time I've seen it since."

"We returned it," Pamela said to Brian.

Kit's mouth moved on its own. "Bollocks you did."

"You're becoming very agitated, Kit," she said.

"Too right I'm agitated. You're accusing me of something I never did with something I never had."

Pamela looked to the ceiling. "So how do you explain those patterns? They're more or less the designs you've made to date."

Kit dropped the balled-up sketches. "Someone's set me up. They've gone back and drawn these up, close enough to what I made to make it look like I cheated. They think I'm a threat."

Brian pulled a pile of cards from his desk and leafed through them. "According to the scores awarded by the judges, you're not exactly the best designer."

"I won the first challenge."

"Not as far as Nancy was concerned." The honesty in Brian's eyes did little to comfort Kit.

Kit swallowed hard, but refused to digest defeat. "And

don't I know it. She reminds us all the time. I wouldn't put this past her."

Pamela laughed. "Don't be preposterous. Nancy's a handful all right, but she wouldn't have the time or the motivation to do something like this."

"So how do you explain why she hates us so much? She's had it in for me since my audition."

"Sometimes people don't get along," Brian said, "and Nancy doesn't get along with anyone except Osred East." He grimaced at the name. "I wouldn't take it personally."

"And I'm not clairvoyant," Kit shot back. "How could I prepare for challenges when I didn't know what they'd be?"

Pamela waved a dismissive hand. "An educated guess would do that. We always have a sportswear challenge, an evening wear challenge, and so on. The inspiration might be different each time, but there are only so many types of garments we could have you design."

Kit grasped for the last few flickers of hope from Brian. "Emilia's in with some of the production team. She said they told her she'd get a good edit."

Brian shook his head, then stood, soaring into the air. "We select our production team for their commitment and honesty to Bacchus and the show. No one—and I mean no one—would ever do that. Emilia tried to psych you out. Looks to me like it worked. You cheated, you got sloppy, and now you're caught."

Kit bit his lip to stop himself from crying. Crying wouldn't help. He stomped on the sketches, his shaking hands finally coming to a stop after running restlessly through his hair. "What about being innocent until proven guilty?"

"This isn't a court of law," Brian said. "It's cut and dried."

Pamela retrieved one of the crushed sketches. "Brian, if I may. Kit is a likeable and hardworking contestant and has been since his audition. The crew says he's been a pleasure to work with. True, he's had the odd wobble as far as Barker's concerned. Perhaps we should give him the benefit of the doubt."

"And the search of his room didn't turn up anything else?"

"You searched my room?"

"*Our* room," Brian said, gigantic fists clenching. "Let's be clear on that. A fellow contestant found the album hidden under your *unused* bed."

The cogs in Kit's head jammed. "Why would anyone look under there? A cleaner, maybe, but another contestant? I mean, why would someone do that?"

Brian looked at them both. "That's a fair point."

"What about video footage? You've looked at that, right?"

Pamela shuffled on the spot. "Inconclusive. There's no footage of anyone going near your bed."

Brian rolled a shoulder back, squeezing it with his other hand. "Okay. Let's back up and see if—"

The office doors flew open and Nancy Shearsmith swept in, a vulture in a black Prada top with feathered cuffs.

"Is it true?" she said, looking from Pamela to Brian. "Has he made is into fools?"

Rubbing his chin, Brian blinked slowly. "We're struggling to understand how Kit could do something like this."

"It seems so out of character," Pamela added.

Nancy's eyes and mouth froze in a dramatic expression of stunned surprise. "'Out of character'? We're talking about someone who bypassed the security systems in the house and snuck off on location for a quickie—"

"Not that quickie," Pamela muttered.

"—with another contestant. That says a lot about his character."

Brian looked out at the view. "True, but—"

Growling, Nancy approached him. "There are no buts, Brian. He has to go. I have a junior designer available to replace him at once."

Turning, Brian's blue gaze met Kit's, dragging him into a lake of fear. "It requires further investigation. Kit has put sufficient doubt in my mind."

Nancy stepped up to face Brian. "I have no such doubt, so I'll make it easy for you. I am not prepared to suffer another indignity at the hands of this production."

"Whoa," Pamela said, mouth dropping open. "Are you saying what I think you're saying?"

Nancy turned her glare's full force at Kit. "It's me or him."

twenty-eight
. . .

HOW COULD Barker concentrate once Pamela took Kit?

Patrick paced. "They have to tell us what's going on. Have to, right?"

Izzy stuck out her bottom lip. "All very odd. I hope his family's okay. He has a brother, doesn't he? And his mum's still going. Maybe something happened?"

The moment Barker spotted Gunter hovering by the entrance, he hurried over to him. "Do you know anything? Because if you do, tell me." Gunter looked away. "And you know why you have to tell me."

Gunter glanced around, checking the others weren't within earshot. "I can't tell you anything specific, because I don't know. What I can tell you is there's reason to suspect Kit hasn't been entirely honourable."

"Honourable? What's that supposed to mean?"

"He cheated."

Cheated? Kit? Barker's thoughts raced from uncertainty to anger. "That's bullshit. You know it, and I know it."

"That's as maybe, but it wouldn't be the first time a contestant has done something rash to stay in the competition."

"Not Kit. No way."

Gunter hesitated. "I'm going to say something and you won't like it."

"Go on."

"This isn't the first time someone you trusted betrayed that trust."

Gunter hadn't been unkind, but bile rose in Barker's throat. The phonecall in Miami, the trial, the loss. Ludo hadn't been the best father in the world, but he'd always operated by the highest moral code—or so he had everyone believe. And all lies. Gunter was right. Why would Kit be different? Barker fished in his pocket for an indigestion tablet. All gone.

Gunter's phone rang. During the conversation he produced a roll of indigestion tablets from his trouser pocket, then placed them in Barker's hand.

After he hung up, Gunter signalled for the cameras to join him with the contestants. "Designers. To make up for the disruption, you'll have an extra ten minutes to make your fabric selections." No one moved. "Come on, people. Let's make fashion."

Barker bought Kit as much pinstripe fabric as he could afford.

Back in the workroom, someone had removed Kit's table. None of his things—either that he'd brought with him or what the production company provided—remained, like he'd never existed.

Had Bacchus kicked Kit off the show? What other reason could there be to clear away his things? What could he have done? It had to be a mistake, a misunderstanding. Kit was honest. Always.

No one but Emilia worked for the next half an hour, the rest huddling in the breakout room for speculation.

Aden rubbed at his brow. "I never saw him take anything home, did you?"

With a glance at Patrick and Aden, as if they had an answer, Izzy shook her head. "Not so much as a thread. I left a measuring tape around my neck once. Forgot it was there, and he reminded me."

Pamela entered the studio, stride uneven, tailed by Nancy, Gunter, and Bruna. "I'm sorry to have to be the one to tell you this, but Kit's left the show."

Barker clamped his hand over the back of his neck. "Did he leave of his own accord?"

Pamela lowered her head. "I'm afraid he broke the rules."

Barker bolted from his desk to a back corner of the studio, pain burning in the back of his throat. "No, no, no, no, no."

Pamela raised her voice over his. "We have always operated, and will continue to do so, a zero tolerance policy for rule breaking."

Even Patrick couldn't settle, still pacing in front of the accessory wall. "What's he supposed to have done?"

Nancy's hard smile radiated superiority. "Mister Redman had a stash of designs in his room."

Patrick folded his arms over his stomach, then leaned towards Nancy. "Bullshit."

"It wouldn't be the first time a simple smile and charming demeanour hid a fluent liar. Judging by some of your reactions," Nancy said, observing Barker's distress, "some of you fell harder for those lies than others."

Palm pressed to her chest, Emilia gave Nancy a polite smile. "I for one never bought his chirpy little Northern routine."

Barker pressed his back against the wall, the floor softening under his feet.

Izzy hurried to him, wrapping him in a hug he barely registered. "I'm sure there's been a mistake."

He melted into her body, rag-doll limp.

255

Pamela joined them. "I'm sorry, too. I've rooted for you both since your auditions. Is there anything I can do?"

From the outset, Barker intended to get in, win the show, and get out. Meeting Kit changed all of that. If Kit planned the same, why waste time on their growing relationship? It made no sense. "I want to see him."

Pamela patted his shoulder, awkward. "We'll have finished filming in a week. You can see him then."

Lifting his head from the crook of Izzy's neck, Barker gritted his teeth. "No, I want to say goodbye. Now."

Pamela looked back at Nancy, who shook her head. "He's already on his way home."

With a gentle clap of her hands, Bruna drew everyone's attention. "I'm sorry, designers. I know I speak for all of you when I say this is a confusing time. But we've already cancelled one challenge. We can't afford to do so again. The time we've lost will extend your deadline for this challenge, but you still have a deadline."

Aden turned away, smacking the wall. "Fuck's sake. You have to be kidding."

Nancy rocked back on her heels, her smile so wide it devoured more than reassured. "I'm sure you'll all rise to the occasion."

Only Gunter stayed in the studio, but when Pamela passed Nancy, she said something to her and Nancy sneered in defiance.

Gunter prised Barker away from Izzy, then steered him into the breakout area. Barker picked up an apple from the fruit bowl, then put it back, the little room threatening to fold in on him.

"If you're going to do this," Gunter said. "Win this show, you need to be fully present."

"I can't. Not without him." The words caught in Barker's throat. He couldn't—didn't want to—go on without Kit.

Taking an unsteady step towards him, Gunter stuttered. "He's still in the building, but not for long."

Barker fled, wrenching open the workroom door and screaming Kit's name. Izzy called after him, but Barker had no use for anything she said. He had to see Kit.

By the time he reached the floor the production company used during filming, a security guard pursued. One man wouldn't keep him away from Kit. Barker flung open door after door, each one empty. Sweat gathered on his brow. *This isn't happening!*

Up ahead, a shadow moved across a frosted window. Barker sprinted forwards, driving into the door with his shoulder and seizing the handle.

Kit sat hunched in a small office chair opposite Layla. She leapt up when Barker stormed in.

Heat flushed through his body. "Get out."

Layla's hands twisted together. "You're not supposed—"

Barker dragged her by the arm, pushed her straight into the oncoming security guard, then locked the door.

Kit's face buckled when Barker pulled him to his feet and crushed him to his chest.

Sobbing, hands clutching at Barker's shirt, Kit howled in anguish. "What am I going to do?"

Layla and the security guard hammered on the door.

Savage, Barker hammered back. "Sod off the pair of you. You can have him when I'm done."

Kit's sobs faltered his words. "I can't believe it."

"What happened?"

"Pamela took me to see Brian. There were sketches in my grandpa's photo album. Made it look like I've cheated."

Throat closing up, Barker spoke through his teeth in forced restraint. "But you didn't have the album."

"Pamela said they'd given it back. Someone found it under

my bed. Told them. Nancy barged in and made Brian choose me or her."

Nancy. Always showing up when things couldn't get any worse.

"I'll talk to Pamela," Barker said, holding Kit back to get his attention. "Demand to see the footage." His hand came down on the door when he hesitated. *It wouldn't be the first time a simple smile and charming demeanour hid a fluent liar.* Light-headed, he lowered his voice to a whisper. "If you did it, Kit, now's the time to tell me."

"What?" Kit's voice cracked on the word.

"I need to know."

Kit shrank into the opposite corner of the office. Ten feet may as well have been a mile.

Barker swallowed hard. "I know you're upset, but if I go out there and look like a fool…"

Kit's voice tore ragged. "They've accused me of cheating and you're worried about looking like a fool?" Hard eyes met Barker's. He was the enemy now. Most loved to most hated. "You bastard."

"Please try to understand—"

"Try? Why try? Because I'm not academically dazzling? Because I didn't go to a fancy school like you? Because I'm smaller than you, so my brain must be, too?"

Another, louder hammer on the door, and Pamela shouted. "Barker? Open this door at once."

Kit's eyes burned Barker to ash. "Get out."

Dread locked Barker's stomach up tight. "All I'm asking is—"

"Not to get in the way of you winning." The sweat on Kit's forehead teased his curls in front of his eyes. He pushed them back.

"Believe me, I—"

"I don't want to hear it. Turn around and take your

bleached hair and your contact lenses and your fake tan with you."

It would have been kinder for Kit to kill him.

Barker rested his head on the door, skull vibrating with each pound from the other side, driving shame deeper into him. He shouldn't have asked the question. He only had himself to blame. "Fine," Barker whispered, opening the door and not looking back. "See you around."

twenty-nine

. . .

THE LAST SUNDAY IN JULY, Kit struggled through the Intimate Theatre's stage door, a dress's weight threatening to buckle his legs.

"Sonia?" he managed, his thin voice echoing through the corridors.

"In here," came a voice from a dressing room.

Kit heaved the dress through the narrow, sliding door.

Sonia Stone—about to play Elizabeth the First in the Palmers Green Community Theatre's production of *Elizabeth's Such A Queen!*—leapt up from her orange plastic chair.

Sonia curled her arms under the dress, sharing the load. "Why didn't you call me to come and help? This thing weighs an absolute tonne."

Together they hooked the dress onto the solid metal rail running along the side wall, then fell into different chairs to catch their breath.

As soon as he'd recovered, Kit took in the room. The same whitewashed brick walls, same mirror running along the wall opposite the rail, and the same cloying smell of waxy makeup.

The same room, but not the same Kit.

"Why've you got the fluorescent light on?" he said. "The lights around the mirror are nicer."

Sonia ran her hands through her newly coloured Titian hair, then smiled. "They are fabulously flattering but once they've been on for half an hour your makeup slides right off. Can you imagine what it'll be like when we're in our costumes? At least it's only me and Daisy in here. All three chaps are in the other room." Sonia slumped back in her chair, then snatched up her script, using it as a fan. "How's Daisy's dress coming along?"

Kit swung his legs back and forth under the chair. "No idea."

Sonia stopped fanning herself. "It's only a few days until dress rehearsal. You know how picky she is, let alone that Maureen."

"No one beats Nancy Shearsmith."

Throwing her script down on the makeup bench, Sonia leaned towards him. "How are you doing, darling?"

Kit avoided her gaze. "Fine."

"Are you keeping occupied?"

"I'm starting a temp job tomorrow. My mate Hannah works there."

Smiling, Sonia clapped her hands. "That charming girl from the telly company? How lovely."

Kit kicked the floor, scuffing his good shoes. "But it's for the company that makes *Runway Rivals*." He coughed, then pushed back his uncut hair, praying Sonia wouldn't notice the heat rising to his cheeks.

Sonia's smile dropped. She pushed back a strand of hair he'd missed. "Is that wise?"

Kit raised his hands, then let them drop into his lap. "It's the best-paid job I can get. They agreed to put me in Kids Entertainment on the condition I stay away from General Entertainment."

"And if you don't?"

"They'll sack me on the spot." He'd never live down a second firing from Bacchus.

Sonia's eyes, warm as fresh tea, failed to raise his spirits. "Even so…"

Kit let his head fall back. He stared at the white ceiling marbled with grey cobwebs. "It's a job. You know how it is."

Sonia picked up her script, then resumed fanning herself. "I wouldn't know, darling. I haven't had a proper job since I married Tom and gave up flying."

Kit head tipped forward, mouth loosening with surprise. "I didn't know you were a pilot."

Sonia's musical laugh burst from her chest. "You've never seen me at the wheel. These days, they call it 'cabin crew'. In my day being a stewardess was a surefire route to bagging the most eligible chaps or, if you were lucky, a pilot."

"Was Tom a pilot?"

"No, more's the pity, but he was First Class. I met my first husband in Economy. He fell in love with someone else. These things happen, and I moved on. I met my second husband in Business. He died, and I moved on. I met Tom when he asked my opinion on a watch he'd bought in New York, then he asked me if I'd go out with him if he bought me the matching ladies' version. I agreed."

Kit laughed at Sonia's audacity. "You went out with a guy just for a watch?"

"Not just any watch, darling. Cartier, eighteen karat, white gold, set with six carats of diamonds."

"Sounds expensive."

"It cost him more than the flat I lived in. But do you know something?"

"What?"

Sonia stood, smoothing down her leaf green sweater. "It

won't be anything as fabulous as what you've made for me. Help me put it on."

It took Kit forty minutes to dress Sonia in her chemise, boned corset, petticoat, farthingale, stockings, gown, sleeves, neck ruff and wrist ruffs. When he finished, he turned off the overhead light, then flicked on the mirror lights.

Sonia gasped, hand flying to her chest. "Good God, that's remarkable. There's no denying who I'm supposed to be, but it's so modern. So Vivienne-Westwood-meets-Alexander-McQueen." Her hands ran up and down the sleeves. "If I don't pilfer this after the run, you must promise to make me one just like it."

Kit used to love revealing costumes to actors. Now it left him cold. He'd wrenched this costume design out of him. He didn't want to make theatre costumes. He didn't want to make anything at all. "Okay, but better. No ruffs."

"Oh, I don't know. Tom's ancient enough to remember them the first time around."

Kit gave her arm a limp tap. "You can't say that. He's your husband."

Sonia winked at him in the mirror. "Young billionaires are scarce."

A joyless shroud cloaked Kit. "I don't want someone like that."

"Are you sure about that, darling? I mean, there's that chap from the show."

Kit cast his eyes to the floor. "That's different."

Sonia patted his cheek. "Never trust rich men. If you want loyalty and affection you'd be better off with a dog."

"What about Tom?"

"Oh, he fancied himself as something of a playboy. I caught him *in flagrante* with his secretary and took him for all he had."

It's in flagrante delicto. "Not half?"

Playing with her hair, Sonia examined her reflection. "Let's just say I knew about some of his other business affairs. I threatened to tell the board of his company." She applied coppery red lipstick to the middle of her lower lip. "His secretary might have had him by the penis, but I had him by the balls."

On his way home, Kit kept his head low, avoiding eye contact, so no one stopped and stared and pointed. After two weeks, and in the dead of night, he moved out of Grandpa's house and in with Hannah.

When he turned into Hannah's street, a huddle of five men broke apart, each one raising a camera. Horrified, Kit tripped over his own feet, falling against a lamppost.

The paparazzi knew he'd moved here?

Awkward, Kit pasted on a counterfeit smile, then proceeded forward, cameras flashing his face, the men hurling questions at him.

Kit reached Hannah's house, fumbled with the door key, then bolted inside. He leant with his back against the door, waiting for the men's voices to die away. When would it end? After Fashion Week? When the new series started? *Please, God, let people have short memories.*

Kit found Hannah fast asleep on the living room sofa. Despite nodding off, she still had one hand on the TV remote, protecting it from him. He'd broken their agreement, that he wouldn't watch *Runway Rivals* or Tabitha's *Coming Undone*, so Hannah took no chances.

"Hey," Kit said, lifting Hannah's hand then sliding out the remote. "I'll turn off the telly and we'll go to bed, yeah?"

Hannah muttered something, then turned over, her face squishing against a cushion, smudging it with mascara. "Humph."

Kit tidied the kitchen, washing mugs ringed with tea stains and plates dusted with crumbs. Foam clung to his forearms.

He'd added too much washing-up liquid. Barker did that the first time they washed up together.

Hannah appeared in the doorway, eye barely open. "Big day tomorrow."

Kit didn't look at her or else she'd see the tears streaming down his face.

thirty

...

THE NEXT MORNING, when Kit and Hannah got off the Tube at Oxford Circus station, she took his hand.

"It'll be fine," she said. "There's no way Brian would agree to you working at Bacchus if he didn't trust you."

Or felt guilty. Kit nodded. "Let's just get it over with."

Hannah led him down Argyll Street, air smudged with early morning traffic fumes, then left into Great Marlborough Street. When they passed the stage door of the London Palladium, three backstage crew, all in black, stood smoking in the street. The *Runway Rivals* crew wore black. Barker smoked.

Kit and Hannah passed a newsstand. Judging by the covers, Barker graduated from specialist fashion publications to TV magazines. His grey eyes, full of heat, suffocated Kit's thoughts.

Bacchus Broadcasting's office stood fifty yards down the street on the left.

Kit pulled back, stopping Hannah in her tracks. "I can't."

Hannah hugged him, darning the holes in his courage. "You can. I promise." She took out her phone. "Come on, or we'll be late." She pushed open a gigantic glass door, then pulled him through.

Kit ducked his head, but still caught glimpses of the brass vine-leaves he'd seen the last time he'd been here.

It's me or him.

"New starter," Hannah said to the man on reception. Then the security gate swung open.

In the empty lift, doors emblazoned with logos of Bacchus's shows, Hannah pointed at the metal plaque next to the buttons. "Kids Entertainment is on two, one floor below General Entertainment. We just call it 'Kids' and 'General'. Do not, whatever you do, go to three, even if it's asking me for lunch. Call me or email me." She punched the button for the second floor. "You'll be busy. Even though it's the end of July, the months running up to October half-term and Christmas are horrendous. Even if people clock who you are, they'll be too busy to bother you."

They got off at the second floor. Hannah led Kit past a kitchen and a breakout area, all painted scarlet.

Someone tapped Kit on the shoulder. Kit turned, coming face-to-face with a blonde man wearing board shorts and a sleeveless t-shirt with *Minted Sting* scrawled across it.

Vonnie Valero, Minted Sting's lead singer, judged the makeover challenge.

The man smiled. "You're Kit, right? Loved you on the show. I mean, I didn't think you had a chance in hell, but you and Barker? Magic. Shame you fucked it up, but it's still nice to meet you." He held out a hand.

"Sol," Hannah said.

Sol grinned at her. "Hey, Han."

"Piss off."

Sol took a step back, then looked around. "Okay, okay. See you upstairs." He jerked his head in the kitchen's direction.

"Our boiler's on the blink, so you'll have to come down if you need a cuppa. Later, yeah?"

Hannah tutted. "Great. He'll tell everyone you're here."

The head of Localisation—an Australian woman sporting a blunt-cut bob—gave Kit the honour of sorting through twenty-five thousand tapes and cross-referencing them with their audio tracks.

"We need to know what languages we've dubbed the shows into, so we know the gaps to fill." She handed him a scuffed laptop with a dirty keyboard. "It's not exactly fashion design, but—" She paused, a humourless smile stamping her face. "—you've earned it." She led Kit to the tape library without another word.

The rest of the morning stretched into eternity. Thanks to Sol, several people sought Kit out, then loitered behind him, whispering insults. He kept his head down, trembling hands recording information in a spreadsheet, typing with one finger. Hand-stitching at breakneck speed? No problem. Typing? Not so much. He found a few General Entertainment tapes mixed in with the Kids tapes: a *The Weakest Twink* here, a *Desert Island Dicks* there.

Aden auditioned for *Desert Island Dicks*. Barker hated Aden. Barker, Barker, Barker. The lad was everywhere.

By lunchtime, all Kit wanted to do was flee down Carnaby Street and never look back. Instead, Hannah took him to a little flatbread eatery across the street.

Hannah ordered 'Fungher Games' flatbreads for them both. "Go get us some seats," she said to Kit. "There are some tucked around the back."

To his relief, Kit nabbed two seats in a cramped, gloomy corner—just what he needed right now. Anything for people not to stare at him.

Five minutes later, Hannah appeared carrying two steaming flatbreads smothered with mushrooms. Kit's went untouched.

Hannah tucked in, keeping eye contact. "How bad was it on a scale of one to ten?"

As he fiddled with the edge of his flatbread, a single tear ran down Kit's face. "Two thousand, five hundred, and nine."

Hannah chewed. "Could be worse."

Kit wiped his cheek. "Grandpa's dead, I lost my job, and I got kicked off the biggest show in the country for something I didn't do."

"And?"

"And what?"

"Say it."

Pushing his flatbread away, Kit sat back, then stared at the table. "I messed things up with Barker."

"But look on the bright side."

Kit searched his mind for something good. Nothing. "What bright side?"

Hannah gobbled down the last of her flatbread, then licked her fingers clean of tomato sauce. "Your mum's in the nuthouse."

Kit's mouth fell open. "I can't—" A sudden laugh ripped through him. He covered his face with a menu in case people looked over. "I can't believe you said that."

Grinning, Hannah wiped her fingers on a napkin. "But you laughed." She scrunched up the flimsy paper, then dropped it on her plate.

Kit crossed his arms, tucking his fingers under his armpits, then slid down in his seat. "All the stuff that's happened, like it's some nightmare I played along with. That time, when I caught some of the show, it was like looking at someone else."

"Good someone else or bad someone else?"

Kit rubbed his face. "I don't know anymore."

Wiping her mouth, Hannah eyed Kit's lunch. "So, what's the plan?"

"Plan? What plan? I don't have a plan."

Hannah glanced at her phone. "We've got half an hour before we have to go back." She pushed aside her plate, got a sketchpad and pencil from her bag, then put them both on the table between them. "Plenty of time to plan."

"What's the point?" Kit thumped his head on the wall behind him, sick of thinking about everything he'd messed up. "It's over. I'm done."

Opening the sketchpad to a blank page, Hannah brandished the pencil. She drew five small boxes, then wrote next to each one. "Grandpa, job, Runway Rivals, Mum, Barker." She ticked the second box. "You didn't have a job. Now you do. That leaves your grandpa, *Runway Rivals*, your mum, and Barker. Which one do you want to tackle first?"

Kit leant forward. With nothing better to do than wallow in self-pity, he'd indulge Hannah. "As much as I want Grandpa back, I'm not getting into voodoo."

Hannah put a cross in the first box. "Agreed. A vengeful demon will possess me as it attempts to get to you. What about your mum?"

"She won't see me."

Hannah coughed into her napkin. "What? Why not?"

"I called Greg. She said I've brought shame to the family prostituting myself to get on telly then 'fucking all the mens'."

"Wow," Hannah said. "You told me she was a piece of work but... Jesus." Going back to her pad, Hannah took Kit's flatbread, took a bite, then put a cross in the fourth box. "See? Three out of five in about a minute. What's next? *Runway Rivals* or Barker?"

"This is pointless, Han."

"No, it' not. Don't you want to do something?"

Kit cut his flatbread in two, then raised the unbitten half to his mouth. "*Runway Rivals.*" He took a bite, chewed, swallowed. "Maybe if I had a look at the camera footage for the house—?"

Hannah huffed. "Not gonna happen, mate."

"Right, then. Not much I can do on that front, unless I get Nancy to admit it."

Picking up the last of her lunch, Hannah nodded. "You'd do that?"

"Why not?"

Hannah took the remains of Kit's flatbread, then ate it. "I've missed feisty Kit." She ticked the third box. "That leaves Barker. Any ideas?"

Kit should leave things be. What was the point of stirring up something when it could settle? He'd walked into everything so blindly, pulled along like a thread through a loom. But what could he do when the way forward meant a journey back? It would be selfish to make Barker feel something when not feeling worked.

"I can't talk to him," Kit said. "I don't know where he is."

Hannah held her pencil over the Barker box, but said nothing.

Was it selfish to pursue someone you might love and who might love you back? Why not be the shuttle for once, racing through the loom, making something strong, something pretty?

I enjoy being surrounded by pretty things.

Kit deserved justice, but Barker deserved compassion.

"So I need to find out," Kit said, sitting up, resting his elbows on the edge of the table. "Pam should know where he is, but she won't crack. There's that Layla. Maybe I could get around her." He tapped his fingertips together, forming a steeple. "But I need someone who's on my side. Really on my side."

Hannah "Don't take this the wrong way, but everyone hates your guts. Like, *everyone*. Apart from me, who's on your side?"

Kit took the pencil, then ticked the Barker box. "Gunter."

thirty-one
· · ·

STANDING outside Gunter's dusky blue front door, a tingle swept up the back of Kit's neck, then dropped into his stomach, a ball of electricity.

Gunter opened his front door, shirt collar open, sleeves rolled up to his elbows, waistcoat. He held a garden trowel in one hand. "Kit? What are you doing here?"

The electricity in Kit's guts amped up his resolve. "Sorry for turning up like this."

Gunter scratched his temple. "It's been a month."

"Three weeks." Kit nodded at the trowel. "I should go. You look like you're busy."

"Busy-ish. Mostly confused and more than a little concerned. How did you find out where I live?"

"Whoever registered the domain name for your website, didn't register it privately. My friend Hannah helped me look you up."

Gunter's mouth dropped open.

"You should do something about that," Kit said. "Can you spare me some time?"

It took a moment for Gunter to compose himself. "I was gardening. Look, are you all right?"

"I need to talk to you, if I can." Kit paused. "If I may."

Gunter's eyes brightened. "Come in. I'll make a pot of tea."

Kit stepped through the door, then closed it behind him. A black and white hallway floor stretched away, and dark wood panelling lined the walls. Kit may as well have been back at Stitchworthy.

Gunter disappeared through a doorway to the left. Kit followed.

The living room furniture, oxblood leather Chesterfield suite and a mahogany coffee and side tables, shared the same flawless sheen. Only the vintage Persian rug showed signs of wear, a sepia track running from the high-backed armchair to the kitchen.

Over the mantlepiece hung a painting of a young man with golden hair.

Gunter's calm energy permeated his home. Some might have called it old-fashioned, but it suited Gunter's soft warmth. If anybody else lived here, they'd look out of place.

Gunter returned from the kitchen with a silver tray bearing an ornate teapot, milk jug and sugar bowl, and a plate of macaroons. "It's a self-portrait," he said, tipping his head towards the painting.

"You look so different," Kit said.

"It's not my self-portrait."

"Oh, right. This is all a bit…"

"Surreal? I know. I work very hard to keep my private and professional lives separate."

"I'm sorry for intruding, Mister Lyffe. I—"

Gunter waved a hand at him. "Gunter, please."

As Gunter moved about the room, Kit couldn't believe he and Kit were the same species. Gunter, charming and handsome as always, and in total control.

"You must like art," Kit said. "And artists. Creative people, I guess. I don't know how you didn't lose your temper with all of us."

"I didn't need to. You were all too busy losing your tempers with each other." He gestured for Kit to sit. "Is there something I can help you with?"

Kit picked up a macaroon the colour of happiness but couldn't bring himself to eat it. "Thank you for using your Lyffe Line to save Barker from elimination. You got him into the final."

"Why wouldn't I? He deserves to be in the final after—"

"Everything he's been through." Heat flushed around Kit's neck. "Is that why you did it? I mean, you saved him on the last week, made it three people in the final and not two."

Gunter poured them both tea. "He's a talented young man deserving a shot at Fashion Week."

"Have you seen him? I mean, have you done that thing where you visit the finalists' homes to see how they're doing?"

"I might have." Gunter made the simple act of offering Kit a cup of tea a token of sympathy. "If you don't mind my asking, how long have things between you…?"

Kit took the cup and tucked the macaroon into the saucer. "Since our auditions, I guess. We were at tables next to each other. It wasn't exactly love at first sight, but there was something about him."

Gunter examined him. "And then you tortured each other for a week."

"Eight days." Kit scratched his neck, replaying their last fight. "I can't forget about him."

"You've been watching the show?"

"I promised myself I wouldn't, but he's everywhere."

Gunter sipped his tea. "I'm not surprised. He's perfect for the show—handsome, talented, fascinating backstory."

Kit turned his teacup in its saucer. Time to get to the point. "Do you know where he is?"

Gunter shifted in his chair. "I can't tell you, even if I wanted to."

"You don't want to? I mean, you let us sneak off that day at the hotel."

Gunter set down his cup. "No, I let you sneak back."

"You weren't yourself. Why?"

Gunter glanced at the painting above the fireplace, hands flexing as though to curl into fists before his fingers straightened. "That's a very personal question."

What a stupid thing to have asked. Gunter had been a wreck that day.

Gunter sagged back into his chair, covering his nose and mouth with one hand. He sat forward and locked his gaze on Kit. "I know what it's like to love, and I know what it's like to lose that love. I'm sorry, but I can't help you."

Tears spilled from Kit's eyes. "He was all I had." He couldn't take it anymore. He didn't want Gunter to see him cry, so he put down his tea and sobbed into his hands.

Kit dabbed his eyes with the handkerchief Gunter offered. "It's raining."

Gunter skimmed a hand over the rectangular lump in his waistcoat pocket. "I hate the rain." His voice brightened. "Would you like some cake?"

"I'd love some."

The kitchen, as immaculate as the living room, shared the same Victorian character, despite a wood-burning stove replacing its cast iron predecessor, and marble countertops. An oak table scarred from years of use served as an island, two chairs at one end.

"I baked yesterday."

Kit's stomach rumbled. He placed a hand over it.

"You're thin," Gunter said. "Aren't you eating?"

"I've never felt hungry until now. I've been living on toast and tea."

Gunter opened a cake tin, cut a slice, then placed it on a floral china plate along with a dessert fork. He handed the plate to Kit.

One smell of lemon drizzle cake and Kit's gummy mouth flooded with saliva. "Is there anything you can't do?"

Gunter chuckled. "The list is extensive. I stick to what I can. Come, sit." He pulled back a chair and waited for Kit to sit.

Kit sank into the chair, then ate a piece of cake. It tasted as good as it smelled, but it wasn't enough to ease the constant ache in his temples. "I shouldn't have gone on the show."

Gunter cut a slice of cake for himself, then took the other chair. "The kindest thing might have been for us not to have cast you."

"Maybe, but I've only got myself to blame."

"Blame doesn't heal your wounds." Gunter's fork hesitated over his slice of cake. "As you know, Barker's in the final three, so he's working on his final collection. With neither a home nor a studio space of his own, he's been staying with a friend."

"He said he didn't have any friends." *Did that Caspian still count?*

Gunter turned a palm upwards. "That's what I've been told. Only Pamela knows where he is. She gave him a prepaid mobile phone, so he's contactable, but—"

Kit put down his fork and leaned forward. "If I gave you my number, could you get it to him?"

"Elbows off the table," Gunter said, gesturing for Kit to sit back. "You're asking me to do something I shouldn't."

"You helped us at the hotel."

"Barker wants—"

"Barker wants me. What do you think we'd have done if we hadn't run into you at the hotel?"

Gunter looked at the ceiling and sighed. "Forget the sex, Kit. There has to be a connection."

"I can't let go of the only person who's makes me worth something."

Gunter thumped the table, shaking Kit's fork off the plate. "You mustn't rely on others for that. They might open your eyes to it, but you have to believe it and hold it in your heart." Rain streaked down the kitchen window. Gunter's eyes shifted to it, glazing with a layer of tears. "Christ, I hate the rain." He blinked his tears away, biting his lip. When he spoke again, his lower lip quivered, words slowly making their way out of his mouth. "I'll see what I can do."

For several sweet seconds Kit's mouth cracked into a genuine smile. "Thank you. Thank you so much."

Gunter's jaw set firm. "But that's all I can do. I can't interfere. I won't interfere. If it's meant to be it's meant to be."

They finished their tea and cake in silence. Afterwards, Kit placed his things in the sink. "I'm sorry to have turned up unannounced and taken up so much of your day. I'd better get going."

Gunter rose. "You're welcome. I'll walk you to the door. I've always taken my role as mentor—and teacher before that —to be as much about pastoral care as academic support. With that in mind, consider exactly what you'll say to Barker when you see him. He's under a lot of pressure, Kit. I would advise a gentle approach." He tilted his head to one side. "How's your collection for Fashion Week coming along?"

An ache stabbed through Kit's temples. "I haven't started."

"You don't have long. Today's August second. Fashion Week starts September eighteenth. That's six, almost seven, weeks."

"What's the point?" Kit's voice echoed through the hallway. "It's not like I can win."

"You are talented, Kit. Believe that and hold it in your heart."

Kit wanted to believe it, but the heaviness in his chest wouldn't let it rise. Besides, Barker filled his heart, leaving room for nothing else. "I know I don't know you very well, but can I—may I—"

"'Can' is fine."

Kit pulled Gunter's face down to his, then kissed him on the cheek. "Thank you."

Fresh tears in his eyes, Gunter hugged him. "Make sure he's worthy of you."

When Kit stepped onto the pavement, he pulled up his collar and waved goodbye. Gunter closed the door, but Kit didn't walk away. Should he go back and offer to spend more time with him?

Gunter drew the curtains.

Kit set off for the Tube. He'd only taken five sloshing steps when Gunter called after him.

"I can't promise anything, but I think I have an idea."

thirty-two

· · ·

BARKER BARED his teeth at the zip. If the bloody thing puckered one more time, he'd take the entire dress out into the courtyard and torch it.

Runway Rivals gave each designer ten thousand pounds to buy fabric and outsource a third of construction. Barker used eight thousand to hold off a bailiff. With no money left to outsource construction, he had no option but to make every piece himself. Barker did his best to avoid the stress of the task ahead, but it crept into his mind when things went wrong. Right now, it was this stubborn bloody zip.

He hesitated in front of the rickety sewing machine Sybille procured for him. She'd had it serviced, but it had seen better days. When he turned the wheel to raise the presser foot, he avoided the machine's cracked case—it cut him the first time. The foot pedal stuck halfway and needed so much pressure to release, the machine had two speeds: melancholic or manic.

How to free the mangled satin? Examination of the bobbin proved the fabric hadn't been punched down through the plate, so he wound the needle to its highest position, lifted the presser foot, then eased the fabric out with care.

Coffee. He needed coffee. The magic of ground beans would clear his mind and fix the sewing machine. Or him. Either would be a blessing. And a filtered coffee? That would give him more time to think than the instant variety. Thinking didn't qualify as procrastination.

Barker mustered the courage to tackle Caspian's coffee machine, but its dials and nozzles better suited the artisan coffee shops Barker used to frequent than a domestic kitchen. A barista conjuring coffee was one thing, Barker's magical mastery was another. A halfhearted rummage through the kitchen drawers didn't turn up an instruction booklet, so the search proved useless. A machine like that needed a week's residential training *and* a manual. Instant coffee would do.

He shouldn't grumble. Natalia, Caspian's latest, impossibly rich, Russian fling had flown Caspian out to Dubai for the foreseeable future, leaving his apartment free for Barker's use.

"Private jet," Caspian said with a faraway look in his eyes as he handed over his key the week before. "A Gulfstream three. One hundred and twenty-five million. I'm hard just thinking about it." In return for a place to work, Barker agreed to look after Caspian's pug, Sterling.

Conditioned to appear in the kitchen every time a cupboard or drawer opened, Sterling waddled into the room in expectation of a decadent treat, drool swinging from his down-turned mouth.

"You can stop that right now. The only thing you're getting from me is a long walk."

Barker kidded himself. He hadn't managed a proper night's sleep since arriving. Sterling insisted on sleeping in the same room as Barker, snoring even louder than he farted. No walkies today. Barker gave in, pushing back the head of a dog-shaped jar, wincing when *Who Let The Dogs Out?* screeched from its tinny speaker. He retrieved a biscuit, tossed it to Sterling, then went back to the sewing machine for another round. "What I need is a—" *Damn it.* "—Kit."

The zip stuck in the machine. "Fucking, fucking, bloody, fucking, fuck!"

Barker held dress in one hand and the courtyard doorhandle in the other when his mobile rang.

"It's Pamela. I need to send Gunter and a crew out to you in two days. Will you still be at the Shoreditch address?"

"Absolutely. The owner's abroad."

"Great. They'll be with you Thursday morning."

"Super. How are you?"

"Sorry?"

"Is everything going all right? With you? With the show?"

"Yes, yes." Pamela paused. Her voice softened when she spoke again. "Sorry. I wasn't expecting you to ask. Things are ticking over nicely, thanks. Are you all right?" This wasn't small talk. Her voice dropped into the kindness she'd shown on audition day.

"I suppose so. I miss—everyone."

Her voice brightened. "So Gunter will be a friendly face. And you'll see the others at Fashion Week."

"Even Fay?"

"Even Fay. And Kit, obviously."

Kit would be at Fashion Week. "Pam?"

"Yes, Barker?"

"I bloody love you."

He floated back to the sewing machine and put in a perfect zip.

On Thursday morning, Barker gave Sterling a long walk and a charcoal biscuit, the walk to soothe Barker's worry, and the biscuit to curb Sterling's wind. He doubted either Gunter or the filming crew's sound operator would appreciate rapid fire flatulence.

In the bathroom, Barker smoothed his hair left then right before settling on a relaxed, tousled look. He took out his contact lenses, then put on his glasses.

Leave me out of it, you fake bastard.

He rummaged through his rail of clothes, choosing a comfortable, all-black look.

An hour later, Gunter arrived. "Who died?"

"I always dressed like this."

"You're too thin to wear black and too pale. Where's your tan?"

"It washed off."

"I see. The glasses are a pleasant touch. They make you appear serious, but the rest is dreary and not what we want, especially after the press you've received."

"I know. I've been doomscrolling for weeks."

"Doomscrolling?"

"It's a thing."

Barker went upstairs to change. Gucci, tropical print, silk bomber jacket with leaves—all shades of green—spreading across the chest and down the sleeves. Every shade of green. Even olive.

Gunter approved. "Let's do my arrival. One camera on me, the other on you. Try 'surprise and delight' when you see me. Or delight. Surprise doesn't read well on its own."

It took a few takes, but Barker got used to being back on camera.

Gunter bent to pet Sterling, pulling back when the startled pug yelped. "And who's this adorable… thing?"

"Sterling doesn't do people bending over him. I'll put him outside. Does anyone want a coffee while I'm at it?"

· · ·

Barker showed Gunter his collection. Swathes of organza, mousseline, and tulle pinned onto dress forms.

"I'm not there," Barker said, chewing his thumb. "But the silhouettes are pretty much what I'm after."

Gunter walked around the three dress forms, nodding. "Exquisite and very seductive. I like the draping, but I can't decide if it's sweet or aggressive. You've resolved every surface…"

"But?"

Rubbing his forehead, Gunter screwed up his eyes. "Your construction hasn't improved. I'm concerned it could go against you if it's apparent on the catwalk. We gave you a budget to cover fabrics and a third of outsourcing. Have you received any of your outsourced garments?"

"I haven't outsourced any construction."

"But this is a twenty-one piece collection, and you have—what?—three pieces here?"

Too much coffee and too little breakfast lightened Barker's head. "That's right."

"You only have six weeks before you're due back the day before Fashion Week. You can't possibly finish these and another eighteen pieces to a standard good enough to win."

"Can we talk?"

"You're not a pattern maker and you're not a tailor." Gunter picked up Barker's sketches. "And these designs are complicated."

Holding his hand up to the camera, Barker lowered his voice. "Can we talk in private?"

When Barker opened the doors to the courtyard, Sterling regarded him with disdain, then leapt off the back step into the long grass, head held high as he strutted away.

Barker tapped out a cigarette and offered one to Gunter, who refused. "I've used the money for something else. I had to."

287

Gunter frowned. "Go on."

"I'm in debt. I have to hold people off."

"This debt. Has it put you into a… legal position?"

Barker flicked ash onto the patio, grinding it into the slate surface with the toe of his shoe. "Not yet, but it's only a matter of time. I have to win the show with what I've got, which is fabric and sod all skills."

"My influence only extends so far with—"

"I'm not asking you to fix the show, Mister Lyffe. I'm not my father."

Gunter took Barker's cigarette, breathing in a slow lungful. "But he has, I mean, your extended family must have some cash."

Barker leaned back, resting his shoulders on the wall. "I got myself into this mess. I will get myself out." He toed the patio again. "Winning the show's a chance to make the money I need as quickly as I need it."

Gunter handed back the cigarette, then joined Barker in leaning against the wall. "If you win, you won't have sufficient funds with which to launch."

Barker took another drag. "I'll have a little left over. Besides, there's no guarantee that winning the show will mean I make it as a designer. The best case is I win the show, pay off my debts, and make enough of an impact at Fashion Week to attract an investor."

Gunter crossed his arms. "They'll want a cut."

"Whatever it takes. I'm in it for the long game."

Gunter fell silent as he watched Sterling trundle around the garden. "That's possibly the ugliest dog I've ever seen."

"You haven't smelled him yet. He's got the digestion of a pensioner and he's only three. Shall we head back in?"

"We shall, but I don't know how you'll swing this."

Barker folded back the patio doors, and Sterling bounced past them both, heading for the kitchen. "Neither do I."

Gunter leaned across Barker, then closed the doors so the crew couldn't hear him. "I have a Plan B, if you're interested."

"I am."

"Kit."

Blood rushed in Barker's ears. This wasn't the coffee or the hunger. "You've spoken to him?"

"I understand he promised to help you in any way he could."

"You've spoken to Kit?"

Gunter took a step forwards. "He wants to make good on that promise."

Barker's thoughts swirled so quickly he struggled to follow them. If he accepted Kit's help, would he come here? Would he stay over? Would Bacchus put in cameras?

Gunter clicked his fingers to get Barker's attention. "No one knows about this, and they never can. My job is on the line."

"I wouldn't breathe a word."

"And you may not outsource over one third to him. It's only fair to the others. I'll understand if you decline, but from what I've seen in there, you won't finish in the time you have left. What should I tell him?"

Barker stood in silence, brain stumbling to a decision.

thirty-three
. . .

HANNAH BOUNCED into the kitchen wearing her Comic Con outfit, took one look at Kit sitting with Alex, then promptly bounced back out.

Unfazed, Alex wolfed a Jaffa Cake as if she hadn't already polished off a plate of cheesy nachos. "I'll say this, pet. Your latest collection's bang on, but you could have told us you'd hired another model. Who is he?"

"There's a *she* under that helmet. She's my new landlady—"

"And friend," came a muffled voice from the hallway.

"—and friend, Hannah."

When Hannah reappeared, she'd removed her helmet to reveal a very pink face. "Awkwardness abounds. Do excuse. Excited about finishing my costume and feeling showy-offy."

Kit sipped his tea and frowned at Hannah's costume. "What is it?"

Alex pilfered another Jaffa Cake. "It's an Evocore from *Dreadlife*."

A tiny, choked sound gurgled in Hannah's throat. "That's…

impressive. You overheard that from a younger brother, perhaps?"

The Jaffa Cake disintegrated between Alex's even rows of white teeth. "No, pet. It took me twenty hours of side quests to find that little bugger."

Hannah pulled out a chair, lowering herself into it so as not to damage her costume. "How many emblems are there to collect?"

"One hundred and sixteen."

"Alternate costumes?"

"Twelve." Alex popped another Jaffa Cake into her mouth.

"Vials of Chromablaze?"

"Thirteen."

Hands slamming on the table, Hannah stood. "Twelve! There are only twelve."

Alex plucked another cake from the packet. "Unless you travel to Mount Embertech during the Vengeance of Autonomy quest."

Hannah sat back in her chair. "Oh. You got them all?"

"Every single one."

"Shut up."

Alex smiled. "Make me, bitch." Another Jaffa Cake disappeared.

Hannah slapped Kit's arm. "Where did you find this woman?"

He rubbed the spot where she'd hit him. "Under a fire escape. You're stronger than you look."

"Is this some magical fire escape under which not-unattractive female gamers lurk?"

Kit groaned. "Alex, meet Hannah. Hannah, meet Alex. Me and Alex worked together on the show."

Hannah reached for a Jaffa Cake without taking her eyes off Alex. "You're a designer?"

"I'm a model."

Hannah's hand stopped shy of the plate. "You modelled Kit's white suit and did the sportswear challenge." She sat back. "I cannot, in all good faith, eat while you're in the room."

Alex picked the Jaffa Cake Hannah's eyes lingered over, then put it in her mouth. "No matter how much I eat, I can't seem to put weight on."

"Ugh. I kind of hate you right now."

"That's a shame," Alex said. "I was hoping to challenge you to a head-to-head."

"You're on, not-unattractive friend of my friend." Perking up, Hannah stood and gave them a twirl. "What's the verdict on my costume? Outstanding, right?"

Alex raised an eyebrow at Kit. "Do you want to be Shearsmith or shall I?"

"How about neither and my friend gets a fair trial?"

"He's no fun. I love it, pet. You look adorable."

"You see," Hannah said, pushing the plate aside so she could place her hands on the table. "'Adorable', although much appreciated, isn't exactly what I was going for."

"What were you going for?" Alex said.

Hannah leaned forward. "I was hoping for badass bitch."

Alex sat forward to meet her gaze. "Badass bitchery will need more spikes and sharper lines."

Hannah pulled Kit's sketchbook across the table. She tore off a corner of the last page. "Here's my Playstation user ID. Add me so we can indulge in a little arse-kickery when we're both online. But now I'm off to inject some of that aforementioned badass bitchery into my costume." Picking up her helmet, she stood. "Strong chat."

"Okay," Kit said as she put on her helmet and marched away. "Hang on."

Hannah's head poked back around the door. "What?"

"The seam on your tail's coming undone. I told you hot

glue isn't the way to go. I've got the right shade of cotton in my room if you want—"

Bottom lip jutted out, Hannah's chin dimpled. "I told you, I—"

"—to borrow it."

"What?"

"The cotton's there if you want to fix your tail."

Hannah lingered in the doorway. "Thanks. I'll go find it."

When her footsteps died away, Kit snatched the last Jaffa Cake out of Alex's hand. "What was that?"

"What?" Looking over his shoulder, she eyed the biscuit tin on the kitchen counter.

Kit pointed from the open doorway to Alex. "Some kind of lesbian mating ritual?"

"She's lesbian? Cool." Unable to reach the biscuit tin, Alex sat back then rubbed her flat stomach. "What's going on with you?"

"Hannah got me a job with her at Bacchus—freelance—until I can get back into tailoring."

"Is that not a conflict of interest, you being at Bacchus?"

Kit got the biscuit tin and plonked it between them. "Everyone's shitty to me, but I'm past caring, and they owe it me. The Southern bastards kicked me out without so much as a fair trial. The least I can do is take their money."

"I suppose that makes weird sense."

"What's going on with you?"

She stared at the biscuit tin for a long time. "I can't say."

"Come on, pet. Help me out."

"There's been this big production meeting."

"And—?"

"Gunter suggested another format change."

A spark of hope lit in Kit's chest. Gunter had promised he'd do what he could.

He tried to act disinterested while opening the tin. "What did he say, like?"

"Barker and Izzy are struggling to finish their collections. Gunter suggested they bring back a couple of eliminated designers to help them finish."

"And…?"

"Nancy's was having none of it."

Kit's resentment towards the head judge rushed back. His skin itched all over. Once again, Nancy had snatched an opportunity away from him. One day he'd come to terms with being kicked off the show, but any chance to see Barker, to try and convince him he was innocent…

Gunter failed, but he'd tried. Kit owed him for that.

As if she'd read his mind, Alex grabbed the biscuit tin. "Brian overruled Nancy."

Kit fought to breathe.

Alex thumped him on the back as though he was choking. "You wouldn't go back, would you? They might make you work with Barker. Knowing them, they'd pair you up for more fireworks."

The nightmare of having a camera stuck in their faces morphed into a daydream where they shut themselves away, worked out their differences, and made a lot more than fashion. "I can handle him."

"You keep telling yourself that, pet. How's your collection coming along?"

Kit wasn't interested in his collection. "Still sketching. Do you really think they'd put me with Barker?"

"I mean it, pet. Don't go back until Fashion Week. You two are never going to get along as long as you're up against each other."

When they weren't fighting, being up against Barker felt pretty good.

"Are you listening, Kit? I mean it."

Alex left, making a point of calling upstairs to say goodbye to Hannah who—no sooner had Kit closed the front door—reappeared to question him at length about her.

But Kit was somewhere else, behind a summer house in a quiet garden, a bedroom in moonlight during a powercut, crushed up in a doorway on a rainy day.

Unsatisfied with his absentminded answers, Hannah retreated to her room.

Kit tidied the kitchen to keep busy, to distract himself, to forget any hope that Gunter could help.

When his phone rang, the biscuit tin crashed to the floor.

"I'm sorry," Gunter said. "Barker said 'no'."

thirty-four

. . .

FIVE WEEKS LATER, Kit arrived at Store Studios for London Fashion Week.

Outside the entrance, Fay shouted at a huge security guard. "What do you mean, how do I spell my fucking name? It's F for *flange*, A for *arsehole*, and Y for... *chromosome*."

"I know her," Kit said, grateful to see a face he knew. "It's cool."

Fay poked the security guard in the chest. "See? I could do your job better than you."

The guard ticked off Fay's and Kit's names, standing aside to let them in.

"Sorry for fucking up your arm," Fay said, sliding her hand into his. "I've had some counselling. Gonna channel my anger into something a bit more productive than pintucks. Are we cool?"

Kit had better things to worry about. "No bother, pet. Have a good show."

Fay squeezed his face in her hand. "Love you, babes. Laters, yeah?"

Kit found the backstage area assigned to him. Three empty

rails waited for his collection, picked up the night before by courier. He psyched himself up for the day ahead. Whatever happened, and whoever he saw, he swore to keep his composure.

Two makeup artists wandered past, drinks steaming in their hands, the waft of strong coffee and vape juice threatening to bring up Kit's crispy bacon sandwich.

One took a drag on his vape stick, then blew out a sickly sweet haze. "I said to her, I said, 'Your models rock up covered in glitter and I'm supposed to get them in a smoky eye and nude lip in ten bloody minutes?'"

"That's nothing," said the other. "I did a shoot in a park in Milan. Try blushing Cara Delevingne when you're being chased by bees. I resorted to a can of hairspray and a lighter."

"To blush Cara?"

"No, to torch bees."

Barker hadn't wanted Kit's help. Gunter had failed. Had he really tried, or had it been a ploy for Kit to leave him alone? Either way, Kit hadn't seen Barker unless he counted that time Hannah was out, and he watched an episode of Tabitha Frost's *Coming Undone*. A montage of series highlights included Fay's meltdown and extended footage of Kit's fall from grace. He should have switched over, but the footage of Barker smoking alone on the patio, Barker shouting at Aden, and Barker lying wide awake in bed, pinned Kit to his seat for the full hour. By the end of the episode, Kit went through a box of tissues and both shirtsleeves.

Kit wandered Store Studios, glimpsing other contestants organising their shows—hanging and steaming garments, fitting models, making last-minute adjustments—but he hesitated to approach. This wasn't the time for a catch up. He marvelled at the collections of the greatest designers in the world: Westwood; Givenchy; Chanel. Who was Kit to be here?

To his relief, Bacchus provided dressers and male models.

When Kit returned to his rails, two dressers unpacked his freshly delivered collection. He caught wide-eyed looks between them. They didn't like his designs.

His limbs ached with fatigue. An entire night of preparation, and for what? For a show that maintained secrecy until ready to reveal its finalists and winner. Until then, another day of humiliation stretched ahead.

No sign of Barker. Gunter's unprecedented move to save him from elimination using his 'Lyffe Line,' meaning three finalists instead of two, caused a media frenzy.

The backstage manager, a woman in a—surprise, surprise—black jumpsuit and designer trainers, called for Izzy, then lined up her models. Izzy, who stood in the opposite wing with Bruna, blew Kit a kiss.

He wanted to cry.

The *Runways Rivals* theme tune boomed around the space. Bruna, microphone in hand, hopped up onto the catwalk.

"Welcome to the *Runway Rivals* finale. May I introduce our judges? Founder and editor of *Shear Style* magazine Nancy Shearsmith." Steady applause. "*Shear Style* fashion editor Osred East." Muted applause. "And our guest judges, singer and activist Vonnie Valero." Tremendous applause. "And Marco Blue." Nothing. "Last but not least, our mentor Gunter Lyffe." Wild cheers and whistles. "Our designers have been waiting for this day their entire careers. What do you say? Shall we start the show?"

Bruna reappeared backstage, handing the microphone to Izzy. Seconds later, Izzy's nervous voice echoed through the room. "Hello, everyone. My name is Izzy Bowers. I'm from here in London, and my collection is inspired by this beautiful city. It's called 'Come As You Are'. Also, it's my birthday." Applause. "I'd like to thank my mother, who's in the audience, for all her support in getting me to this moment. I love you, Mum. Enjoy."

Izzy came off the catwalk on Kit's side of the stage and rushed to hug him. "I've missed you so much. How are you? No one believes what happened. Are you showing after me? You look tired. Let's go to makeup."

Kit drew back, fighting tears. He'd never appreciated what a wonderful friend Izzy had been. "I missed you, too. I'm a mess, I didn't do it, my show's next, I've been up all night, and there's no time for makeup. But never mind me. This is your show. Enjoy it." Hands on her shoulders, he spun her around to face a huge monitor showing a live feed from the catwalk.

The closest thing Kit could call Izzy's collection was 'street couture'. Beiges, greys, and hot pinks. Shorts, dresses, knee-length trainers. "I love it," he said. "Those shorts are amazing."

"I only made them yesterday. I'd made cigarette pants and Nancy tore them apart during the pre-show appraisal. *Literally tore them apart.*"

"Once a bitch."

Izzy didn't take her eye off the monitor. "She exploded when Gunter saved Barker. Almost melted her jewellery."

They hadn't shown that on TV.

At the end of her show, Izzy joined her models on the catwalk, then took a bow. Whoops and cheers rose from the audience.

Mukta jostled her way through Kit's male models, then leapt between him and Izzy. "That was beautiful, Izzy. And Kit! I'm so excited I could scream."

When the music changed into Kit's opening, he let out a shaky groan. Anxiety deadened his mind and body. He grasped a strut holding up the wall on that side of the catwalk, the metal's cold shivering up his arm. He turned to the girls.

They spoke as one. "You can do this."

Could he? He tugged on his jacket. Everything moved in

slow motion, the backstage area spun, his models gathered around him, blurred bodies waving in his vision.

Izzy handed him the microphone.

His applause was polite at most. The show hadn't explained his departure in full, but people weren't stupid.

"Hello. I'm Kit Redman. My collection..." A sea of blank faces looked back at him, each one a spotlight of expectation. He rubbed his thigh. *You can do this.* "I called my collection 'Deconstruction'. It's inspired by the love we find and the love we've lost and—" He met Gunter's eye. The mentor's lips set in a grim line. "—it's for someone I failed. Thank you."

When he stepped down, he addressed his line of models, voice steady. "Ready, lads? Go give them a show."

One by one, the men took to the catwalk. The first outfit, a traditional suit and umbrella which everyone expected morphed, look by look, to narrow strips of fabric—only the seams of suits and nothing more. The last outfit was nothing more than black string over a white shirt.

Like Izzy, Kit joined his models. When he arrived at the end of the catwalk to take a bow, no one made a sound.

Kit froze. Just like Sonia's dress, he'd dragged the designs out of him. But it wasn't that bad, was it? Didn't anyone understand? The audience's faces blurred, snapping back into focus when someone grabbed him from behind to stop him falling off the catwalk.

"Hey," the model said. "It's all right. Let's get you backstage."

Halfway down the catwalk, Nancy and Osred sat together. Nancy caught Kit's eyes, then whispered something to Osred, who roared with laughter.

Gunter's seat was empty.

With the remaining contestants' shows to go, the backstage area was still chaos. The woman in the black jumpsuit ushered Kit's models away to hair and makeup for their next show.

The model who helped Kit offstage, gave him a quick hug. "Ignore them, all right? It was a wonderful collection." He shook Kit's hand. "Name's Olly. See you around, Kit, and don't give up."

Alex appeared, eyes narrowed, until she spotted Kit and hauled him to a running order pinned on a black curtain. "I'm in Aden's show next. As long as it's not Emilia's. Go get yourself some Champers and watch the last few shows. We'll grab a burger later."

"I brought Jaffa Cakes."

She kissed him full on the mouth. "If you had a fanny, I'd marry you. See you later, pet."

Champagne wouldn't sit well in his stomach, so he grabbed a bottle of water and found a spot next to Izzy in front of the monitor.

She held his hand, her eyes as bright as Nancy's jewellery. "Whatever happens, no one can take this away from us. We've shown at London Fashion Week."

Fay's show, a modern twist on a floaty, floral collection would have made any finalist proud.

Aden's show followed, as bombastic as the lad himself. Metal rings tethered to beaded column dresses undulated in time to his soundtrack.

Fay rocked up, beer in hand. "Brace yourselves—Bitchwhore's up next."

The music and lights faded. Pitch black. Deathly quiet. When a spotlight winked on, a lone woman stood holding a violin.

Kit squinted at the monitor. "That's not Emila."

Aden joined them to watch the show, gently nudging Kit with his shoulder. "God forbid Emilia should do the same and introduce her show."

The model raised her bow with a flourish and played. Mournful sound rose from the catwalk and filled the studio.

When she finished, a pulsing beat shook the audience in their seats. The violinist played to the soundtrack, strutting along the catwalk, her low-neck, sleeveless dress looming behind like some floral spectre.

Izzy's hand went to her mouth. "Christ Almighty."

The next model also held a violin, playing along with the first, her dress even more dramatic—brocade bustier, tulle skirt catching the air, unfurling into a seven foot train.

The camera cut to Nancy and Osred, who scribbled in their notebooks. Kit's heart sank. *Please don't let Emilia win.*

By the time Emilia's show drew to a close, twenty-one models played their violins towards a crescendo so dramatic everyone leapt to their feet.

It would be a long time before Kit forgave Emilia for the way she'd treated him, but her show was spectacular.

Fay drained her beer. "Vile."

thirty-five

. . .

EMILIA DIDN'T JOIN Kit and the others at the monitor. Not that he cared. She'd been as nasty as Nancy. He wanted Izzy to win.

A familiar scent washed over him. Clean skin and leather. The compulsion to look over his shoulder crashed into a fear that froze him in place.

Nothing had changed. Barker didn't want his help. Barker didn't want him.

Kit's stomach churned. *Runway Rivals* took him from one uncomfortable place to another, and this was the most uncomfortable of all.

Crew dragged structures wrapped in swathes of calico onto the catwalk. Subdued lighting bathed each pale shape.

Barker, like Emilia, didn't introduce his show. His first model—tall, bespectacled, cropped brown hair—ambled down the catwalk, resplendent in a crimson mandarin collar blazer, black shirt unbuttoned to his chest, and black jeans. The model stopped at the halfway point, then raised a microphone to his mouth.

"Hello. I'm Barker Wareham."

Aden jabbed his finger at the screen and looked back at the rest of them. "What the fuck has he done to his hair?"

Barker addressed the judges, looking each one in the eye. "I don't like lies. Not my father's, not the press's, not the people who broke their promises." Acid rose in Kit's throat. "And I'm ashamed to tell you I'm the biggest liar of them all. I'm broke, and I'm homeless. I didn't trust anyone until one man saw through my lies and helped me see the truth. This collection is called 'Honesty, Always'. Thank you." Barker fumbled with the microphone as he walked offstage. When his eyes met Kit's he pushed his glasses up his nose, then disappeared into the crowd.

Fay tapped her empty beer bottle against the palm of the hand. "I'm taking that's you?" she said to Kit.

Barker's music, a reeling orchestral score, rose through the room before dissolving into the tinkling sounds of a music box.

Two boys ran onto the catwalk, identical twins, both fair. They ripped the calico off the structures: a throne at the back of the catwalk and a sewing machine table at the front. Each boy took a seat.

Izzy cleared her throat. "Since when does Barker do childrenswear?"

The next model, a woman, wove her way along the catwalk, making an elongated figure of eight around the boys. The boy at the sewing machine kept his head in his work, ignoring her. The boy on the throne gave her a dismissive wave.

The pattern on the dress caught Kit's eye—a mosaic of marbleised fabric pieced together on tulle. The pattern of Roman temple floors.

Models in organza and mousseline ball gowns followed, the fabric printed with inlaid stone effects floating around their bodies. Models in fitted jackets and crisp trousers joined them. Models in bra tops under sweeping leather coats cut to look like tiles joined the catwalk. Models in delicate bias dresses embroidered with roman numerals bolstered their number. The last model, draped in an impeccable white suit, took the last spot.

Izzy made a sound in the back of her throat. "That's extraordinary."

We've all got a little Roman in us.

Unable to form words, Kit dipped his chin, convinced Izzy would hear his racing heart if he opened his mouth. The detail on the dresses jolted his emotions. When he met Barker it would be like walking into a storm he might not escape.

The boys might have been clumsy, but the meaning stretched throughout Kit's entire body. The boys were both Barker—one judgemental, one hard working.

The music rose to a crescendo, dropping off with the lights except the one shining on the sewing machine. Stunned silence fell over the auditorium until Osred East jumped to his feet, yelled "Bravissimo!" then promptly burst into tears. Nancy tried to drag Osred back into his seat, but he shook her off. Everyone stood—Bruna, Vonnie, Marco, and Brian and Tabitha there in the second row. Everyone but Nancy.

Mukta cheered. "That was mental."

Kit wiped his face. It was the most heavy-handed, beautiful thing he'd ever seen.

A shaven-headed Barker hopped up onto the end of the catwalk, then took the machinist boy's hand. Together, they joined the boy on the throne and the woman in the white suit. All four took a bow.

Barker inclined his head in appreciation of the applause and, palms down, quietened the audience.

"The truth is, I've looked for easy ways out of my problems, much like my father did. One man taught me nothing but hard work gets us what we want. I want my fashion label and I want him. I don't know if I can have either, but I'll keep working until I do."

The remaining shows passed by in a blur. Pamela collected those who hadn't made the final, then led them out to waiting cars.

"Where are we going now?" Kit asked.

"Back to The May Fair for the afterparty. I'll join you later, after we finish filming the judge's deliberations."

Patrick pulled Pamela to his side. "But Barker won, right? You saw how the audience reacted?"

"It's not about theatre," Pamela said, exasperated. "It's about fashion."

Aden scowled. "Bollocks. It's about what makes good telly, and that was amazing."

Before the party got underway, Layla showed the five contestants into a small, private lounge. Impressive and elegant, assorted chairs littered the space—some comfortable and some upright with padded seats and carved backs. Country landscape paintings adorned the walls, and design books hunkered down on a large cherry-wood table.

Everyone drank Champagne and laughed over Emilia's horror the first time Fay wanted to get 'stuck into' it.

Mukta groaned. "If Emilia wins, there'll be no getting away from her. She'll be rubbing it in that she beat Izzy and Barker."

Aden drained his glass. "It'll be awful."

Fay gave his hand a sharp tap. "You don't think Izzy's in with a chance?"

"I love her, but she won't swing it."

"Don't ever, ever tell her that will you?" Mukta said. "Not even after the dust settles. Do you promise?"

Aden went still. "That I love her?"

"No, about her chances." She paused. "And… you love her?"

Cheeks and neck flushed, Aden dipped his chin, polished off his drink, then poured another.

Kit stared at the panelled wall in front of him. What would he say when he saw Barker? Tension and anxiety built while his mind emptied. The second hand of a black-framed wall clock lingered with every passing moment. He looked away, vowed not to check it again, then picked out a book. He scanned the same page three times, then checked the clock.

"How much longer are they going to be?" Aden said. "I'm bored."

A creak shifted Kit's eyes to the door.

Tabitha stepped in. "Oh, God, it's so exciting. They've just arrived back. The party's about to get going. Come through!"

Aden and Fay left first, followed by Mukta and Patrick. Kit stepped forward, but Tabitha stopped him.

"There's someone who'd like to see you," she said with a broad smile. "Wait here. I'll get them."

Kit paced the sea-green floor, then sat on the edge of a high-backed chair, hands on his knees.

Not knowing what to say to Barker might be a blessing. Whatever he said would be natural, assuming he could speak at all.

The door handle turned, and Kit leapt to his feet.

thirty-six

. . .

"I LOST."

When Barker rehearsed what he'd say when he saw Kit, "I lost" wasn't in the mix. It shamed him to say it and when Kit didn't react a mountain of pressure threatened to burst through his skull. But what shamed him more was the way he'd left things with Kit. The way he'd doubted him, asked for a confirmation of his innocence when Kit had the most integrity of all.

Instead of the reaction he expected, for Kit to fix him with his angry glittering eyes and tell him he deserved to lose, Kit stared at him like he'd produced a blue whale from his pocket.

"How?"

Barker relived the winner's announcement but couldn't get the words out. He ran a palm over his shaved head and, as much as he tried to hold it in, his disappointment came out as a low moan. Static buzzed in his head, a side-effect of the fear and stress he'd lived through the past eleven weeks. Longer, if he counted Ludo. The winner's announcement took something out of him he didn't know he had left.

In a second, Kit was across the room, arms around him. The

world blurred, melting away. Everything, gone. Barker gasped for absent air.

As Barker unravelled, the threads of every happy memory spooling away, Kit was there. He led him to the sofa, his arms holding Barker together. Anyone else would have left him to rot in his despair. Not Kit. Kit stayed with him, like the time he braved the storm of Barker's panic when the yellow dress ripped.

At last, Barker curled up against him. "I'm sorry for —for—"

"For losing?" Kit ran his hand over Barker's scalp. "Or for this?"

Barker smiled inside, albeit for a moment. "You saw right through me that first night when you came into the bathroom. The way you looked at my glasses. And later, when you called me a fake. Every time I looked in the mirror... I wanted to be real."

Kit stroked his head again. "It's like velvet."

"What am I going to do?" Barker took off his glasses, then pressed the side of his face against the gentle thump of Kit's chest.

"Like you said, you'll work hard and pay what you owe. Either that or we'll steal it off..."

We'll.

Kit's body stiffened. "Please tell us it was Izzy who won."

"I wish."

"I can't go out there," Kit said. "Emilia hates us. What did she do when they announced it?"

Barker sniffed. "She waved Izzy and me off the catwalk, whispering she could have beaten us in her sleep."

"Bitch by name..."

"They picked it up on mic and made her reshoot it." Barker curled deeper into Kit. "She didn't even want to win like I did. I thought I could do it."

Kit raised Barker's face to his, eyes glistening with tears. "You'll make it. We both will."

If Kit hadn't held Barker's head, it would have fallen back into his neck. "I couldn't help everyone with what I had."

"Help everyone?" Kit's eyebrows met. "That Caspian lad. I thought I overheard him say something about what you did for his family?"

Barker sat back and wiped his face. Could he ever move on from the loss his father caused? "Caspian's family was one of many my father persuaded to invest, and it all went wrong. When my trust fund matured, I had to do something."

"Trust fund?"

Pins and needles ran over Barker's scalp. *It was your money, not his.* "Four point two."

Kit did a double-take. "Million? You spent four point two million quid helping people? We all thought you'd pissed it up the wall or spent it on clothes."

"Only one-fifty."

Kit's mouth dropped. "'Only' one hundred and fifty thousand pounds on going out and shopping?" Kit edged away from him. "You said you owed about one hundred."

Where was he going with this? "Yes."

"So you spent one fifty out of four point two million on yourself? That's—" Kit counted on his fingers. "Three and a half percent on yourself. Another another hundred on credit? That's—" He counted again. "—six percent." Kit threw up his hands. "Why didn't you put everyone straight?"

Barker shuddered at all the faces running through his mind. "It wasn't only Caspian's family. I couldn't help everyone. I was in so deep and so fast, I couldn't risk word getting out. I tried to do the right thing. I did."

Kit didn't speak.

"Not like you, Kit. Right from the start, you helped me with my dress."

Kit reeled away. "Don't make me out to be some kind of angel. I helped you because you helped me… and I fancied you. It was nothing compared to what you've done."

All the times Kit compared himself to the others, all the times he found himself wanting. Barker wanted him most of all. "Kindness is kindness, Kit."

Kit leant his forehead against a panelled wall. "Kind people don't abandon their sick mam to go on telly. Nice people don't cut the power in the hope they'll get off with a cute lad. Nice people don't come back twice as hard when someone's horrible to them. Nice people don't—"

This wasn't happening. Not now. Barker ran to hold him, muscles tensed to hold him still. "Nice people make friends. Nice people get Fay to come out of the toilet when she's sobbing her heart out. Nice people stand by their word. Nice is good and honourable and everything I've ever wanted in someone."

Kit slumped back against Barker, body shaking. "And where did that get me?"

"You didn't get what you wanted, Kit, and neither did I, but maybe this will be the making of us both."

"There is no us." Pushing Barker off him, Kit covered his face with his hands.

Barker prized Kit's hands away, holding him by the chin, forcing eye contact. "I started falling for you the day we met and I still haven't hit the ground yet. Catch me."

Kit wiped his face, olive eyes wide, and made a sound like a choked laugh. "Did you get that out of a book?"

The tension snapped. Barker laughed, too. The suspended horror he'd willed to end collapsed around him. "I swear to God, as long as there's a heart beating in this chest, I'm willing to lose it to you."

Another laugh, but it was kind. "Where are you getting these lines from?"

Barker took Kit's face in his hands. "I want you in my life. Where's that on the cheesiness scale?"

"Two thousand, nine hundred, and ten."

He remembered. "I've got something for you." Barker reached into his jacket pocket, then drew out a small velvet bag.

Kit eyed the bag. "That's not a team leader token, is it? That'd kill my buzz."

"Please shut up and open it."

Kit pulled on the drawstring, then tipped the contents of the bag into his palm. Two gold cufflinks tumbled out. "Where...?"

"At our audition. I took these off to roll up your sleeves. With everything going on, I forgot to give them back to you. I've kept them ever since."

Eyes glistening, Kit rolled up his cuff to reveal buttercup yellow threads tied around his wrist. "I found them stuck to my shears."

The humble echoes of a late May afternoon sweetened Barker's memory. "Can I kiss you, Mister Redman?"

Squeezing Barker's hands, Kit surrendered his smile. "I started falling right along with you. How else could you drive me nuts?"

Barker's wiped a tear from Kit's cheek. "I let you down, didn't I, over your grandpa's photograph album?"

Kit's Geordie accent thickened with emotion. "Divven't worry, man. None of us is perfect." He touched Barker's neck. "Are you ever going to tell me what this tattoo's supposed to be?"

The soft panic of admitting the tattoo's meaning faded away. "A few months after my father's sentencing, I tried designing a tattoo. I wanted something inspirational, but I couldn't get there. Fuelled by wine and frustration, I scrawled it out with marker. And that was it, the perfect symbol of how I felt—of wanting to scratch myself out."

Pamela hammered on the door.

Barker rocked back, gesturing to the door. "She does a lot of that, doesn't she?"

When Kit kissed him again, the hammering in Barker's chest drowned her out.

thirty-seven
. . .

WHEN KIT OPENED THE DOOR, Pamela poked him in the chest. "For God's sake, it's The May Fair all over again. I need the pair of you out here for afterparty shots, although you both look a right old state." She rummaged in her pocket, then produced a small plastic bottle with a nozzle at one end. "Eye drops. Always carry them at the final. We had to go on without you for Emilia's speech."

"I'm proper gutted," Kit said, trying to sound like he gave a shit. "I was looking forward to it."

The acid in Emilia's voice cut through the babble. "Considering you're the size of a leprechaun, I'm surprised being green with envy doesn't suit you." She glared at him, the *Runway Rivals* trophy clutched in both hands. "I cannot believe you had the audacity to suggest I planted those sketches in your album. I'm too good a designer to sink to your diminutive level."

Kit gestured for Barker to go on with Pamela, who exchanged looks before stepping away. He needed to clear the air with Emilia, but he had to stay calm if it was going to work. "You're right. You won. This proves you're the best designer."

Emilia's mouth fell open in genuine surprise. Kit pulled on the hem of his jacket. "But you lost, too."

Her eyes searched his. "What on earth are you wittering on about?"

Kit controlled his breathing, forcing it into a steady rhythm. "You lost sight of the truth."

Emilia's left eye twitched. Blinking rapidly, she clutched the trophy to her chest. "What do you know about truth, you wretched little fraud?"

"Whatever people think about me, I know I'm honest. Do you?"

"I have no idea what you're talking about." Looking around, Emilia spotted Layla snogging the miserable cameraman. Emilia waved her over. "Layla, get your hands off that Carl and fetch me a makeup artist. This mascara's playing havoc with my eye." Layla disappeared into the crowd. "Now," Emilia continued, "where were we?"

"You're sad and scared and lonely like the rest of us, but you won't admit it."

"Oh, you poor, poor thing. Is that what this is all about? You're jealous of me because I'm still friends with Barker and you're on the scrapheap?"

Kit closed his eyes, positivity flowing through him. "I'm trying to help you. I mean it. Your father put you in that school to get close to Barker, put it in your head you could marry him. He made you believe it was your right."

"How dare you."

"It was the easiest way to be accepted by the old money."

Emilia's ponytail swished as she looked for Layla. "Nonsense. Daddy would never do that."

"Barker cares for you in his own way, but it'll never happen, Emilia."

"Don't you ever—"

Behind the Seams

"He's sorry for you, and you're sorry for yourself. You just have to be honest about it."

Emilia sagged, back bowed. Kit strained to hear her over the chattering crowd. "Daddy's never forgiven me."

"You can't force him to be straight." Kit reached for her arm, but she flinched away. "And you can't get rid of the competition so you can try."

Emilia shielded herself with the trophy. "I had nothing to do with that photograph album."

Something puzzled Kit about Emilia's gait, as though she struggled to hold an uneven weight. "What? I wasn't talking about the album."

"You need to get used to losing," she said, easing towards her full height but falling short.

"Why did you bring up the album?"

"Shut up." Emilia's head snapped from side to side. "Layla!"

"What did you do?"

"Shut your mouth."

"Tell me, Emilia. What did you do?"

Brian Foster charged through the crowd, followed by Aden and Patrick. "What's going on?"

Without warning, Emilia spat in Kit's face. "You disgusting little queer. Putting sketches in the album wasn't enough. It should have been anthrax."

Emilia screeched, then a sudden snap of pain jolted across Kit's face. He staggered sideways, then crashed to the floor. Emilia stood over him, eyes blazing, one hand returning to her side.

Brian grabbed her by the arms.

Aden helped Kit to his feet. "I knew it. I never believed you'd cheat."

Pamela and Tabitha swept into view, a security guard and a cameraman in hot pursuit. "What's happening here?"

Aden prodded Emilia's shoulder. "This bitch fucked Kit over. She admitted it and attacked him."

Tabitha waved wildly at her cameraman to record.

"I did not."

"But you struck him?" Tabitha said, ramming a microphone into Emilia's face.

"He was so vile, I had to."

Pamela examined Kit's face, her expression sour. "I'm sorry, Miss Winchmore, but we must disqualify you for breach of the rules." The crowd mumbled in hushed tones.

"That makes—" Pamela scanned the crowd. "Where the buggery bollocks are they?"

Barker leant against the wall by the emergency exit and tapped out the last cigarette in his packet. Perhaps the money he'd make from a few magazine interviews would help him keep up his credit card repayments until he found a job. If it came to it, he'd swallow his pride and ask his grandparents for the rest, but that would be the last resort. His mother didn't need any more stress. Besides, he'd still have to pay them back.

How long would it take to earn the money and still live? If it wasn't too soon, he could suggest he and Kit find somewhere cheap to stay and they'd save a ton of money if they only ate toast. Someone in the audience might offer him a job. He should go back in, find Kit, and work the room together, but right now he would enjoy the hell out of his last cigarette.

A girl wandered past, sweating profusely in a fancy dress outfit. The girl with her caught his attention.

"Alex?"

Alex blushed. She and the girl held hands. "Hi, Barker. We got—delayed. Where's Kit? Are they having to tear him off Emilia's bleeding body?"

The girl with her laughed. "He wouldn't go that far. He's feisty, but that's not his style."

Barker cocked his head. "You know Kit, too?"

"I'm Kit's friend, Hannah. You're Barker. I've seen, and heard, a lot."

"In that case, you're not a fan."

"I wasn't. I was. I wasn't."

"And now?"

Hannah raised her free hand and tilted it from side to side. "You know."

The emergency doors smashed open, then Fay rocketed out onto the pavement. She looked at Hannah in such confusion, it took her a moment to spot Alex and Barker. "Emilia's lost it and gone for Kit."

Barker's cigarette dropped from his fingers. His thoughts scattered, beads tipped on a polished floor.

He ran back inside after Fay, gesturing for Hannah to follow. "Don't just stand there. We might need a—whatever you are."

They hurtled along the corridor only to be met by two security men carrying a thrashing Emilia.

"It wasn't only me," she howled at Barker as the men dragged her around a corner out of sight. "It wasn't."

"The patterns in Kit's album," Fay said as they sprinted ahead. "She did it. Admitted it when she went for him."

Pamela and Layla appeared at the end of the corridor. "Barker," Pamela said. "We need you."

"And I don't give a shit," Barker said. "Where's Kit?"

"He'll be fine. Now, pull yourself together and follow me." She looked Hannah up and down. "Whose collection are you wearing?"

A weak smile crept onto Hannah's face. "I'm not a model. I'm a friend of Kit's."

Pamela whimpered in something like defeat. "Layla will take you to see him. He's with the first-aider."

Alex stepped in front of Layla before she could get to Hannah. "I know where it is, pet. I'll take her."

Barker gave Alex a quick hug, then patted Hannah's head. Hannah gave him an unimpressed grimace.

"Look after him, okay?" Barker said to Hannah. "I don't know what's going on, but I'll be back as soon as I can. Don't let them take Kit anywhere without me."

thirty-eight
. . .

BARKER FOLLOWED Pamela back to the party. Why bring him here when he should be with Kit? The gabbling crowd fell silent when they saw him, anticipation in every face. He'd already lost. How worse could it get?

Then Mukta gave him the thumbs-up from where she stood alongside a grinning Izzy.

Pamela led him to the front of the room where Brian Foster stood, expression hard.

A camera with a built-in light closed in on him. Barker raised a hand to shield his face from the glare. "What's going on?" he said to Brian.

"Emilia's attack contravened our zero tolerance policy against violence," Brian said, brusque as ever.

Barker cocked his head at the big man. "You have a lot of zero tolerance policies, don't you?"

"And rightly so. Emilia's in serious trouble, and I'm reporting her for assault."

"Speech," someone called from the back of the room.

Barker looked around at the expectant crowd. "Why would I make a speech about Emilia?"

"She admitted to putting the doctored album under Kit's bed. The birthday present Layla delivered was not the dress Emilia wore later, but Kit's album."

"And—?"

"Both Emilia and Layla admitted to being in cahoots since day one. With the help of her boyfriend Carl, Layla erased the footage of Emilia entering Kit's room to place the album under his bed. I've sacked them with immediate effect. Emilia is disqualified."

Gunter joined them, pressing the trophy into Barker's hands. "That makes you our series seven winner."

It took a second for Gunter's words to sink in.

"What about Izzy?" Barker said, look back at her and Mukta.

"Come on, Barker," Izzy called, cupping her hands around her mouth. "You smashed it."

Gunter nodded. "You really did."

The trophy, heavier than it looked, kept him from floating away. Barker let the happiness soak into him, closing his eyes, savouring the beams of joy snuffing out his loss and shame and doubt. He'd done it. He'd won.

When he raised the trophy above his head, the room exploded with applause.

Mukta's voice soared over the noise. "Speech." The entire room took up the chant.

Barker climbed onto a chair. "Foremost, can someone please get Kit?"

Pamela hurried back the way they'd come.

Every face mirrored Barker's happiness. He loosened his grip on the trophy. "I'd like to say thank you."

Aden shouted from where he'd joined Izzy. "Why? Because we lost?"

"Something like that. But it's for you, I mean, everyone who took part. It wasn't easy. It, uh, wasn't anybody's idea of fun. And for you lot in Bacchus Broadcasting, thanks for looking after us, and, you know, waving cameras in our faces at inopportune moments."

Aden raised his glass. "And something else, when Kit cut the power."

Izzy covered her eyes when people looked over and whooped.

Flanked by Alex and Hannah, Kit came in through a side door. His swollen face bore a lopsided smile and the thumbs-up he gave Barker said he was okay.

Barker winked down at Aden. "Busted, although nothing's been waved yet."

Kit echoed Izzy's embarrassment, and eyes moved from her to him. "Haddaway, man."

"I'd like to thank Gunter, the best mentor a designer could ask for. We must have been the liveliest bunch of designers you've ever had to deal with. Thank you for your patience and understanding. You taught me more than fashion. You taught me what matters in the world. Everyone needs a Gunter." A cheer went up from everyone.

Gunter pressed his lips together and dabbed his eyes with a handkerchief.

"Everyone in this room, from the judges to the crew, personifies hard work and dedication. Congratulations to every one of you for a job well done."

Pamela waved at him. "Oh, darling, you don't have to thank us."

Aden squeezed past her, Izzy in tow. "Can I say something?"

"Go on."

Aden dropped to one knee, and the room fell silent. "Izzy Bowers. You might not have won the show, but you've won my heart. Will you marry me?"

Izzy's hand flew up, one to her chest, one to her mouth. The assembled crowd caught their breath.

"No, I bloody won't," she yelled. "Get up and stop playing to the camera."

Aden's mouth slackened. "But I love you."

"After three months? Don't be ridiculous."

Voice trembling, Aden lowered himself onto both knees. "Are you breaking up with me?"

"For Heaven's sake, we're not at school. We date like normal people and see where it goes."

Barker jumped down from his chair to join them. "That's what we're going to do."

Barker pulled Aden to his feet, then gave him and Izzy a hug.

"Sounds like a spinoff to me," Fay called to Pamela and Tabitha. "*Izzy Or Isn't She?*"

When Aden's head snapped around to gauge Pamela's reaction, Izzy groaned. "Don't encourage him."

thirty-nine
. . .

GRATEFUL FOR THE attention moving back to Izzy and Aden, Kit looked for an escape route. He wanted was to be alone with Barker and snog the face off him. A door at the back of the room offered an opportunity to slip out. He caught Barker's eye, then shouldered the door open.

"Not so fast." Gunter slipped between them, then stopped in the doorway. Kit stood inside the room, but Gunter blocked Barker from entering. "What was that, Kit?" he said, brow gathered in a frown. "A superb collection could have given you opportunities."

Head down, Kit shifted his weight, a naughty schoolboy in the headmaster's office. "Nothing spoke to me."

"Design is the same as tailoring, Kit. You don't wait for inspiration to strike. You turn up every day and work at it."

Barker coughed, as though to remind Gunter who stood behind him. "Kit doesn't joke about work."

Nancy squeezed past Barker and Gunter, then strolled into the room.

"Nancy has something she'd like to say," Gunter said, his expression softening in something like—satisfaction? Nancy glared at him. He nudged her forward with an elbow, then let Barker into the room. Gunter closed the door behind them, leaving the four of them alone. "Go ahead, Nancy."

Nancy splayed the fingers of her left hand, checking her nails.

Gunter raised his voice. "Nancy..."

"All right, all right." Her attention turned to Barker. "That was the best collection I've seen since McQueen's two thousand and nine Autumn Winter."

Barker's jaw set hard. "So why didn't I win straight off the bat?"

Nancy sighed. "Emilia's was better."

"Bullshit," Barker said.

"I knew it from the start." Nancy raised her chin. "I said it myself at the audition. If I could mix your DNA with each other, I'd achieve perfection." She adjusted a ruby bracelet clinging to her wrist. "Both you, Mister Wareham, and you, Mister Redman, showed impressive levels of design and construction. There's nothing in the rules preventing you from outsourcing work for free, Mister Wareham. There will be next year. Outsourcing to Mister Redman proved fruitful."

Barker moved to stand next to Kit. "I didn't. Kit offered, but I refused. I was determined to prove I could sew."

Nancy squinted at Kit. "Really?"

Kit shrugged. "It's true."

"Hard to believe."

Barker cut in. "It is true. I made that collection myself. All of it. I didn't sleep until my shears came alive and told me I could make pinstripe puppies out of magic coffee beans."

Nancy tilted her head to one side. "Exhaustion can do that to a designer..."

Gunter tutted. "For pity's sake, Nancy. Spit it out."

"All right." She looked at the ceiling as she spoke. "I've decided you're worthy of investment."

This wasn't making sense. She'd gunned for Barker as much as she had Kit, dismissing them as designers and tearing them down at every critique. Now she wanted to invest?

"Why?" Kit said.

Nancy gave him an exasperated groan. "I've been toying with creating a fashion house, but time and talent are in short supply. With Barker as Creative Director and Kit as Head of Garment Technology, the fashion industry would sit up and take notice. What do you say?"

Kit must have tripped coming down the stairs and bumped his head. This had to be a dream; he couldn't speak. "Me? I wouldn't work for you in a—"

Barker squeezed his hand. "That's very generous, Miss Shearsmith, but we're launching our own label."

"You are?" Gunter said.

Kit squinted up at Barker. "We—are?"

"We are. RedWare."

Gunter beamed. "From your surnames? I like it."

Nancy jutted out her bottom lip. "I suppose that could work as a *Shear Style* sub-label."

Barker sucked air in through his teeth. "Still not loving the idea. Kit?"

As much as Kit wanted to be the bigger person to impress Barker, he wanted to cut Nancy down to size. *I have very little confidence that you're the investor we're looking for.* He stayed silent.

Nancy appeared to take Kit's lack of response as a refusal and started back towards the door.

Kit stepped forward. "That doesn't mean we can't come to some beneficial agreement."

Nancy stopped, looked over her shoulder. "Such as?"

"You introduce us to other investors. If they work out, we give you exclusive coverage of all forthcoming collections."

Gunter lowered his voice. "Nancy."

She leaped back in time to avoid Osred barging into the room.

"I can photograph the shit out of this," he said, beckoning three models to follow him into the room. The first wore a dress of marbleised fabric on tulle, the second wore a bra top under a sweeping leather coat, and the third wore an impeccable white suit.

"Look at it," Osred said, standing back to let Nancy see. "It's begging for an editorial."

Nancy looked from Kit to Barker and back again. "Exclusive? All the time we need to shoot the collections and exclusive rights on the images? No other press at your shows? No social media?"

It might be a deal with the devil, but as an investor, Nancy couldn't call the shots. "Fine with me."

For the first time since their auditions, Nancy's expression softened. Smiling at them both, she took their hands in hers. "Barker? Kit? I can't wait to see what you do next."

Kit doubted Nancy wanted to see what he'd be doing with Barker next.

Barker smiled as though he'd read his mind, but he kept his eyes on Nancy. "It will blow your mind."

Barker lost track of the time somewhere after the third bottle of Champagne. When he and Kit stumbled out onto the pavement, sunrise coppered the horizon, threading it through with silver and gold. As Barker watched, the rising sun turned buttercup yellow.

Kit slumped against him. "Remind you of anything?"

Barker kissed the top of Kit's head, then wiped his mouth. "Maybe we should find you a different hair product?"

Marco Blue bounded over, eyes so bright he must have

taken something. "I'm launching a fresh line of hair products next season. Maybe we should team up?"

Eyelids heavy, Kit peered at Marco. "Are you propositioning my husband?"

Unexpected. Barker held Kit close. "Husband?"

Kit patted his chest. "Shush now, future husband. I'm talking to this one."

Barker helped Kit to stand on his own. "Let's take a raincheck on that, Marco."

Looking Barker over, Marco pouted. "If I'd have known there were studs like you at LUCA, I'd have studied fashion, not business."

Kit gave Marco the finger. "You and me both."

Barker guided Kit away from the crowd forming on the pavement, then steered him into a quiet doorway. Pressing their bodies together, he kissed Kit's mouth, giving him a preview of things to come. "Do you know, sometimes it takes a guy to fit properly."

Kit grumbled something unintelligible, then kissed him back. "Bespoke or off the peg?"

"Either works, although the latter might need a few adjustments." He played with Kit's belt buckle. "Once some seams have been unpicked."

"This meta—thingy," Kit slurred.

"Metaphor."

Thumping Barker's chest with a weak fist, Kit's shook his head. "Not working, is it?"

Barker smiled into Kit's hair. "Not at all, and I was going for something spectacularly profound and romantic." A familiar black BMW pulled up. Its passenger window slid down, the driver beckoning for Barker and Kit to get in. "Our car's here. Do you want a minute to say goodbye to anybody?"

"And miss another minute I could spend getting your kit

off? No chance." Kit tottered towards the car. "We'll see them soon. I've offered them jobs at RedWare."

God help us. "Come on, Mister Redman. Let's make—"

"Love!" Kit cried out, fumbling with the car door.

"If you're up to it. After, we make fashion."

Kit tugged on the doorhandle. "You design it. I make it."

Giving the handle a sharp pull, the car door flew open. A couple tumbled out onto the pavement.

Barker jumped back. "Nancy?" Her poker straight hair stuck out in all directions.

Kit sobered as the man who'd landed on top of Nancy stood and dusted himself off. "David?"

"There you are." David gave Kit an unsteady hug. "I was telling Nance how hard it was to let you go from Stitchworthy."

"Nance?"

From where she lay on the pavement, Nancy clutched at David's trouser leg. "Help me up, you fool."

David hauled her to her feet. "Nance and I go way back. Carnaby Street, nineteen sixty—"

Patting his arm, Nancy rearranged her hair. "They don't need dates, darling."

Alex called out from the crowd where she stood with an arm around Hannah. "I can see your knickers, 'Nance'."

Kit steadied himself on the car door. "I need to sit. It's like I walked in on my old life and my new life shagging."

"Doubtful," Alex called again. "She's wearing Spanx. It'll be tomorrow before he gets her knickers off."

Gunter sailed to Barker's rescue, bundling everyone away from the car. When he returned, he helped Barker get Kit into the back seat. "Go home, the pair of you. You must be exhausted."

Kit fell onto his side, eyes closed. "I can't sleep. I'm too excited."

Barker climbed in, then stroked Kit's side. "Shush now. You'll be fast asleep in a minute."

Kit woke in the afternoon, rolling over to cuddle the man next to him. Six foot two. Forty-inch chest, thirty-inch waist, thirty-four-inch inside leg. Handsome face, nothing fussy. Two faint lines across the brow, freckles above his cheekbones and over the bridge of his nose, and the hint of a cleft chin. Cropped hair and pale skin.

The man's eyes opened. Sharkskin grey. Kit promised himself they'd design RedWare's first collection on that colour. The man caught Kit's eye. He smiled.

And Kit couldn't help but smile back.

forty

. . .

BARTY RIBBLESTONE CLIMBED out of the taxi, then straightened his clothes.

He'd pored over his wardrobe for a week before settling on what to wear: white t-shirt; patchwork, Cuban collar shirt; and high-waisted, pin-rolled chinos.

This was it. He strode across the pavement, pushed on the glass doors, then froze. Reception stood empty save for a lone receptionist speaking on the telephone.

Mid-conversation, she noticed him and held up a finger. *One minute.*

Barty sank into a scarlet leather sofa, taking in grey walls and mirrored pillars. Framed blowups of this season's collection adorned each wall: airy, experimental pieces with a workwear aesthetic blended with tailored, wrap-fronted blazers and slouchy trousers.

The receptionist coughed to get his attention, then beckoned him over. "Welcome to RedWare, Mister Ribblestone. I believe this is your first day."

Despite the cool September morning, and generous air-conditioning, the skin on Barty's back tingled with perspiration. "I'm on the apprentice scheme."

"I'm pleased to welcome you. Mister Redman is already on his way."

"He is?"

"He cleared his calendar for you." She handed him a small rectangle of plastic attached to a scarlet lanyard. "This is your security pass. Keep it safe. If you lose it, you'll face the wrath of Miss Fairfield."

He knew that name "Fay Fairfield?"

"Fay Fairfield is our head of security. Her bite is worse than her bark, so mind your manners."

Kit Redman jogged down a flight of stairs and hugged him. "Bartholomew."

"Barty, please."

When Kit pulled out of the hug, he held Barty by the shoulders. "Not 'Barty the Third'?"

"Please, no. I hate all of that. Thank you for giving me this opportunity. I promise I won't disappoint you."

"We're lucky to have you." Kit took a step back, looking him over. "You look the part. I see you had a growth spurt."

"Yes, I'm—"

"Five foot six, thirty-four-inch chest, twenty-six-inch waist, twenty-eight-inch inside leg."

"That's amazing."

Kit lifted a shoe and tapped the heel. "What's amazing are stacked heels and shoe risers. I'm a towering five foot five in these. I get them from the guy who made Prince's shoes." He dropped his foot, then tugged on the hem of his jacket. "I suppose I'd better give you the tour."

Barty followed him up the stairs to a rabbit warren of spaces painted bright white. Full height windows flooded each space with light. Rows of small sewing tables lined the walls.

Quiet, focused people worked on their different garments. Some cut, some stitched, and some pressed.

Kit whispered, all theatre. "Best talent in the world, this lot. Don't tell them." Everyone in the room looked up and smiled. "It's London Fashion Week next week, so it's all go, but this is where we'll start you off."

Barty paused at a dress form by the door. A sheer grey dress clung to the form.

A smile creased Kit's eyes. "No matter what the colour trends are, I insist we make one garment a year in sharkskin grey."

"The colour's amazing."

"You have excellent taste."

"What is it?"

"It's Vonnie Valero's wedding dress. Any other questions?"

Barty gazed around the room, looking for the rest of the equipment. "No sewing machines?"

"We make everything by hand. Shears, pins, and a needle and thread. That's all you need."

A dark-haired teenage boy chuckled to himself. "And a lot of time. What the average, Kit? Three hundred hours?"

Kit smiled, his lips a grim line. "Halton, meet Barty. Barty, meet Halton."

The boy shook Barty's hand, warm and rough from his work. "Please to meet you. I'm Halton Winchmore."

Barty hesitated. "As in *Emilia* Winchmore?"

Halton eyebrows raised for a second. "Don't let her infamy cloud your judgement. We're poles apart. You'll probably meet her later."

"She works here?" Barty said, swallowing hard.

"No," Halton said. "She failed the police record checks, but she's in the building, so watch your back."

Kit bobbed his head. "He's right. Halton's just graduated

from our apprentice program. He'll be your buddy and help you settle in, but I'm doing your tour. Onwards."

Barty trotted out of the room at Kit's side. "So, why no sewing machines?"

"I hate the things. I have a soft spot for antique Singers, but anything modern makes me want to hurl. Each technician works on one garment from conception to catwalk. We make our clothes with love, so people don't mind the long hours."

"How long?"

"In the run up to a Fashion Week, we can be here until ten o'clock if Barker wants alterations." Kit stopped at a door with the sign *Atelier Renos*. "Are you ready to meet one of our *première tailleur ateliers*?"

"A what?"

Kit grinned. "I know it's a mouthful, but he likes it. Renos has twenty-four staff, so I guess it's only fair he has a twenty-four letter title."

A well-groomed, big-bellied man rounded a corner, a pale blue dress in his meaty hands. He scowled when he saw Kit, his face crumpling. "To bloody hells with your man. Second time he see this dress and he want more changes. Should have asked when he saw bloody *toile*." He noticed Barty. "This the new one?"

Kit gave Barty a nudge forward, and Barty held out a hand, waiting for Renos to gather the dress over his left arm so he could do the same. "It's an honour, Mister Savva."

Renos poked out his lower lip. "I'm impressed. You know my work?"

"You don't remember me? I came to visit Stitchworthy when I was little."

"You're still little."

Kit straightened. "Renos…"

"Sorry. Sorry. Go on."

"You went to Chanel after Stitchworthy," Barty said.

"Which then became a sub-label of Nancy Shearsmith's *Shear Style* fashion label. From Savile Row tailor to Chanel to RedWare. Quite the pedigree."

Grinning proudly, Renos opened the door to his office, then going inside. "You tell Kit he needs to give you a raise."

"It's his first day," Kit said, following Renos into his office and beckoning Barty to follow.

"So?" Renos placed the dress on his desk. "Take no notice of what I said about him upstairs. He still lose his temper from time to time, but he wants things right. That's how it should be. Every line of every sketch means something. Every detail. Pay attention to them. Pay attention to me. Who his buddy?"

"Halton," Kit said.

"Pay attention to him. He best apprentice we have in long time. Reminds me of Kit when he was your age."

"I was eighteen, Renos. Barty is sixteen."

"Good. No time to learn bad habits. You shown him the *flou*?"

"Later. I want him to meet Barker first."

"He's in a mood."

"I can handle him." Kit strode out of the room and along a corridor to another staircase. "Questions?"

"What's a *flou* and who's the other *première*?"

"I'm the other one, although I prefer the term 'tailor', and the *flou* is mine. It's where we make the delicate stuff. After you've served your time with Halton and the others, I'll move you in with me."

Barty looked back down the corridor. "Where's your office?"

Kit sat on the second step of the staircase, patting the step for Barty to join him. "I don't have an office. I enjoy being with my team. How are you doing?"

"Great. It's interesting."

"No, Barty." Kit rubbed the back of his neck. "How have you been since the funeral?"

The question came out of the blue. Barty tried to stop the water pooling in his eyes. "Fine."

"I was twenty when I lost my grandpa."

"He was everything to me."

Kit's arm wrapped around Barty's shoulders. "The Barty I knew was a kind man, and he thought the world of you. He told me. If you ever need to talk to anyone, you can talk to me. Okay?"

Barty dabbed his eyes with the back of his wrist. "That Renos is a character."

"He's Greek, man. It's all passion and devotion. Works all the hours God sends unless his boyfriend can drag him away. I fancy a cuppa. Come on."

Upstairs reflected the same decor as reception, but with many more mirrors.

"Teas and coffees are up here," Kit said. "Barker wanted the cafe moved downstairs after someone spilt Vietnamese weasel coffee over Victoria Beckham."

"Shit. Did he fire them?"

Kit laughed. "Barker can't fire himself."

A redheaded man in a white robe burst out of a side door and crashed into Barty. Barty staggered back, but the man caught him. "Sorry, mate."

Barty looked up. Even under his robe, the man's physique impressed. "You look familiar."

Kit put a hand on Barty's shoulder. "This is Aden Cooper. Series seven contestant on *Runway Rivals*, and now a successful underwear model."

Aden winked down at Barty. "You might not know my face, but you know my abs and—"

Kit cut him off. "Aden's the only model who doesn't have to pad his underwear."

Behind the Seams

"Cheers, Kit. Gotta go. Vonnie's gonna kill me if I'm late to the wedding rehearsal." Backing down the corridor, he waved to Kit. "Loving the dress, mate. Can't wait to get it off her."

As soon as Barty and Kit arrived at the cafe, Kit poured them drinks. "Let me give you a warning. When we go into the design studio, it'll be intense. Halton's sister is here from *Shear Style*. She's doing a piece on our new collection. She and Izzy, our head of media relations, don't get on. Bacchus Broadcasting is here filming a documentary about the run-up to Fashion Week. You'll be pleased to know Pamela, their head of production, is a sweetheart, but she has something like four camerawomen with her. And she's directing Tabitha Frost's 'Where are they now?' piece for *Runway Rivals*. Now that Bruna's left the show, Tabitha's fronting it. She'll be in there somewhere." Kit set down his mug. "Tell me more about yourself."

Barty rubbed his hands on his thighs. Kit hired him without an interview. Could this conversation ruin everything? "Ever since you arranged that visit to Stitchworthy, I knew fashion would be my future. My grandfather knew, too. I picked apart one of his shooting jackets once and he didn't bat an eyelid. It's a passion."

Kit sipped his tea. "I get that. I come here for pleasure, not because I have to. Renos could run everything, but I want to be here."

"I have wanted to do this all my life."

"Good. Finished your tea? Let's go."

As soon as Kit pushed open the door into the design studio, the room beckoned Barty inside.

Hundreds of sketches plastered the walls, camerawomen wound their way through the gathered people, RedWare staff,

341

all wearing vibrant colours, stood out from the production team who all wore black.

Barty stepped forward, eager to join the throng.

"Interesting," Kit said. "That's not how I first reacted to the fashion set. Let's find Barker."

A tall woman in a lime-green brocade jacket headed them off. "I love that shirt. Did you make it?"

"Yes," Barty said.

She clapped her hands. "It's lovely. Very on trend. I'm Emilia Winchmore."

Watch your back. "It's a pleasure. I know you from *Tatler* and your coverage of last year's Givenchy collection. Excellent work."

Emilia beamed. "I like you already." Her ponytail swished as she spoke to Kit. "Can you please do something about Izzy? If I didn't know better, I'd say she was avoiding me. All I need is the press pack for the show, which looks tremendous. Nancy and Osred will be thrilled—again. Do you have any idea where I might find her?"

Kit's chin dimpled. "We're about to see Barker. I'll ask him to get her up here."

"Super."

At the back of the room stood scarlet double doors emblazoned with Barker's name and *couturier*. Kit pushed them open, leading Barty into the biggest office he'd ever seen. A cocoon of a room, painted warm, dark grey.

Barker Wareham, mocha hair buzzed short, pored over a sketch. His brow furrowed in two deep lines. When he looked up, his frown melted away. Sketch forgotten, he bounded around his desk to kiss Kit full on the mouth. "Hello stranger."

Kit blushed. "Howay, man. It's only been two hours."

The blaze of Barker's attention turned to Barty. "Is this him? Let's have a look at him. He's far too cool to be a *tailleur*. I might steal him away from you."

Barty shook his hand. "I'll never be up to your standard, Mister Wareham. Inspiration rarely strikes."

Barker shook his head, then spoke to Kit. "What was it Gunter said?"

"'You don't wait for inspiration to strike'," Kit said. "'You turn up every day and work at it.'"

"Hear that, Bartholomew? If you put your mind to it, you'll design the socks off me."

Something moved in the corner of Barty's vision. He jumped.

A woman he hadn't noticed stepped forward from where she'd pressed herself behind the door. Her yellow suit flashed against her rich, dark skin. "Socks are so last season," she said. "Is Emilia still looking for me?"

Barker perched on the edge of his desk. "Why can't you just email her the press pack?"

"You know what she's like, she wants the fancy, boxed one with the memory stick." She shook Barty's hand. "Hi, I'm Izzy. Barty, right? I would do a release about you joining us, but too soon—?"

Blinking slowly, Kit nodded at Izzy. "Too soon."

Barker handed the sketch to Barty. "What's your opinion?"

A slim-fit suit adorned the page—a bold check with a pale blue waistcoat. To the sketch's left, staples held swatches of fabric in place.

Barty ran his fingers over the checked fabric—closely woven, flexible, and soft. "Lightweight tweed. Nice."

Barker took the sketch back. "I like you. So, Barty, how do you fancy coming on a company jaunt after Fashion Week?"

Surprised by the invitation, Barty looked around the room, his eyes settling on Kit. "I'm flattered, but I'm not into white-water rafting and the like."

Barker's laughter filled the room. "Neither are we. Do you have a passport?"

"I do." He looked at Izzy and Barker before his gaze settled on Kit. "Where are you going?"

"France."

"For—?"

"To visit my mother," Barker said. "She's just bought a pad in Cannes, so we thought it might be an excellent spot for—well—you know."

"I'm not sure I do."

Kit sat next to Barker, then took his hand. "An excellent spot for our wedding."

about the author

Stuart holds an MA (Distinction) in Professional Writing, and his debut novel, *Body of Water*, was one of ten books long-listed for the Polari First Book Prize.

His third novel, *Behind the Seams*, reached the 2021 BookLife Prize Fiction Contest semifinals.

He is a lifelong superhero nerd and a devoted action figure collector.

twitter.com/misterwakefield
instagram.com/misterswakefield

Printed in Great Britain
by Amazon